PRA
NEW YORK
BELA

DEMON STORM

"..non-stop tense action, filled with twists, betrayals, danger, and a beautiful sensual romance. As always with Dianna Love, I was on the edge of my seat, unable to pull myself away."
~~Barb, The Reading Cafe

"...nonstop adventures overflowing with danger and heartfelt emotions. DEMON STORM leaves you breathless on countless occasions."
~~Amelia Richard, SingleTitles

"There is so much action in this book I feel like I've burned calories just reading it."
~~D Antonio, Goodreads

"...I have to thank Dianna for keeping this series true to the wonderful world, witty dialogue and compelling characters that I have loved since the first book." Chris, Goodreads

RISE OF THE GRYPHON

"...It's been a very long time since I've felt this passionate about getting the next installment in a series. Even J. K. Rowling's Harry Potter books. It's a story you don't want to end and when it does, you can't help but scream out 'No! NO THEY DID NOT JUST DO THIS TO ME!! NO!!!!'" ~~Bryonna Nobles, Demons, Dreams and Dragon Wings

"...shocking developments and a whopper of an ending... and I may have exclaimed aloud more than once...Bottom line: I really kind of loved it." ~~Jen, Amazon Top 500 Reviewer

"I want more Feenix. I loved this book so much...If you have not read this series, once again, what are you waiting for?" ~~Barb, The Reading Cafe

"..fantastic continuation of the Belador series. The action starts on page one and blows you away to the very end." ~~Fresh Fiction

THE CURSE

"The Beladors series is beloved and intricate. It's surprising that such a diverse and incredible world has only three books out." ~~Jessie Potts, USA Today, Happy Ever After

"The precarious action and genuine emotion in THE CURSE will continuously leave the reader breathless...a mesmerizing urban fantasy story overflowing with heartfelt emotions and dramatically life-altering incidents." ~~Amelia Richards, Single Titles

"If you're looking for a series with an epic scope and intricate, bold characters, look no further than the Belador series...This new addition provides all the action and intrigue that readers have come to expect...a series to be savored by urban fantasy and paranormal romance fans alike." ~~Bridget, The Romance Reviews

ALTERANT

"There are SO many things in this series that I want to learn more about; there's no way I could list them all... have me on tenterhooks waiting for the third BELADOR book. As Evalle would say, 'Bring it on.'" ~~Lily, Romance Junkies Reviews

"An incredible heart-jolting roller-coaster ride...An action-packed adventure with an engrossing story line and characters you will grow to love." ~~ Mother/Gamer/Writer

"An intriguing series that has plenty of fascinating characters to ponder." ~~ Night Owl Reviews

BLOOD TRINITY

"BLOOD TRINITY is an ingenious urban fantasy with

imaginative magical scenarios, characters who grab your every thought and more than a few unpredictable turns ...The paranormal action is instantaneous, while perilous suspense continuously escalates to grand proportions before the tension-filled and satisfying conclusion. The meticulous storyline of Book One in the Belador series will enthrall you during every compellingly entertaining scene." ~~Amelia Richard, Single Titles

"BLOOD TRINITY is a fantastic start to a new Urban Fantasy series. The VIPER organization and the world built ... are intriguing, but the characters populating that world are irresistible. I am finding it difficult to wait for the next book to find out what happens next in their lives." ~~Diana Trodahl, Fresh Fiction

"BLOOD TRINITY is without a doubt one of the best books I've read this year... a tale that shows just how awesome urban fantasy really can be, particularly as the genre is flooded with so many choices. If you love urban fantasy, don't miss out on BLOOD TRINITY. I can't wait to read the second book! Brilliantly done and highly recommended." ~~ Debbie, CK2s Kwips & Kritiques

WITCHLOCK

BOOK SIX
THE BELADOR SERIES

NEW YORK TIMES BESTSELLING AUTHOR

DIANNA
LOVE

PP

DEDICATION

This book is for Lisa Kulow who shows the world a
beautiful smile no matter what she faces.

THE BELADOR SERIES
IS AN ONGOING STORY LINE,
SO IT'S BETTER IF YOU READ THE SERIES IN ORDER:

BLOOD TRINITY
ALTERANT
THE CURSE
RISE OF THE GRYPHON
DEMON STORM
WITCHLOCK
ROGUE BELADOR (April 2016)

MIDNIGHT KISS GOODBYE
(novella in DEAD AFTER DARK)

FIREBOUND
(short story – free at www.AuthorDiannaLove.com)

CHAPTER 1

How am I supposed to find a demon among all these Santa elves and Christmas decorations?

Evalle Kincaid rubbed her gritty eyes and repositioned her sunglasses. She kept moving through throngs of locals from Atlanta's suburbs, all enjoying the first weekend in November at Memorial Hall in Stone Mountain Park. She'd been here for four hours and it was only nine-thirty. A half hour yet until closing.

The park was decorated to celebrate the start of the holidays, and every tree was lit up. She'd never seen so many bright lights and happy freaking people.

Shoot, every surface glowed or sparkled. She wore dark sunglasses to protect her oversensitive eyes *and* to protect the locals from seeing those same green eyes glow.

Humans didn't know about the strange beings that existed in their world. Like her. She was a Belador, one of an ancient line of warriors living secretly in the world today. But most Beladors looked human. Her weird eyes and deathly aversion to the sun came from her mixed blood.

Not her favorite topic to think about.

She squinted to avoid looking right into the hottest lights, because they kept messing with her vision.

If someone viewed the historic park from above, Memorial Hall would look like a glittering jewel against the dark night.

She'd be hearing Jingle Bells in her sleep tonight.

But even that would be better than the nightmares she'd had for the past week.

"Are you the Secret Service, babe?" a mouthy young guy wearing a dark pullover and dress pants asked Evalle.

"No." She smiled and tried to pass.

"A Hell's Angel?"

"No." Without the smile this time.

He finally went on his way.

Okay, so she had on jeans, boots, a black jacket and dark glasses after sunset. She didn't get the memo on wearing perky holiday colors, but that wouldn't have changed her choice in clothes anyway, since this was her standard fare.

She caught sight of her potential demon again.

Or maybe between the lights screwing with her eyes, lack of sleep and wanting to go home, her brain was trying to help by convincing her that some poor schmuck might be a demon in glamour.

Wearing khaki pants and a fleece hoodie, said schmuck looked like every other middle-aged, balding, slightly overweight man she'd seen tonight, but she could swear the face on this one had flickered for a second.

All of VIPER had been up in arms for the past week. Something had been killing trolls in Atlanta, and the last body was found butchered near the Chattahoochee River on the north side of the metro area. Thankfully, this was not summertime when a human out rafting or kayaking might have happened on the body.

Humans didn't know about the trolls—or the demons— because Evalle and other VIPER agents like her stood in the gap. VIPER was a secret coalition of powerful beings who protected humans from nonhuman predators.

Sometimes they had to protect the nonhumans, too.

That's why Storm was gone.

With the blood of a Navajo shaman and an Ashaninka witch doctor, along with the ability to shift into a black jaguar, Storm was the best tracker on the southeastern VIPER teams. He could identify a majik scent and track it as easily as he could a human or animal one, and he could handle whatever had taken down a troll.

That didn't stop her from worrying about the man she loved.

She gave her watch another glance. Twelve hours and six minutes until he would be back in Atlanta. Nine in the morning couldn't come soon enough. The last six days had been the longest of her life.

And the most conflicted.

She missed him. But she'd also spent every day since he left stressed about his return. This whole relationship thing was still new and left her off-kilter some days.

She hated that. Hated to feel clueless about things most twenty-three-year-old women took in stride. She could kill a demon six different ways, but she had no skills to cope with the changes that living with a man had brought about.

Storm had moved in with her just hours before he'd been asked to leave and track the troll killer.

Less than one day of living together, and it had been a major fail.

On her part.

Giggles erupted nearby. Evalle turned to find three little girls laughing and talking to one of Santa's elves. Without a preternatural loose in here, all the families visiting tonight would normally be perfectly safe with Stone Mountain's top-notch security staff.

Evalle gave the elf a once-over and got nary a ping on her internal radar. She smiled at the girls, who were obviously having a great time. *I'll keep you safe, too.*

What would it have been like to grow up as a normal girl? One who hadn't spent her first eighteen years locked in a basement?

Khaki Guy stepped into view again and pulled Evalle's gaze from the girls. Finally, he was where she could get a really good look at him.

Not quite six feet, average-looking male with brown hair. He stood on the edge of all the activity as he eyed the bustling crowd entering and leaving Memorial Hall, where Santa was holding court.

His appearance fit right in with the suburbanites, but no one else out here stood that still or watched with predatory intensity.

Monsters came in all types, human and nonhuman.

Evalle had faced both.

This guy's gaze latched onto the three little girls and tracked their forward movement.

He wore a blank expression.

Energy buzzed in the air for a moment, then disappeared so

fast she couldn't pinpoint where it originated.

In the next second, the man's face blurred.

Gotcha.

"You'll have to wait your turn for Santa, lady," a female voice said from close behind.

Evalle wheeled around, blowing out a breath that fogged in the chilly air. "Don't do that."

Adrianna Lafontaine's lips angled up on one side with her signature half smile. "What? Catch you zoning out?"

"Don't sneak up on me," Evalle scowled and turned back quickly to look for Khaki Guy, but she immediately regretted admitting that the Sterling witch had managed to do just that— sneak up on her. "I was not zoning out. I was watching a potential perp ... *Crud!*"

The space where he'd been standing was vacant, and the little girls were gone, too.

"What?" Adrianna asked, stretching her head forward.

"This ... guy was watching three little girls." Evalle caught herself before saying demon out loud.

Adrianna kept her voice down. "Are you sure he wasn't human?"

"Sure enough."

But Adrianna must have caught Evalle's hesitation. "If he *is* human, that's for the park security, not us."

Adrianna was right, but Evalle didn't care. Human or not, that creep was not going to hurt those little girls on Evalle's watch. And his face had blurred. She was tired, but not *that* tired ...

"He was not a human," Evalle said with more conviction and started forward.

Adrianna's boot heels clicked behind her as she took quick steps to keep up with Evalle's much longer stride. "Where are you going?"

Evalle tossed an answer over her shoulder. "To find *him* and make sure he isn't around those kids. *Any* kids."

Adrianna groused, "I hadn't planned on running through Stone-freaking-Mountain tonight."

Either give me patience or something to kill. Evalle kept her gaze on the crowd, searching for her guy, but slowed a little until Adrianna came up beside her and she caught an eyeful of the witch.

Surprisingly, the petite fashionista *had* donned jeans, boots and a leather jacket that might just be custom made for her perfect five-foot-three body.

In spite of dressing in the same clothing items as Evalle, Adrianna's jeans were black where Evalle's were blue denim with worn spots earned honestly. Bright blond hair swooped around the shoulders of Adrianna's red, leather jacket that sported a white, faux-fur collar. Her matching red boots had been designed for runway effect as opposed to running ability.

They were now in the middle of the throng heading toward Santa, so moving fast was impossible. Pausing to stand on tiptoes, Evalle swept a long look over the tops of heads, still not seeing Khaki Guy's balding globe. She huffed out a breath, muttering, "Excuse me," over and over while she weaved through the excited park visitors. "Trudging through the Okeefenokee swamp waist-deep in muck has to be easier than moving through this crowd."

Adrianna warned, "Stop scowling. You're scaring the natives." She scooted ahead, spearing her way politely through middle-school kids who probably thought the witch was one of them until they got a look at her body.

"They're not looking at me," Evalle said, passing Adrianna and taking the lead again. "They're trying to figure out if you're Santa's biker babe. Did you get a red Harley broom to go with that outfit?"

"You're a bucket of laughs tonight. Don't tempt me to put a spell on that mouth of yours," Adrianna snipped, but without malice, and followed close behind. "And don't be a hater just because my clothes don't look like I've been dragged through a field."

Evalle's black Gortex motorcycle jacket had seen its share of battles and her scuffed boots concealed sharp blades for fighting.

Adrianna asked, "Have you heard anything from Rowan or Nicole?"

"No. Should I have? Is something up?" Evalle swatted away hairs that had slipped loose from her ponytail. She ignored the three guys she passed whose jaws dropped in Adrianna's direction.

"Maybe." Adrianna paused and must have realized no one was listening to them or that only Evalle could hear her over the kids squealing in delight. She continued, "The white covens across the country are forming councils in major areas now that the Medb have dumped warlocks and witches into Atlanta. The fighting between Beladors and the Medb faction is spilling over into the witch population. Until now, no witch has ever had to declare if he or she was dark or white."

Evalle stopped again and turned slowly, scanning the crowd. With the same happy faces and winter clothing, they were starting to blend together.   What was Adrianna saying? Something about the Medb?

The Medb were the oldest and deadliest enemies of the Belador race, and even though Evalle had recently found out she was half Medb, she held no sympathies for that coven. Didn't matter. The witches would have to work out their own issues, because VIPER had bigger problems.

As one of six agents covering the park tonight, Evalle had to determine if she'd actually seen a demon, and whether it was the same one that'd been sighted an hour ago in the town of Stone Mountain.

When Adrianna didn't say anything else, Evalle ran back over the conversation. She'd been only half listening about the witches. "So? What's the problem?"

"If the witches form a council here, which they will because Rowan is pushing for one, then VIPER will recognize the council, which means VIPER will expect me to tell them where my loyalty lies."

Evalle lifted her hands. "Just declare that you're a Sterling and be done with it."

"It's not that simple. Never mind," Adrianna murmured, then looked around as she switched topics. "Think the Medb coven is behind this demon tonight?"

Evalle growled in frustration. "Who knows? VIPER should never have welcomed the Medb into the coalition. The Medb spend a few days acting like good Samaritans, killing demons that *they* created, and VIPER conveniently forgets how many years of blood has spilled between the Beladors and the Medb. Apparently they've *also* forgotten that dark witches are dangerous and untrustworthy as a rule."

Adrianna lifted a sharp eyebrow at that slam.

Evalle rolled her eyes at the Sterling witch, who had used her dark powers to help Evalle—and VIPER—more than once. She amended her statement. "Present company excepted."

Having once been the bane of Evalle's existence, Adrianna was now ... a friend, though Evalle still had to work at the trust part. Wind swatted more loose hairs around her face. When Evalle stretched her neck, she looked up past Memorial Hall to where spotlights illuminated the carving of three Confederate soldiers on one side of the bald mountain.

Power snapped around Evalle again and she jerked her head around, searching and rubbing her arms. "Did you feel that?"

"That buzzing?"

"Yes. Like some kind of energy."

Adrianna shrugged. "Probably a ghoul in the area."

"I don't think so." Evalle moved through the crowd, ignoring the stares at her dark glasses.

They'd stare even more if she took them off.

Adrianna tagged along. "When will Storm be back?"

"By nine in the morning, last I heard."

"Good, because I've waited as long as I can, but I—"

Evalle's phone chimed with a text, but the default tune that played meant it was not Storm. She lifted the phone and gave Adrianna an index finger signal to hold her thought. Then she read the text: *Your week is up.*

Oh. Hell.

"You look like you just heard from the Grim Reaper," Adrianna quipped.

"Worse. Isak." Evalle pushed the off button and put the phone back in her pocket.

"You haven't gone to dinner with him yet?"

"No."

"Why not? You told him you'd get in touch within a week after he helped us contain that witch doctor."

"I know that," Evalle groused back at her and returned to her surveillance. She rubbed her eyes again. "I didn't get a chance to talk to Storm before he had to leave town and I'm not about to have him come home to hear that I was having dinner with another man while he was gone."

"With a hot warrior no less," Adrianna teased. "You're afraid to tell Storm."

Evalle didn't have the energy to argue.

Isak would not wait long. The last time she'd ignored him, he'd sent his black ops team to snatch her off the street.

Then he'd served her a mouth-watering Italian meal.

A profiler would have a field day with the men in her life, but the only one who mattered was Storm.

Evalle widened her stance and said, "I'm dealing with the Isak situation as soon as Storm is back." Sounded perfect. Confident. Decisive.

A total lie.

Adrianna snapped her fingers. "Anyhow, as I was saying, I need to meet with you and Storm about our deal."

There went Evalle's fantasy about the down time VIPER had promised her this week. But Adrianna had helped Evalle and Storm several different times. They both owed her major debts. Plus Adrianna had yet to say what she wanted, and Evalle smelled a secret. "I'll check with Storm. If he's good to go, I am."

"I don't have much time—"

The suspicious guy stepped back into Evalle's line of vision once more, stared in her direction, then turned to walk away from her and Memorial Hall.

Evalle lifted her hand. "Wait a minute."

Adrianna huffed, "What *now*?"

Evalle kept her eyes on Mr. Khaki Pants as she told Adrianna, "There he is. I'll be right back."

Adrianna leaned to look in the same direction Evalle had been watching. "I'm supposed to be your backup."

"Look, this may be nothing more than my eyes playing tricks on me because of all these damn lights," Evalle explained, "But that's the guy. I saw something odd happen to his face earlier."

"What kind of odd?"

"It was just a blur. I can't call in a blurred face or I'll never hear the end of it at headquarters. Just stay here and keep an eye on the crowd. If I'm not back in fifteen minutes, call in the cavalry."

"Fine, but I'm not going to deal with Tzader going off on me if you get hurt."

"He won't." Tzader Burke was Maistir of the North American Beladors, and one of Evalle's two best friends. "He'll go off on *me*," Evalle assured her and hurried forward, weaving her way through miniature Santa stalkers.

If she could just catch one more flicker of change in that guy's outward appearance, she'd know for sure what she'd seen before hadn't been an optical illusion created by all the mash of lights around her.

Her special sunglasses shielded her eyes from normal city lights at night, but this place was uber-bright. Give her pitch dark anytime, where she could see without eye protection.

Taking off her glasses would reveal unnatural neon-green eyes, but more critical, it would leave her blind and vulnerable. As dead tired as she was, the glare from the screaming-white strings of Christmas decorations in this park might be tricking her eyes.

Wind whistled through nearby bony branches, jangling leaves that hadn't fallen and offering an eerie background to the jolly event as Evalle moved away from the crowd noise.

She curled her chilled fingers, working out the stiffness in case she had to use the spelled dagger hidden inside her jacket.

Khaki Guy hadn't acted like any demon she'd ever gone after.

Decisions, decisions.

There'd been no demon sightings in the Atlanta area for five whole days—until this evening here in Stone Mountain.

Everyone had thought the recent infestation had been put to bed. VIPER was adamant about getting this corner of the country back under control before the trolls made good on their threat and informed the humans that monsters lived among them.

That would be pandemonium.

The man she trailed slowed to watch a family walking toward Memorial Hall, then he kept moving.

If the potential demon-in-khaki-slacks wasn't raising hairs on the neck of anyone in this crowd, then either this guy was just another park visitor or this group didn't have a lick of spidey sense. As long as the coalition did its job, these people would continue to go on about their lives, content in their ignorance of anything unnatural in their world.

Keeping pace with her target but far back enough to be unobtrusive, Evalle searched ahead. The only obvious destination in his direct path was the park's Summit Skyride, where high-speed cable cars zoomed visitors from ground level to the top of the mountain and back.

Thankfully, that attraction had been shut down for the night.

She'd heard VIPER agents rave about the view, but she'd pass. She got nauseated fifteen feet off the ground.

Strangely, she had no fear of heights when she shifted into her gryphon form and flew, but she wasn't allowed to do that in the human world, even if no humans were around.

The guy slowed when he encountered one of the park's uniformed personnel near the entrance to the skyride structure.

Evalle held up. The minute that security guard sent her suspect back toward the festivities, she'd return, too.

But that didn't happen.

Khaki Guy said something to the guard, then continued walking until he stepped up on the platform that led to the parked cable cars.

Evalle picked up her pace, sliding from shadow to shadow so no one would see her using unnatural speed. When she reached the security guard, he stood perfectly still, staring straight ahead. She waved a hand in front of his face. He was breathing, but locked in time like a living statue.

She had all the confirmation she needed that Khaki Man was not what he seemed.

She sent a text to Adrianna that she definitely followed something nonhuman, but she had yet to determine what it was exactly, so stand by for an update.

Evalle shoved the phone in her back pocket and closed the distance.

Demon, troll or *other*, he was not disappearing again.

CHAPTER 2

When Evalle reached the platform, Khaki Guy was trying to open the doors on the parked cable car. They were probably powered by hydraulics.

No human could break those apart.

Khaki Guy held his hands back-to-back and pushed his palms out, inching the doors open. The mechanism controlling the gears cried in protest.

Just great.

Now she'd have to call in Sen, the VIPER liaison and a roaring pain in her backside, to fix that before she left. Sen could thaw out the security guard and purge the man's memory while he was at it.

She called out, "You can't ride without a ticket."

Ignoring her, the guy leaned forward, growled in strain, and shoved the doors open with a bang before he turned around. He still looked just like Joe Suburbia, but then he opened his mouth.

Guttural demon voice came out. "Who are *you?*"

She respected any being's strength, but she had to clue this creature in before he decided to go toe-to-toe with her. Sometimes clearing up any misconception saved getting her favorite clothes bloody. "My name's Evalle. If you'll come quietly with me, I won't hurt you."

"I don't have to do what you say."

"That's where you're wrong. She pulled off her dark sunglasses so he could experience the full effect of her glowing green Alterant eyes, a mark of being half Belador and half Medb. Don't even get her started on *that* issue. The fact that she was an Alterant had played havoc with her life for as long as she could remember. "I'm with VIPER and I have authorization to take you in."

He stared at her, or more like *through* her, not blinking, which was creepy on a human face. Then he asked, "We'll go together?"

Did he think she worked on the honor system?

Sure, I'll give you an address for the hidden VIPER headquarters in the North Georgia Mountains and you'll turn yourself in while I go home and take a long hot bath.

If only. "Yes, we'll go together."

He nodded and turned back to the cable car.

"Hold it. This way, buddy," she called over to him.

The words flew right past him as he climbed inside.

Just once she'd like a demon, or whatever he was, to cooperate. Evalle pulled out her dagger just to be prepared and walked over calmly, standing in front of the door. "Come on out and let's go."

The seats in the car lined the walls, wrapping around the inside. He sat on the far side near the front with his body leaning against the window.

Was he demented?

She'd dealt with a Cresyl demon once that had acted confused, but the Cresyl had been under a spell. A Medb spell come to think of it, from what Evalle had put together since then.

She considered using her kinetic power to lift him off the seat and float him out, but he was acting docile at the moment, which was *way* better than the alternative.

Agitating unknown beings often turned out badly.

Stepping inside the spacious car, she walked over until she could see his face. He lay hunched over against the window, eyes shut and breathing softly.

Asleep?

At least now she could use her kinetics to get him out of here, but that would be simpler with both hands free. She slid her dagger into the sheath inside her jacket and raised both arms shoulder high with her hands stretched toward Mr. Khaki Pants.

She powered up her kinetics, expecting him to be a lightweight, but she strained to lift him two feet off the floor, then turned to walk him toward the door. If she could get this guy away from the cable car structure and into the woods close by, she could pin him to the ground while they both waited for Sen in a spot where no one would see them.

Once she had Khaki Guy contained, she'd call Tzader telepathically and give him the location. Sen hated Evalle and would dismiss any request from her unless he thought there was a chance she'd committed a crime where he could lock her up in VIPER prison.

She'd almost reached the opening with her captive when power burst all around her in a blast of lightning bolts, knocking Evalle backwards off her feet.

She dropped her guy, who hit hard.

He bounced once and landed on his feet as he came alive with eyes glowing bright yellow. The bottom of his face warped down and sideways, growing twice as big as it had been before. Jaws opened to reveal two rows of barracuda-sharp teeth when he roared an ungodly sound.

Now *that* was more like the demons she knew and loved.

He dove at her.

CHAPTER 3

Evalle shoved up a kinetic wall in an attempt to block the demon diving at her. He slammed against it and visible cracks splintered across the invisible shield.

What the ...

She had no way out except past that snarling jaw full of teeth and those inch-long claws. She rolled fast, toward the front of the car before he crashed through her invisible barrier and pinned her. She locked her hands in a fist and swung both arms, batting a kinetic blast at the demon.

He flew backwards and landed on the floor. Finally. She kept her kinetic wall in place just in case ...

The demon sat up.

Are you kidding me?

And ... now she could see black ears. A Réisc Dubh demon?

She'd read about them, but had never seen one because there hadn't been any around for something like eighty years.

Sparks crackled and zigzagged back and forth through the air, buzzing close enough to singe the skin on her face and hands.

Where was that power coming from?

A spell maybe, and one that didn't play nice with her Belador powers, because it was corrupting her kinetics. She'd pull out her dagger, but killing him had to be her last choice.

If her memory was right, Réisc Dubh demons had been created as servants or slaves, and didn't have a lot of power.

Someone had super-juiced this one.

If she handed this demon over to Tzader alive, then the Beladors had a chance to find out if the Medb had a hand in this. There may not be a telltale burnt lime scent, but she had a strong feeling this might be another game move by the Medb.

The beast that lived inside her body surged to break out, but shifting into a gryphon would bring the wrath of VIPER down on Evalle's head. They *still* had not given Alterants permission to shift while in the human realm, even though they knew she and the others were fully in control of their gryphon forms.

Nothing would change until the petition passed to recognize Alterants as a race with rights.

Shifting wouldn't help right now anyway, because her gryphon form had a wingspan to fit a ten-foot tall shape. This car was too small to allow her to move in that form. She could, however, shift into battle form, just enough to allow her more strength.

Her arms, neck and legs thickened, straining seams on her jeans and stretching her jacket. She wrenched the jacket off and slung it aside as the demon stood and turned to face her.

The khaki pants still fit his lower, human-shaped body, but he'd ripped out of the fleece hoodie. Veins stuck out thick as fingers all over a gray-tinged chest that belonged on someone who bench-pressed three hundred pounds.

Was this really a Réisc Dubh? The black ears were the giveaway, but what was he doing so bulked up?

She'd worry about his actual identity once she had him under control.

That might have been a sound plan if the car hadn't jerked forward right then, tossing her off balance and slamming her into the demon, who clamped down on her shoulder with sharp teeth.

Ouch, dammit.

She slammed an elbow into his middle and heard a bone crack before he went flying against the window. Her shoulder throbbed and the smell of fresh blood hit the air.

Cold wind slapped her in the face.

Sparks still shot around her like out-of-control electric charges.

Evalle spun around to the open door.

The night sky moved past her, and lights from Memorial Hall were shrinking. The cable car sped up. She sidestepped and grabbed the doorframe. Her stomach lurched at the distance growing between her and the ground. Stars danced through her vision.

Bad time to get light headed.

The headlines would read *Deadly Demon Killer Succumbs to Acrophobia, Plunges to Her Death.*

Her stomach did another spin cycle.

Her attacker screeched behind her.

Killing him was back on the front burner.

She turned fast, but kept a death grip on the doorframe. He held his head, shaking it back and forth. What was wrong with him? One minute asleep, the next trying to kill her, and now he acted as if he had a migraine.

He started yelling, "Your fault. Your fault."

She had nowhere to go and didn't want to see the world growing smaller outside the car so she stayed put.

His shouting hadn't been so bad, but then he changed it to, "You die. You die." His body arched and twisted, lifting inches off the floor and hanging there a moment.

This had to be the strangest demon she'd ever met.

He landed hard, as if whatever held him just let go. His chin dipped to his chest and his body moved sluggishly.

Finally, she might get the upper hand.

She risked a quick look forward. They were over halfway to the mountaintop and had a front-row view of the carving straight ahead, which was better than looking down.

Evalle eased toward the front to get away from the open door. Her palms were slick with sweat.

She'd taken two steps when darting bolts of energy burst through the air again. *What the hell?*

She ducked to avoid one coming at her face. Then an explosion of lights burst inside the car so bright she blinked against it.

When she could see again, the demon was on her.

A boot caught her in the chest, knocking her backwards. She hit the floor and slid sideways out the opening, clawing for anything to grab. Her fingers caught a vertical seat support at the last second, yanking her body hard as she swung into the buffeting wind. If she hadn't changed into battle form, she doubted her arm could have held against the wind dragging her weight.

Don't look down now or it's all over.

The demon kept making crazy sounds she couldn't interpret as actual words, but if she had to guess she'd say he was engaged in a one-sided argument with someone.

Forcing her free arm against the wind, she struggled to reach for a second handhold.

His head snapped up and those yellow demon eyes stared at her.

He moved forward and lifted a foot above the wrist to her only handhold.

She threw a kinetic hit with her free hand that felt as if she'd slugged a steel beam.

He stumbled back, then dropped down to all fours. Not what she'd hoped for, but in another minute they'd reach the mountaintop platform where she'd be able to stand on firm ground.

Her fingers slipped where they were clamped around the chair leg.

So much for wishful thinking. She gripped it tighter.

He snarled and crawled toward her.

The platform came into view, but Stone Mountain was a volcanic burp that had resulted in a rounded shape. She had to let go before smashing into the structure that would break every bone in her lower half, but not until the top area leveled out. Drop down too soon and she'd miss the fence circling the crest of the mountain and slide off the side with nothing to push her kinetics against to break her fall.

And this creature would escape.

Protecting humans came before delivering evidence of who created this thing.

Evalle dropped her free hand out of sight and called her dagger to that hand, clamping her fingers around the grip when it touched her palm.

The demon opened his jaws, saliva streaming down in long drips.

Yellow eyes on fire.

Her handhold slipped again and her heart tried to climb into her throat.

Getting back inside the car was out of the question. She had to time her jump so she landed safely and on her feet. The last gigantic cable support tower at the top of the mountain came into view. The ground would level off on the other side.

Thirty more seconds and ...

The demon lunged faster than he'd moved the whole time and chomped down on her injured shoulder again. Pain burned through her muscles.

She swung hard and stabbed him between the eyes, ordering her dagger, *"Stay!"*

He screamed and jumped back, grabbing at the dagger and yanking. A futile effort. That dagger would only come out when she ordered it to do so.

Her grip slipped to a three-finger hold. She looked down in a panic.

Stone Mountain curved away.

What were those spikes shooting up from the base of the cable tower? The front of the car reached the tower and bounced, causing the car to jerk and sway.

A whip of wind slammed her sideways and snatched her loose.

No, no, *no.*

She shoved her kinetics at the tower and pushed away from the spikes just in time ... flying backwards. Her back struck the top of the chain-link fence that would have stopped her from falling if she'd come down inside it.

She hit, bounced and landed, rolling.

Downhill.

Wrong direction.

Swinging her arms out, her good one whacked a pine tree with a trunk an inch thick. Enough to grab and flip over to her stomach.

The tree snapped and she was back to scrambling for a handhold anywhere. She bumped over craters in what was otherwise a relatively smooth surface compared to most mountains.

Her shirt bunched and rock raked her exposed stomach. She dragged her hands, fingers digging for any purchase in the unyielding stone.

Lightning strikes had pockmarked the mountain's face with

the sporadic craters, and rough edges raked her clothes and tore her skin.

She slapped at any imperfection in the smooth surface for a handhold. Four fingers snagged another pine tree, this one with a thicker trunk but still only six feet tall.

Good news? It was her uninjured shoulder. She wheezed and panted, dragging deep breaths in and out.

She'd noticed this tiny line of trees beneath the cable lines earlier, when she'd looked up at the mountain from below, and thought it amazing that anything could grow on this slick rock.

Chugging in another gulp of air, she thanked her lucky stars something had grown here.

The damn tree trunk creaked, threatening to give way.

Clawing with her other hand, she gritted against the pain and found a three-inch deep crater with her fingertips.

Would this nightmare ever end?

On second thought, she shouldn't be wishing for a quick end while dangling off a mountain.

Everything hurt, and her shoulder burned hot from the demon bites, but at least she was not falling.

For the moment.

Sucking hard breaths in, her arms and body shook from the terror of clinging to a mountainside. Fighting a crazy demon had only pissed her off, but almost falling to her death sixteen hundred feet down?

Yep, that took the starch out of her.

Her dark hair blew all over the place and covered her face. She'd lost her ponytail band somewhere along the way. That might be a plus if her wild hair kept her from seeing just how much trouble she was in.

She had to heal her shoulder, but to do that required calling up her beast. She'd done it many times, but it was a lot harder while terror from the height spiked through her body. It wouldn't work with her insides in chaos.

She needed to calm down.

This would be a great time to shift into her gryphon form and fly away from the mountain face, but there was the stinking permission problem again.

Also, she might crash before fully shifting and getting her

wings to function properly.

Sweat ran down her neck in spite of the chilly temperature.

Blood trickled from her hand where her weight forced the rock edge to cut into her fingers. She had to get out of here before it severed all the digits.

But she had nothing to push against with her kinetic power to shove herself up from this spot. She calmed down and called out telepathically. *Tzader, can you hear me?*

She heard something garbled in her mind.

Bad sign. She should be able to reach a Belador, especially Tzader. Her shoulder felt on fire from the demon saliva.

Was that interfering with her ability to use her telepathy?

She had no way to tell anyone how to find her. By the time Adrianna sent someone, would they even know to look on top of the mountain?

Something bumped her arm and she jerked. She tried to look up, but couldn't see anything with her hair doing a Cousin It imitation.

If the demon was still alive and coming for her, she had no tricks left up her sleeve and no dagger for backup.

"Hold on!" a hoarse voice shouted down.

Her heart thumped with hope.

But if that was a human ...

She didn't have time to think long on someone being in danger if the demon still lived. Tiny pebbles bounced over her body ahead of the sound of someone's boots scuffing down the side of the mountain in a hurry. Now she realized what had bumped her arm. A rope.

Who had gotten here so quickly, and with a rope?

"Hold on, sweetheart."

Could it be? She blew hair away from one eye to see Storm lowering himself down next to her, slowing as he came closer, carefully reaching for her.

Her heart held a celebration.

She smiled in spite of being in pain and terrified of falling. Amazing what love would make you overlook.

When Storm was level with her, he hooked an arm around her waist and said, "I've got you."

The greatest three words in her world right now.

She took a deep breath of relief and sagged into him.

"Can you climb up the rope?"

For him, she could move this mountain. "Sure." She grabbed and her hand slipped, slick now with blood.

Storm cursed. "Why haven't you healed your wounds?"

"I haven't caught my breath long enough to call up my beast for healing." *That sounds so much better than I've been too petrified of falling off this mountain to calm down long enough to call up my beast power.*

She'd wasted her breath.

Storm had the ability to tell if she was lying and that answer had barely skated near the truth, but rather than call her on the lie, he said, "Let go of the tree and heal your wounds while I hold you."

Before Storm, she'd trusted only two people—Tzader and Quinn, Beladors who were like brothers to her.

Storm held a place in her heart that no one else had ever claimed and no other man ever would. She wrapped her arm around his shoulder, curving into him as she released her other hand, hissing at the pain.

He muttered something darker than his last curse and started chanting softly in his native Navajo language.

As soon as she relaxed, she got busy calling up the beast energy that flowed through her body, repairing the shoulder muscles first, purging her body of the poison from the demon bite, then sealing the cuts on her hands and the torn skin on her belly. Her shoulder and hands would still hurt for a while, but she'd be able to function.

When he kissed her temple, she realized he'd stopped chanting. He held her tightly for a moment then eased up and asked, "Ready now?"

"Definitely."

"Push up on my shoulder to get started."

Going up was only slightly less terrifying than sliding down, but she kept her eyes on the rock and the rope. She had to get back over the fence, but thankfully, half way back the incline leveled out enough for her to move faster. When she finally reached actual level ground, she released the rope. Storm had tied it to an observation post where people could look through mounted binoculars.

She hurried ahead toward the platform where the cable car had parked, but Storm appeared right beside her just as she started to clear the fence enclosing the platform area.

Storm caught her good arm and pulled her around. "Whatever it is will wait, and must be long dead since I didn't see anyone or anything on my way to you and nothing is out here causing havoc."

Too tired to argue and thankful to see Storm again, she let him draw her into his arms. But how had he ended up here at this moment? "How did you—"

"I'm done waiting for this." He covered her mouth in a hungry kiss, taking her under so fast she drowned in the feel of him.

What a way to go.

Her body revved up and she'd love to snap her fingers and land in their bed, even if it meant teleporting, which she liked almost as much as heights. Not even. But teleporting was not one of her powers.

His hands ran up her back, strong fingers holding her and letting her know just how much he'd missed her while he was away.

She'd had very little experience with kissing until Storm showed up in her life, or with being touched for that matter, but she craved his kiss and touch. Craved the way he held her, with both power and tenderness. He drove his fingers into her hair, which had to look like she belonged in the psych ward by now, but he didn't seem to notice.

His kiss became gentle, and now he devoured her in slow bites. Her world spun on its axis and settled into a comfortable roll as he slowed the kiss, nipping at her lips. She had a hand on his chest. His heart pounded at a savage pace and she knew it was for her, all for her.

She would never be anything like the chic Adrianna, but Storm had made his choice for his mate. *Me.*

She needed to keep that thought front and center.

When he stopped, he dropped his forehead against hers. His hands still held her in a possessive grip, and he let out a hard breath. "You scared the hell out of me."

Scared the hell out of her, too, but now was not the time to admit that. Now was the time to convince him she was fine and to soothe him. She knew only one way to push Storm's mind away from her brush with death.

She wrapped her arms around his neck and leaned into the kiss again, enjoying her own private feast on his mouth.

He was warm and hard and all hers.

When she shivered this time, it had nothing to do with the brisk wind whipping around them. His body burned like a furnace.

Right here, in his arms, was all she needed. It was the one place she felt safe when safe had never been in her vocabulary.

When he'd moved into her underground apartment a week ago, chaos had erupted in the brief hours he'd been there before Tzader had called for Storm's help tracking. Living together wasn't going to be as simple as she'd thought, and what had once seemed perfect for her and a pet gargoyle now felt cramped, since Storm had moved in and Quinn's cousin, Lanna Brasko, was also staying there.

He broke the kiss once more and turned to eye the cable car. "I shouldn't have let you talk me into leaving."

"Tzader needed you to help the Beladors."

"He assured me you'd be safe while I was gone."

"He sent Adrianna to help tonight." And this was why she'd convinced him to go help Tzader's team. She needed Storm to give her the space to perform her duty without him hovering.

That's going to be a tough sale after tonight.

She'd fought too hard and too long to be accepted as an equal among the Beladors, and now that she'd finally achieved that, she would *not* let anything make her look weak. Storm had argued that they were VIPER partners, and that should trump his leaving for any other reason.

But they'd gone from being partners to mates, which meant he couldn't be objective about her role with VIPER.

Storm wanted her locked up somewhere safe.

That wasn't happening, and it was just another issue they had to figure out.

Sirens blared at the base of the mountain.

She swatted hair off her face and muttered, "Sen's going to

love this."

"Screw him. We all have a job. His is cleanup."

When any of the agents ran into a problem that required powers or majik they didn't possess, Sen got called in. No one Evalle knew had any idea where he came from or what he was, other than difficult, arrogant and a walking grudge against Alterants.

Or maybe Evalle was the only Alterant who brought out his hostility.

But one flick of his fingers and the cable car would be restored and functioning. Then Sen would remove any memory of tonight's demon from the security guard, wake him up from his half coma, and erase any memories from any other people who'd seen Evalle almost fall out of that cable car.

Storm gently brushed her hair back and smoothed it behind her ear. His face lost its moment of charm and turned serious. "What the hell were you thinking to go chasing something solo?"

She knew he was just protective but that comment still got her back up. They had to find a middle ground on this, because she would not sit on the sidelines while other agents stuck their necks out.

She calmly reminded him, "I had backup."

"Where?" He opened his arms and looked around. "I don't see Adrianna anywhere up here."

Sarcasm just pissed her off. She tried for a logical counterpoint. "You were the first real partner I had in VIPER. I've worked solo for a long time."

"Not anymore."

She clamped her lips to keep from arguing. She wanted to spend a nice evening with him. Not fight about something that would not change.

He wouldn't let it go. "You can't be chasing demons with no backup."

She stepped back and crossed her arms. "Since when?"

"Since becoming my mate."

They'd had this disagreement by phone three days ago.

He didn't want her working alone. Ever.

She was not going to be treated like some princess who couldn't deal with a few cuts and bruises.

Storm had been overprotective before they were mated, but he'd seen her kill things bigger than demons. She wouldn't lose her temper with him, but she was not going to start calling in help every time she had to face something preternatural.

She didn't want him to take issue with Tzader either.

Wait a minute. Tzader should have told her that Storm was back in town. "Did you tell Tzader when you arrived?"

"Yes. That's how I knew you were here. I asked him not to tell you so I could surprise you."

That was sweet.

He glanced at the cable car then back to her, angry again. "And I'm the one who gets surprised when I find you close to falling sixteen hundred feet."

She pushed the topic away from her near death. "How did you make it back into town before tomorrow morning?"

"I had everyone on the troll killer team push around the clock for the last two days so I could get back early."

That's why he looked so tired. She had to leave all the heavy talking until tomorrow and just get him home. "Did you get the killer?"

"Yes, but he was dead when we found him. I'll tell you about that later. I left the group so I could return faster on my own."

She thought on that. "Did you shift and return as a jaguar?"

He nodded.

"Why? They had vehicles."

"They also stop all the time to eat and for every other reason. Worst road trip ever. Tzader told me where you were supposed to be, but you *weren't* with Adrianna when I got here."

She caught the undertone to expect more conversation later and held her tongue so he could get it all out. Storm was the most patient man on the face of the earth when it came to her, unless he thought she was in danger.

She'd been living in a dangerous world her whole life.

That was not going to change anytime soon.

Storm said, "Adrianna pointed out the skyride and told me you'd gone after something you thought was a demon. I took off and reached the skyride platform just as your cable car was too far out for me to leap and catch. I ran to find the trail up the back side of the mountain while you took the scenic route."

She knew how preternaturally fast he was, but that surprised even her. "Where'd you find a rope on the way here?"

"When I saw you hanging off the damn mountain, I raced back to the skyride building and used majik to open the storage area that had rescue equipment." He studied her. "What were you doing hanging from a cable car when you hate heights?"

When had he figured out she was freaked by heights? She growled. "I didn't do it intentionally. I can now take dangling from a cable car and clinging to the side of a mountain off my bucket list."

She totally missed with lightening the mood.

The fierce look in Storm's eyes went up another level.

She put her hand on his crossed arms and said, "I would have hung there until someone came along. I was not going to let go and lose you."

His eyes softened and he swallowed hard. "I'm glad you didn't let go."

"Never."

He looked as if he wasn't convinced and started to say something, but didn't get the chance.

Power flashed around them in a burst, and a rogue wind slapped their clothes.

CHAPTER 4

That whip of power could only mean that someone had sent Sen to deal with the mess on top of Stone Mountain.

Evalle reminded herself that killing the VIPER liaison would only delay her going home.

She took one look into Storm's eyes, which had immediately darkened. He knew who had arrived, too, and she'd have her hands full keeping peace between these two. She took a breath and prepared to face Sen as she turned around.

Storm stepped up beside her, but at least he didn't try to step in front of her.

Sen's body materialized near the platform thirty feet away and on the inside of the fenced area. He stood in black jeans, boots and a black short-sleeved T-shirt, oblivious to the cold seeping into Evalle's body. His hair, often a different length within a twenty-four hour period, now fell loose around his shoulders. Today he stood almost six-six, and would tower over most of the agents. She'd seen him shorter, so he'd probably chosen uber-tall today just for her, so he could lord his position as if she and Storm were cockroaches avoiding his boot heel.

Sen cast a glance around then said, "Tzader called me from a Tribunal meeting. This better be important."

So either Tzader had heard her signal for help after all, or Adrianna had made the call.

"I caught a Réisc Dubh demon stalking humans around Memorial Hall," Evalle replied, giving Sen as simple a statement as she could to limit what he'd criticize.

"*If* that's true, what're you doing up here?"

She clamped down on her irritation at his immediate

suspicion with anything that involved her. "The demon walked around with a glamour then jumped into the cable car. When I tried to contain him, he attacked me and somehow got the cable car moving. We fought all the way up here."

Sen stood with his arms crossed. "A Réisc Dubh and even *you* couldn't stop him?"

Sen made her sound like a bumbling fool, but this Réisc Dubh had not been what she'd expect from that kind of demon. "He was glamoured to the point that I couldn't tell his race at first, but once I realized what he was, he showed his form, and was tougher to take down than he should've been. He had more power than any demon I've faced before. He ripped up my shoulder before I finally killed him by stabbing him with my dagger."

"Who else saw him besides you, Alterant?"

Storm stiffened at Sen using the word Alterant as if it were a slur. When Storm moved forward a fraction, Evalle squeezed his arm in a silent plea not to engage. Sen had shown his god-like powers more than once and Evalle didn't want him flexing his muscles. With a tiny finger flip, he'd smashed Storm, in jaguar form, up against a brick wall.

Evalle had thought Storm died, and he almost had.

Storm had assured her Sen would never get a second chance to kill him, but keeping these two apart would be better for everyone involved.

Storm let out a breath that sounded threatening, but he eased back off the balls of his feet. His body was still rigid with the urge to act, but he kept his temper restrained.

Sen chuckled.

Tension swept from Storm.

You are such a jerk, Sen. She'd have to deal with having asked Storm to back down in front of Sen later, once she and Storm were alone.

Sen repeated his question. "Who else saw the demon?"

"Just me. Why?" Evalle confirmed.

"The Tribunal doesn't want Beladors retaliating against the Medb by conjuring up bogus demon issues."

"What?" Evalle shouted at Sen. "Are you serious? Beladors have been working around the clock to clean up the–" She paused before saying they'd been cleaning up the mess left by the Medb, because that was not going to help the Belador case with a Tribunal that needed an attitude adjustment. "Problems left from last month," she finished.

A sound rumbled from deep in Storm's throat that reminded her of a predator on the hunt, waiting to attack its prey. Anyone with sense would realize that might be the only warning before Storm's control snapped like a paper leash.

"So you can prove this isn't some trumped-up issue?" Sen asked.

"Take a look at the body." *Dickhead,* she finished silently. "The guy was strange, even for a Réisc Dubh. One minute he was entirely human then the next his head and shoulders lost their glamour. His head expanded until his jaws were a foot wide and showed off a double row of teeth. He'd act demented sometimes, then out of the blue, he'd make lightning bolts fly around that interfered with my kinetics."

"He made lightning bolts fly around *and* made a cable car ride up here on its own?" Sen scoffed, then directed his next question at Storm. "That wasn't a Réisc Dubh. What kind of demon has that type of power?"

Storm smiled, but there was nothing nice about it. "You'd be surprised at what some demons are capable of given the right motivation."

Any minute all this testosterone poisoning would combust into a blood bath with one wrong move.

Just over a week ago, Storm had to be dragged back from the edge of turning demon forever. He carried that tainted blood as a gift from his Ashaninka witch doctor mother, but the Navajo half he'd inherited from his shaman father kept him from the dark side.

At the moment, he looked like he was ready to embrace his dark genes.

Evalle cut through the tension by pulling everyone back to the problem at hand. "I have no idea if he was entirely Réisc Dubh, but he had black ears. The bottom half of his body didn't change into anything. Take his corpse to the druids at headquarters and see what they think."

That broke the silent battle raging between the two men.

Sen leaped up ten feet to the platform.

Evalle used her kinetics and catapulted herself over the fence, then up onto the platform, too.

Storm landed silently next to her.

Nice to have jaguar agility.

Sen walked over to the cable car and stuck his head in for a moment then backed out. "Where is he?"

Storm frowned and glanced at Evalle then they both walked over to the car, where no body was inside. The chair leg she'd clung to was still bent, but the rest of the damage had vanished and there was no blood. Even her jacket was gone.

She shook her head and pointed. "He was right there."

"You fought him?" Sen asked.

"Yes."

"He tore up your shoulder?"

"*Yesss!*" she said, losing patience with Sen's snippy tone.

"Where's the blood?"

"You see it on her shirt," Storm said, his voice loaded with disgust.

"That could have been staged."

"You son of a bitch," Storm said, taking a step forward.

Sen said, "Do it. Give me a reason to ask the Tribunal to lock you beneath headquarters."

Where Storm would stay forever.

Evalle whispered, "Please don't." She put her hand on Storm's arm again and felt his muscles quivering with fury.

Sen mimicked in a bad imitation of Evalle, "Oh, please don't Storm, or you'll get your ass kicked."

Storm turned to stone, not looking her way, but he moved his arm out of her grasp.

Now she'd pissed Storm off by giving Sen ammo to humiliate him.

One day, Sen would go down in flames and if she controlled all the water in the world she wouldn't allow it to dribble on him. "I didn't make up any of this, Sen. The Beladors are not faking demon attacks. No one can lie to a Tribunal. All they have to do is ask Tzader."

Not that she wanted to send Tzader to face a Tribunal with all the personal troubles he had right now, but the mix of three deities that made up a Tribunal wouldn't intimidate Tzader one bit. He'd set everyone straight.

"It's coming to that very soon," Sen warned. "The Tribunal has to keep changing out gods and goddesses just to accommodate these problems. Neither Macha nor Maeve can be in a Tribunal due to conflict of interest, so the other gods and goddesses are not happy about all the new Belador and Medb conflict."

Bloodshed and loss of lives for centuries deserved a better word than conflict.

Sen pointed out, "This is my only warning. I had better not be called back to deal with another alleged demon sighting by an Alterant any time soon."

She said, "If you don't want us hunting demons, or any other creatures, then why don't you have your Medb buddies deal with them? As for the Tribunal, if they'd end the tug-of-war over the gryphons, all this conflict might die down."

Macha had claimed ownership of the Alterants-turned-gryphons first, but Maeve awoke from a two-thousand-year nap and decided she had equal claim since they carried Medb blood. That witch could posture all she wanted.

Evalle would not join the Medb and would fight any challenge Queen Maeve brought.

Whiny Tribunal deities.

Yes, this was the first time in many years that the deities had been called upon so much, but if they didn't like being imposed upon, they should fix it.

Then again, Evalle had suffered their attempts at fixing things in the past, which hadn't been fun, especially the way they twisted words to suit their purposes. She kept her mouth shut.

"I'll be sure to pass along your advice to the current Tribunal," Sen said, way too smug.

Adrenaline from moments ago drained from her body, leaving exhaustion in its wake. She wanted to go home. "I'm done. Just so you know, when you get this area back in shape, the demon-you-don't-believe-exists left a security guy comatose at the lower platform. That's all yours."

She walked off before Sen could cause any more problems for her. Storm fell into stride next to her, just as silent as he'd been for the last few minutes.

What had happened to that demon's body?

Not just the body.

She slapped her head. "Crap!"

"What?" Storm asked, looking around as if some threat had arisen.

She waved him off. "I just realized. My spelled dagger is gone, too."

He said nothing, but what could he say?

Whatever she'd stabbed shouldn't have been able to walk away. Not under its own power. Besides, that dagger had been a gift from Tzader. He'd given it to her not long after they'd met and she not only depended on it, she cherished it.

Storm moved smooth as water slipping down the side of the mountain, sure-footed and determined, but although she was a city girl through and through, she kept pace with him, looking over in time to catch him watching her.

Things were uncomfortable again.

She hated this weirdness. He'd been upset with her for sticking her neck out, almost since the day they'd met, but it had never been like this, with her having to tiptoe around him. She said, "Do you have to go back out hunting tomorrow?"

"No. Tzader will let me know if anything new comes up on the killing."

She stumbled in spite of her night vision, but Storm caught her by the arm and steadied her. He asked, "When was the last time you slept?"

Soundly? Not for a week.

But he hadn't asked that so she gave him an answer that wouldn't set off his internal lie detector. "I woke up twelve hours ago. Not much else to do during the day since I can't go outside in the sun." But she was so tired she could sleep standing up right now.

Storm's worry became a living thing hovering around her. She had to get his mind somewhere else. "Sen isn't kicking up a fuss over you working with Tzader instead of answering to him?"

"I don't answer to anyone. Tzader gets that. The morning we left to go hunting, I made it clear that my loyalty belonged to the

Beladors now and that I'd help VIPER if it suited me or benefitted the Beladors."

She smiled at that until Storm added in a harder tone, "And I also made it clear that I would not leave unless I was guaranteed you would not be working alone."

Don't say a word. She kept telling herself to wait until they had both caught up on rest, then they'd talk.

She sucked at talking, but she was tired of the ache in her chest every time she thought about their going back to the apartment together.

Storm had been on edge, and it had started ten minutes after he'd walked into her apartment a week ago. He'd locked down his emotions so fast she hadn't gotten a good empathic read on him, but it hadn't taken a rocket scientist to recognize that look of I-might-have-made-a-mistake on his face.

Her stomach clenched at the memory.

He had to be thinking twice about staying at her place. She'd tried to convince herself that wasn't the case, but she'd never been one to avoid the truth.

This tension had as much to do with their living arrangement as it did with his extreme need to protect her. Evalle had to make some changes, but she couldn't just shove Quinn's cousin Lanna out the door. Not with a powerful wizard looking for the teenager. Evalle had promised to keep Lanna safe for Quinn, who had been her friend as long as Tzader had.

And Feenix was never leaving.

But she didn't want Storm to leave either and Feenix hadn't liked Storm being around her at all.

What if she had to choose between Feenix and Storm?

She couldn't do that.

Storm could use majik to soothe Feenix, but she wanted them to get along without any outside influence and had no idea how Feenix would react to Storm's majik.

She'd made it halfway down the mile-long path to the bottom of the mountain when Storm stepped in front of her.

She pulled up fast. "What?"

"You're upset."

"I'm not," she lied out of knee-jerk reaction before rolling her eyes at the flat line of his lips. She admitted, "Okay, it's been a long week. I'm just ... thinking a lot."

"What are you thinking about?"

How cramped my apartment is becoming with four bodies moving around.

How the only day we spent there started in chaos and ended in uncomfortable tension.

How I couldn't cook a decent meal or look like Adrianna even if I had a fairy godmother.

Evalle hunted for something that could be the truth and not open that discussion yet. She ran the thought through her mind to make it true, then said, "Adrianna needs to meet with us right away."

"She'll wait." He didn't challenge her statement. Instead he leaned down and said, "I've had something on my mind, too, that we need to deal with right now."

Please don't say you don't want to go home with me. "What?"

"You and me. Naked."

CHAPTER 5

"Get away from there before Sen or another VIPER agent senses you," Donndubhán warned, fighting a homicidal urge after losing one of his best demon specimens.

Imar backed up, but kept watching through the trees where that bastard Sen and two VIPER agents moved around the top skyride platform on Stone Mountain, cleaning up the mess before humans could panic. Imar said, "That's four dead demons and for what? We're going to end up just as dead if anyone in the Medb coven gets word of this."

"Getting caught is not an option. Death would not be our punishment," Donndubhán pointed out. "Queen Maeve would put us in a cycle of eternal torture that would make dying a gift."

Imar narrowed his eyes. "I trusted you when you said we could do this and get out of the Medb coven forever, but this isn't working. We can stop now and the queen won't know. Someone's going to tie these demons to the troll killings. Then what? The next thing you know they'll find out we're not turning trolls into demons, but using our own—"

"Shut up," Donndubhán snarled, "You really believe we can stop now and be safe? Queen Maeve has something in play that she won't share with anyone except Ossian. She has him moving around Atlanta in some disguise that's a secret from the rest of us." That ass-kisser Ossian had been awarded the top position in the Scáth Force of Medb elite warriors. Neither VIPER nor the Beladors knew what Queen Medb had inserted into the Atlanta area under the guise of being just another Medb warlock or witch moving here.

"We shouldn't have left that troll body by the river,"

grumbled Imar.

Donndubhán had just finished sacrificing a troll to create this last demon when an old troll saw them. Donndubhán captured the noisy bastard and had Imar spread the old troll's scent in three directions to buy them time, then he'd placed a spell over that troll, convincing him to go with Imar to find his missing troll son.

Then he'd sent the pair on their way with orders for Imar to take the old troll to South Georgia, five hours away, and kill him there.

Donndubhán told Imar, "As long as the Beladors and VIPER are the only ones investigating the troll deaths, Queen Maeve and Cathbad won't give two shits. But if word of new demons gets back to her, we'll be screwed. That's the part we need to keep hidden. Queen Maeve and Cathbad won't believe a Medb is creating the demons unless they catch one alive, and I won't allow that to happen. What you should be thinking about right now is how you can help me with the next demon."

Donndubhán had served the last coven queen for six hundred and sixty- six years. Then the original Medb ruler, Queen Maeve, and her confidante, Cathbad the Druid, had reincarnated.

This queen would never die, but warlocks like Donndubhán would.

He had no intention of spending what mortal life he now had left as servant to another witch.

Just another grunt for the royalty.

Imar chewed on his fingernail, a disgusting habit, but everything about Imar disgusted Donndubhán. With a body as substantial as a fifty-gallon steel drum filled to capacity, Imar's forehead jutted out over thick eyebrows like a bad human experiment and his shoulders were hunched in a way that modern clothes couldn't fix. Stick him in jeans and an oversized T-shirt and he looked like a thug. That body was better suited for the robes they'd worn in Táur Medb, their coven's home on another dimension.

Donndubhán, on the other hand, had taken to this human world. He'd like it even better if he had any semblance of a real life. Queen Maeve and Cathbad still lived as if it were two thousand years ago, assuming all their people were loyal followers, happy to continue waiting on the royalty hand and foot.

Every leader required a lackey, which was why Donndubhán tolerated Imar, and also because the annoying warlock had considerable power when needed.

Donndubhán couldn't do this alone and not get caught.

This way, if anyone ended up in perpetual misery it would be Imar. Donndubhán could cast a control spell on his sidekick so fast Imar would never know what hit him, and Imar would confess to creating the demons all by himself.

Imar stopped gnawing his grubby fingernails long enough to complain some more. "We have to find more trolls for testing the spell, but the troll families keep contacting VIPER about the disappearances."

"You think VIPER really cares if someone thins out the troll population in Atlanta?"

Imar frowned but didn't argue that point. "No, but what if Queen Maeve suspects one of her own coven is working rogue in her territory? She'll call us all in and we won't pass her lie test."

Donndubhán had thrown that caution to the wind when he came up with this plan. There was no way to go back. He needed a powerful coven to join, one that would accept him as a peer. That wouldn't happen until he could prove he was no longer with the Medb, and had an army of glamoured demons at his beck and call. What he hadn't told Imar was that once they had absolute control over his special Réisc Dubh look-alike demons, Donndubhán would use majik to bind his creations to him, and turn the entire group into a force even the Beladors would think twice about attacking.

He'd make this work.

To pull it off, he had to find the perfect dark witch coven that would take him in and help him fake his death in such a way that Maeve would never find him. She'd find Imar, whom Donndubhán intended to use for his final sacrifice. Once Donndubhán was in contact with a coven worthy of his talents, he'd pull out his big gun—Noirre majik. Every dark witch in the world would trade her own child to get Noirre.

Only the Medb queen could make that trade.

Anyone else caught sharing just one Noirre spell outside the

Medb coven would die in a truly painful way.

But offering to share Noirre would convince *any* other dark coven that he had turned his back on the Medb, and then his army of demons would give him power within the coven.

He would rule others for once.

And he had the perfect witch in mind who would give him an introduction to the Sterling coven. All he had to do was manufacture evidence that Adrianna Lafontaine was behind the glamoured demon trolls. With just the right proof, he'd be able to blackmail her into helping him, because no one but a fool believed a dark witch would really help VIPER.

CHAPTER 6

Evalle had been enjoying the last of her hike down the mountain trail with Storm until a witch appeared in front of her.

Sixty seconds ago, she'd been smiling over Storm's not-so-subtle admission that he wanted to make love to her and wasn't above making that happen right here in the woods.

Since Evalle wasn't into public sex, and her apartment was seventeen miles away in downtown Atlanta, she was in a hurry.

Adrianna stood where the trail ended, across the street from a parking lot. Evalle gave Adrianna the evil eye and the witch smirked, damn her.

"Glad to see you're in one piece," Adrianna said as Evalle and Storm stopped beside her. They stood on a sidewalk that ran parallel with the road around this side of the mountain. In daytime, this place was busy with locals wanting to hike up the back side of Stone Mountain.

The Sterling witch struck her usual pose, hands clasped together in front of her, everything proper and precise no matter what she was doing.

Evalle told Adrianna, "Thanks for telling Storm where I was."

"Like I was going to deny someone who turned into a crazy man when he heard you were off on your own?"

Evalle slashed a look at Storm, who neither acknowledged nor denied Adrianna's claim. But everything in that face had shut down. Where had her teasing Skinwalker gone—the one who'd surprised her by switching the mood from upset and frustrated to urgent and wanting in no more than a heartbeat?

She had a sinking suspicion that seeing Adrianna reminded Storm of just how close Evalle had come to dying.

Adrianna must have picked up on the unease rippling through the air, because she moved ahead. "Since we're rarely all three together at one time without others around and time is becoming an issue, I want to talk about our deal."

"How about after we get some sleep," Storm said, making it clear he was not up for an argument. He reached over and tugged Evalle to him, kissing her hair. "She's whipped."

Evalle started to protest, but she'd rather talk later, too. Still, her new witch friend had said she was on a tight timeline.

Storm's suggestion failed to faze Adrianna. "I didn't delay in helping after Sen smashed your jaguar body on a brick wall and your spirit guide asked me to hide you until you healed. Nor did I put off Evalle when she needed help locating you in Mitnal."

"You're right, but just to be clear, I'm not feeling uber appreciative about your sending her into demon hell," Storm muttered.

Adrianna's calm countenance shifted into the first signs of anger. "Maybe we should have left you there."

"No, we shouldn't have," Evalle said and lifted a hand to halt Adrianna. The witch rarely showed any reaction, but she was just as testy as Storm. Evalle got why Storm was, but not Adrianna's reason.

Evalle turned to Storm. "She *is* right. We should find out what she needs and pay our debt."

Storm wiped a hand over his eyes and mouth. "Yes, we should. Sorry, Adrianna. There never seems to be the perfect time to do anything and I didn't mean to sound as if I wouldn't make good on our agreement. I appreciate all you've done."

Adrianna answered, "Thank you."

His gaze roamed over Evalle's torn and bloody shirt, now covered by his jacket, but he conceded. "Let's go somewhere close and eat. I'm starving."

"Me, too," Evalle agreed, glad to feel harmony return. "I know a place just east of the park that's open all night."

"Works for me," Adrianna agreed. "I have my car here. I can drop you at Storm's SUV."

When they reached Adrianna's Lexus sedan, she slid into the driver's seat as Storm held the front passenger door for Evalle.

Adrianna murmured, "What's up with him?"

Evalle whispered, "Think he's tired. He ran all the way here from South Georgia in his jaguar form."

Once Evalle and Storm transferred to his truck, Storm drove silently as Adrianna followed them to the Metro Café Diner, which stayed open twenty-four-seven. Evalle's mouth started watering as soon as she entered the café. She slid into one of the red vinyl booths with Storm on her right and Adrianna across from them.

Vintage rock played softly in the background, entertaining a dozen customers enjoying late-night meals. A little quiet for a Saturday night, but it was close to midnight at a diner in a peaceful suburb. Not some party club in downtown Atlanta. Two young men sat at the bar nursing beers and thumbing their smart phones. They'd paused long enough to scope out Adrianna and Evalle until Storm had unloaded his alpha stare in their direction.

The men decided to stick to safer entertainment on the internet.

Adrianna requested hot tea, but Storm and Evalle made up for her meager request with their food orders. Between shifting from human form to jaguar and racing back to Atlanta on four legs, Storm must have burned a ton of calories. Evalle hadn't eaten a decent meal since he'd left, mainly because she'd been eating her own food.

Grabbing a meal now took the pressure off of her cooking at home.

Score.

With the waitress out of the way, Adrianna leaned forward and said, "Give me a moment and I'll create a privacy spell that will allow the waitress to pass through when she returns."

Storm's fingers covered Evalle's hand, warming her from the soul out again. Maybe he *was* only tired, as she'd told Adrianna.

Adrianna leaned back, closed her eyes and murmured a soft chant. When she sat forward again, she asked, "Can you free up some time very soon?"

"I can, but Evalle doesn't need to help," Storm answered before Evalle had a chance to speak.

She gritted her teeth and said, "We both made commitments to Adrianna. We're both paying up. End of discussion."

A flash of anger rushed off of Storm. Too bad.

He had to get past this uber-protective mode he was in. Had she known becoming his mate was going to flip a switch and throw him into overdrive when it came to her safety, she wouldn't have ...

Okay, she *still* would have become his mate.

Regardless, they lived in a dangerous world, and Adrianna had come through more than once on tight timelines. Evalle would not put her off any longer if Adrianna had something pressing.

Plus, Evalle had wanted to know Adrianna's secrets for a long time. No Sterling witch joined VIPER just for the exercise.

Evalle said, "We should be able to get a couple days off after the last few weeks of nonstop work for VIPER. What do you need us to do?"

Storm said nothing, but he did lean in to listen.

Adrianna drew herself up, shoulders back like a polite child waiting to recite English homework. "I came to VIPER for a reason. They needed a dark witch and I needed to find someone powerful enough to help me, but also a being I could trust to not betray me. That limits the field greatly. I didn't expect to find two, but it will give us a better chance of succeeding."

Evalle had heard some of the Beladors speculating about Adrianna's reason for joining up, but no one ever had real knowledge. The witch kept to herself and had been judicious in making friends, but she'd clearly decided that Evalle and Storm deserved her confidence.

Not a bad bet since Adrianna had held Evalle's confidence more than once.

Other than the occasional half smile, Adrianna rarely expressed emotion. She might appear to be a petite, even fragile, woman, but Evalle had seen the uber-feminine blonde pull out a can of witch whoopass and the sight had been impressive.

After fighting a yawn, Evalle wanted this moved along faster. "I think the three of us have proven we can trust each other, so what is it you need us to do?"

"Help me reach my sister who is being held captive by another witch."

Storm leaned in, intent now. "Is the goddess over the Medb coven holding your sister?"

"No."

She felt relief rush off of Storm as he leaned back. "From what Evalle told me, you took on the witch doctor who had me trapped in Mitnal. With that kind of juice, why do you need our help?"

"Because my sister, Ragan, and I are twins. Ragan is the more powerful twin. The witch holding her is drawing Ragan's power and will soon be more powerful than any other single witch—maybe even any other *group* of witches—if she isn't stopped."

Evalle asked, "What will it take to rescue Ragan?"

"To steal her from a realm protected by ancient guardians who were once living members of a powerful coven."

CHAPTER 7

Storm sat forward, staring at Adrianna. He had no idea who really lived inside that body and mind if she thought he'd go along with taking Evalle into another hostile realm. "Are you serious?"

Evalle's jaw had dropped. "Is it even possible to get to her?"

Reaching both hands behind her head in a moment of what looked like exasperation, Adrianna grabbed her blond hair and wrapped it into a quick knot of some kind at the base of her neck. When she brought her hands back to the table and folded them together, she took a deep breath.

Storm felt frustration flow out of Adrianna like water, then she said, "If this was easy I'd have done it alone by now. If I allow that witch to continue cooking my sister's majik, Ragan will end up a shadow, unable to die or to cross the veil to rest even if she *could* die."

"I'm in, but that's ... insane," Evalle said, voice falling off in disbelief.

Adrianna said, "I understand, but–"

"No," Storm growled. "*I'll* go with Adrianna."

"No!" Evalle crossed her arms and turned those gorgeous eyes on him that, even through the dark lenses of her glasses, dared him to dare her. "We *both* agreed to help. We *both* owe her. It sounds like it's going to take everything we can throw at this witch to stop her and save Ragan."

Storm leaned toward Evalle until they were nose to nose. "You don't even know what you're going up against."

"I rarely know what I'm up against. What makes this any different?"

He had no argument for that, but neither was he giving in. "I'm the one with witch blood and majik."

"Actually," Adrianna said, interrupting, "I was thinking I'd take Evalle with me so you could stand guard, Storm."

Taking a second to keep from blasting Adrianna, Storm took another approach. He'd drive the conversation toward better planning. "From what Evalle told me, you took on a witch doctor who was an evil piece of work supercharged by a demon king, and you won. That's pretty damn powerful. Why not bring in more witches to help?"

Adrianna rubbed her temple and said, "For one thing, the witches I've gotten to know since coming here are white witches who are not about to get involved in anything they'd see as dark majik. Number two is that if they do get involved, they'll probably end up dying."

"Well that's encouraging," Evalle interjected.

Adrianna shoved a quick flash of attitude back at Evalle, but continued in that disturbingly calm tone. "I'm not saying that getting Ragan back doesn't come with danger, but these witches have no idea what they'd be up against and frankly, after watching them try to form a council, I doubt they could agree on anything soon enough to be of use to me."

Evalle snapped her fingers. "Oh, yeah, you never finished telling me about that. Something with Rowan and Nicole, right?"

"That's because you weren't listening."

"I am now," Evalle answered dryly.

"I don't know anything about a council," Storm admitted.

Adrianna acknowledged his comment with a tilt of her head. "There have been no major covens, white or dark, in this region for a long time. Only small, independent groups, though some of those are powerful. Now that the Medb is dumping a constant flow of dark witches into Atlanta, all the small covens and solitary white witches are banding together to form a council under the pretext of policing their own." She gave a snarky chuckle. "Let's say they're *trying* to band together. The truth is they want to concentrate their power, which is not a bad idea for defense if the Medb attempt to undermine the white witch community, but now Rowan and her peers are bugging me about getting involved."

Evalle waved her hand at that. "But why would they want a Sterling witch? And, for that matter, why aren't you calling in big guns from your own coven?"

"Because I'm not aligned with the Sterlings either," Adrianna admitted softly. She met Storm's eyes as she finally answered, "Bottom line is that I don't have any other witches to call in." Her throat worked in a hard swallow, and he sensed a wave of grief wash over her, then as quickly as he'd felt it, the emotion was gone. "And by next week it may not matter."

"Why?"

"Because of what we have to do."

Tired of dancing around a topic that sent his blood pressure boiling every time the idea of Evalle being involved came up, Storm asked, "And what exactly is that?"

Adrianna's sigh carried a weight that sagged her shoulders. "Let me start from the beginning and explain everything first. As I said, my sister Ragan is being held in another realm. A parallel universe that was created by the ancestors of the witch who took her captive." Adrianna paused, sliding her intense blue eyes to Storm when she admitted, "I would do this alone if I could, but there is too much at stake to risk failure."

Storm studied her a moment. "What's at stake besides your sister?"

"The supernatural powers within this world. Freedom. Humanity. Take your pick."

"*All* the powers?" Evalle asked.

"Yes. Anyone with non-human powers would be at risk, depending on their vulnerability."

Storm asked, "What witch could be that threatening?"

"One who can wield Witchlock."

Storm took a moment, searching for any memory. "Never heard of it."

Evalle lifted her shoulders, indicating she hadn't either.

Adrianna placed her hands on the table top, stacking them neatly again. Storm got the feeling she was drawing power in some way to soothe herself. "Few have heard of it. Witchlock originated in the ninth century Current Era, and was practiced in secret until the thirteenth century, then the coven where it originated disappeared.

"Later, major covens such as the Sterlings, the Medb, the Diamond Bright Truth and Viaje de la Luz all assumed that any descendants who possessed remnants of Witchlock power had become a nonissue after so many decades."

"Whoa." Evalle lifted a hand. "The Medb and Sterlings are dark witches, and you know I'm not slighting you because you're a Sterling."

"I know."

"But the Diamond Bright Truth and Viaje de la Luz are not dark witches. So what's the tie between all this?"

Adrianna explained, "Most of the world believes that there are only light and dark witches, because few contemporary covens are even aware of a third group known as KievRus. That name came from the Kievan Rus area that Ukraine and Russia consider the first East Slavic state."

Evalle yawned. "Aren't Sterlings from that area?"

"Sterling blood can be traced back to medieval Scotland, which was inhabited by the Norse-Gaels–"

"Vikings?"

"Basically, yes, but the Sterlings eventually migrated to Ukraine, which is now their home even though many live in different parts of the world."

Storm noted how Adrianna talked of the Sterlings as if she had not been born one. Something was seriously off between her and her coven.

"Got it." Evalle yawned again, sounding as beat as she looked.

Storm would call a halt to this and suggest they meet after everyone had some rest, but there was no way he'd get Evalle to let go of this tale when they were finally going to find out so much about Adrianna.

His earlier irritation had evaporated once he had Evalle safe and close beside him. Normally he could control his temper around her, but not when she constantly put herself first in danger and last in value. He was slowly changing that, helping her understand that she mattered, but since he'd mated with her, all he could think about was just how precious a gift he had, and how he'd never survive losing her. The thought of anything happening to her was ... he couldn't even consider it.

Still, the possibility had been at the forefront of his mind the whole time he'd been gone.

Then he'd come home to find her one slip from plummeting to her death.

Drawing in a calming breath, he put his arm around Evalle's shoulders and pulled her to him. She smiled up in response and his heart took note, beating like a war drum.

Adrianna made a noise in her throat, which drew a grin from Evalle. The witch said, "Are you two still with me?"

Storm said, "Yes." Then he ticked off a condensed version. "A third player in the world of witches, apparently neither white nor dark, which originated in the ninth century in Kievan Rus. What makes this coven different from others?"

"KievRus originally formed with the idea of being an objective force for the people, which meant doing whatever they felt necessary to protect the masses from oppressive rulers and other threats, whether that involved using white or dark majik. Instead of sacrificing a human or an animal to power the origin, the two who started all this each gave of their own blood and created a spell that bonded their blood with all of the elements, but especially that of the air."

Evalle lifted her head from where she'd propped it on her hand. "Why air?"

"Because, of all the elements, air can affect water, fire and earth."

"Okay, so what has all that got to do with your sister or you?"

"I'm getting to that. I'm trying to give you as short a story as possible, but this happened over many centuries and you need to understand what we'll be up against. The bottom line is that the empire known as Kievan Rus had a population of both Slavic and Scandinavian people. It was founded by Vikings ... depending on which history you follow. But let's say mine is correct."

"What if it's not?" Evalle asked with a bit of taunt.

"Let me make this simple. It. *Is*. Correct."

Evalle snorted at Adrianna's rare show of temper and Storm couldn't stop his chuckle.

Adrianna shot them both a glare and said, "During the time the Slavics and Vikings co-existed, a secret coven of powerful beings grew from those two who gave their blood. One of the original blood donors was a woman who called herself Heide and was loosely described as a descendant of an immortal Norse sorceress named Gullveig. Heide might have been part fae as well. She married Volkov and he was believed to be a shaman from Ukraine, but today we'd call him a witch."

"That'd be a scary mix," Evalle said. "So they started a coven, right?"

Adrianna nodded.

"Is it still around?"

"The KievRus coven was believed wiped out when the Mongols invaded Kievan Rus."

Storm thought a moment. "Are you talking about the Khan witch hunts?"

"No. Those events were quite public and the Mongols did not fear going after those witches because the public was aware of them.

"Over the years, just to protect their identities and location, the KievRus coven fed rumors to convince the general public they were only a myth. But one witch got a burr up her backside, probably because she was not powerful enough to ever hold a position of leadership. She betrayed them."

"Got it."

Adrianna continued, "Mongol soldiers were sent covertly to behead the coven members, and the soldiers returned after being gone for four months, claiming to have killed the entire coven. But they did not bring back even one head, nor could they recall the path of their journey. Things were quiet, so everyone believed they'd been successful. They weren't, but the coven lost its leader—the one who wielded Witchlock—and at that point they truly became more myth than reality. They took what was left of their group and went underground."

Adrianna looked introspective for a moment before going on. "Fast forward to the late twentieth century. Two decades ago, rumors circulated that the KievRus coven was active again. Across all this time, elders in the Sterling coven have refused to dismiss an ancient foretelling that a leader would arise to once again wield the power."

Storm asked, "They haven't had another to wield Witchlock in all this time?"

"Not until now. The new leader has arisen, and the time approaches when she will come into power. She's called Veronika, and she's a direct descendant of Heide. Publicly, the KievRus refused to involve themselves in the world or its politics. But many Sterling elders suspect that the KievRus have *always* had a hand in directing world events from wherever they hid during each century, and that their majik has ultimately influenced many changes in the mortal world. Now Veronika is in position to take control."

"You've met her?"

"Yes. As I mentioned, the Sterling family line has Norse origins just as KievRus do. Veronika and some of the Sterling coven share blood."

Storm leaned forward. "I hope I'm wrong about where you're going with this."

Adrianna glanced at Storm, then back at Evalle before she answered.

"When Veronika's family surfaced again twenty years ago, they stated that the new leader had been born, and offered to allow the Sterlings to continue to exist without threat from Veronika once she came into power *if* the Sterlings would hand over blood in exchange when the time came to pay up."

Storm breathed a soft curse. *Sometimes it sucks to be right.*

"Your people sacrificed someone in their own coven to Veronika?" Evalle asked, clearly appalled.

"Blood wasn't actually shed, but an agreement was struck and blood was *handed over*," Adrianna explained. "When Veronika came to collect, she demanded the most powerful of our next generation. That is my sister, Ragan. Veronika locked her into a timeless stasis so Veronika could draw on Ragan to form the power nucleus for the rebirth of Witchlock." Adrianna paused, then added, "At least, I originally thought the stasis was timeless."

Evalle sat forward again, obviously thinking it through. "Why would they do that? Hand over their most powerful resource to another coven when that leader hadn't come into power yet?"

"The elders believed the foretelling and that Veronika would be the one to wield Witchlock. They knew that if they didn't take her deal, she'd find another coven who would, and even Ragan's power would not be enough to protect them. They saw it as win-win."

Evalle huffed at that. "The only losers being you and your sister." She rubbed her eyes under the glasses again. "You said the KievRus were altruistic. How...?"

"I said they *started out* that way. When they went underground, something changed, apparently. They still talk the talk and maybe some of them actually believe that Veronika is meant to do great things for humanity, but I can feel what she's doing to Ragan, and I can tell you that what she means to do...there's nothing good about it."

Storm shook his head. This was not good. He reminded Adrianna, "You have yet to say what Witchlock *is* specifically."

"The Sterling historians explain it as the ability to take possession of another being's power and control that person's gifts or abilities. The term *Witchlock* comes from a convoluted translation of ancient Slavic words, which basically means for a witch to lock onto any energy and take control."

"The drain on your sister notwithstanding, I've never heard of a witch *that* powerful," Storm argued.

"I had not either," Adrianna agreed. "Not until I saw the Sterling coven, which is feared by all who know them, hand over their next leader just to protect themselves."

No wonder Adrianna never said much about being a Sterling. Storm cheered her decision to turn her back on *that* family. He had his own dark genetics that had almost sucked him into a bottomless abyss.

If not for Evalle, he'd be there now.

He kissed her head and felt her smile wrap his senses.

"How tough can this Veronika be?" Evalle asked.

Adrianna said point blank, "Although she's dangerous in her own right even now, her current powers are nothing compared to what they will be when she takes possession of Witchlock. At that point, she'll be pretty much invincible."

"Not to a god or a goddess," Storm qualified.

"I honestly can't say, Storm. Veronika is descended from

Heide, and Heidi is suspected of actually *being* Gullveig, who was burned three times and still came back to life, Veronika is not to be underestimated. And as I said, she may also be part fae. There are some things no one outside the KievRus coven will ever know."

Storm ran a hand over his face, trying to wrap his head around the threat Adrianna clearly believed was imminent. Hard to argue with her when every word she spoke rang true to him.

Evalle sat up and started tapping the table with her fingers in a fast rhythm. "Where's this place your sister's being held?"

"She's in a realm called Jafnan Mir, which is both Nordic and Russian. The words translate into Forever World. It's similar to *Iron Wood* in Norse mythology, but Veronika's ancestors created the Jafnan Mir realm." Strain peeked through Adrianna's calm exterior when she stifled a yawn.

Evalle asked, "How long has this been going on?"

"Ragan was taken seventeen months ago."

"Your sister has been a prisoner for seventeen months? How can you be so calm all the time?"

Adrianna didn't say a word at first, but her fingers curled into tight balls. "It takes every ounce of my control to remain as calm as possible. Ragan and I are twins, but we're more than that. We were bound with majik while in the womb because we were the seventh daughters of a seventh daughter. The Sterlings knew we would be extremely powerful, but they were afraid two baby girls would divide the power. They were wrong."

Storm understood. "You were double the anticipated power, right?"

"Correct, but Ragan and I kept it a secret for a long time so that they wouldn't separate us." Adrianna kept talking at an easy pace, but her fingers remained fisted so tightly her knuckles were bone white. "My sister has been locked inside her own mind for seventeen months. Like being frozen while wide awake. I can hear her every minute of every day. I can feel her breathing. If I'm upset, she feels it through the bond and my agitation would increase her stress, but she has no way to release it. For that reason, I must remain at peace to help her survive. She would have given up living immediately if she could have. She has no control over anything and when it's bad she ... "

Evalle whispered, "She what?"

"She screams. She rarely sleeps. She moans constantly, but it's the screaming that is so ... difficult to endure."

Storm had run for hours to get here and had been angry to find Evalle left alone to fight a demon, then he'd been terrified to find her falling off a mountain. He was not looking forward to the circus in her apartment when they went home, and definitely not ready to let her near a bunch of dark witches, but hearing Adrianna's story made all of his problems appear trivial and manageable.

He couldn't say that he would have been able to maintain the quiet calm she exuded every time he saw her. He asked, "What do we have to do to reach Ragan?"

Adrianna's gaze faltered for the first time. She was hiding something. She stretched her fingers and clasped them loosely again. "Veronika's ancestors will stand in the way to prevent us from reaching the center of the realm. I know where Ragan is only because she was placed in the realm before Veronika blinded her. If we do get past the guardians, the minute Ragan realizes I am near, Veronika might also know. I've searched and traded favors for any bit of information, but I don't know everything. The one thing I do know is the guardians are there to keep anyone from touching Ragan. If you're going to walk away, now is the time to do it."

Time to wrap this up. Storm could smell the food almost ready to come out and Evalle's stomach growled.

Storm said, "To avoid arguing, let's say that we're both on board to go after your sister and getting her out of there. You said you'd like me to stand guard. Why not take me?"

"To travel there takes stepping out of our bodies and crossing through a different plane."

Evalle's face fell. "Is this going to be like me doing that astral travel thing to find Storm in Mitnal?"

"Similar, but no. I'll be guiding you instead of unknown spirits. With Storm staying behind to protect us, he can help send us there and insure you get back."

"How does he do that?"

Adrianna pointed at Evalle's chest. "You're wearing something akin to a chakra stone, right?"

Evalle's hand moved to her chest. "He glued an emerald on me."

"I did *not* glue it," he corrected her. "I used *majik*."

Rolling her eyes, Evalle said. "He majik-glued a stone on my chest to use like a tracking device."

He scowled. "That's not–" Then he caught Adrianna's smirk and looked over to find Evalle grinning. He leaned close to Evalle's ear and said, "You'll pay for that."

She murmured, "I sure as hell hope so."

"Any*hoo*," Adrianna stressed, eyes twinkling for a moment before turning serious again. "If we can't leave the realm on our own, I'm banking on Storm jazzing up the majik on that stone so that you can alert him that we're in trouble. He'll pull you out the minute he senses it."

Now Storm understood why Adrianna wanted him to stay behind. She was creating a safety net for Evalle. Evalle could hold her own with pretty much any supernatural being, but if she got into real danger, the stone *would* alert him and he'd yank Evalle out so fast she'd lose a day of time.

That was *if* he went along with her going, which was still a no in his book.

The other thing he'd noticed about Adrianna's plan? She had no safety net for herself. "Would I be able to pull you both out?"

"No. You'll only be withdrawing one person."

Caught in the middle of another yawn, Evalle snapped her jaws shut and gave Adrianna a hard look. "What *are* you really saying?"

Adrianna had returned to her subdued self, fingers steepled and tapping silently against each other. She stilled all her motions and addressed Storm. "We need to do this. Veronika would have a battle taking over your power, Storm, but she wouldn't tackle that fight first. She'd go after Evalle, who is vulnerable."

Evalle said, "What? I'll show you and Veronika vulnerable with my boot."

"You misunderstand me, Evalle. I'm not saying you're weak. I'm saying that you are vulnerable because you care for so many people. The KievRus majik preys on emotional vulnerabilities. When Veronika possesses Witchlock, she'll learn everything about every powerful being that she chooses as prey. She'd especially want someone like you with Belador and Medb blood, plus you're a gryphon to boot. When you least expect it, she'll set a trap and catch you with your mental shields down. Once that happens, she'll use your powers and your gifts to kill everyone who trusts you ... starting with Storm."

Chills crawled up Storm's spine at what Adrianna described. If she had her information right, that would be catastrophic and he could see why Evalle would be a prize to capture. "How do we stop her, Adrianna?"

She inclined her head toward him, indicating he'd finally asked the right question. "Veronika has only one weak spot right now and it's her connection to Ragan. We have to use that link to destroy her no matter what."

Evalle sat up as the waitress arrived.

Once the young lady left, Adrianna dipped her tea bag into the mug of hot water and continued in a low voice. "We have very little time."

"Explain," Storm said and took a bite of his baby back ribs. They tasted damn good, and he was starving.

"Witchlock requires specific astronomic and astrologic conditions to come into full power. Those conditions happen no more than once each millennium and not always then. Veronika's people kept the time frame secret for many reasons, but mainly so another coven wouldn't tamper with the power. I've spent every free minute trying to pin down her end game. I now have that. We have until the upcoming solar eclipse to stop her. It's directly following a blue moon."

Storm had just lifted his fork, but lowered it before asking. "Do you mean—"

"Yes. The solar eclipse is in two days and will be visible in this hemisphere. If we miss that window, Veronika will have no more use for Ragan. At that point, everyone with any power will be at risk, including some of the gods and goddesses. If I can get to my sister before that and open the bond link, she'll trust me to do whatever I have to do at that point." Adrianna put her tea bag down and dried her fingers on the napkin, then lifted her chin to face both of them.

Evalle toyed with her napkin, but she had deep thought lines marring her forehead. "Where is Veronika right now?"

"My sources say she's in the KievRus compound in Ukraine, but the best view of the total eclipse will be in the US, so she'll be on this continent in time for that."

Storm considered all the things that could, and would, go wrong on any mission, especially one with little confirmed intel. "What if you can't get Ragan out of the realm, Adrianna?"

"I have a backup plan."

Evalle said, "Which is?"

"I've kept the link between Ragan and me shut down to a bare minimum connection so that Veronika doesn't catch me not looking and find a way to latch onto my powers, too. If I can't get Ragan out alive, I'll open that link all the way to bond completely with her again. Together, we should be able to destroy Ragan's connection to Veronika. That may not stop Veronika from accepting ownership of Witchlock, but it will significantly limit her range of power."

"That might kill Ragan," Storm pointed out.

"There's no question that it will."

"I hate to point out the obvious, Adrianna," Evalle said in a sarcastic and weary voice. "But that means you both die. How is that a good plan?"

Putting her tea aside, Adrianna replied, "If I don't stop Veronika, my sister will turn into a shade, plus none of us will be able to defend ourselves against Witchlock. Even the Medb may be vulnerable, but their new queen might just join sides with Veronika against the Beladors. I'm not suicidal, and I want to free my sister more than anything, but I'm accepting the responsibility to do what I have to if this doesn't work."

Storm had heard enough. "I'll go with you, but not Evalle, and the plan will be to rescue your sister and return both of you here."

"Wait a damn minute," Evalle said, lighting into him. "You don't get to say what I can do and not do."

Adrianna said, "I haven't told you—"

"I'm not dictating your life, I'm trying to keep you safe," Storm told Evalle, who had moved so that the light shining on her face showed the dark shadows of exhaustion. He hated for her to be run so hard and could tell how close she was to going ballistic mainly because she was too tired to prevent it.

Storm held his temper and kept his voice low. "I'm the most qualified to go with Adrianna since I carry very strong witch blood and powerful shaman blood."

Adrianna leaned in. "If you would just listen–"

"No, he won't listen to anyone," Evalle snapped. "Especially me. What I say doesn't count all of a sudden."

"That's not true," Storm argued.

"Yes, it is. I'm telling you I'm just as qualified to kill anything out there as you are and you *know* that. But you're dismissing me outright."

Storm wiped a hand over his mouth. "I need you to–"

"*Shut. Up!*" Adrianna said just loud enough to cut through their angry words.

He turned to her and could feel Evalle's frustration roll into anger, ready to lunge at the witch. He put his hand on Evalle's arm and felt the pulse of her temper beating hard beneath the thumb he rubbed back and forth over the vein to calm her. She was upset because of *him*, not Adrianna, and the Sterling witch didn't need Evalle's misdirected anger at this point.

She stayed there an extra second, then quieted and sat back in her seat.

Adrianna leaned in, hands clutched together. "I've spent a very long time researching this and I get one shot at making it happen. I am not going to let whatever issues you two have get in the way of going after my sister. You said you'd help. If Evalle isn't going, then tell me now, because I'm running out of time and I have to know."

Storm held back his thoughts, allowing Evalle a chance to reply first.

Maybe he *was* being overbearing, but he would not lose her.

Evalle said, "I fulfill my commitments and I told you I would help you when the time came. I'm in." She turned to Storm and her silence challenged him.

He gave in for now. "We'll both help you."

The smile he received from Evalle lit up his world. He couldn't back up on his word to her or Adrianna, so he nodded to let Evalle know they'd do this together.

Evalle asked, "Does that mean you give your word to not

fight my going with Adrianna?"

"Yes."

He got a double blast of happy Evalle for that admission. She didn't need to know that he already had a shaman in mind who could be the anchor in this world, which would allow Storm to travel with Evalle and Adrianna. He had faith in his ability to protect her anywhere, even in the Jafnan Mir realm.

Now that they had peace between them again, he leaned over and kissed Evalle's cheek. "Sorry."

She whispered, "Me, too."

"Maybe we can get done now that you two have made up," Adrianna muttered.

Evalle lifted her eyebrows. "Hmm?"

The witch smirked and said, "Thank you both, because I'm sure I can't pull this off alone or I'd have already gone after my sister. I waited, because if there is a chance to bring Ragan home alive then I do want that first and foremost. She's all I have."

Storm said, "Tell us everything you have in mind so we can plan."

"I have a couple of locations that should be perfect on a Sunday evening, but I'll have the best one figured out this afternoon. We can't wait until the last moment, so we'll do this after sunset." Shifting her gaze to Storm, Adrianna could finally finish explaining. "As for the plan, what I was trying to tell you is that I can only take one person into the realm with me and it has to be a woman. So Evalle and I will travel there together and you will be our protection in this world."

What. The. Hell? Now that he'd given his word, how was he going to stick to it *and* keep Evalle safe?

CHAPTER 8

"Where. Is. Brina?" Tzader Burke asked Macha, the Celtic goddess he'd sworn his allegiance to and the person responsible for the homicidal fantasies he was trying hard not to act upon.

With alabaster skin as pale as his was dark, Macha's high cheeks and narrow nose would be thought patrician by today's standards, but she'd lived far longer than aristocrats of recent centuries. Mink brown hair woven into finger-thick braids hung in front of her shoulders and down her back to her waist.

She changed her hair as often as a flea jumped to a new spot on a dog.

And she had a temper that rivaled Tzader's.

He'd been cautious over the years to not shove her into a corner in a way that would result in Macha unleashing her fury, but the time had come for her to step out of his way.

That didn't mean Macha would see his side.

Avoiding his question for the third time, the goddess replied, "Treoir castle has never been this vulnerable. I need you in Atlanta since I have to remain here to watch over Brina and Treoir Island. You're the next one after me and Brina who can represent the Beladors at the Tribunal." The goddess floated across the expansive living area in Treoir Castle, ruffling her bright green gown.

She turned to him, voice as hard as the unforgiving ruler she could be. "We are still at war with the Medb. Even more so now that they've gained permission to enter the human world. We can't ignore our duties."

He'd never ignored a damned duty since he'd picked up his first Belador sword at eight years old, but he was not in the mood to battle wits with her. Not now. He knew the threat hanging over Treoir.

For two thousand years, this island had been hidden in a mist over the Irish Sea.

Two. Thousand. Years. Then breached two weeks ago by the Medb coven.

That group of dark witches gave their allegiance to a deadly queen, now reincarnated into a goddess, who wanted everything Macha had, starting with Treoir Castle and Island.

Tzader had never cared about living in a castle or possessing piles of money. He'd grown up on this island because his family had defended Treoir Castle and fought alongside Treoir warriors for more generations than Tzader could count.

In all his life, he'd wanted only one thing he couldn't walk away from–Brina.

When Tzader's father was killed in battle, the elder Burke's immortality had passed to Tzader. At the same time, a powerful defense ward placed around the castle prevented any immortal except Brina or Macha from entering, and that ward had stood between Tzader and Brina ever since.

Four long years.

The ward was gone now, and Tzader would not wait any longer.

He should suck it up and drag out what was left of his patience since he had to go through Macha to reach Brina, but Macha was the reason he had no patience left. He reminded her, "I'm here to see Brina."

"We're talking about the Tribunal!"

No, you're trying to avoid discussing Brina, Tzader wanted to say. Macha's avoidance meant she was hiding something, and the longer she took, the more Tzader's chest tightened with worry. "Fine. Tell me what the problem is now with the damn Tribunal."

Her eyebrows moved up slightly at the curse, but amazingly she let it go. "I have just been informed a new Tribunal is expecting our representative in forty-nine minutes."

Now what? "Why?"

"The Medb are complaining that Beladors are killing their witches and warlocks unprovoked."

"That's insane. VIPER *knows* that every Belador warrior stands to face severe punishment, *death* even, for breaking our code of honor." He shook his head and scowled. "No Belador is going to take that risk knowing his or her entire family will face the same consequences."

"VIPER may recognize that, but the deities who make up each Tribunal won't care one way or the other. They're annoyed at spending so much time dealing with the human world and now that the Medb have sent a proposal for peace, the Tribunal wants me to rubber stamp it."

"What proposal?"

"The Medb suggest the Tribunal assign a liaison between the Beladors and the Medb coven." She resumed floating inches above the floor as she air-paced.

"And?" He had a sick feeling about where this was going.

"They claim since Evalle is the leader of the gryphons and shares the blood of both pantheons that she should step into the role of liaison."

"No." He braced himself for an argument.

Macha came to a sudden stop. Her emerald-green gown swirled around her ankles, sparking with tiny bursts of light where other gowns with bling would merely twinkle. She lifted her chin and held his gaze with her steely one. "That is not your choice to make."

Nothing ever was. "You would hand her over to the Medb after all she's done for us?"

"I didn't say I intended to agree. However, you should remember who makes the final decision here."

Like he needed a Post-it stuck on his forehead when he looked in the mirror? "I know who runs the show."

"You're in an impertinent mood."

"I'm in an *impatient* mood. I want to see Brina."

"So you're not interested in *my* decision regarding Evalle?"

If he had the time, he'd walk over and shove his fist through the closest stone wall. It would feel better than suffering this frustration. "Yes, Macha, I'd like to know."

"I refused to agree to the Medb offer."

The goddess hadn't rejected the offer out of any desire to protect Evalle. He waited to hear Macha's explanation.

"The last thing I want to do is give the Medb access to any Belador resource. There's no telling how they might figure a way to use Evalle against us."

And there it was.

With Evalle somewhat safe and that out of the way, Tzader replayed his broken record. "About Brina."

"What progress is being made with finding evidence of the Medb dumping demons in Atlanta? I'd like a detailed report before I have to teleport you to the Tribunal meeting. That is your duty, after all."

"I know my duty," he said in a voice so deep the words came out in a growl. "Here's what I know. We have no solid evidence that the demons dumped in Atlanta a week ago were products of the Medb. Then it seemed they went away for five days. Now new demons have shown up, but the Medb are no longer popping on scene to kill these new ones the way they were a week ago to show the Tribunal the Medb coven could be an asset for VIPER."

She muttered, "Smoke and mirrors game."

"I agree, but we still lack evidence. VIPER isn't helping, but one of our warriors cornered a demon."

"Oh?"

"It was a Réisc Dubh that—"

"*Those?*" she scowled. "Why call forth something with the mentality of a slug?"

"I don't think they called it up. I think these things are being created."

Macha pulled back at that. "Why would... I don't care why. Interrogate it."

"We can't. It was necessary to terminate the demon."

"A Réisc Dubh? What warrior couldn't contain a Réisc Dubh?" she said with so much fury the walls trembled.

Evalle, but Tzader was not giving her up. He had only the details that Storm had texted him after the Skinwalker found Evalle on top of Stone Mountain. "A warrior who put survival ahead of intel. This particular Réisc Dubh turned aggressive and the top half changed into something that could kill a Belador."

Macha harrumphed and the air vibrated.

Tzader crossed his arms. "And it had no Medb scent. No scent *period*. When we got a call earlier this week about a gutted troll, I asked the Skinwalker Storm to track the killer. At first, I thought a demon had gutted the troll to fuel a spell to turn something else into a demon. But the scent leading from the corpse turned out to be another troll's. They found him way south of the city ... dead."

"Why waste manpower to track down a troll killer?"

"Because the troll deaths coincided with the new demons that have been sighted. I think those two things are connected. I've ordered our Beladors to not link unless they're positive about what they're fighting." Tzader would not risk losing an entire squad of Beladors. They gained power by linking with one another in battle, but all of them would die if one was killed while they were linked.

"That's your first priority, to get to the bottom of this soon and deliver evidence to a Tribunal that the Medb are behind the demons," Macha mused out loud as she lifted another few inches off the floor and stared beyond him, lost in thought, then her gaze returned to his. "I'd hoped the Tribunal would come to their senses before now and boot the Medb out of the human world, but that clearly isn't going to happen. All I get from them are messages saying the Tribunal wants an end to the bickering between the Beladors and the Medb."

"They think this is *bickering*?" Tzader asked, appalled. "Blood has flowed for centuries because of a *war*. What the hell do they want?"

She sent him a sharp look as a reprimand for his language. "They want to have peace in the human world. Deities are not particularly happy to keep coming in to settle what they consider petty disagreements. I don't blame them since I would have destroyed something or someone by now if anyone wasted my time. Our most immediate fight is over the gryphons."

That fight translated into a new way to screw Evalle yet again. Tzader asked, "What do you think will happen with the gryphons? Or, let me be more specific. With Evalle."

"I refused to let the Medb have her or them, but I can't fight the entire coalition of deities if they decide otherwise. I sent back that I'm willing to discuss a peace treaty, but not their proposal."

Good luck ending up with any peace treaty that had teeth, but he'd leave Macha to her negotiations for now.

He glanced at his watch. Twenty-eight minutes.

"Did you just check your watch while in my presence?"

"You're the one concerned about my making the Tribunal meeting on time," he reminded her.

Her glare slid down her haughty nose and hit him between the eyes. She warned, "You're immortal, Tzader, but only against a weaker adversary, which I will never be."

His patience had clung by threads since the beginning of this discussion and he'd like to tell Macha she was welcome to his life, a miserable place without Brina.

But Brina was the reason he'd shown humility to the goddess and would suck it up one more time. "I was not being disrespectful, Macha. I'm simply tired from working around the clock, which has left me no chance to see Brina until now and you have yet to tell me where she is other than in the castle. If I sound short, it's unavoidable at the moment."

Not an apology, because that was asking too much.

"You should take note of the allowances I've made for those close to you."

Where was she going with this? He asked, "Such as?"

"Quinn. He should not be allowed to live after falling into bed with the enemy."

Tzader had forgotten that this would come up again. "I told you after that last battle here that Quinn met Kizira when he was very young and he did *not* know she was Medb when he fell for her. Quinn has always been truthful with me and was even prepared to submit to death by your hand at one point."

Her gaze flinched.

Didn't expect that did you, Macha? Tzader continued, "Quinn is solid and has paid the highest price for that moment in his life."

"You put him in as Maistir once," she said, allowing it to stand as an accusation.

"And I would do it again." Tzader would hand that position to Quinn now if he thought his friend could handle it, but Tzader pushed that aside. "Thank you for allowing Quinn to take Kizira's body back."

"I trust that you will insure the witch's body is dealt with appropriately."

Macha meant that Kizira's body should be burned and the

ashes scattered, but she failed to say that so Tzader answered, "Yes."

Whatever Quinn did would be appropriate and kept away from the world.

Tzader asked, "Can we get to Brina now?"

He must have finally gotten through to Macha because she let out a long sigh and said, "She's in the library. She goes into a rage with objects flying around when she can't recall things. One minute she almost has a grasp of a memory then it slips away, leaving her without an anchor to any point in time. The battle to regain her memories is wearing her down physically and emotionally. She sleeps often, waking in terror."

That sucker punched the air out of him. "She'll remember. I'll help her." He stepped toward the door.

"I'll allow you to see her as long as she doesn't become any worse."

She'll allow me? Tzader swung back around. "You will allow me to see her as often and for as long as I want when I am not on duty. You owe that to me and to her. I have never asked for anything from you for myself, except that Brina and I could be together. Not *once* since my father and her father died together as Belador warriors have either of us given less than our best to you and the Belador tribe."

Macha's hair fanned straight out like the spokes of a wheel. Her body glowed with energy flooding her. Walls shook and the floor rumbled as if it would explode from the pressure.

As he waited for her to strike at him, he added, "The sooner you help me bring Brina back to us, the sooner we'll marry and start a family. You want babies to rebuild the Treoir dynasty and secure the Belador power here forever. I want the woman I love in my life and to father her children. We have the same goal for different reasons. I intend to get started on that goal right now. Please teleport me to the entrance of VIPER headquarters in twenty-five minutes."

That calmed Macha when nothing else would. She nodded. "We need Brina back and soon. Her mental state seems to grow worse each day she goes without remembering. I'll trust you to take care with her."

"That's a given." He strode quickly through the halls, passing two of the royal guards along the way. He gave them an abrupt nod when he'd normally have stopped to chat. He'd expected to find Brina alone, which she technically was, but Allyn McDonahue stood outside the open door to the library.

Macha had sucked Tzader dry of any patience.

This guard deserved none. Not after trying to poach Brina.

Tzader knew the minute Allyn realized who approached because the guard tensed and straightened his shoulders.

When Tzader reached the entrance to the massive library, he paused to take everything in. Brina sat on the far side of the room in a cushioned window seat with a leaded glass backdrop.

That was new. There hadn't been a window in this room for years.

Tzader kept his voice down. He had no problem taking this guy to task, but he didn't want to cause a disturbance so near to Brina. He told Allyn, "I warned you about being around her."

"I am not *around* her, but guarding her. There is a difference, Maistir." Allyn had said that in a tone of tolerance more than respect.

"Find someone else to guard. In fact, spend your time outside training your men, overseeing the gryphons, picking up rocks, I don't give a damn what you do. Just stay away from her. Understood?"

Allyn had gone rigid as a post. "Understood."

Tzader stepped back, giving him room to leave. Once the guard was out of sight, Tzader stepped into the library and walked with loud enough steps to alert her that someone had entered.

Brina's head lifted. Flame red hair fell to her waist in soft curls, looking as if the locks were threads spun of fire and copper. Her heart-shaped lips parted with surprise and green eyes as bright as a lush valley in spring studied him.

In that moment, he saw her go from hope to disappointment when she couldn't gather her memories of him.

A traitor within the Beladors had used Noirre majik supplied by the Medb to trap Brina within majik threads while the Medb attacked Treoir Island and Castle. Tzader had killed the traitor, but not before Brina, along with Quinn's teenage cousin Lanna, had tried to escape by teleporting. They'd ended up lost in another realm.

Evalle had brought Storm to Treoir as a last ditch effort to bring the two women back, which had ended successfully. But Brina's memories had deteriorated.

Were *still* deteriorating.

Tzader kept walking and forced his lips into a smile.

He had little time to make headway with her, but it could be too much time if she became agitated. She'd been through a lot and he would not press her for more than she could handle.

But his warrior queen was strong.

Somewhere inside that body still lived the woman who had waited within the walls of this warded castle for four long years, seeing him only in hologram form, just to do her duty as a Treoir.

His woman had been raised a fighter.

She sat cross-legged on the cushions. In her lap lay an enormous album that had leather binding softened by a century of wear. The large pages made her hands appear as small as a child's holding a normal-sized book.

He tried not to think about how fragile Brina looked. She'd never been fragile, but everything she'd been through recently showed in her sad face.

She closed the album and held up her hand in a silent order, forcing him to stop three strides short of her.

He obeyed her silent request, but it took all of his control to hold back from bundling her into his arms and drawing her close to bring peace back into her face. "I'd like to visit with you."

She blinked, closed her eyes, then opened them, frowning. "I know you ... but I'm not bringin' you clear to mind."

Her Irish lilt curled around his heart and hugged him. "You do know me and, if you'll let me, I'll help you remember a lot of things."

Standing this close and not touching her reminded him of the years he'd suffered without her in his arms and his life, sating his loneliness for short periods only when one of them visited in holographic form.

His father had bequeathed his immortality to his only child without Tzader's knowledge.

Tzader had come to terms with the unfairness in life, and now cared only about today and tomorrow.

Brina studied him. "Tell me somethin' that I should be rememberin'."

A thousand memories rushed forward, all clamoring to be the *one* that brought her back. "There is a huge tree not far from here where we once swam as teenagers. It was *our* spot."

He'd made love to her there the first time, and again in his dreams just over a week ago, but his dreams didn't count. She had to remember what happened for real.

Her eyebrows dropped low as she thought hard on something. Sending him a wary look, she asked, "Were we at the tree ... recently?"

"What do you call recently?" he said, curious to see where this was going.

She shrugged. "In but two weeks past."

"No." Not unless he could show her his dream.

"Oh." She sounded disappointed.

"What's wrong?"

"I recall bein' in a place such as that only a wee time back with a man and we were ... " Her voice trailed off and she couldn't meet his gaze. "It matters not since it was not you."

Who the hell had she been to their spot with, and what had they done? "What did you do at that tree?"

Her cheeks blushed and jealousy stormed his body, because he knew exactly what she'd been doing *with a man*. He demanded, "Who was this man?"

She put aside the album she was holding and stood. "Do not dare to raise your voice to me."

He heard her, but he had been put off by Macha and would not leave her without finding who had dared to take her to their tree. "I want a name, Brina. Now."

If she said Allyn, that guard would regret his audacity for the rest of his short life.

She pointed to the doorway. "Get out!"

That order had rung with the power of Brina the Belador warrior queen everyone missed, and would have made Tzader happy to see one part of her return, if not for what she'd said.

Raising his voice had been the wrong move.

He took a step closer and hoped Macha didn't show up to

interfere. Brina's eyes widened with the shock of anyone defying her.

Keeping his tone gentle, Tzader spoke as he eased closer to her. "You might be confusing the time, because that's one of *our* memories. That tree was our favorite place, our secret place to meet. But the last time was four years ago."

She shook her head, now distracted by his words. "Why would we have gone there then and not recently?"

He held her gaze as a bridge between them, moving another step closer as he spoke. "Because your father helped Macha ward this castle against immortals before he went to battle the Medb four years ago, and without knowledge of that, my father asked for Macha's promise to pass his immortality to me. I couldn't touch you until I broke the ward."

The soothing sound in his deep tone had to be working because she appeared mesmerized and murmured, "How did you ... break the ward?

"I rushed through it to protect you when the Medb attacked Treoir." He lifted a hand and ran it over her hair, surprised to see his hand tremble, but this was their first real touch in four years. "I died when I crossed the ward, but through a miracle I was revived. Just not fast enough to reach you before you were attacked with Noirre majik." He paused to lean closer. "I killed the traitor and I would kill a thousand more if they tried to harm you."

Then he kissed her.

A gentle kiss. A little hello from their past to remind her of their first kiss, but she leaned in and his heart banged against his chest with more happiness than he'd ever believed he'd feel again.

Brina remembered him ...

He cupped her face and continued the kiss, slowing only to say, "The last time we were at our secret place we made love under that tree. Your first time and I'll never forget it. Never give you up. I love you, Brina."

She froze and pulled back.

He didn't try to stop her.

She touched her lips. Confusion and wariness struggled in her gaze. "But we were not married then, correct?"

"No, but we pledged ourselves to each other before we made love."

"Pledged? I hold the power for the entire Belador tribe and I gave myself without marriage?" She took a step back, her legs bumping the window seat. Humiliation crawled up her neck in red splotches. "You took advantage of me when I was what? Eighteen?"

Heat crawled up his neck at being accused of something so disgusting. "No. It was consensual. You were an adult."

"Why didn't we marry then?"

"I told you. Our fathers screwed up or we would have been married by now."

She challenged, "We couldn't have married somehow? What if I'd been pregnant?"

"Then we *would* have married."

"But only if I was pregnant?"

"What? No." Tzader took a step forward and reached to calm her, but the room spun out of focus and his step ended up on dirt and rocks outside the mountain headquarters of VIPER.

He roared in fury.

CHAPTER 9

Two hours before daylight, Evalle quietly opened the door to her dark apartment. She slipped inside ahead of Storm, who made no sound as he followed. They tiptoed past the futon Lanna had requested for her bed, where she was currently crashed out, dead to the world.

Feenix slept next to Lanna, curled up on his beanbag chair with his little wings tucked in and clutching his favorite alligator stuffed toy.

Evalle smiled at the peaceful scene. It gave her hope that this living arrangement would be fine after all. Lanna wasn't staying forever and Feenix would get used to Storm being here. Her little gargoyle had just been frightened the first night.

Squawking, screeching and flapping wildly for the best part of an hour as he wrecked everything he ran into.

Lanna had tried to help by making Feenix's toys fly, but that had turned the place into even more of a circus.

Evalle didn't want to think about that right now.

She'd spent this past week dwelling on it every waking minute, which had been pretty much the whole time since she couldn't remember the last solid sleep she'd had. Not when she suffered nightmares of Storm changing his mind about living with her. She'd come up with a plan. That's what Quinn and Tzader, her best-friends-slash-surrogate-brothers, had taught her.

Tackle a problem by coming up with a strategy.

Their advice always sounded good on paper, but once she waded into trouble up to her neck, she generally just started killing everything until she could walk away.

Not exactly a strategy for sorting out a personal crisis that was probably all just in her mind.

Probably.

Moving in stealth mode down the hall, she stepped inside her bedroom and left all the lights off except the fused-glass night-light Feenix loved. It threw a kaleidoscope of color over the room.

Storm shut the door and started shedding clothes.

She'd begun doing the same, but paused to admire the view of the hottest man alive.

Cut muscle wrapped him from neck to ankles and the man was entirely at ease nude, but who wouldn't be with an Adonis body like his? He had beautiful teak-colored skin covering a powerful physique. Reaching up, he flicked the leather thong away that had held his black hair, letting it fall past his shoulders.

He smiled without looking her way.

He'd caught her ogling him and clearly liked it.

Evidently she was taking too long to undress, because the next thing she knew he was in front of her, unzipping her jeans and pulling them down.

She laughed, happy for the first time in a week, and stepped out of the jeans, which he tossed aside. She couldn't recall Storm being so messy.

He caught her face with his big hands and stared deep into her eyes. "I like the sound of you happy."

"You're the cause of it."

"I like that too." He kissed her, using his mouth with the precision of a maestro, tuning her body to a fever pitch that would sing the minute he plucked a few choice cords. She ran her hands up his chest and marveled at the fact that he was hers.

His hands touched and explored. Every part of him moved in perfect sync.

One particular part thudded against her abdomen, letting her know just how much he'd missed her. She eased down and grasped him in a firm grip and he stilled.

All that power at her mercy.

She moved her hand slowly up his length.

He groaned, a deep feral sound, then lifted her until she had to release him and hook her legs around his waist. Then he headed for the bathroom, which was nowhere near as spacious and well appointed as the one in the house where he'd been living.

Another negative of Storm being stuck underground with her.

He'd showered here that first day, but alone, because she'd been busy trying to calm Feenix.

She had a moment of panic, berating herself for not allowing Quinn to incorporate all the upgrades he'd intended for this apartment. She'd been so determined to stand on her own two feet and take no charity, that she'd refused any luxury Quinn had tried to push her way under the excuse of being her landlord.

Which he was, but she received a monthly stipend like every other Belador warrior and could pay her bills.

Storm sat her on the vanity and eased away, leaning down until his face was all she could see. He shook his head. "What are you worrying over now?"

He couldn't read minds. She knew that.

But he was a strong empath. If she told him she was embarrassed by the cramped quarters, he'd tell her it didn't matter. He'd blow it off. He couldn't outright lie or his Navajo gift for detecting a lie would backlash on him with physical pain. That didn't mean he hadn't figured out how to skirt the truth by being clever when he felt it necessary.

She opened her mouth and closed it.

He said, "If you don't want to say what's bothering you, that's fine. It's better than feeling like you have to shade the truth with me, because you don't and you know that right?"

"Right." She knew it in her heart, but her mind was not in sync with her heart lately. She finally admitted, "I'm tired and not up for any discussion." Not now when they finally had a moment to themselves.

Tap. Tap. Tap.

Evalle looked past him toward the bedroom door. "Now what?"

"I'll check. You get the shower started."

Storm wrapped a towel around his waist and walked slowly enough for Evalle to start the shower noise before he opened the door. He found her critter outside.

The half-pint gargoyle lifted his chin until his bright orange eyes stared up, unblinking. When Feenix spoke it sounded like a teenage boy, but came out as an order. "Evalle."

She'd warned Storm that her pet didn't have a big vocabulary, and after that first meeting Storm had also learned the little guy frightened easily. For that reason, Storm tried to sound calm and patient when all he wanted was to be alone with Evalle. "She's getting a bath and going to bed. Evalle is tired. You should go to sleep, too."

"Evalle," Feenix repeated, not moving an inch. This time those orange eyes flamed bright then narrowed.

Evalle described Feenix as harmless.

Storm had survived by being able to read what truth lay beneath the surface in a confrontation with an animal or a powerful being. Deadly animals on the prowl attacked.

So did frightened ones, and Storm's presence unnerved Feenix.

Storm wasn't sure where a gargoyle fell in the food chain, but he wasn't taking any chances with something capable of torching a pizza with fire from his snout. Yeah, he'd heard that story, too. Evalle had thought it charming when Feenix tried to cook her a pizza in the oven with his own built-in blowtorch.

Storm thought it sounded dangerous if the gargoyle ever lost his temper, but things had been so tense between him and Evalle since he walked in carrying a duffel last week, that he would not start in on her pet.

As long as the gargoyle didn't harm Evalle.

Feenix showed no sign of budging.

This wasn't going well.

Evalle would come looking to see what the problem was if Storm didn't return to the bathroom soon. He rubbed his eyes with the heels of his hands, feeling the long hours and two hundred miles he'd spent running in jaguar form before stopping at his truck, where he always kept an extra set of clothes.

He couldn't have survived waiting until later this morning to see Evalle.

He dropped his hands, determined to find peace with Feenix, but someone saved him from round three.

Lanna padded down the hall from the living room. Blond curls stuck out in six directions and the teenager wore powder-blue warm-ups. She squatted down, yawning, and patted Feenix on the shoulder. "Evalle has been working many hours. She is tired. We will visit tomorrow, yes?"

For Lanna, the little guy's eyes turned into pure charm.

What a con artist.

Feenix smiled at her and said, "Yeth. Morrow."

She smiled at Storm, letting him know she'd handle it.

Storm mouthed the words *thank you* over Feenix's head. He was just closing the door to the bedroom when he heard a sharp sound and opened it again to find a burn spot two feet off the ground.

Lanna turned the corner, still holding Feenix's hand. At the last second, the gargoyle gave Storm a long look and poofed a streak of black smoke at him, then disappeared into the dark living room.

Might as well accept the truth.

This was not going to work for long, but Storm wanted Evalle relaxed and happy tonight. The discussion on living here could wait for now. He shut the door and used a quick chant, creating a spell to prevent any sound escaping this room.

Now for his welcome-home gift waiting in the shower.

He opened the glass door, stepped into a cloud of steam, and found Evalle under the showerhead with a hand propped against the wall and water gushing over her. He curved his arms around a wet and naked Evalle from behind.

Holding her was all his best dreams wrapped into one.

Still leaning forward, she reached back to touch his thigh with her free hand, always touching him now that she knew him intimately.

He'd taught her to enjoy touching and was damned proud of her.

She'd overcome a hellish childhood that included being raped by a man she'd thought was the family doctor.

If the guy hadn't died in a wreck back then, Storm would ...

"Can't breathe," she laughed and patted the arm around her waist.

He immediately eased his hold, pushing his mind away from murderous thoughts.

Now was not the time to think about anything but this woman. Reaching up, he cupped her breasts and brushed a finger over each nipple, teasing each one into a hard little bead. She arched back against him and trembled.

Storm had run Tzader's team hard for a week and it had been worth every argument and gripe.

The only one who hadn't argued was Trey, because he had a woman he loved just as much waiting at home, too.

Getting back to Evalle just one minute sooner would be worth any effort. He kissed her neck and bit lightly at the same moment he pinched her nipples just enough to wring a cry out of her.

She sucked in a breath and stilled suddenly.

He leaned close, whispering, "I soundproofed the bedroom and bathroom."

She let out her breath and her voice purred. "You think of everything."

Only for her.

"Keep your hands on the wall," he told her, because he knew how tired she was. He'd first thought to encourage her to climb into bed and get the sleep she clearly needed. As much as he'd wanted her, he could have been content holding her while she rested.

But the one night they'd spent here had stressed her out and left her with a wary look of worry he hadn't been happy about leaving.

Right now, he wanted to remind her that she was loved, and that she was his. Next he'd drain her of all the pent-up energy surging around her. His empathic gift kept picking up on that.

Once that was gone, she'd sleep soundly, tucked up against him where he'd be able to rest with her safe and content.

She lifted her head. "I want to feel you so much you have no idea."

I beg to differ.

That had been a plea as much as a statement and he ached to be inside her, too, but not yet.

Allowing one hand to pay homage to her breast, keeping her gasping and trembling, he ran his other hand down, fingers tracing every inch of her firm body. She was built for agility and power, but all that toned body came with plenty of curves.

Evalle fought with all she had inside her to protect others and do her duty. She rarely softened completely except at a moment like this when she felt safe enough to let her guard down.

Only for him.

Humbling to say the least.

This magnificent woman was all his to hold forever.

His fingers swept around her waist and across her taut butt, then he slipped between her legs and found the bundle of nerves that were as slick wet as the rest of her. He wanted to take her to the edge with his tongue, but she would not last long tonight so he brushed the pad of his finger over the sensitive spot and she slapped her hands against the tiled wall.

Two more strokes and she shuddered, calling out to him, so very close that he slid one long finger inside her, pulling it out slowly then pushing back in.

Power shook the glass.

"Easy, baby," he soothed her, which was in contradiction to the way his fingers demanded she let go.

He moved to the nipple that had been neglected and teased it.

She bowed back, arching with her hands flush against the wall. She keened a long sound.

The wall cracked just as she crashed over the edge. He didn't let her stop until she gave everything up.

When her knees buckled, he caught her and turned her around, then lifted her into his arms where he could kiss her. She curled a noodle-limp arm around his neck.

Her lips smoothed into a content smile.

He'd make it his goal to keep her that way.

He kissed her deeper, missing everything about her more than he would ever expect to miss a person in only one week. Good luck expecting him to go away again any time soon. All he had to do was come up with a living arrangement that would work for both of them. That had never been an issue in the past, but they'd never tried to coexist under one roof before.

She let him lift his head. When he did, he was treated to a glazed look of satisfaction that he'd put on her face.

She struggled to draw in one breath after another. "Is that all?"

"Can you handle more?"

"I know you didn't just ask me that."

There was his badass, always up for a challenge. He lowered

her to her feet and kissed her again with water sluicing over them both.

She pointed her hand at the glass door, which swung open, then she bent a finger as if calling something to her.

He lifted his head in time to catch the condom flying into the bathroom.

She asked, "Want me to put it on or can *you* handle that?"

"Tough question. It's been a whole week since I've been inside you. I might not survive it."

Her eyes glowed and her lips quirked up. She snatched the condom out of his hand and tossed the wrapper out the door, closing the glass door before she sheathed him.

He hadn't been kidding about not surviving her hands on him. Then she jumped into his arms and he busted out laughing and told her, "I've missed you."

"Really?"

That sounded too serious. He held her with one arm underneath her and brushed her hair back. "Don't ever doubt it or that I love you."

"I love you, too." Again, too intense.

He'd get to the bottom of all this anxiety filling her gaze tomorrow. For now, he'd just love her.

She squirmed and moved, trying to lower herself.

He used both hands to lower her, stopping just close enough to let the tip of his penis tease her.

She grabbed his shoulders and gave him her threatening look. "If you keep holding me back, my kinetics might kill us all."

Not giving up her bright-green gaze, he lowered her and pushed inside slowly until she took all of him.

Sweet mother of... mercy.

Then she moved up and down, whispering, "Faster. Harder."

He took over and changed the rhythm, driving toward pleasure that damn near blinded him.

He could face anything tomorrow as long as he had Evalle in his arms tonight.

CHAPTER 10

Quinn stepped out through the patina-green doorway of the private mausoleum that now held a Medb priestess who should not be there. Late morning sunshine glared in his face and knocked back the chill in his soul. A peaceful Sunday seemed appropriate for laying Kizira to rest, and the sculptured statues, massive monuments and ancient oaks of Oakland Cemetery would watch over her.

With downtown Atlanta only a mile away, Quinn could keep her close and out of sight. This cemetery had shielded secrets since the mid 1800s when the first Atlanta residents were buried here.

Oakland would protect Quinn's secrets, too.

His eyes stung. He squeezed them shut.

He'd shed all the tears that he would allow to fall. It was time to face the consequences of his failure.

Kizira dead.

So young. So beautiful. So full of love.

He hadn't deserved her love, but she'd given it without restraint. He swallowed against the perpetual knot of pain that had lodged in his throat. "Kizira, why ... "

You know why, you bloody bastard. She stepped between you and the jaws of a gryphon. Saved your miserable unworthy hide.

Damn if a tear didn't defy him and slide down his cheek.

Straightening his shoulders, Quinn found his backbone and leaned through the open doors to place one of his oldest Belador triquetras on the floor inside. Then he pulled the old iron doors together with a clang and used his mental kinetics to lift the triquetra blade and hook it over the handles on the inside of the doors.

Using that old triquetra to guard her body seemed fitting.

All of his new ones had been freshly warded a few weeks ago, so they could not be moved using kinetics, because Kizira had been compelled by her evil queen to breach his wards. Quinn shook his head at the ugly irony. He could safely use the old triquetras again because the only person who knew how to get past them now lay dead inside this tomb.

The ward on the triquetra would stand stronger than any lock to prevent someone foolish enough to touch what was his.

He couldn't keep her in life, but she was his in death.

There would never be another love for him such as her. He'd fallen in love with the enemy a long time ago and realized too late that what they had was genuine.

Too late for Kizira.

He'd be lucky if Macha didn't punish him, or strike him down, for his relationship with a Medb.

Not just any Belador enemy. Their most hated.

But Quinn hadn't known Kizira's true identity when, as a young man, he'd met and fallen in love with a dazzling woman who had just come of age. Two weeks of bliss, then she'd given him a bracelet braided of his hair and said goodbye.

She'd told him then that she belonged to his enemy's coven, but he would never be her enemy. He should have taken those words to heart, because *she* had, and it cost her.

He stepped away from the tomb and lifted the fragile bracelet from his coat pocket, running his thumb carefully over the tightly knit strands.

Kizira's final words to him as he'd held her dying body kept torturing his mind. He could see her face, pale and waning as death called to her.

"Promise me . . . " she'd said.

"Anything." He'd brushed his lips over hers, savoring the feel.

"Find Phoedra. Keep her safe."

"Who's Phoedra?"

"Our daughter."

Pain struck his chest again as he watched her die once more in his mind. Agony clawed his heart, a beast with an insatiable appetite for misery. Quinn curled his fist to keep from slinging power madly at anything and everything.

His fault she died.

Unclenching his fist, he grappled for control of his own emotions. He had no place to lay blame other than at his own feet, and would not lash out at an innocent world just because his soul was damned beyond redemption.

He'd find Phoedra, who would be twelve now. Once he located her, he'd determine if she was safe, though he had no doubt that Kizira had hidden her well to keep her from the filthy clutches of the Medb.

Kizira expected Quinn to go and take possession of their daughter.

He stared at the bracelet. How could he tell his daughter that he was her father and the man responsible for her mother's death?

Sliding it back into his pocket, Quinn strode out of the cemetery.

"Is that Belador the one Queen Maeve put a bounty on?" Donndubhán asked in a hushed voice.

Imar nodded. "Vladimir Quinn. The queen wants him. She said it's because he killed one of our warlocks last week. If she wants him, why doesn't she send all the Scáth Force after him instead of just Ossian?"

"Queen Maeve favors Ossian." Donndubhán had proven himself as an elite Scáth Force warrior time and again, yet Ossian had been the one to gain Cathbad's eye.

Cathbad the Druid had been selecting the warlocks he believed most suited to belong to the Scáth Force, and Donndubhán had easily made the cut, but Ossian had somehow been picked as the top ass-kisser. Ossian always had been an attention whore. But whatever the queen wanted, Ossian couldn't deliver it without help.

And that's how Donndubhán had ended up as Ossian's confidante. Ossian needed the eyes and ears of someone capable he could trust.

Imar huffed out his irritation. "Will Ossian tell you why Queen Maeve wants Quinn?"

"No, but I'll bet the queen wants this Quinn for something besides retribution for killing one of her warlocks. We're little more than disposable rats to her." Donndubhán scratched his five-day-old beard and watched Quinn get into a limo, which drove off. If Maeve cared about losing a warlock, she'd have taken it up with the Tribunal now that the Medb coven had joined the coalition.

"If she isn't after revenge, then why would she want Quinn?" Imar asked. "He's a Belador."

Donndubhán stood and stretched his legs, saying, "My intel shows that Quinn is one of the most powerful Beladors because of his mindlock ability. We need to find out more about him and figure out what Maeve wants."

Imar agreed, "And before another Medb group gets their hands on him. I want that bounty."

"If he's as dangerous as I've heard, any Medb other than the Scáth Force is on a suicide mission if they go after him."

Imar muttered, "Maybe even them, too."

Donndubhán ignored the stupid comment and looked down the path to where Quinn had exited a mausoleum inside the cemetery. "What's in that tomb?"

"I don't know. I came straight here as soon as I got a call from the troll who said he had something to offer. When I got here, the troll said Quinn had walked into the cemetery while his limo waited, then entered the mausoleum, so whatever is in there was already in the tomb before Quinn got here."

"You dealt with a troll?"

Imar looked insulted. Touchy damn warlock. Imar said, "Of course I did. I offered him safety. I told him we're going to do what the Beladors won't and protect trolls, but that he has to help me and keep quiet or we won't keep him safe. I've got him convinced he can't go home or he puts all his family at risk and that we have people watching over him. He's showing me hiding spots of his troll friends so I can tell our warlocks to watch out for them."

"Interesting idea."

Imar shrugged. "We need more trolls if we're going to make this demon plan work and that's the best way to find them. I'm not stupid."

That was debatable, but Donndubhán said, "Good job, Imar."

Donndubhán turned around, checking to see that nothing else had entered the cemetery. There were only ghouls and orbs. Not something he could get rid of in a place like this.

What could be important enough for this Vladimir Quinn to visit that tomb? And why did Maeve really want this man? Donndubhán would find out both, which meant he'd hold all the cards when he captured Quinn.

Donndubhán knew how to set a successful trap and never get caught.

What Imar didn't need to know was that Quinn would be far more valuable as a trade. Once Donndubhán had decided if the Sterling coven deserved his skills and genius, he'd trade them Quinn. No dark witch worth her salt would pass up a chance for that kind of power.

CHAPTER 11

Evalle brushed her damp hair in front of her bathroom mirror, feeling more rested than she had in days. Steam boiled from behind her where Storm showered.

Alone, or they'd never get out of the bedroom.

If not for the other two in the front room and Adrianna expecting them in two and a half hours, Evalle would stay in here all day with Storm.

But she had to make the most of her time while she waited to leave here under cover of darkness.

Two hours should be long enough to figure out how to bring peace into this apartment.

Evalle's negotiating skills were as nonexistent as her culinary abilities, but everyone currently living here was dear to her, so she had to find a way to keep them all happy.

As soon as she and Storm finished dressing, she'd help Lanna whip up something edible in the kitchen, because whatever Lanna didn't know about cooking she made up for with her majik. It would be nice to know if she was a mage or a wizard, but Lanna's mother didn't know who Lanna's father had been. The woman had disappeared just over eighteen years ago from her home in Transylvania, and when she'd shown up again she was pregnant, with no idea where she'd been.

Lanna had displayed some scary power, but she was sweet in spite of being a busybody.

Evalle stepped into the bedroom and smiled at the clothes thrown in every direction. Storm had been intent on getting naked last night and she'd loved every minute of it, plus another round of lovemakng this morning when she'd rolled over to find him watching her with a look of contentment on his face.

She wanted to live with him.

Was that too much to ask of the universe?

Once everyone finished eating, Evalle would move Lanna and Feenix into the bedroom to watch movies so that Evalle and Storm could have the living room alone.

If they tried to talk in here, they'd end up in bed.

Not that she had any complaints about that, but nothing would get decided and she'd spend another day with this lead ball of worry rolling around in her stomach.

She hated this feeling of being in limbo.

Evalle hunted for a shirt in her banged-up, pressed-wood chest of drawers. She'd dug the piece out of the dump late one night, cleaned it up and painted it blue. The drawers worked.

Wasn't that the point?

Pulling on one of her BDU shirts, her personal indulgence when she could find them in a vintage shop, she turned as she buttoned it.

Storm stepped out of the bathroom, hair falling in straight black lines. He had that look on his face that said he'd picked up on her anxiety a moment ago.

She brightened her expression and said, "I'm fine. Don't give me that look."

"If you were really fine, I wouldn't be giving you this look."

"I told you I'm thinking about things."

He lifted both eyebrows. "Oh?"

"Not *that*."

He stepped over and hooked a hand on her waist, pulling her forward possessively. Then he lowered his head. "I'm losing my touch if you're not thinking about *that*." Then he kissed her and sent heat into all the right areas of her body.

"You proved your point," she laughed against his lips. "I am thinking about *that*, but we don't have time right this minute." She put her hands on his chest, feeling the taut skin over hard muscle. "Time for coffee and breakfast." The idea of cooking eggs and bacon terrified her, but Lanna had talked her through one almost successful attempt.

The eggs had been rubbery and the bacon had turned out black. Not just done, but black.

She'd pull it all off the heat sooner this time.

She killed demons for crying out loud. She could cook a damn egg.

She wanted to be the perfect mate and she had no idea where to start.

Storm kissed her forehead. His brown eyes softened with a thought. "We need to sit down and talk today."

That dropped the lead ball of worry straight to her feet. Hadn't she been thinking they needed to talk?

Yes. So why the sudden panic?

Because if she was honest with herself, she'd been hoping she was wrong about the weird tension and that he'd brush off her concern and Feenix would smile and be crazy about Storm and ... yes, that was all fantasy.

Storm loved her and had always made it clear that he loved her just the way she was.

But he'd never *lived* with her.

He sighed and looked away.

Before he could ask why she was upset again, which he would know with his empathic gift, she said, "We do need to talk. I know you aren't happy with this arrangement—"

His face whipped back to hers. "I didn't say that."

Truth, but that didn't mean he hadn't thought it. She said, "Just get dressed and we'll talk, okay?"

He let out a long breath and kissed her on the cheek. "Okay." Then he walked around, searching the room. "Where's my belt?"

She'd pulled out her socks and sat down on the edge of the bed to put them on. She looked around the room, too.

She did not want to lose his belt, which should be easy to locate. It had a silver buckle carved as the head of a jaguar, with two yellow diamonds for eyes. Storm had once popped out a diamond to give her to use as the buy-in for a beast match. She'd questioned the value back then and he'd only said it was enough to get them what they wanted.

She'd found out later the yellow diamonds were rare and ridiculously expensive, but the buckle? Priceless.

His father had given it to him when he was ten, saying he'd had it made by a silversmith in his father's Navajo tribe. She'd find a nice safe place to put it where he could easily find the belt when he chose to wear it, which wasn't often.

Scanning the area again and not seeing the belt, she asked,

"Where'd you leave it?"

He lifted an eyebrow at that. "On the floor with everything else last night. I was in too much of hurry to pick up my clothes." Then he winked at her.

Maybe she was making too big a deal over her perception of the problem. Maybe there was no problem and her insecurities were rising up to choke her.

She trusted Storm. Now she needed to prove it by showing him that she wouldn't react every time a problem arose. They'd eat, talk and get everything out on the table so they could make a decision on how to move forward. Storm would live here and they'd make this work.

He muttered, "The belt should be right here," and kept looking around, but the room was not that big.

Sliding on a boot, Evalle glanced over at the door.

It was ajar.

She said, "Have you gone out to the kitchen this morning?"

Storm's gaze went to the same spot and he started that way. "No."

He strode out the door and was gone by the time Evalle came to her feet to follow.

Storm yelled, "*Are you kidding me!*"

That was not his joking voice. That was his I-want-to-kill-something voice.

Feenix squawked in a high-pitched, terrified screech.

Evalle raced out to the living area to find Storm holding his half-eaten belt and glaring at Feenix, who was flying around, shooting out short bursts of fire with each squawk.

Feenix would catch the place on fire if that continued.

Lanna chased around beneath him. "Come here, Feenix."

This was far worse than the first night Storm had spent here. All of Evalle's concerns had been nothing compared to this. She glanced at the buckle—or at the thirty percent of it that was left.

No way to fix that, so she stepped past Storm to catch Feenix.

Standing in the middle of the room, Evalle waved Lanna back and called out in a gentle voice, "It's okay, Feenix. I'm here. Come to me, baby."

Lanna moved over to the side, for once not trying to interject her advice. She had a good heart, but interference was her middle name.

Evalle had saved Feenix from a crazy sorcerer who'd created
the gargoyle then decided Feenix was inferior because he hadn't
turned out to be a killer, like the huge, deadly creatures the
sorcerer sent out to attack.

Feenix had been marked as food.

It had taken him a while not to react to any sudden movement.

The squawking got quieter. He flapped back and forth across
the room for a moment while she kept talking to him in a
soothing voice. "Come on, sweetie."

He made one last circle and flapped slowly down to her open
arms. She hugged him to her. He shook like a miniature
earthquake, complete with occasional puffs of smoke and
frightened grunting. He tucked his wings. She stroked his back
and cooed to him until the only noise was a low rumble in his
chest.

When she turned to Storm, no emotion showed on his face,
but he was gripping the ruined belt with white knuckles that
attested to how difficult it was for him to contain his anger.

Feenix lifted one of his pudgy little hands and spit something
into it, then deposited that in Evalle's hand.

The second yellow diamond that had been an eye in the
buckle.

She walked over and placed it on the counter between her and
Storm.

When Storm didn't pick it up or say anything, she said, "I'm
sorry, Storm. I know it's not replaceable."

He broke his gaze from hers, looking away when he took a
breath then said, "No big deal."

Then he turned and walked into the bedroom, but not before
she'd caught the grimace on his face from the pain that lie had
cost him.

Lanna started in, "I am sorry, Evalle. I was listening to iPod
music and did not realize Feenix left room."

Evalle turned to Lanna. "It's not your fault. Feenix is my
responsibility. You've been wonderful to stay here all week and
keep him company."

"And hide from wizard."

"That, too, but you might have been more comfortable

somewhere else."

"This was good place to stay. I like being with you and Feenix. And Storm." Lanna had spent the past week with Evalle, because Quinn had needed time away to mourn Kizira's death and a safe place to leave the young woman.

Lanna reached for a wide headband, which she pulled over her head then up over her curls, not taming them so much as containing the mass. She'd put on a pair of jeans that rode low on her hips, and a bright red sweatshirt.

Evalle had gotten used to having Lanna around, but she needed more room for this many people. Still, Evalle said, "You're always welcome." It was true.

"Thank you, but I am too many wheels."

Evalle cocked her head until she realized what Lanna was saying.

"You mean a third wheel?"

Tugging the headband until she had it the way she wanted it, Lanna said, "Yes. Third wheel. You and Storm need your time and I am ready to go. Cousin is back in Atlanta."

"Quinn's back? You're sure?"

"Yes, I feel him." But she didn't look happy about it.

"What's the matter, Lanna?"

"Cousin is sad, very sad." She studied on what she was saying and added, "Dark."

That did not sound like Quinn, but the man had watched the woman he loved die in his arms. Evalle would be dark, too, in his place.

In fact, she'd be just as dark inside if this didn't work out with Storm. He'd made her his mate.

Could he *un*mate her?

The question she should be asking was—would he?

Storm took three deep breaths to bring his blood pressure back down so his head didn't explode.

He looked at the belt buckle his father had given him.

In fact, his father had sent a request back to a relative in their Navajo tribe in Arizona while Storm and his father still lived in

South America with the Ashaninka people.

Yes, it was something with deep sentimental value, but his father had taught him to care for people, not things.

He traced a finger over what was left of the ruined piece of art and swallowed hard, trying to let go of how much he cared for this buckle.

The silver and diamonds meant nothing to Storm, only that it was a tangible reminder of his dad.

It might be easier to let go of his anger if Storm believed it had been an accident, but the gargoyle had snuck in here and taken his belt out of the bedroom.

One of the diamonds was still in place, staring at him like a macabre, one-eyed mask.

Storm had to get out of here and clear his mind.

Evalle's empathic gift was not as strong as his, but she would know what he was feeling. Even he couldn't hide his anger right now and the longer he stayed here the more it would upset her.

His phone buzzed.

He checked the text from Tzader: *I need you to go over what happened with hunting the troll killer. It would be simpler if we did it at headquarters. No point in bringing Evalle out during daylight. You can relay any new information to her.*

At least now Storm had a reason to leave. That had to be better than saying he needed some air to clear his head. He sent back an affirmative.

Then Tzader added: *Quinn's on his way to headquarters and wanted to know if you would bring Lanna with you.*

Storm replied: *Yes.*

He stuffed the belt and his clothes back into the duffel and left it in the corner, then grabbed his leather jacket and shrugged it on.

When he reached the living room, Evalle was still walking and humming to Feenix, who'd snuggled even closer.

Storm asked Lanna, "What do you need to do before you're ready to go?" Storm glanced at Evalle then looked away. "I've got to leave for a bit."

Evalle swung around to watch both of them. "Why?"

"Tzader texted me about coming into headquarters and asked if I'd bring Lanna. Quinn will meet us there."

Lanna gave Evalle a smug look. "I told you Cousin was back." Then she picked up the handle of an old rolling suitcase. "I am packed."

Evalle eyed Storm. "I didn't get a telepathic message, but Tzader texted *you*?"

He could see how that might not sit well with her. "Because he needs me to debrief everyone on the troll killer hunt."

"I'll go with you." Evalle started toward the bedroom and Feenix's wings flapped quickly. She stopped and patted him again.

Maybe getting out of the way would help her calm Feenix down, too.

Storm added, "Tzader said it wasn't necessary for you to come out in daylight to make this meeting since I can catch you up on anything when I get back."

"Did he *specifically* say not to bring me?"

"No, but he just doesn't want to have you travel in daylight when you don't have to." Why was she being so edgy about this? He'd think she would be glad to avoid the sun and headquarters, which meant interacting with Sen.

Hell, Storm would just as soon pass on this meeting.

"Fine."

He hated that word. It was the most dangerous word in the female language. "What's wrong?"

She glared at him.

What had he said wrong?

Evalle glanced at Lanna, then back at Storm. He got it. They had an audience. There was nowhere for a private conversation unless he cast a spell to protect their words, which he didn't have the time for right now even if Evalle looked receptive, which she didn't.

He had a stop to make before he went to headquarters, and that stop had become even more important now.

He grabbed his keys off the counter, causing them to jangle.

Feenix lifted his head at the sound and looked from the keys to Storm's face. Feenix hadn't touched silver keys that had been left out in the kitchen, yet he'd gone for Storm's belt in the bedroom.

Evalle cleared her throat and said, "Don't forget the other

diamond."

Storm picked it up only because he didn't know if it would bother her more if he left it sitting there. He had never questioned his instincts around Evalle, but at the moment he was off balance and didn't like it. "I'll be back in time to pick you up and meet Adrianna."

She gave a wooden nod.

He stepped over to her, but on the opposite side of where Feenix had dropped his head onto her shoulder. Storm gave her a long kiss on her forehead and whispered, "Get some more rest, okay?"

"Right."

Another curt answer. He couldn't do anything about this until he managed to take the strain off Evalle and that wouldn't happen by him staying around right now. "Call me if you need anything."

"If I do, I'll send a message to Tzader since you'll be with him."

He started to say something, but she tipped up her chin in challenge. Evalle didn't deal with emotions well and being uncomfortable made her combative.

Much like a cornered animal.

He hated that he was the cause of more anxiety.

She added in a flat voice, "Just flip the switch that activates the power for the elevator. I took the warding off the controls when we came in last night so that *you* could leave when you wanted."

Storm closed his eyes for a minute at the turbulent emotion beneath her last words.

...you could leave when you wanted.

She'd designed a complicated, warded security system that involved a constantly changing code to prevent anyone or any*thing* from accessing the elevator. That would be no problem for Storm if not for requiring the ability to manipulate the lock with kinetic power, which he did not possess.

He'd joked that she could build one hell of a prison.

She hadn't caught the joke.

He *would* fix this mess as soon as he returned. The sooner he left and handed off Lanna then made his report, the sooner he could get back here. With Lanna gone, he'd have an easier time talking to Evalle.

Lanna walked to the door, keeping track of every word said and not said. She started to speak and Storm shook his head, pointing for her to leave. She sighed and obeyed his silent order.

When Storm reached the door, Evalle still had her back to him.

Feenix watched Storm over her shoulder. The gargoyle patted Evalle while keeping his gaze pinned on Storm and saying, "Mine."

Evalle hugged him back. She probably thought Feenix had been speaking to her. "Yes, I'm yours baby."

But Storm and Feenix both knew for whom that message had been intended.

That gargoyle may not know a lot of words, but he knew the power words when it came to Evalle.

Feenix pfft quietly in Storm's direction and a puff of smoke curled from his snout.

Storm shut the door and caught up to Lanna.

He knew for sure that he could straighten out this tension between him and Evalle, but he had no idea what to do about Feenix's territorial behavior.

How did you have a conversation with a gargoyle that had the vocabulary of a three-year-old child?

But Feenix was far wiser than a child.

And that little critter meant the world to Evalle. Storm was the last person who would ever separate them or be the cause of conflict between those two. He definitely did not want to put Evalle in a position of having to choose between him and Feenix.

She'd been put through enough in her life.

He wanted her as relaxed and happy as she'd been the last night they'd made love in the backyard of his Midtown house.

He should have realized the turmoil he'd cause her by moving in when she'd never lived with anyone, not even a family.

They hadn't discussed it.

He'd spent hours making love to Evalle that night outside, because he hadn't wanted to take her around the taint the witch doctor had left inside.

Evalle invited him to move in with her, and all he could think about was finally being able to keep her close all night long. Or all day long. He didn't give a damn as long as he could hold her and love her the way she deserved to be loved.

But his presence was creating discord in the one place that had served as her safe haven before he showed up. She loved with her whole being and she'd suffer in silence before uttering a word of complaint.

She deserved to be happy in her own home.

He would make sure that happened.

CHAPTER 12

Castle KievRus, Ukraine

Veronika lifted the hood of her signature red robe and let it fall behind her. She studied Tegus Bilguun, the twenty-six-year-old, male sorcerer draped spread-eagle against the gray stone wall in the dungeon of her family's Ukraine castle. Chains anchored to the wall secured his wrists and ankles so that he hung a foot off the floor, wearing only jeans. With blond hair, aristocratic nose and chin, plus amber-gold eyes, the man gave her an attractive view.

This castle was one of six similar holdings in different parts of Europe, and her ancestors had lived here for over a thousand years, but they hadn't built this structure.

Her bloodline came from that of royalty, not laborers.

Her ancestors had also been a bunch of bleeding hearts, but she hadn't been born with that affliction.

"Who the hell are you?" the sorcerer yelled when he realized he was no longer alone.

"Veronika of the KievRus coven."

"There's no such coven. My family would know."

"We have been in existence since the ninth century."

"Sorry, but I'm not a history fan. Give me back my cellphone and I'll look it up. Oh, that's right, I won't be able to hold anything again after you fucked up my hands!" he screamed. He tried to move his hands, then gasped in pain. "You will so pay for this, bitch. Your death will be slow and painful."

"I think not," she answered, stating the obvious. She'd had his hands sandwiched between boards, then drilled all the way through with half-inch bolts holding them encased. Blood still dripped from between the boards, running down stones that had been cut and placed many centuries ago.

This dungeon had held other powerful beings in the past, but none so significant as *this* sorcerer.

She'd have preferred for Tegus to be free to use his hands, because that would provide a true test of her powers. But she couldn't risk having miscalculated her progress and allow him to harm her.

Her window of time narrowed with each day.

He shouted, "What do you want?"

"You'll be the first to become part of the greatest power ever seen in this world, which will rise again very soon."

Blood drizzled faster down the wall when he banged the wood against the stones with his struggles.

She informed him, "You only hurt yourself. You can't destroy the wood slats. That wood will not catch fire or break, short of Thor striking it with his hammer."

This sorcerer might be young, but just one flick of his fingers could kill.

Even something as simple as the right combination of words could be used as a weapon.

She should know.

At the age of six, she'd stopped the heart of her family's pet wolfhound, even though she'd misspoken the words given to her by an old crone who knew Veronika would be the one to revive the KievRus. So often, it was the intention that really counted in a spell.

The family had warned her against testing her majik as the time for Witchlock drew close, but she would not be careless in these tests.

Tegus spit out a slew of derogatory remarks. Words to shield his pain and save his pride. When he wore himself down, he yelled, "Use my blood for a curse and my family will find you. When they do, they'll wipe whatever KievRus you claim still live from the face of this world."

He thought she intended to use his blood to fuel a spell?

She was no dark witch who wasted her time on such things. That was for those who lacked vision for witchcraft. Those covens were no better than the mealy-mouthed white witches who refused to dirty their hands with dark arts. No, Veronika had known her destiny from the moment she'd read the history of the original KievRus coven.

Her people would never fear retribution or betrayal again.

She would see that day.

As the only person of this generation who could restore the KievRus coven to its former glory, she could afford no mistakes. The time was nearing for when she'd be gifted with the power of Witchlock, but she had much to do before that moment.

She kept the sphere tucked close inside the deep sleeves of her robe. Withdrawing her empty hand, she pointed a finger at Tegus.

Power vibrated in the room.

"Don't be a fool. My family will retaliate!" he shouted, though the sound had been reed thin and hurting. His words were losing punch. He rasped, "You can kill me, but you'll never live to enjoy a moment of whatever you're trying to do."

Tucking her hand back inside the sleeve of her other arm, she smiled. "I'm not going to kill you. At least, that's not my goal."

He squinted, frowning at her, then shook his head. "Then more the fool you are, because I will rain down terror upon you and your family the second I am free."

"No one can find my family. They've hidden from your kind, and from mundanes, since the time when your ancestors tried to destroy our coven."

He stopped cursing her and stared with profound confusion. "What *are* you talking about?"

"You really *should* study your family history. In the thirteenth century, Mongols captured Kievan Rus here in Ukraine. One of our own betrayed us, intending to become the harlot queen of the Mongolian ruler, but he was wise enough to put her to death once she'd served her purpose. Before that happened, she told him how her coven had used our majik to manipulate events and would use their power against him if our people found him to be an unfit ruler. Your Bilguun grandfather, many times over, led a group of soldiers to behead my entire coven." They killed three family members before the rest of the coven found out and dealt with the soldiers.

"You have got to be kidding. That was eons ago. What is this? A replay of the Montagues and Capulets?"

"Hardly, as I am no one's Juliet. Certainly not yours."

"What do you know? I agree with you on something." He sucked in a deep breath that sounded like an attempt to fortify his battle to maintain equal ground in spite of the pain creasing his face. "What the hell do you want then? Revenge?"

"Retribution for deaths long past is too simple for what I seek. My ancestors expect me to bring our coven back to power so that we may live free of persecution. This is not about an execution of justice, but to take control of all witchcraft."

First.

Then she'd pick off the most powerful, one at a time.

Tegus laughed, his derision falling off of her as easily as water off a duck's back. He shook his head in disbelief. "You're kidding, right? Sure, you caught me in a trap, because I was not expecting someone to be stupid enough to put their hands on the son of a Sterling witch and the Mac An Aba Mage. If you do succeed in killing me, one of them will come for you, and you'd better hope it's my father and not my witch mama."

I certainly hope so, but not until I reach my full potential.

She kept that thought to herself. The Sterling coven would hiss and carry on if they knew she'd captured one of theirs, but they had clearly failed to inform him of their agreement with Veronika or he wouldn't have been so easy to snare.

They were not a concern right now.

She maintained her calm only because she knew what was coming, while he did not. She asked, "Have you exhausted all your threats? Shall I begin?"

That sobered him. "I don't need my hands to deal with you."

And now would come his attack.

As he began calling up dark spirits to aid him, she pulled out the hand that held a diaphanous white sphere the size of a cantaloupe. It spun on her palm. Energy boiled around the sides and wisps of white smoke wicked into the air.

He paused, his eyes focused on her hand. "What is that?"

"You know the tale of Witchlock, don't you?"

"*Witchlock?* That's … impossible." His gaze jumped to her face and he lost all the arrogance of a moment ago. His eyes darted back to the steaming sphere in her hand and shock took over his expression. "It can't be. That was lost to everyone. How did you ... "

"I don't have time to discuss this. Once this experiment is successful, I'll have to bring in the next specimen, which shouldn't be as much of an effort. Children are actually a joy to use as experiments."

Tegus became very quiet.

Now that she had his full attention, she continued. "You see, this is not about *wielding* Witchlock. When the moment comes for me to embrace the Witchlock power, I will have no trouble with one like you." A partial truth. But she did still need to learn how to control the power she received from Ragan. Then she wouldn't lose consciousness the first five minutes she took possession of Witchlock and it overwhelmed her. She'd read the history. The more power she gained now, the stronger she'd be during the eclipse.

"You're insane," Tegus accused her.

She ignored his lack of understanding and finished explaining what this test meant. "All I'm doing right now is learning the way this power will travel through a bloodline, such as along the energetic connection from you to your son. You should be very proud of him. His powers are quite strong for an untrained eight-year-old who is half human."

"No. Not him. Take anything you want from me, but spare him. *Please!*"

And there it was. This was the vulnerable point in Tegus. She would locate that in every powerful being she chose to exploit.

"I can't possibly fail to finish this experiment once I take control of your power."

Tegus started shouting curses. Not profanity, but the real ones that had been created by his ancestors and intended for the destruction of entire armies.

Now she had a worthy adversary.

She extended her index finger on the hand holding the sphere, ignoring everything except funneling the energy from the sphere through her body and out to her finger, then sending that stream inside Tegus's mind.

His livid cursing was cut off mid-word by his own scream. He arched his body against the restraints anchored in the wall. "Get out of my head!" Veins stuck out all over his chest. His muscles twisted and moved like snakes inside his body.

Howling came from a distance. He was calling in spirits. They wouldn't be able to harm her, not with this much raw power running through her body, but they could distract her.

Her body trembled from the strain, and she drew harder and harder for each breath, desperate to maintain control. Blood trickled from her nose and her head felt as though it would split in half any second.

She grew light-headed, but she kept drawing all the energy she could into her body, pulling harder on Ragan, and sending that energy up through her hand.

Blue light shot from her outstretched finger and struck Tegus's head, lighting up his face.

His body shook so hard the heavy chains rattled. Foam poured from his mouth. His body bowed and twisted unnaturally, muscles and tendons stretching. He fought her with all he had and she admired the warrior in him.

A gut-wrenching scream ripped from his throat right before the blue light vanished and his body slumped. Blood ran from his eyes, which now bulged out of their sockets.

Veronika cupped the hand holding the sphere against her chest and brought her other hand up to support her trembling arm. She licked away the trickle of blood running over her lip as she stood there shaking, and her stomach lurched a little at the metallic taste.

She took in the slumped form of Tegus.

Drat. His chest no longer moved with breathing.

How disappointing.

She'd she'd lost control when she pushed too hard. Once she reached her full potential, directing it would be simpler, but her body could not tolerate more energy drawn off Ragan yet. She looked at the sphere, where threads had begun forming inside the round ball of energy, and her mood lightened. That was the first sign of the final metamorphosis for the sphere.

Maybe she wasn't so far from success as it appeared, but Tegus's child would be of no use now. Still, she hated to pass up a chance to play. She so rarely got to enjoy herself.

This was not the time to lose focus or rush anything.

Impatience would be dangerous.

She had only one chance to take possession of Witchlock.

Once she did, she would have the power to own anyone's witchcraft, and eventually, the power of deities.

One in particular.

CHAPTER 13

TÅμr Medb, home of the Medb coven

Maeve studied the wall of jewels in her private quarters within TÅμr Medb and felt the eyes of a predator on her back. She swung around to meet the living eyes of her dragon-shaped throne. The chair sat between her scrying wall and the doors that led to the rest of the tower realm where the majority of her coven resided.

At least, that's where they resided until she could wrangle the power from that bitch, Macha.

The dragon watched her with an unholy look in his glowing silver gaze with its black diamond pupils.

She strolled around to the front of the throne, forcing him to move in order to continue eyeing her. Laughing, she said, "I have noticed your silver eyes. Did you tire of the original color? Or have you finally managed to control one part of your body?"

Those eyes narrowed, with some vicious thought, she had no doubt.

What, Daegan? Do you have something to say after all this time?"

That viper-sharp gaze stared back, unblinking.

"Very well, I will allow you to speak if you don't annoy me, but it will not undo the entire spell so don't get excited." She pointed a finger and whispered a string of words.

The dragon's eyes glowed brighter, then dimmed and he blinked.

She cocked her head. "Have you forgotten how to speak?"

"No," came out low and gravelly. "I remember everything."

"I have no doubt." She studied him, considering the best tack to take with this traitor who had thought to see her dead. "Would you like to share something you've seen during the years I was unavailable?"

"No."

"Then returning your ability to speak was a mistake."

"No, casting a curse on me was your mistake and I will live long enough to see the favor returned."

The confidence in his words sent chills down her spine. He'd almost overpowered her once.

Never again.

But she would not allow him, or any other man, to unnerve her in her own domain. "I do love a man with your confidence, Daegan. I'll make you a deal. Tell me something about Kizira that I can't find out from the scrying wall and I'll grant you a boon."

The dragon's eyes brightened at that offer, then took on a thoughtful look. When he moved his gaze back to her, he said, "Flaevynn compelled Kizira so that the priestess could not heal herself during the final battle, because Flaevynn believed Kizira had betrayed Flaevynn and the coven during visits to the human world."

Maeve added that bit of information to what she'd learned about the young woman being allowed a year away on her own at nineteen.

What had Kizira done during that year? And had she betrayed the Medb for the Belador warrior who had held her as she died?

A deep noise came from Daegan's throat, reminding her it was time to pay up.

Maeve said, "Alright, what do you want and don't be ridiculous. If you ask to break the spell, I'll deny the boon."

"My request is simple. I have not slept since I became a chair. Allow me to sleep when you do not need me to observe."

She thought about any potential problem with that and couldn't see one. Perhaps she'd found a way to squeeze information from him by allowing him to enjoy sleeping, then she'd dangle another bait later as a treat.

Lifting her hand she waved her fingers and tiny lights twinkled around his head then disappeared. She said, "Don't make me regret that."

"I am but a humble servant."

He used to say that when he'd used his sword arm for her.

Before his loyalty turned.

She'd teach him not to try her patience.

With one snap of her fingers in his direction, he hissed at the sudden reinforcement of the initial spell that condemned him to live forever as the queen's throne, unable to speak or enjoy life as a virile male ever again.

She warned him, "You may slumber when alone, but I warn you to choose your words more carefully next time you speak to me."

The tall double doors opened on their own ahead of Cathbad walking briskly toward her from the hall leading to her quarters. He rubbed his hands in glee. "Ossian has inserted himself into VIPER as an independent contractor. They think he's an independent warrior mage from the Julian Alps in Italy."

"That was quite clever of you to gift Ossian with the ability to shield his Medb scent and change his physical appearance ... as long as no one at VIPER becomes suspicious of him."

"Ossian is the best of our elite warriors. He will not let us down. With access to VIPER intelligence, he's able to feed information to his scouts. One group has reported that Vladimir Quinn has returned to Atlanta, and they have located him."

"That's encouraging, but I'll be more enthusiastic once I find out the connection between him and the priestess Kizira."

Cathbad's grin broadened. "You didna let me finish. He was seen leaving a mausoleum in a cemetery. I'm thinkin' that's where he laid her to rest."

"He didn't burn the body and scatter the ashes?"

"Maybe not." Cathbad held out his hand and a crystal glass appeared with two fingers of brown liquid. "But I'm thinkin' we may be premature in capturing Quinn until we know how to access the mausoleum."

"Why can't we just teleport into the vault?" she asked, thinking out loud.

"There's no telling what kinda trap a Belador might have set."

"You have a point. Still, I want to see it. If Kizira is in there, we'll either capture Quinn and gain what I want or find a way into the mausoleum and find my answers there."

"That's my Maeve, thinkin' like the sly queen who rules with a wicked fist."

A snort sounded, drawing both Maeve and Cathbad's attention toward her throne, where a puff of white smoke drifted from the tip of the dragon's nose. Daegan's eyes were as hard as his stone body that formed the elaborate throne.

Cathbad commented, "I'm not so sure allowing him to live all these years was a good idea."

"Of course it was," she told him, her sharp words making it clear she would not be criticized, not even by Cathbad. "Killing him would have been merciful and I will not be accused of that fault."

Chuckling, Cathbad agreed. "Only fools would believe that of you." He turned from eyeing the dragon. "Back to business. I hear the Tribunal is quite angry over this conflict between you and Macha and wants a solution."

"Oh? Should I be concerned?"

"No, I think you may be quite pleased with a gift I have for ya. Donndubhán, one of our Scáth Force warriors, has brought us an opportunity that you can use to gain advantage over the Beladors and very possibly force the Tribunal to see it your way with the gryphons."

"Where is this gift?"

"In the dungeon."

CHAPTER 14

VIPER Headquarters, North Georgia Mountains

Tzader nodded at agents as he strode through VIPER headquarters, where the chilly air inside this mountain failed to improve his scorching bad mood. If Storm hadn't been able to pin down a scent from the troll killing, no one could.

Not Storm's fault.

The Skinwalker had run hard day and night trying to find the killer, which the Beladors needed more than ever now, or the Medb would point a finger at the Beladors for that murder, too.

He'd suffered through a half hour with the damned Tribunal deities, who were no happier with him than he was with them.

The hell with them.

They wanted the Beladors to play nice with the murdering Medb. They wanted the gryphon issue settled. They wanted Macha to shake and be friends with Maeve.

Like any of those crazy gods and goddesses would do that in Macha's position?

Well, he wanted a few things too, like a chance at a normal life with the woman he loved. That was never going to happen as long as he had to cater to every person between here and Treoir. He couldn't remember the last time he had a day off, much less a real day with Brina.

If Brina needed anything right now, no problem. Same for Evalle and Quinn, but the rest could go screw themselves.

When Tzader reached the main receiving area, agents walked through an arched exit that appeared when their resident troll, Jake, activated an overhead door hidden by Sen's majik.

The surly troll had been harder to deal with than usual since trolls around Atlanta began disappearing last week. He, no doubt, held Tzader and everyone else in VIPER responsible.

Tzader caught Storm's chin lift from where the Skinwalker stood to the side as others streamed past on their way out, now that the debriefing was over.

Storm started in the minute Tzader reached him. "Evalle needs some time off."

Tzader couldn't agree more, but he didn't care for Storm's demanding tone. "Why"

"She's getting run into the ground and she's hunting demons alone. You told me she wouldn't do that while I was gone."

"I don't like her going off on her own either, Storm, but I also know trying to dictate to her is never a good idea." Tzader hoped Storm heard the extra message in that.

Storm rubbed his neck. "I know she's stubborn, but she's stressed out right now and a few days off would help."

That didn't sound right. Tzader's mood turned darker by the second. "We all knew she was stressed while you were gone. Now tell me why she's stressed with you home."

Storm's gaze flickered just enough to indicate he'd struck a nerve.

Tzader pushed harder. "What's wrong with her?"

"Nothing that a little time off won't fix."

Tzader waited for three agents to pass by before saying, "We're having issues with the Tribunal. The Beladors are, that is."

"Damn those fuckers," Storm snarled.

"Not that I don't agree, but this is not the place to share your honest opinion."

Storm washed a hand over his face. He looked and sounded as tired as he claimed Evalle was, but when he dropped his hand his sharp eyes were aware of everything around him. He spoke softly. "I'm tired of them jerking her around like a puppet."

"No more than I am."

"Then take her off the teams for a while and out of the fire."

Tzader made a decision. "I'm going to tell you something, but you can't share it with Evalle until I have a chance to tell her."

"I won't if she doesn't hear about it first and ask me."

"She won't. The Tribunal has run out of patience with what they consider a pissing match between the Beladors and the Medb. They accepted the Medb into the coalition and aren't going to back up on that, but this custody battle over the gryphons and daily accusations from the Beladors and the Medb has pushed a vote for a liaison to settle disputes."

"About damn time."

"It might be, if they hadn't decided that Evalle should take the position and run interference between the Beladors and the Medb."

"What. The. Fuck?" Storm's chest heaved with harsh breaths. His fists curled then uncurled. "Now what does she have to do?"

"It hasn't been formally decided. I presented Macha's point that Evalle has been a Belador too long to be an objective liaison, but I think the Medb are behind this push for Evalle to be the liaison."

"Why would they want that when she's clearly on your team?"

"My bet? To get Evalle in TÅµr Medb again."

Storm's eyes turned as black as the threat in his voice. "I'll take her where no one can find her if they try that."

Tzader considered the ramifications of the drastic measure Storm threatened, but anyone who knew Storm at all would realize it was no empty threat.

Even so, no one had ever escaped being hunted by VIPER.

And Sen would find a way to convince a Tribunal that VIPER should go after her.

Plus Evalle wouldn't agree because she'd never be able to return. Tzader said, "We haven't lost the battle yet to keep her out of TÅµr Medb. Macha and I are in agreement so we're fighting it."

"Those are *possibilities*," Storm stressed. "I'm talking about an absolute."

Tzader had to get Storm to see this from Evalle's position. "Don't you think Quinn and I haven't considered that before? We talked to Evalle about it once and she said she was never going to live in a prison again. She'd rather take her chances and stay here with the people who matter to her than hide for the rest of her life."

The hard glint remained in Storm's eyes. "I'll do whatever it takes to keep her safe."

"What if she hates you for doing it?"

Storm looked thoughtful. "Her safety comes before anything else."

"Even her happiness?"

"She'll be happy."

"Not if you snatch the only life she's ever had out from under her. You may not like to hear this, but she would leave you and come back even knowing the risk. You can't lock her up. We've all figured that out. She hates that we're all so protective of her and tries that much harder to prove that she can handle anything." Tzader took a step closer and warned, "Be careful with her heart. If *you* hurt her, it will be worse than anything the Tribunal has ever done to her. Then you'll find out just how dangerous Quinn and I are as a team. We'd bring the full force of the Beladors down on anyone who hurt her, even you."

Storm's fierce determination didn't waver, but he let out a long breath and ran his hands over the hair he had tethered into ponytail. "I want her happy. She's never been in a relationship before and she needs time to settle in and realize I'm not going to abandon her at the first hint of trouble."

Tzader believed Storm, and his respect for the Skinwalker ticked up a couple of notches, but he didn't like that last part. "What sort of trouble?"

Storm looked down, his face a wash of internal debate, but he finally said, "I've dealt with Isak Nyght, Tristan's crap, Medb crap and fought everything from Svart Trolls to warlocks to keep her safe and keep her with me, but I may lose the battle to a two-foot-tall gargoyle."

Ah. Now Tzader got it. "Feenix unhappy you're there?"

"The little critter is territorial as hell around her and making it clear he doesn't want me there."

It would be funny if not for the misery in Storm's voice. Tzader had just as tough a battle with trying to get Brina by his side. For the first time since Storm came along, Tzader was in his corner. "What are you going to do?"

"I have a plan. Not sure it's a good one yet."

Before Tzader could say more, Quinn walked up with Lanna

trailing close behind. The young woman dragged her beat-up suitcase behind her.

Just to poke at Quinn, Tzader asked, "You can't part with a few bucks to buy Lanna a decent suitcase?"

She paused, not saying a word, which was so unlike the young woman who generally stuck her nose anywhere it was not wanted.

Tzader's gaze swung to Quinn, who would normally scowl at him and make a sarcastic dig at Tzader in return, but Quinn's reaction was completely un-Quinn-like.

His friend frowned at the rolling baggage as if he hadn't seen it before. "Yes, I should have done that by now. We'll find a new one today."

Where was Tzader's best friend, and who had stuck the Grim Reaper in Quinn's place? Tzader didn't expect Quinn to be over Kizira's death, not by a long shot, but this Quinn concerned him.

Storm broke into the stilted silence. "I've got to get back to Atlanta. I have some business to take care of before dark, then Evalle and I need tonight free. We've made a commitment and we can't reschedule."

Even Quinn's eyebrows lifted at Storm's statement, because he sure as hell hadn't *asked* for tonight off.

But the guy had a point. Evalle deserved a break and for everyone to cut her some slack. Tzader nodded. "Check in with me tomorrow."

"Will do." Storm strode out the opening that appeared as a group of agents passed him on their way in.

Quinn asked, "Something going on with Evalle?"

Instead of discussing Storm and Evalle, Tzader said, "Maybe. I'm trying to keep her from being stuck as the liaison between the Beladors and the Medb, but the Medb are pushing hard for it. They say since she leads the gryphons, she should be the representative to work out the gryphon possession issue and the Medb and Belador conflicts."

"No." Quinn gave his vote in a voice as hard as the rock surrounding them. "Let the deities deal with it."

"My feelings exactly, but the thing that bothers me is Sen."

"He doesn't like anything to do with Evalle."

"See, that's the thing. I would have expected him to be

pushing for her to take that position, because it would put her in a bind, plus force her to spend time in Treoir and possibly TÅµr Medb, but he smiled when I told the Tribunal that Macha said no. That bothers me."

"You've got a point." Quinn cleared his throat and quietly said, "We need to find somewhere away from ... here."

Tzader nodded, thinking Quinn and Lanna wanted lunch. Maybe some casual time would give his friend a moment's reprieve from grieving. "Where to?"

Lanna stepped forward. She glanced all around, watching until no one was near them and said, "I must use some majik for Cousin. I do not like him unhappy."

What the hell were these two talking about doing?

She started for the door, chatting away. "Then we will go to hotel and I will shop. I have not been outside in forever. This will be wonderful day. You will see, Cousin."

Quinn muttered, "No, it won't."

But he didn't elaborate.

Tzader waited for Quinn to leave and followed him.

Quinn had been adamant about Lanna not using her majik because a crazy wizard was after her, and he would know when she drew hard on the elements. But it sounded as if Lanna thought she wouldn't do enough to bring any attention to her location.

The only way Lanna could make Quinn happy was by bringing back Kizira. That wasn't happening.

CHAPTER 15

Tzader climbed out of his 1970 Hemi 'Cuda when the road, if you could call it that, ended deep in the woods ten miles from VIPER headquarters. A smattering of leaves clung to the branches, but November had just started and those would be gone soon.

Quinn stepped from a metallic silver Audi S8 that was probably still running on its first tank of fuel. He paid it no more attention than he would a rusted-out pickup truck.

Lanna jumped from the car and hurried to catch up to Quinn's long strides. "This is much better, Cousin. I am tired of being inside."

"I'm sorry for keeping you indoors so much, Lanna, but I can't risk Grendal getting his hands on you."

"I am not worried, Cousin."

"I'm not either. If he shows his face around me, I'll be the last thing he sees before his head explodes."

Tzader could appreciate Quinn's need to protect Lanna from the wizard, but Quinn had struggled with using his mindlock in the past. He paid an emotional price when he entered anyone's mind and suffered guilt if he had to terminate a threat with his powers.

He had *never* sounded so willing to kill without question.

Lanna's smile dimmed but she pushed through the brittle moment and asked, "What did you need me to do?"

Quinn became very quiet, staring at the ground. "I need you to find someone, and tapping that much of your majik may draw attention from Grendal. But I won't let him harm you."

"I understand." She might mean what she said, but she was not happy about it now that she realized Quinn needed more than *some* majik. Once she pulled from the elements, she'd have to be kept locked away safe, and the poor girl was desperate for a little freedom.

Tzader asked, "Why ask Lanna when we have VIPER resources?"

Quinn sighed heavily and raised devastated eyes to meet Tzader's before he swallowed the emotion that had brought on that look. "I haven't shared this with anyone, but as Kizira lay dying in my arms ... " He took a breath and Lanna's eyes turned watery. Then Quinn continued, "As she was dying, she said I had to protect someone she referenced as *her*. I thought she meant Evalle, but she said the name was Phoedra."

"Who is that, Cousin?"

He tried to smile. Major fail. "The daughter we had that I never knew about."

Lanna's gasp covered Tzader's reaction. Lanna sputtered, "When did ... why ..."

Quinn lifted his hand to stop the questions. "We met thirteen years ago by accident. I was in Chechnya, running patrols in towns where strange attacks on people were happening that no one could explain, so of course the Beladors sent us in to investigate."

Tzader said, "I remember hearing something about that, but the European Maistir was handling the problem."

"Right. I'm not up to telling the whole story about how I met Kizira."

That was understandable when every time Quinn said her name he grimaced as if someone had stabbed him. "We spent two weeks together during which I had no idea she was Medb. As royalty, she could shield her Medb scent. I had stepped in to stop a warlock from attacking her and almost died battling four at one time. When I woke up, she had me tucked into a cabin and was healing my wounds." He stared off into the distance and said, "Evidently we produced a child."

"She should have told you," Lanna whispered. "You would have cared for this girl."

"Yes, I would have," Quinn agreed. "But Kizira was wise to keep our daughter hidden from the Medb and she kept our relationship secret to pro ..." His voice broke. "To protect me." He cleared his throat again. "Anyhow, Kizira died before she could tell me Phoedra's location."

Tzader asked, "She couldn't have left you a letter or something?"

"Not being a Medb priestess. Flaevynn, that miserable whore of a mother, had access to Kizira's thoughts. Kizira was clever. I'm sure she had ways to hide those thoughts from a surface scan, but she would never trust leaving anything tangible when it could mean the life of our daughter."

Lanna put her hand on Quinn's arm and he smiled sadly at her. She said, "I will find her. Do you have something of hers for me to touch?"

The teenager had proven herself fearless when it came to protecting others, but she earned Tzader's admiration with her loyalty to Quinn at that moment. She put his needs above her safety and wish for freedom, but she had the full protection of the Beladors even if she didn't realize it.

Tzader studied the young woman. "Can you do that, Lanna?"

"Yes. I have many gifts. Some do what I want. Some do not, but no one is better at finding others than I am."

No lack of confidence there. Tzader liked this kid. "You should train."

"That is what Brina told me would happen when we came back, but ..." Her voice trailed off and Tzader was sure it had something to do with the look on his face. "I am sorry, Tzader. She will remember that she cares only for you."

"Lanna," Quinn warned and she quieted.

"She did nothing wrong, Quinn. Right now I welcome any encouragement."

"I know. I also know what it feels like when a wound is constantly reopened."

Tzader didn't want to shift the focus to his problems, not when Quinn had suffered so much and now had to find a twelve-year-old child he never knew about. Tzader told Lanna, "Brina is a woman of her word. She'll see that you're trained."

"I would like that." Turning to Quinn, she said, "Cousin?"

That was all the prompting he needed to get back on track.

Quinn pulled a braided hoop a quarter inch thick and the size of a bracelet from his pocket. He held it up. "Kizira managed to tell me to hold on to this bracelet. She wove it of my hair when we were first together. I now see black threads through it, which I believe must be the color of my daughter's hair."

Every word came out of Quinn with pain, but saying "my daughter" sounded as if it damn near broke him. His hand shook. He said, "Anything you can tell me will help because I have no clue where to begin, but I know Kizira has Phoedra somewhere not just anyone will locate."

Nodding at Quinn, Lanna closed her eyes and murmured something too low for Tzader to hear. The air, dead calm just a moment ago, now swirled and picked up momentum, shaking the leaves.

All at once, Tzader heard whispers here and there. He turned right and left, then looked at Quinn, who gave him a sign to wait.

When Lanna opened her eyes, she said, "I ask for help and have been told yes. If I cannot see your daughter and where she is clearly then the spirits will help me, but I must show them what I can first." She held out both hands, palms up and next to each other.

The second Quinn dropped the braided bracelet into Lanna's hands, black smoke bloomed into a cloud and billowed up, blanketing them in a dark fog. Voices screeched everywhere.

Lanna started screaming.

The smell of burned skin singed Tzader's nose. He fanned his arms to find her.

When he could finally see her she was on the ground holding her hands to her chest and crying. Quinn had the bracelet in one hand, holding it far from her and his other arm around her shaking shoulders.

"I'm sorry. I'm so sorry." Quinn kept repeating his apology in a voice raw with horror.

Tzader squatted down in front of them. "Let me see, Lanna."

She was taking short, halting breaths and shaking hard, but she opened one hand that looked as if acid had been poured on it in the outline of the bracelet.

Tzader said, "Let me send her to our druids in Treoir. Darwyli should be able to heal her hands faster than anyone here."

Quinn's eyes were swollen and full of agony. "I should never have done this."

Lanna, trooper that she was, sniffed and wiped her nose on

her sleeve. "Was not your fault, Cousin."

"Yes, it was. I should have had someone else look at it first. I just ..."

"You protect your daughter. I know. Do not let anyone else touch that."

Quinn turned her to face him. "Why?"

"It carries Medb majik so strong I think only Medb can use that to find her. I am sorry. But I know you do not want to hurt others."

Hugging her close, Quinn said, "I'd rather cut my arm off than ever harm you. I'm so sorry."

"No problem, Cousin. I want to see Darwyli. He will heal my hands and I want to stay to see Brina. She needs help."

Tzader said, "If that's okay with you, Quinn. I'd love to take Lanna to Brina after she's healed. Lanna would be safe from Grendal there, too."

Lanna nodded, staring up at Quinn with large blue eyes.

He leaned over and kissed her head. "You'll be safe in Treoir."

"And not locked inside, yes?" she asked, face full of hope for any freedom.

Quinn agreed, "No. That wizard can't touch you there." He asked Tzader, "Would you watch her for a moment? I have a thermal blanket in my car."

Tzader did, too, but Quinn looked like he needed a stiff drink. Barring that, a moment to breathe would help him. "Sure. Might want to bring her some water, too."

As soon as Quinn walked away, Lanna turned to Tzader. She shivered from shock, but she blew hair out of her eyes and said, "You must help Brina."

Did she think he didn't realize that? "I know."

"I mean, you must help her in dreams. She will remember if she sees you in same place. I feel that will be good."

"What do you mean if she sees me in the same place?"

"When traitor attacked us and we were gone, I told her how to find someone in dreams to help because Cousin was not sleeping so I could not reach him. I told her to find someone she cares much for. Had to be you. She slept. Did you not see her in dream while we were gone?"

Unbelievable. "Yes. It was vivid, but I was so tired I thought I was hallucinating."

"Do you see her in dreams now?"

"Haven't slept long enough to dream."

"Does not take long, but you must want to see her badly for her to find you. Does she dream now?"

He tried to process that he could be with Brina in a damn dream state. "Macha said Brina is having nightmares."

"She looks for you in dream, then maybe panics when she is alone. Go to her."

"But she doesn't remember me when she wakes up."

Quinn returned and wrapped her in the thin Mylar blanket, then held a bottle of water for her to drink from. "We need to get you to Treoir."

Quinn helped Lanna stand. She looked shaky and still rocked forward and back gently, but she told Tzader, "Brina will find you in dreams. She wants you."

Just how much did this teenager know about him and Brina?

Lanna's mouth quirked. "She tells me nothing. Your face tells much."

"You're scary, you know that?" Tzader said, unable to keep the smile from his voice. If Lanna could help him bring Brina back, he would personally insure the young woman got trained and anything else she needed.

"Finish up, Lanna," Quinn said gently. "We have to take you to Sen so he can transport us."

Sending Quinn to Treoir was not a good idea, especially if Quinn had to talk to Sen for more than three seconds.

Tzader offered, "Let me take Lanna so I can get her to Brina where I know she'll be in good hands. Brina's prickly these days and if she doesn't recognize you it could be a problem."

Quinn frowned, but said, "I understand."

"Would you do me a favor and keep an eye on Evalle?"

"Of course. Why?"

Lanna perked up, all ears.

Tzader took one look at the teenage snoop and sent Quinn a telepathic message. *I talked to Storm. Evalle isn't adjusting well or something. I have no damned idea, because I don't think Storm is treating her badly.*

That's a change of tone coming from you.

Tzader glared back. *I never said Storm was a bad guy. I just didn't like any hardtails around Evalle, but now that she's mated I want to be sure she's happy. I haven't had time to talk to her and to be honest I need some time on Treoir with Brina.*

Quinn's joking ended. *Go. I can handle things here.*

Once Tzader had Lanna packed into his car, he called to Evalle. *Are you busy, Evalle?*

No. I'm sitting on my hands staying out of the sun like a good little girl since you didn't want me outside.

She sounded pissed. He said, *Did you want to come to headquarters and visit Sen?*

No, but neither do I want people telling me what to do everywhere I turn. I'm tired of everyone else making decisions for me. Is Storm still there?

No, he said he had some business to take care of then he was heading home. Said that you two had plans tonight.

What business? Really pissed.

How should I know, Evalle? I'm not his keeper.

No, he doesn't have one, but everybody thinks I need one, including him.

Tzader's protective instincts kicked in. *Are you okay?*

Yes! I'm fine and I have some business of my own to take care of tonight. What did you need?

Now he wished he wasn't headed to Treoir yet. He'd like to revisit that conversation with Storm. But it wouldn't happen right now. *I'm taking Lanna to Treoir and I'd like you to talk to Quinn.*

Why?

There was a time that Evalle would have been thrilled at the idea of Quinn visiting her apartment instead of questioning why. What the hell had happened?

Tzader said, *Quinn's grim. Just see if you can get him to open up and talk about Kizira. Ask about Phoedra, because he'll want to tell you.*

Who's Phoedra? she asked in a softer tone.

Ask Quinn. It's better if he tells you, but don't mention that name to anyone else.

Okay, but I may have to leave soon.

I understand. If you don't catch up with him tonight, then maybe tomorrow.

Tzader withdrew from Evalle and sent one more message to Quinn. *I don't know what the hell is going on, but Evalle is upset. Find out what it is and if Storm is the cause. If he is, I want him picked up and taken somewhere you and I can have a private talk with him.*

Affirmative.

CHAPTER 16

Evalle paced across the apartment while Feenix stacked building blocks made of wood and plastic.

She checked her phone again. No call from Storm.

Her phone buzzed. She answered without looking. "Where are you?"

"In my living room," Nicole answered with a chuckle. "Clearly I'm not who you were expecting."

Nicole would realize even more if she were here with Evalle, because *this* white witch had a lot of gifts, but Evalle valued her most as a friend. Evalle said, "No, I thought this was Storm calling."

"Speaking of him, how's it going?"

Evalle gave her reflex answer. "Fine."

"That good, huh? Do you still have Lanna with you? I can keep her for a day or two."

"No, she left this morning and it *has* been crowded down here, but she's not a problem. It was good to have her here so that Feenix had someone." Evalle paced again, noticing Feenix had taken a whirly toy that Lanna made for him and was trying to make it fly.

Lanna could do that. Evalle could only throw it or pull it across the room with her kinetics. Feenix kept trying to make it spin in the air and when it didn't, his shoulders drooped.

The minute she got off the phone with Nicole, Evalle would play with him until she heard from Storm or Adrianna.

Then it would be go time.

"Evalle?" Nicole called out.

"I'm here. What's up?"

"The council of witches being formed is coming together, but I'm concerned about Adrianna."

"Why? Everyone knows she's a dark witch."

"We would welcome her as a liaison between the Medb and us, but she won't open a dialogue."

"Adrianna wants nothing to do with the Medb. She's pretty much her own person."

"She's not going to have the option very soon. The witches on this council are significant players and Rowan will head it up. As a sister-in-law to a Belador, Rowan will be the liaison between the council and the Beladors, but with the Medb leaders now able to enter the human realm, the chances for conflict between the Medb and Beladors increase. The council wants to insure fair representation for both groups to prevent VIPER from interfering. Witches have not had to join the coalition and they want to keep it that way."

"The Tribunal should come up with a plan for fixing all this since they're responsible for bringing our worst enemy into the fold," Evalle said so sharply that Feenix jumped. She covered the phone and said, "Sorry, baby. Everything is okay."

He nodded and went back to picking at his toys, but not with the enthusiasm he'd had while Lanna was here.

Nicole said, "I understand, but you know better than to depend on the Tribunal for anything by now."

"True."

"The longer we delay in forming a plan of our own, the more agitated the witch community becomes and that's never a good thing. Especially when we have a significant number of Medb in our midst and we have a rogue group of solitary witches being whipped into a fervor by a young, untrained one."

"What's that all about?"

"Just immaturity out of control. The rabble-rouser is a witch called Hermia. Rowan has to hold a hard line on all witches for any hope of this council working and preventing VIPER interference, and she's facing having to take a stand and push Hermia's group to fall into line. Rowan would rather Hermia recognize her lack of training, take responsibility and encourage her people to separate into reasonable size groups who can govern themselves, but Hermia is charismatic and smart enough to make the right noises and push the right buttons with the solitary witches, most of whom just want to be left alone. She's not ready for coven leadership, but the call of power has gone to her head and she thinks she can take a shortcut by becoming their leader."

Evalle finally calmed herself enough to hear the concern in Nicole's voice. "Where will you land in this new mix?"

"Rowan knows I'm not a dark witch, but I'm not much for committees and politics either after the white witches turned their noses up to me as a child. I've agreed to be on Rowan's advisory board, which was her way of bringing me in without making a statement by doing so." Nicole sounded amused at Rowan's maneuvering. "I'll help Rowan because she's the only one watching out for the best interests of everyone."

Trey McCree was a Belador with unmatched telepathic power and usually the central call-in point for all Beladors during a crisis. He was also married to Sasha Armand, Rowan's younger sister, who had erratic witch skills at best, based on what Evalle had heard.

Rowan, on the other hand, was the most powerful white witch that Evalle had ever met.

She'd hold a firm line when it came to gaining what she wanted to form this council, and right now, it sounded as though getting Adrianna on board was high on her priority list.

Adrianna did not need one more pressure at the moment.

In another day or two, none of this would matter if Adrianna, Evalle and Storm failed to stop Veronika and Witchlock.

Evalle considered telling Nicole about Veronika, then changed her mind. There was nothing to be gained, and Nicole would stress, or use her powers trying to help and potentially end up a victim to Witchlock if she drew Veronika's attention.

They had to rescue Ragan. Evalle wanted the specifics of the plan, and she wished Adrianna would call already. She told Nicole, "I'll talk to Adrianna, but no promises."

"I understand, but tell her that this council is serious. If she can't meet them halfway, she'll need to leave this area for her own safety. Once the council is formed, Rowan intends to inform VIPER that anyone outside of the council's jurisdiction will fall to them."

"I'm not seeing the problem or reason for Adrianna to leave, because she works for VIPER."

"Think about it, Evalle. What will those Tribunal deities do if any witches become a problem at that point?"

It hit Evalle like a blast of cold water. "They'll call in the Medb and make it the Medb's problem since that will be the most powerful and organized dark force on the coalition."

"Exactly. And at that point, the Medb will see Adrianna as an obstacle. They will seize any opportunity to eliminate a powerful witch from another coven, especially one who works with VIPER. Rowan and the others want to establish a power base—and their autonomy—before the Medb become entrenched in this region. Other areas of the country are forming similar councils, which will all send a representative once a year to a summit meeting."

Nicole was different from other witches in that she had some unusual gifts that didn't fall under traditional witchcraft, and her significant other was Red, a human woman who hated all this *woo-woo*, as Red termed it.

Evalle asked, "Is Red good with all this?"

"She will be. I've explained that it will protect me to join with more of my kind. Adrianna is going to need that protection, too." Nicole changed subjects without slowing down. "I have to go in a moment. Why do I sense that you are unhappy?"

So hard to keep anything secret around a friend with Nicole's abilities. Evalle said, "Hold on." Then she told Feenix, "I'll be right back."

He lifted a chubby, four-fingered hand in his okay sign, still intent on stacking the toys that Lanna had suggested Evalle buy for him. Lanna had realized he needed some way to practice motor skills and reasoning.

Evalle should have figured that out.

Just like she should know how to be Storm's mate. She entered the bedroom, pushing the door shut and dropped on the bed. "I think I made a mistake, Nicole."

"About what?"

"Storm moving in with me. He had a nice house that was above ground where he could come and go. I have to live underground, but he doesn't. And I know he's *willing* to do it, but that's going to get old quickly." *Might have already.*

"Have you talked to him about it?"

"No. We haven't had a minute alone since he brought me home that first night. If I ask him about it, you and I know he won't complain. Then he'll work even harder to hide how much he doesn't like it here."

"You might be wrong, Evalle."

"Feenix ate half of Storm's silver belt buckle. It had a jaguar head carved into it. The buckle also had two yellow diamonds in it, but thankfully those don't taste good to Feenix. Still, it was a piece of art and worth a fortune, and most important, Storm's dad had it made for him."

"Oh, yeah that's bad, but surely he understood that Feenix is like a child."

"An insecure and very possessive gargoyle child," Evalle clarified. "I have no skills for figuring any of this out. I can't cook an edible meal. We live a nocturnal life because I can't be in the sun. Storm is always understanding and accepting of everything in my life. What does he get from me?"

Nicole laughed.

Evalle said, "Besides *that*."

"I'm sure it's not as bad as you think. Storm isn't going to leave you over an apartment."

"I didn't say he would break up with me, but I don't want him being miserable just so we can be together. You wouldn't want that for Red."

"No, I wouldn't," Nicole said in a solemn voice. "Talk to him so that he knows you realize what he's giving up and figure it out together. The only two skills you need to make a relationship work are communication and honesty."

Evalle nibbled at her thumbnail, thinking on that. Nicole was right. She'd talk to Storm and they'd figure it out, even if it meant him moving back to his own place.

She'd been over-the-moon happy about him moving in.

The idea of him not living here made her stomach hurt, but she could hide her disappointment from him if that was the best way for them to stay together.

She could do anything when it came to Storm.

Her phone beeped. Evalle said, "I've got a call coming through. I'll talk to Adrianna and let you know."

"Thanks."

Clicking the buttons, she was glad to see it was Adrianna, who started in without a hello. "I've found a place for us to cross into the Jafnan Mir realm. It's the new sports arena being constructed to replace Atlanta's sports dome."

Evalle pulled up a mental image of the construction right next door to the current Georgia Dome in downtown. "Storm is ... " Evalle was not going to admit she had no idea where Storm was presently. "He's at VIPER headquarters, but I'm expecting his call any time to let me know he's on the way back. Where do you want to meet?"

"Sundown is in twenty minutes and I haven't eaten all day. I'd like to grab dinner, formulate our plan and go to the site."

"I'll send him a text to tell him to meet us at *Six Feet Under*. It's across the street from the Oakland Cemetery. Go ahead and order. We usually eat much later."

"Got it. I'm on my way."

Evalle jumped up and changed into her riding gear. If she texted Storm before she left, he might ask her to wait for him to pick her up.

She needed her freedom as much as he did.

She'd text him *after* she got to the restaurant. Rushing out to the living room, she slid to a stop and Feenix stood up, gripping his favorite stuffed alligator in one hand.

He took in her clothes and his face lit up. "Go ride?"

"Not right now, baby. I have to meet someone for business."

"Oh."

Just kill me now. That one word loaded her shoulders with guilt. "We'll play with your blocks when I get home, okay?"

"Ith okay." His eyes and mouth turned down.

She squatted down. "Come here."

He trudged to her, dragging his alligator by the tail, and stepped into her arms with his wings tucked. Then he dropped his head on her shoulder and one horn nipped her neck.

She hugged him close and said, "You know I will never give you up, right?"

He pulled back and two little teeth poked down over his bottom lip when he smiled. "My Evalle."

"Yes. And you're my Feenix. I'll be back soon, but I want you to promise me not to eat anything silver except the lug nuts."

His gaze scooted away from hers and he sounded very innocent when he said, "Okay."

She knew better. "Feenix?"

His sly gaze cut back at her. "Ye-eth?"

"Please don't touch anything that is not mine or yours, especially not Storm's."

"Wath accthident."

The little devil was sly enough to avoid giving his word. She said, "I need your promise."

He tapped his little foot and finally said, "Promith."

"Thank you. Storm is going to live with us and he will treat you nice. It would make me happy for you to be nice to him, too."

Feenix made an exaggerated sighing sound. "I thaid promith."

"Great. I'll see you soon."

"Where ith Lanna?"

"With her cousin, Quinn."

"Come back?"

Evalle's throat tightened. He was ripping her heart into little pieces with how lonely he sounded. "I'll ask her when I see her."

"Yeth." Feenix nodded and grinned.

It took so little to make him happy. *I'm sucking at that, too.*

CHAPTER 17

Evalle made the short trip to *Six Feet Under*, arriving as Atlanta calmed down for Sunday night. This late in the day in November, temps had dropped into the thirties, so riding over on her Suzuki Gixxer just before sunset in full-body Aerostich, deer skin gauntlet gloves and a completely enclosed dark helmet had actually been nice.

Not so much fun to be fully covered like this in the middle of August.

She did appreciate Tzader trying to save her making the run to headquarters, and if she never saw Sen again it would still be too soon, but she didn't care to have everyone thinking she was vulnerable the minute she stepped out of her apartment.

She'd killed plenty of creatures, hadn't she?

The last demon took your dagger and disappeared, and you came damn near to dying by falling off a mountain.

Okay, her job had pitfalls, but she was no princess to be put on a pedestal. She was having a tough enough time just being a mate.

Inside the restaurant, the smell of fresh-cooked fish and other kitchen aromas had her close to drooling. She found Adrianna sitting at the bar, nursing what appeared to be club soda.

Evalle set her helmet down.

Adrianna was halfway through a bowl of chicken fajita soup and put her spoon down. "Is Storm on the way?"

"Crap..." Evalle pulled out her phone and punched in a quick text about meeting her and Adrianna.

As expected, Storm replied that he'd pick her up. When she sent back that she was already at the restaurant, nothing came right back, then all she got was: *K, be there in 40 min.*

Bad sign. He was irritated.

She told the witch, "He's on the way."

Adrianna talked between bites as she finished her meal. "I've got a question. I heard Beladors around VIPER saying stuff about you being able to walk in the sun after you turned into a gryphon, but no one sees you outside in the daylight now. Are you just nocturnal by nature?"

"That ability went away. I'm night bound from here on."

Adrianna frowned. "I don't understand."

"Remember when you told me the spirits would expect payment for guiding me through their world to locate Storm in Mitnal? You warned me to choose my sacrifice. I made an open-ended pact and they jumped on it."

Adrianna studied her with compassionate eyes. "I wondered what happened after you made the offer for the spirits to take whatever they could from you where you stood."

Evalle lifted her shoulders, trying to own the feeling of unconcern so no one threw her a pity party. "I have no regrets since Storm is back here and alive. I was willing to lose all my Belador powers to find him, but the spirits took something from me that I'd never really had anyway, so really they've only inconvenienced me. Nothing more."

Nothing except what you most longed for after living in the dark your whole life..

Now who was hosting a pity party?

Sure, Evalle would like to be able to watch the sunrise or sunset with the man she loved, like a normal person, but she hadn't been dealt a normal life.

To balance things out, she got Storm forever.

Pretty good get on that point.

Any more mental complaining and she'd have to put her brain into time out.

"Can you be in the sun in your gryphon form?" Adrianna asked.

"I have no idea. I can't shift in this world without permission." That was another constant irritation on top of all she'd been through. She had the ability to shift into a beautiful gryphon now instead of the hideous beast form she'd once been relegated to, but even though Macha had accepted Alterants into her pantheon and petitioned for recognition, Evalle still couldn't shift, not even to show Storm.

I'm sick of other people ruling my life.

That was why she'd left the apartment on her own tonight. *Some*thing had to be under her control. No one was ever going to tell her when she could come and go.

Not even the sun.

And definitely not Storm.

Adrianna pushed her bowl away and spun on the bar stool, all five-feet-three of her dressed in a denim skirt and a dainty white shirt with full sleeves. She sported short, silver boots with spiked heels.

How did she walk or do anything else in those?

Ready to change the subject, Evalle asked, "Why did you pick the construction site for ... you know what?"

Keeping her voice down, Adrianna said, "It will be free of activity on a Sunday night. There *are* security cameras, which I've taken care of and–"

Adrianna's voice drifted off as her gaze shot past Evalle.

Evalle turned to find Isak Nyght strolling up to them. Men came in all shapes and sizes. This one walked in with the swagger of a linebacker on a day off. Usually, Isak showed up packing enough personal artillery, which included his custom demon blasters, to take out an entire terrorist encampment.

At the moment, he was packing a wicked glint in his blue eyes and a sexy curve to his mouth that had to be distracting the women he passed from whatever their dates were saying. The navy, collared shirt and dark pants might be an attempt to tone down the dangerous edge, but his bomber jacket and built-in attitude brought the threat level right back up.

Evalle had never missed Isak's appeal—she wasn't blind after all—but he wasn't Storm ... who would not be happy to find Isak here. There was a time she wouldn't have cared, but now she did. A lot. Storm was all she wanted in a man, and she wanted her man happy.

She checked her watch. Storm still had another half hour.

That gave her thirty minutes to get rid of Isak. Twenty-five if she didn't want the men to run into each other, which would end badly.

Isak gave a nod in Adrianna's direction.

The witch angled her head in a cool response.

These two had not hit it off during their first encounter, when they'd both shown up to help Evalle corner the witch doctor so she could open a portal for Evalle to bring Storm home.

That had been a trying time, especially when the witch doctor used majik to pin Isak and his megablaster to a wall.

He had no love for nonhumans and correctly grouped witches into that category.

Still, he'd pricked Adrianna's temper when he'd automatically referred to the witch doctor as an "it" even before he knew anything about the race.

Then Adrianna had conjured up some crazy majik to back down the bitch, who'd been determined to turn Storm into a full-blooded demon. Isak's personal code of nonhumans-are-a-danger-to-the-world had never been tested until he'd met Evalle, but he'd gotten interested in her long before he realized she was not human.

His attitude hadn't changed, just allowed for one exception to his rule.

Evalle jumped in first before Isak could start in on her about the dinner date she'd put off forever. "I know I'm a little late getting in touch–"

That snatched Isak's dark attention off Adrianna and back to her. "A *lot* late. You've blown off dinner three times."

Has it only been three times? "Things have been complicated, Isak."

"Did that guy Storm make it back?"

"Yes and he's not *that* guy–"

"Then it's not complicated any longer. You agreed to dinner a week later. It's been a week later."

"I realize that." Evalle glanced at Adrianna, who lifted her eyebrows as if to say *hmmm*? No help there. "What if I absolutely promise–"

"Tomorrow. That's your last extension. Kip asked about you and said to tell you the boys are doing good, but they want to come home."

Who was minding the guilt gates, and why, all of a sudden, were they wide open?

Evalle was getting bombarded everywhere she turned. Kip,

Isak's mother, had spared Evalle's life when she'd been almost shot full of holes by several Nyght weapons, and then she'd loaned Evalle a Nyght megablaster for a mission to take out deadly Svart trolls who'd kidnapped a bunch of humans.

As long as Evalle agreed to come for dinner.

Kip had been in obvious matchmaking mode, and for a woman who barely came to Evalle's shoulder, she was frightening. Plus, as a favor to Evalle, Isak had dropped off two homeless teenage boys with Kip. Evalle and a Nightstalker named Grady usually watched over the boys, but when things heated up in Atlanta, Kip had taken them for safekeeping.

Adrianna asked, "What boys?"

Evalle said, "A pair of eighteen-year-old twins who are homeless."

Isak added, "Warlocks."

"No, they aren't," Evalle argued. "They're witches. Warlocks are *dark* male witches. Those two boys are not like that." She knew this would not go over well, but she asked Isak, "Can Kip watch the boys for another week?"

"Why?"

Anyone else would be arguing with her or snarling over her audacity, but leave it to Isak to immediately figure out that Evalle had a reason for not bringing the boys back right now. Should she tell him a crazy witch called Veronika would have no trouble grabbing control of those two after an upcoming eclipse? Not a good idea unless Evalle wanted a black ops team in the middle of everything just to protect her.

Save me from men determined to protect me.

Evalle said, "I'm tied up on a project right now and want to be available when the boys come back so they don't get into trouble."

Adrianna was listening intently, watching the play between Evalle and Isak.

He stood, blocking Evalle's exit with his wide body. She had to get him turned around and out of here. "I really am sorry for all the delays."

He asked, "What time tomorrow?"

She accepted the end of her wiggle room. "I'll meet you here at dark."

"If you aren't here at dark, I'm coming to get you."

She said, "I'll be here, but I need to get back to my conversation with Adrianna. She's, uh, working on that project with me."

"Hmm." His gaze jumped to Adrianna, who managed to suddenly radiate even more sex than usual, while still giving him a frosty look.

Evalle had no idea what was going on with her.

Isak spoke too low to be heard outside their small circle, but he sounded disgusted when he asked Evalle, "You need a *witch* to help you?"

He'd said that as if he asked whether she needed an ex-con to aid her.

Adrianna remained in a relaxed position, with her elbow propped on the bar and stirring her club soda with a tiny straw. "Yes, she does, because as you had the privilege to witness, I can handle *anything* thrown my way."

"You sure about that?"

Sitting forward, Adrianna spoke softly, which meant Isak had to lean down to hear her when she said, "A foolish man made the mistake of underestimating me. It only happened once."

She sat back and he straightened to his full, humongous height. Daggers flew between their gazes.

Evalle didn't move for fear of getting cut by the sharp-edged glares. She suggested, "Nice to see you, Isak, but I really have to get back to work."

He nodded and turned, then stopped.

She leaned around to see what blocked his path.

Storm.

CHAPTER 18

Storm locked down on his emotions before Evalle picked up on his urge to rip Isak into two pieces and toss each half as far away from Evalle as possible.

Isak mimicked Storm's posture, with legs slightly apart and arms crossed.

Storm would be the bigger man for Evalle, who didn't need to be stressed over this. At least, he would be as long as Isak didn't touch her.

Evalle stepped around Isak and looked up at Storm. "Funny running into Isak here, but he was just leaving."

Isak interjected, "I might hang around and have a beer."

Being the bigger man was overrated. "That's fine. We're leaving," Storm told Isak, who wasn't budging.

Evalle glared first at Isak then at Storm.

Then she must have noticed how quiet things were getting in the normally bustling restaurant.

People were watching.

Waiting on the show to begin.

Could Isak not recognize that the chase was over? Evalle had made her choice, dammit.

Isak gave Storm a narrowed-eyed stare of challenge.

The human outweighed him by about thirty pounds, but Storm's jaguar strength would more than balance out that difference.

Hurting this guy would upset Evalle and she had enough on her plate right now, but Storm needed to get things straight with Isak so he'd stop sniffing around.

If that didn't work, then Storm would have a more in-depth conversation in a less public venue.

Evalle muttered, "Another minute of this and I'll get

testosterone poisoning." She leaned past Isak and called out, "Ready?"

Adrianna slid off the barstool.

Storm angled his head just enough to see Adrianna, whose eyebrows lifted and dropped just as quickly. She tossed money on the counter and slipped the strap of her tiny purse over her shoulder, striding past Isak without a second look.

Isak noticed *her* though, his gaze sliding from head to toe as the petite witch walked away, before he caught himself and returned to posturing.

Storm picked up on male interest in the witch that should have eased his anger, but Isak's gaze slid from Adrianna to Evalle, who rolled her eyes at both of them.

Then she fell into step behind Adrianna, not saying a word.

Storm felt eyes on his back and sent a look across the bar area and around the restaurant. That had everyone immediately shifting their attention to whatever conversation had been going on a moment ago.

Isak's mouth lifted with smug sarcasm. "Nice trick. That all you got?"

Storm stepped up to Isak. "Let's make this simple. In case you didn't get the memo, Evalle is my mate. Don't come near her again."

"Going to be hard to avoid it when she just agreed to go to dinner with me tomorrow."

Shock whipped through Storm first and disappointment followed close behind. What was going on between Evalle and Isak?

Storm was a master at disguising his emotions and shrugged off Isak's comment, telling him, "Don't get your hopes up."

Isak's mouth turned up, beaming arrogance. "Don't bet against me." He walked out.

Storm needed a minute to pull his fury under control before he walked out of here and faced Evalle. She was as genuine as they came, so his first guess was that she owed Isak dinner for something in the past, probably borrowing one of Isak's damned weapons.

With that realization, Storm's blood pressure started dropping. Isak had come around to collect on a debt.

Storm had won her love and he wasn't letting anyone impose on her. If Evalle had an outstanding debt with Isak, Storm would settle it.

Sure that Isak had cleared out, Storm turned to catch up to Adrianna and Evalle, but when he stepped outside the women were nowhere in sight.

Thumbing the keys on his phone, he sent her a text on the way to his truck. *Where are you?*

Busy.

His fingers paused on the handle of his truck and he stared up into the heavens, searching for patience. He could track her and Adrianna, but that would take time and he didn't want to risk those two trying to cross into a hostile realm by themselves.

He climbed into his truck, mentally searching for the right thing to say, and texted: *Isak and I parted on civil terms. Now can I come join you? I missed you today.*

Thirty seconds passed and he stared at the phone, waiting.

Forty seconds.

A minute.

When she finally texted back, she sent an address for the construction location of the new dome, but it was the smiley face she included that eased the tightness in his chest.

Still, she'd been stressed when she left the restaurant and knowing he'd contributed to her tension felt like shit.

He glanced up at the rearview mirror, seeing the face of a frustrated man. "Your trying to build walls around her to keep her safe is not helping."

No, but he could fix that. He'd have to give her space and hope like hell nothing happened to her.

CHAPTER 19

Evalle followed Adrianna over chewed-up ground that would eventually be home to the Atlanta Falcons football team. Once this new dome was finished, the old one next door would be torn down.

The Georgia Dome still looked nice to her, but she'd never been to a football game so what did she know?

"Is Storm coming?" Adrianna asked, sounding concerned but not missing a step with those spiked boots.

"He's on the way."

Adrianna wore a backpack that had been stuffed full. She had her palms turned toward the ground, shining a glow ahead of her, which made up for her lack of night vision.

But Evalle saw just fine even through her dark sunglasses, and Storm would move through the night with the eyes of the predator he could shift into.

Adrianna paused and swung around, adjusting the backpack, then gave a head nod in the direction of something behind Evalle. "Looks like he found us."

Evalle twisted around.

Storm closed in on them with long strides, his knee-length coat billowing open. He was silent as a shadow in spite of how quickly he moved across the construction site.

When he reached them, he stopped and looked around. "There are cameras all over this place, plus they've got to have on-site security."

"I've taken care of the cameras," Adrianna assured him. "Whoever monitors the feed will see the same picture with an occasional bird flying past to break it up. We'll be shielded from human eyes. As for human security moving around, they'll turn back as soon as they reach this area and retrace their steps, thinking they've circled the building."

Evalle tried to get a read on Storm and picked up strong determination.

Storm worked on one speed when he was focused. All out.

He wouldn't let her or Adrianna move forward unless he was convinced they'd both be safe.

That was the man she loved, who might go overboard when it came to watching out for the woman *he* loved, but he didn't love in half measure.

He studied the construction site, where the skeletal structure soared four floors high already, with gantry cranes and scaffolding everywhere. "Is this where you want to access the realm?"

"Yes. I spent several hours here checking for spirits. There were two Nightstalkers, but I made a deal with each one for tomorrow if they stay away tonight. I haven't seen them. Once we get to where we're going, I'll enclose us with a spell that will prevent humans from hearing or seeing us, plus deter most curious supernatural beings from bothering us, but it won't stop someone truly determined."

"I won't let anyone close," Storm said.

Evalle took that to mean he was finally on board with staying here as their guard. "Then let's get this done."

He held up his hand to stall her and asked Adrianna for the specific location, which was on the very top level, of course.

Evalle asked, "Why does it have to be up there?"

Adrianna gave her a look that questioned why she was picking at the plan. "Because that construction level is the newest ground with no specific energies connected to it yet, and it's in the most open spot with nothing above us. Plus the vibration is always higher at elevation, and we can use all the help we can get. So what's the matter?"

"Nothing. Just wondering."

Storm asked, "Would you go ahead of us and get everything set up, Adrianna? We'll be right behind you."

"Sure." She walked away, hands glowing in front of her again.

Here it comes. Evalle gave him her full attention.

"Were you going to tell me?" Storm asked in an even voice,

which might mean Isak hadn't said anything.

"About what?" she bluffed.

He waited, not saying a word.

Nope. That blasted Isak had bragged about the stupid dinner she owed him.

She folded. "I agreed to dinner a long time ago, with his mother in fact, and it somehow morphed into dinner with Isak. I'm paying a debt. That's all. Isak means nothing to me. Yes, I was going to tell you, but–"

"But?"

"Not until after this was over tonight. We just haven't—"

"Haven't had any time to talk," he finished, lifting a hand to smooth over her hair.

She leaned into his hand, wishing they could just spend some quiet time together. "I wasn't keeping this from you. It's just a meal."

"I didn't think you were hiding anything, sweetheart."

She smiled, glad he was not making a big deal out of this, especially after having just run into Isak at one of Evalle's favorite restaurants. She admitted, "I don't even want to do this."

"Then don't."

As if her life was that easy. She was tired of IOUs hanging over her head and wanted to get them paid off. People had helped her and she wanted to show her appreciation even if it meant dinner with Isak when she could be spending the evening with Storm. "I have to go. It's just one dinner and then this will be off my conscience." Plus, she intended to ask Isak to accept her decision and stop trying to spend time with her. "Isak will let it go and I won't make the mistake of getting indebted to him again."

Considering how uber-protective and possessive Storm tended to be, he surprised her by calmly accepting what she wanted to do. Or he was doing a great job of hiding his true reaction.

He studied her face, then asked, "This isn't just about the megablaster he loaned you for the Svart trolls, is it?"

She might as well get this out on the table and be done with it. "No. Isak backed us up when Adrianna and I had to capture the witch doctor. He brought one of his custom weapons, and stunned Nadina long enough for us to contain her. Even then she managed to call up a smoky dragon, but Adrianna shut that down."

"Then *I'm* really the one who owes him. Why don't you let me talk to him about settling this debt another way?"

She shoved her hands up in the air and dropped them. "You know what? Then you go to dinner with him, and while you're at it, you can figure out how to thank his mother for watching over those two homeless witch boys."

"I'm trying to give you what you need." Storm backed off and clutched his head with both hands, walking away then back to her. He dropped his hands and cupped her face, kissing her hard.

If *this* was him trying to give her what she needed, he definitely got it right. His mouth swept away all the anxiety that had been riding her for days, just like he had last night. But they couldn't spend every minute of their lives in the shower, in bed or kissing.

If they could, she'd totally be down with that.

When he let her come up for air, he said, "I hate everything you had to do to come for me in Mitnal. I hate that you constantly sacrifice. I don't like you owing anyone, especially another man, because of me. And I really hate you being out here tonight for this thing with Adrianna." He kissed her forehead and tugged her into his arms. "But you know what bothers me the most?"

That wasn't enough? "No."

"That you're going to do this tonight even though you know I don't want you to take the risk." He squeezed his eyes shut for a second. "I know that's selfish, but I'm a selfish bastard when it comes to you. I'm trying to give you the room to do what you need to do, but not knowing if I can keep you safe is killing me."

Her insides did a happy dance. God, she loved this man. But something had to give.

"When did you start thinking I couldn't protect myself, Storm? I was battling creatures worse than demons long before you came along. I love that you care for me, but I'm starting to feel smothered with you making everyone scared to put a scratch on me. And the bigger question is, when did you start thinking I would stop doing dangerous things or actually not do my job because we're together?"

He rubbed his thumbs over her cheeks and touched her lips with his. "I know you can handle yourself in a fight. You're the most amazing woman and warrior I've ever known, but that doesn't mean I like seeing you hurt. After my dad died, I was an island. Nothing could touch me, because I had no one to lose. Then you came along and—" His throat moved with a deep swallow. "I have no world without you."

Her heart quivered. She said, "Adrianna and I can do this. We'll make it out of there alive."

"You don't even know what you're going up against."

"It doesn't matter. Nothing will stop me from getting back to you." She hoped she was right, but she didn't want to think otherwise. Staring up into his dark eyes, she had to know the answer to a question that had been hounding her. "Are you happy about living with me?"

"Of course I am." He showed no signs of his body punishing him for lying, so that had to be true.

"Let's get this done. Part of why I'm stressing is because I'm not sure what to do once I follow her into this realm."

"I'm in a tough spot here because you need my help to go and I don't want you doing this, but I gave you my word and I'm going to do my part."

"Thank you."

He hooked an arm around her and started them toward the building. "You're welcome. I hope you still love me when you turn my hair gray in a year."

She felt like poking at him. "You don't want me out in the sun. You don't want me to have dinner with Isak. You don't want me working alone. And you don't want me realm traveling with Adrianna. Does that sum it up?"

"Pretty much."

She punched him in the abs, but he was like rock and the grunt came out in a chuckle. She smarted back, "What comes next? 'I want you barefoot and pregnant'?"

"No."

Thank goodness.

Then he added, "I like your boots."

The hair on her neck stood up.

His chuckle turned into a full laugh, then he turned quiet before saying, "I really don't want to change you, sweetheart. But this is not an easy adjustment for me."

"Me either." She put a hand on his arm and when he stopped, she reached up for a quick kiss, but he caught her in his arms and she poured her whole soul into it, letting her wild emotions run loose and showing him how she felt. When she pulled back, they were both breathing hard. She whispered, "Let's just get this done so we can go home."

"Agreed."

She climbed ladders and scaffolding with Storm behind her, constantly commenting about the view. She knew he was doing that because heights bothered her, but it worked.

She made it to the top without having a panic attack.

Glowing candles surrounded an open area thirty feet across. Evalle lost count at twenty-five candles.

Adrianna finished drawing a perfect circle ten feet in diameter with a thick piece of chalk, then pulled what looked like a blanket from her backpack. When she shook it out and placed the material in the circle, it turned out to be round, with strips of gold attached in the shape of a pentagram that glowed against the black blanket.

Evalle pointed at the ground covering. "Is that real gold?"

"Yes. Spun gold threads." Adrianna drew odd symbols all around the outside of the round shape, then she drew another circle three feet in diameter that touched the big one, complete with a perfectly drawn pentagram inside. She pointed at the small circle. "Storm will be in this one. Evalle, you will lie beside me on the blanket. We have to hold hands."

"Why?"

Giving Evalle an I'm-not-in-the-mood glance, Adrianna said, "Because it's the only way I can be sure we show up in the same spot on the other side."

"I see your point."

Adrianna shook her head and asked Storm, "Are you sure you have a strong tie to the emerald on Evalle's chest?"

"I do. I increased the power on it this morning while she slept."

Well, crud. Evalle's hand flew to the emerald that was just a cold rock at the moment. "Were you going to tell me?" she said, echoing his earlier words right back at him.

"As soon as we had a chance to talk." He winked.

Touché.

Adrianna waved her hands. "Can you two work out your domestic differences later?" With silence in place again, Adrianna stepped into the center of the circle, standing on the blanket, then she chanted as she used a small dagger to point to the four cardinal directions, one at a time, then up at the sky and down toward the earth. Power zinged through the air and a dome of shimmering light formed around the area, encompassing the two circles drawn on the ground. The shimmer faded, but Evalle could still feel the hum of the energy as she reached out to touch the circle.

Then Adrianna walked to the edge of the power dome and used the knife to cut an arched doorway in the side. She motioned Storm and Evalle inside. Power crackled as she sealed the opening, then sent Evalle to the blanket with directions to get comfortable.

Evalle gave Storm a long look she hoped telegraphed how much he meant to her, then she stepped carefully onto the pentagram and stretched out on the blanket.

Adrianna told Storm, "I need you to walk over to the side with me so I can tell you the chant."

Evalle popped up. "Why can't I hear it?"

Adrianna made a noise deep in her throat. "Because you'll be thinking about it and, with your bond to Storm, you'll screw it up. You might even harm *him*."

"Oh, never mind." Evalle dropped back down.

Storm backed far enough away to be out of Evalle's hearing, which she could power up with her Belador genes, but she wouldn't do that after Adrianna's warning about harming him.

When Adrianna stepped up to Storm, he asked, "Why did you lie to Evalle?"

"Because she will not agree to leave me with my sister and save herself if this goes badly. I'm sure she believes she can pull us all out alive, but if that doesn't work out I have to destroy whatever is holding my sister for any hope of stopping Veronika. I'm giving you the backup plan for snatching Evalle out and triggering a spell."

"Let me get this straight. You want me to flip the switch that will kill you and your sister in cold blood."

Tension showed in Adrianna's stiff movements and in the strain of her voice. "I wouldn't ask anyone to do that if I had a choice. And *I'm* the one who will be responsible for any death." She handed him a pouch. "All I need you to do is hold this. I'll give you a chant to use when you receive a signal *if* Evalle and I have failed. I need to know that you will say the chant. If you have any doubt about doing this, just remember that when Veronika comes for all of us—and she *will* come for Evalle eventually—you could have prevented it."

"I understand." He might not like it, but he wouldn't let Adrianna down.

"You have to believe me when I say this is your best chance at keeping Evalle alive. That's why I know you'll do what I ask. You won't kill in cold blood, but you will kill anything that tries to harm her."

"Damn right."

"Remember being in Mitnal?"

The hellish memory burst into his mind of a thousand demons lead by their king who enjoyed torture and murder. "Hard to forget."

"Think of all those demons turned loose and multiply that by a hundred. Even *that* would be nothing compared to the apocalypse Veronika will unleash if we fail."

Adrianna glanced over at where Evalle lay on the blanket. "I have no doubt you would die for her, Storm, but the best defense is a strong offense. That means we cut off Veronika's power now. Do that and she'll go into hiding with her people until the next opportunity comes around a thousand years from now, *if* she is immortal."

Adrianna was right.

Some battles were better avoided.

She continued, "I spent the first six months Ragan was captured trying to figure out how to rescue my sister and came to the conclusion I can't allow Veronika to take Ragan to the end of this. So, yes, if we can't get my sister out and destroy the host connection, then my plan is to bind myself to whatever holds Ragan and call out the chant that will activate the pouch you hold."

A kamikaze death. He ground his jaw. "Would your sister want you to do this?"

"Yes. She would do the same in my place. If Ragan dies and we are apart, I will very likely not survive anyhow, due to our bond. I'm asking you to stop Veronika and help me free my sister in some way, even if it means I go with her."

Storm had never expected this from Adrianna, who most of the teams thought was just another cold and self-centered Sterling witch.

She'd proven herself to be a valuable part of VIPER, but she'd also kept herself apart from everyone except him, and now he understood why.

He could also see how Evalle had become friends with the witch. He asked, "What do you want me to do?"

Adrianna nodded at the pouch. "That contains a lock of my hair, a stone from Veronika's ancestral home, and a lock of my sister's hair. The minute you feel energy building in the pouch, start this chant." She said it twice for him. "Not before you feel the energy."

"Got it. Then what?"

Adrianna whispered, "The pouch will burst into flames. I know it won't harm you, not with your bloodline. Drop it and immediately use your tie to the emerald and yank Evalle out. If the pouch does not burst into flames within ten seconds of finishing the chant, pull Evalle out anyhow."

"What about you?"

"No one will be able to save me at that point. I'm going to cloak Evalle with a spell as soon as we enter the realm. The guardians should come after me, but in case something happens to incapacitate me, if they target Evalle, the same spell will blast bright energy in their faces if they touch her. That will allow her enough time to escape and hide until you pull her out."

Evalle would never run and hide.

He wanted to haul her away and lock her in that cramped

underground apartment, but she'd never forgive him and Adrianna spoke nothing but truth. She did mean to put a protective cloak on Evalle. "You're sure you can't take a male with you?"

"I'm as sure as my research. Look, my Sterling blood will be the draw."

Evalle called out, "How long is that freakin' chant?"

Adrianna lifted a hand to stall her and Evalle grumbled something under her breath.

His hellion. She was deadly, but she bled and she could die.

"Evalle's not fragile, Storm. I wouldn't take her with me if I thought she wouldn't come back."

"I know." He stepped inside the small pentagram circle, still holding the pouch. He sent out his energy, searching for the emerald.

The stone glowed beneath Evalle's shirt, shining green light on her chin.

She smiled, moving her hand to her chest. "I feel it."

All systems were go, but he had a sinking feeling about this.

Adrianna stepped into the larger pentagram and sat down before stretching out. Every movement she made was a precise execution.

Was her sister currently screaming in her mind?

If so, Adrianna kept any sign of it off her face.

She reached over and clasped Evalle's hand, then began chanting. Candle flames grew and grew until Adrianna shouted a word Storm did not recognize.

The flames shot ten feet in the air, roaring like giant blowtorches.

Eyes shut, Evalle and Adrianna lifted off the blanket.

Dread clawed its way up Storm's spine. He opened his mouth to call out words that could break a spell in midchant, but wind swirled and both bodies disappeared.

Hadn't Adrianna said their bodies would remain here?

No, she'd *insinuated* that he was here to guard them, and Storm took that to mean their physical forms.

Adrianna had lied by omission.

Storm stared at the empty blanket, afraid to move from this spot now that everything was in motion.

He gave his heart a chance to slow down and calmed himself so he didn't send anxiety to Evalle through the stone, but he needed to feel that tether. He wanted the reassurance that he could pull her out in an instant.

Drawing on his energy, he sent a wave out searching for the link.

He waited.

And waited.

No. Storm called up a blast of power he forced straight at the large pentagram on the blanket to search for Evalle's trail. The energy shot through the empty space and on to the other side, causing a quiet flame to flare up.

His skin chilled.

He had no connection to Evalle.

CHAPTER 20

Evalle heard a quick blast of sound and felt heat. Had the candles exploded? She couldn't feel the blanket.

She couldn't feel anything except Adrianna's cold fingers, which she was now grateful to be holding. But had Adrianna died crossing into the realm?

Evalle opened her eyes. Colors warped past her, but she didn't feel as though her body moved.

All at once, everything stopped.

The sudden loss of feeling connected to reality reached inside where she kept her deepest fears and shook them awake. She flinched and gripped Adrianna's fingers tighter.

"Put your feet down, Evalle," Adrianna said softly.

Looking to her left, she found the witch pivoting from horizontal to vertical. Evalle willed her own body to move and her feet lowered to the ground.

"Will you let go now?" Adrianna asked in a chiding voice.

Evalle snatched her hand away. "I didn't want to do that to begin with."

"Right." Adrianna pushed long hair off her shoulders and turned, eyes searching.

When Evalle's eyes focused, she felt like an ant in a giant forest.

So this was the realm of Jafnan Mir.

Evalle's gaze climbed a hundred feet in the air to where huge palm-frond-type branches sprouted from smooth gray trunks. Trees? Twisted vines with spines crawled up around the trunks.

The entire place appeared to be in sepia tones, like an old, brownish-colored photograph, which added to the ancient feel. The sky was an odd shade of gray.

Strange vegetation everywhere reminded her of a leafy plant

in Georgia used for poke salad. Or it would have if poke leaves were as long as Evalle's arm and had a black base as thick as her leg.

The ground shifted and made a sighing sound.

Evalle pointed down. "What the–"

Adrianna said, "Everything here is part of Veronika's family. Every bush, the trees, any creatures. Our presence will become known to the guardians before long, but let's try to delay that as much as possible."

"Got it. What do we do next?"

"I'm going to cloak you in a spell."

Evalle shook her head. "No, you're not."

"Why?"

"For one thing, I don't like anyone using majik on me, and for another, I have no idea how my powers will react to anyone's majik except Storm's."

"You let the witch doctor cloak you."

"I had no choice, plus I don't need to be cloaked. It might hamper my powers like the witch doctor's invisibility cloaking did."

"Why are you always difficult?"

Evalle let go of the argument and focused on what Adrianna had been up to before leaving the construction site. "Did Storm tell you to put some kind of protective spell on me?"

"No, but I told him I would cloak you and I don't want to face him if you do something stupid and get hurt."

"Stupid? You mean like using my powers to watch your back?" Evalle felt something move nearby and wished for the millionth time to have her dagger. She lowered her voice. "Something's coming. Let's move out."

Adrianna nodded. "Give me a minute to locate my sister."

"I thought you heard her all the time."

"I do, or I *did*, but she got quiet when I entered the realm. Button it up so I can listen for her."

Evalle wanted to get in and out, so she let that mouthy comment slide and opened up her empathic senses.

Lights flashed around her in small bursts of white-blue the size of her hand.

"Don't touch those power pops," Adrianna warned. "I believe

those might be explosions of majik powering the realm."

"Wonderful," Evalle groused. She kept searching the area with her empathic ability and felt a tug on her power. That was weird.

Adrianna took a step in the same direction Evalle had felt the tug.

Evalle started to ask if the witch was being pulled that way when she sensed something moving toward them from behind her. She spun and narrowed her empathic senses in that direction.

Whatever stalked them kept coming and was emitting one single emotion. Aggression.

A noise crackled seventy feet away, then again at fifty.

Evalle told Adrianna, "Something is hunting us. Ask your sister where she is and let's get moving."

Adrianna turned to her, skin pale and blue eyes wide with shock. "I can't find her. She's ...she's not here."

More lights flashed, popping everywhere at once.

The bushes leaned to each side on their own.

Evalle did a double take at what stepped through the opening.

She tried to categorize the creature, but where did you file something with a body resembling a rhino covered in grayish-green plates that shined like metal and the head of a jackal with blue fur?

A massive jackal.

The thing roared and it sounded like two terrifying animals in chorus.

The magnetic pull tried to draw Evalle to her right. She planted her feet firmly to keep from being dragged to the side.

To Adrianna's credit, she stepped up beside Evalle and faced the creature with a determined glint in her eyes.

Lifting her hands, Evalle prepared to use kinetics and hoped like hell that her powers worked in here.

Adrianna whispered, "Don't use your kinetics yet. Every time you use power in here, the realm takes an equal amount for itself. You may only get one or two uses."

That limited her choices, but saving her juice for later wouldn't matter if that thing ate them.

Adrianna pointed a perfect red fingernail at the creature and it snarled.

Then wide jaws opened, but this time a human voice came out that sounded as raspy as an old man who had smoked his whole life. "Who are you?"

Adrianna said, "I am family."

"Not my family."

"Yes, I am."

"Prove it."

Adrianna tapped her chin as if thinking and said, "I know. I'll let you taste my blood. If I prove I am family, you will allow us to pass."

Evalle couldn't decide if she wanted to give Adrianna an award for best bluff ever, or conk her on the head for the stupidest idea she'd heard in a long time. Evalle whispered, "Do I get to cut your head off to feed him for this taste test since you clearly aren't using it?"

Adrianna sent a scathing glare in answer, then her entire body leaned away from Evalle in the direction of that strange pulling sensation.

Evalle grabbed Adrianna's shoulder and brought the witch back vertical again.

Murmuring her thanks, Adrianna smiled at the creature. "What will it be?"

"Veronika did not tell us of new family."

"She has too much to get done before the eclipse, and the young woman feeding Veronika power for Witchlock is growing weak. I am the host's twin. I was sent to keep her strong."

Evalle watched the creature. Did he realize Adrianna was lying through her teeth? Or did he buy that line?

"Give me your blood and I will decide."

That would be *no* he didn't believe her.

Adrianna looked around and caught a branch with a leaf the size of a serving platter, but she didn't break it off. She told Evalle, "Hold the leaf level."

While Evalle did as she asked, Adrianna used a fingernail to slice across her palm and drizzle her blood onto the leaf.

Evalle asked, "Shouldn't we have pulled this leaf off first so it would be easier to feed him?"

"Do not harm any plant or it will retaliate. Everything in here was created *by* their ancestors and *of* their ancestors."

"How can a–" Evalle sputtered to a stop when the leaf veins opened up and absorbed the blood.

It even made a slurping sound.

O-*kay*.

Message received. Don't antagonize the landscape.

When Adrianna nodded, Evalle released the plant and waited.

The creature lifted its head and angled it to one side as if listening to someone. Then he growled and said, "You may pass, but Veronika will be informed of this."

When would the four-legged grump tattle on them? Now or later?

"Where is the host?" Adrianna asked, ignoring his comment.

The jackal's green eyes sharpened with predatory intent. "You would know that if Veronika sent you. *Who. Are. You?*"

Oh. Crap.

Adrianna said in a hushed voice to Evalle, "I can't hear or feel Ragan. She hasn't been silent one second in the last seventeen months."

The ancestor creature shouted, "Veronika did not send you. You are an intruder."

Evalle said, "We need to fight or leave."

"Agreed." Adrianna reached up and yanked a strand of hair from Evalle's head.

"Ouch. What the hell?"

Adrianna whispered words quickly while gripping the strand, then tossed it into the air where silver-blue power poofed at Evalle. She sneezed and swatted an empty space. "I swear I'm going to kill you myself."

The creature lifted a massive hoof and slammed it down, shaking the ground. He roared, "*Intruder!*"

Something shrieked in reply in the distance.

Skin around his mouth pulled back, revealing sharp teeth twice the length of Evalle's fingers. He snarled and leaped forward.

Evalle pushed Adrianna aside and dove in the opposite direction, rolling then coming up on her feet. She spun around, ready to toss a kinetic hit at the creature, but Adrianna had her hands up and was chanting in a language Evalle had never heard.

Using kinetics might harm Adrianna, who had stepped

between Evalle and the creature.

Thrashing plants right and left, the creature dove at Adrianna and red power burst across his head and body. He screamed in agony and backed up, trying to get away from whatever Adrianna had conjured.

He stood all that body up on his short and stocky hind legs.

Evalle wouldn't have thought that possible.

Then he crashed backwards, shaking the entire area with trees swaying and the ground rippling. Evalle danced around to keep her balance.

Adrianna was doing the same then she started sidestepping faster and faster.

The plants parted to make a path.

Any help from the plants could not be good for either of them.

Evalle lunged for her, but Adrianna took off running backwards. The witch yelled, "I can't stop!"

Gaining her feet, Evalle turned to go after her, which was a good thing. That magnetic force gripped Evalle's chest and yanked her in the same direction as the backpedaling Adrianna.

Evalle raced through the strange woods.

Leaves and branches swung out of the way then back across the path to swat her face, her arms, her legs ... even when she tried to duck or avoid them. Thwacking noises and Adrianna's shouts rambled thirty steps ahead of Evalle.

Evalle double-timed to catch Adrianna and grabbed one of the witch's flailing arms. She whipped Adrianna around so they could both run forward.

Trees bent, their long branches reaching for Adrianna and Evalle. She had a vision of being the main dish for a forest. Death by vegetation would be so wrong after all the vicious beings she'd fought and survived.

All at once, the woods blurred into a gold steam that swirled as if the air had been whipped into cream, and the magnetic draw began to lessen.

Evalle slowed as the creamy air swirled around them. She tried to take a step backwards and got a quick yank forward again. She waved her hands, fanning the cloudy mist. Adrianna did the same.

When the mist cleared, they found Ragan.

Ragan looked identical to Adrianna except for being suspended in a giant, translucent sphere forty feet in diameter. It hung a foot off the ground and turned slowly, smoldering as tendrils of white energy smoked away from the surface.

Ragan had the same long, blond hair, but upon closer inspection, her hair had turned white with jagged stripes of black running through it.

Hundreds of gossamer threads tied Ragan to the inside of the sphere.

Adrianna's game face gave way to the pain of seeing her twin. "Ragan?"

Evalle lost all sense of the magnetic pull. The realm had drawn them here, which might mean this was some sort of trap. "We've found her. Now what?"

"I can't hear her inside me. I need to put my hands on the globe and see if that reconnects us."

"What if it kills you?"

Adrianna turned a crazed look on Evalle. "My sister is dying. Veronika's cooking Ragan's majik. Ragan is powering that sphere, which means I should be able to touch it and not die."

Should just did not have the same ring as absolutely.

Evalle kept looking around. "Another guardian might show up so let's figure this out quickly."

Adrianna turned to her. "You're right and we don't have much time. Listen carefully."

"I hate when phone recordings say *listen carefully*. What? You think that will make me listen better?"

Adrianna's jaw clenched. "Don't make me regret bringing you. We'll make one attempt at freeing Ragan and leaving, but if I can't get her out of that sphere we won't have much time before the other guardians come for us. When I tell you to get ready that means I'm going to join with my sister and say the words that will ignite the pouch I gave Storm. The minute that happens, Storm's pulling you out of here."

"That was *not* the plan."

"It was not *your* plan, but it was mine. Why do you think I stepped away to talk to him?"

Evalle would deal with Storm's part in this later, but she refused to accept defeat this easily. Evalle snarled, *"Listen carefully.* Here's the real plan. We get Ragan out of that ball and both of you out of here. End of strategizing."

Swallowing hard, Adrianna said, "I've dreamed of saving her for seventeen months, but we'll be lucky if we get one chance at this before the guardians show up."

"Then let's stop discussing it and get to it."

Nodding, Adrianna said, "I needed you to help me reach this point, and for that I thank you, but now you just have to stay safe while I do this. Storm's expecting you to do that."

I should appreciate all this thoughtfulness, but no one is telling me when to quit.

Adrianna added, "We didn't kill that guardian, because they can't be permanently destroyed inside this realm. All we did was delay him from calling in the others."

The news kept going from bad to worse to unbelievable.

"Are we in agreement?" Adrianna asked.

No one had been straight with Evalle to this point so she just shrugged for an answer, which Adrianna must have taken to mean yes.

Facing the sphere, Adrianna started walking forward slowly.

Twenty feet off the ground in the center of the sphere, Ragan turned as if alerted to a change. She tugged at the tendrils tying her to the globe and jerked around to face Adrianna, but she must be sensing her twin so close through their bond somehow, because Ragan's eyes were white with blindness.

Ragan's freaky gaze stared down at her sister, and she started shouting something. She looked out over the realm then back at Adrianna.

Adrianna called out, "It's me, Ragan. I've come for you."

Power shot here and there like tiny asteroids out of control.

The legs of a thousand spiders crawled all over Evalle's skin. She rubbed her arms, but nothing physical touched her. Her beast came alive inside and started pounding, wanting out.

No telling what kind of problems shifting in here would cause.

She shivered and clenched her fists, fighting the change.

Ragan's crazed face lost its beauty. White eyes glowed, then turned red as hot coals. Her skin sagged. She opened her mouth and yellow teeth looked sharpened to points when she screamed something silent.

What the hell?

Then Ragan extended fists in Adrianna's direction.

Call me jaded, but that does not look like a loving sister.

When Adrianna got close to the sphere, she reached out to touch it, but she was snatched off the ground and lifted high into the air until she hung at eye level with Ragan.

Adrianna stretched both hands out, leaning forward to put her hands on the globe's wall. She couldn't quite reach across the distance and strained so hard her face turned beet red. Something invisible kept blocking her at two feet away.

Ragan stretched and lunged to put her hand on the mirror spot inside the fiery white sphere.

Bad sign. Really bad sign.

Evalle would face her friend's wrath later. She shouted, "Adrianna! Get back down here!"

"I can't do anything."

Ragan's gaze jumped to Evalle. She shouted in Evalle's direction.

Roars and screeches sounded far away and were now moving toward the clearing. That had to be Ragan's guardians coming to the rescue.

Had Adrianna's sister called them in?

This was not the way Evalle had envisioned a happy sibling reunion and Storm had warned her that she wasn't skilled in witchcraft.

But she *was* skilled in kicking ass.

Evalle shouted, "She's going to kill you, Adrianna."

Adrianna yelled back, "No she's not."

Evalle was out of ideas. She could leap up with kinetics, but if she hit the sphere her power might explode everything.

Tendrils of energy swept away from the globe and reached for Adrianna, wrapping around her arms and legs and face.

She started struggling and chanting.

Heavy crashing noises were coming from the woods, heading toward the sphere.

The web of energy wrapping up Adrianna yanked her hard against the surface as Ragan lunged from the other side.

Adrianna shouted, "Bind your power with mine and we'll get

you out!"

Ragan's scream came through loud and clear this time. *"Too late. Veronika's cominnng!! Get out of here!"*

CHAPTER 21

Evalle watched in horror as Ragan's body jerked back into the center of the white-hot sphere and all the threads connected between her and walls of the globe drew tight as bowstrings. Ragan's hands slapped against her sides and her body began spinning.

Heart wrenching screams from Adrianna and Ragan filled the air, threatening to pierce Evalle's eardrums.

Crashing noises kept advancing. From all directions.

Screw this.

Evalle was on her own in this realm and needed no one's permission. She called up her beast and power flooded her body, forcing muscles to warp and bones to snap and change. Being drawn and quartered probably felt like this. Her stomach roiled at the hideous sounds of the change as blood pounded through her ears.

A creature crashed out of the trees a hundred feet away and stood upright, rising to nine feet. He had the head of an ogre, with rust-colored hair sprouting between spikes on his scalp. She mentally marked it as a *he* because a darker shade of hair failed to cover his genitals. The rest of his body reminded her of an oversized honeybadger, which was disconcerting to say the least.

Did these ancestors take a hit of acid before choosing their shapes?

She'd seen what a smaller creature could do. This one came after her, snarling with jaws snapping.

As a gryphon, she had the body of a ten-foot-tall lion with an eagle's head and huge claws. And a badass wingspan.

Flapping hard, she lifted into the air as the guardian creature dove at her and missed.

She swooped down and caught it by the neck, digging in her

hooked beak. She lifted the ogre into the air and slung him far away, then turned to go after Adrianna.

When Evalle reached her, Adrianna was wrapped up like a golden mummy and a million energy threads covered her mouth. Evalle couldn't do anything about that until she had the witch free and away from the sphere. Keeping herself steady with a constant flapping, Evalle used sharp talons to slice through the threads holding Adrianna.

That worked, but Adrianna slipped from her grasp.

Evalle swooped down and caught Adrianna in her claws just before the gold mummy body slammed the ground. She banked away as another creature raced from the forest and leaped at her. Whipping her wings faster, she angled around to take a look back.

A mob of ancestors in a mash of funky realm shapes spilled into the opening. The sphere glowed and turned with Ragan caught in the center.

Roars and screeches filled the air.

Evalle gave one look at Ragan and accepted that she couldn't save her, but she could at least try to get Adrianna out of here.

Flying hard and covering distance quickly, Evalle used her eagle vision to locate an open spot to land in.

She circled to slow her speed as she descended to the ground, then dropped Adrianna a few feet above spongy looking bushes to cushion her fall.

The witch's body hit and bounced off, smacking the hard ground.

Oops.

Adrianna rocked back and forth, still wrapped up in the gauzy threads and making angry noises.

Evalle landed and walked over to where she could place a paw gently on the mummy witch and use a sharp claw to slice threads that buzzed with energy. She pulled loose ones away with her beak.

The minute Adrianna's hands were free she reached up and scrubbed away the threads on her face, then jumped up to her feet.

She yelled, "You pulled me away! I had a chance to destroy that sphere and you ruined it."

Evalle stood there, unable to talk to Adrianna because the witch had no telepathic powers that Evalle knew about—or at least none that worked with a Belador.

Adrianna stomped around with fists clenched and hair askew in an uncharacteristic disheveled show of frustration. She turned on Evalle. "We can't get back to Ragan. They know we're here and Veronika is on the way. I have no idea if she's here already, but she probably has faith in the ancestors being able to kill both of us."

The trees nearby started swaying and whipping their branches back and forth so fast that Evalle's wings caught air.

Adrianna paused her rant and took in their surroundings. "Start changing, Evalle. Now!"

Evalle cocked her head at Adrianna, because she had no way to explain that if she shifted back to her human form now she couldn't do this again any time soon.

She could feel her power draining away faster than normal. In fact, she wasn't sure she could return to human form just yet.

But even if she could, changing out of her gryphon shape would leave both of them vulnerable.

Adrianna's hands were shaking when she lifted them in front of her and began chanting, "From the past to the present, from death to life..." She glanced at Evalle and shouted, "Hurry the hell up. That emerald's going to light up in about sixty seconds and you have to be in the same form to travel both ways."

You could have told me that sooner. But Adrianna couldn't hear that thought so Evalle screeched at her.

Adrianna shoved her face up toward Evalle's gryphon face, hands on her hips. "I'm having a bad day, too, so get over it and start changing if you want to see Storm again."

That did it. Evalle had little practice in shifting back from this form, but she called on her powers and her muscles began contracting.

Oh, that hurt.

Adrianna was busy walking around Evalle, spewing her chant.

Flames erupted in a circle that surrounded them.

Thunder boomed over and over, shaking the ground.

Evalle brought her head up and tears came to her eyes because that part hadn't finished changing and her neck was tight. Why was it taking so long to shift and why did it feel like she dragged her limbs through quicksand?

Adrianna's words hit her. *If you use your power in here the realm takes an equal amount.*

Evalle glanced around her. Trees close by that had been gray now had a vibrant, greenish glow. Was that where her power was going?

One look at how long it was taking Adrianna to start a fire confirmed that the witch was also a quart low on juice, too.

A loud roar joined the pounding thunder.

That was not thunder.

The sky, if what hovered over the top of this place was really a sky, had not a cloud.

Adrianna's flames were only a foot tall and from the way she kept chanting faster and faster it was obvious Adrianna expected more.

Trees and plants literally bent to the ground to get out of the way of a beast running hard. Long orange and black hair flowed behind a body shaped as a tiger, but this one was the size of Storm's truck.

The emerald on Evalle's chest heated and she felt a tug, but she was only halfway changed.

Adrianna grabbed at Evalle, latching her fingers and yanking on what would be an arm again once Evalle finished shifting. The witch continued chanting in a booming voice Evalle would have expected out of someone twice Adrianna's size.

Straining, Evalle forced energy to the parts still pulling back into place. She'd reached eighty percent completion when the emerald glowed bright as a searchlight and vibrated.

Storm must be using everything he had to pull her back.

The tiger-looking beast leaped across the opening.

Adrianna's hand clamped tight, and Evalle fought back a scream of pain. The limb was sensitive in mid-change.

Something sharp sliced her thigh.

Her world blurred and spun out of control.

Lights bright enough to blind flashed by her, and the whirring sound of being in motion roared in her ears, throbbed through her body.

Body? She hadn't finished shifting.

What about not being able to return if she wasn't back in her original form?

CHAPTER 22

What was that loud noise?

Evalle covered her ears then blinked her eyes open. Wait.

She had hands and they were on her ears.

"Can you hear me?" Storm leaned over her. The source of the booming noise. "You are never going anywhere without me again."

She'd argue and tell him he couldn't tell her what to do, but she never wanted to do that without him again either. She croaked, "Adrianna?"

"She's catching her breath, but she's fine."

He pulled his knee-length jacket off. "Put this on until I can get you to the truck.

She sat up and grabbed her head where something tried to beat its way out with a sledgehammer. Storm pulled her to her feet and had her arms in the jacket without much help from her.

"What the hell happened?" he snapped, tugging the leather together and buttoning her up.

Warmth and the scent of Storm. She might sleep in this tonight.

"Evalle?" He ducked his head to look at her, eye level. His fury evaporated. "Are you okay, sweetheart?"

Her thigh felt as if she'd been branded with a long, hot poker and she'd like to curl into his arms and let him baby her, but she had too much pride for her spine to go wet-noodle limp right now.

She said, "I'm fine. I was shifting back to this form when you pulled me out of the realm."

"Shifting from what?"

She whispered, "Gryphon. I don't have permission to shift here but no one specifically said I couldn't shift in some unknown realm with a bunch of ancestors in beast form trying to rip us to pieces." When she took in the sick look on Storm's face, she stepped up and hugged him. "We made it back alive. I'm just drained. When you use majik or powers there, the realm takes an equal amount for fuel, so we're both at rock bottom right now. I see why Adrianna wanted you here for when we came back."

He crushed her against his hard chest and she welcomed the feel of his strength. He kissed her face and hair then said, "You've been gone for hours."

"Really? What time is it?"

"After one in the morning." He hugged her again. "You're safe and I want you to stay that way. Promise me you won't go back no matter what."

That was an easy agreement. "I promise, and besides, we can't go back."

"I should be so lucky," he muttered.

Adrianna wobbled her way over to them. "She means it, Storm. I failed to destroy the sphere holding Ragan. There is no going back. "

Evalle's heart broke at the devastation in her friend's voice. "I'm sorry Adrianna. It was killing you. I couldn't leave you there to be trapped with her."

Adrianna shook her head. "The realm took too much of my power—a lot more than equal measure, maybe because Ragan and I share the same origin. I couldn't strengthen the bond quickly enough. Veronika's hold on Ragan is too strong." She met Evalle's eyes. "At least we tried." She raked a hand through hair that was messier than Evalle had ever seen it. "Ragan is still trapped and the ancestors have called in Veronika. They'll tell her I was there."

Storm said, "Can she find you here?"

Adrianna gave up a weary sigh. "My whereabouts are not a secret."

Storm said, "We'll have your back if she shows up. At least you're both safe and in one piece." He paused and sniffed the air. "I smell burned skin."

Adrianna said, "I thought the last beast that came after us clawed at Evalle. Did it catch your leg?"

Evalle sent Adrianna a death look for pissing off Storm again when she finally had him calmed down. The witch lifted her shoulders in answer.

Storm asked, "Where are you hurt?"

"My thigh. It's not bad." Burned like a bitch, but she wasn't going to whine.

"Sit down so I can see."

Once she was on the ground again, he moved aside a flap of leather to expose her thigh.

Evalle leaned forward to see what hurt so much and damn if it didn't look like she'd been burned instead of cut. "Why isn't it cut and bleeding? I'm not complaining about the lack of blood, but ... "

Adrianna scratched her forehead. "That is strange. I don't know everything about the realm, but it's surprising that it clawed you. It was close enough to bite off your leg."

Lovely thought.

Storm said, "It has a sharp cinnamon smell."

Adrianna murmured, "Not good."

"Why?"

"That's the KievRus scent."

"What does that mean?" Evalle asked.

Adrianna hesitated, then shook her head as she stared at the burn. "I don't know."

"We should get out of here." Storm stood up and looked around. He told Evalle, "If you'll sit tight, I'll help if Adrianna will allow me to pick up any of her things." He raised his eyebrows in Adrianna's direction, obviously asking permission along with the offer.

Evalle had no problem being a slug on the side. She'd tried to help Adrianna once in the past and the borderline OCD witch did not like anyone touching her toys. Storm already knew that, apparently.

"I've got this, Storm," Adrianna said in a no-nonsense voice worthy of a grade school teacher.

He nodded, and Adrianna said a quick chant, using the knife to close the circle she'd created earlier. Storm moved Evalle out of the circle and kept watch as Adrianna moved around the space, collecting her things.

When she had everything packed to suit her, she gladly handed Storm the backpack, and he adjusted the straps then slid his arms through. Once Adrianna had him loaded down like her own personal pack mule, she walked out ahead of everyone.

The Sterling witch might look like she'd been dragged through a briar patch, but she could pull together dignity faster than the queen of England.

Storm helped Evalle stand, and on the way to the truck, he lifted her over anything that might cut her bare feet.

Once she got inside, Evalle had just sunk into the passenger seat and leaned back when she got a telepathic call from Tzader. *Evalle, we have a situation. I've been ordered to a Tribunal meeting. I need you to meet me there.*

That would require teleporting by Sen. Ugh.

Evalle sent back a quick, *I can meet Sen in Woodruff Park in fifteen minutes. I just need to change clothes.*

More like she needed to put clothes on, but that was information Tzader didn't need.

Tzader replied, *That's fine. I told them it'd take a half hour.*

She asked, What's up?

The Beladors are being accused of killing the Medb without provocation and the Medb have demanded a judgement.

That's crazy.

I know. I wouldn't bring you in but the Tribunals are not happy about the tug-of-war over the gryphons and the Medb want to present an offer that involves the gryphons. Since you're the gryphon leader, they want you present. Bring Storm with you.

She rolled her eyes at being called their leader as if that meant she held some position of significance, then she realized the last thing Tzader had said and replied, *Okay, but why Storm?*

The Medb are delivering a body and VIPER has requested Storm to identify a scent and give testimony about the murder.

You don't think a Belador murdered a Medb, do you?

No, but I have to be prepared to deal with it if one of ours lost control and killed a Medb.

Tzader's presence withdrew from her mind.

She glanced at Storm, who might have to send a Belador to his death, because some rules could not be broken.

The Belador code of honor topped that list.

CHAPTER 23

Veronika materialized inside Jafnan Mir to find her ancestors in chaos.

She swept through the forest, nodding at those of her family who had taken the shape of trees and plants in the muted colors of lives long gone. They bowed in respect as she passed. They cleared a path ahead of her, allowing her robe to float over smooth ground.

Flowers burst into bloom in brilliant colors along the way. Those would be the KievRus children who had been lost too soon.

When Veronika reached the center of the realm, where she'd formed the sphere, all the beasts surrounding the rotating ball ceased growling and roaring. They turned to face her, then settled on the ground, docile as guard hounds.

She opened her arms out to each side and her robe sleeves hung halfway to the ground. The smaller version of the sphere spun on the palm of her right hand. She could feel the palm sphere yearning to reach out toward Ragan's giant ball of power.

Ragan still spun in the center, but something had disturbed the peace.

Something had upset her ancestors, or they would not have called Veronika in.

She tilted her head back. The hood fell away and her blue-black hair fell gently down her back. Closing her eyes, she opened her soul to her parents, grandparents, great grandparents, and on, including, aunts, uncles and cousins from many generations back.

Their anxiety became hers.

She clenched against the anger and frustration, then opened her mind, asking, *What has happened, Guardians?*

Reports barreled into her mind one right after another, accompanied by images.

Ragan's twin had tried to rescue Ragan from her destiny.

Veronika's eyelids fluttered with the speed of images flying past her mind's eye.

Adrianna had brought a friend. Someone unknown to Veronika could pose a threat to her plans, but wait ... her great, great, great uncle had marked the second woman.

Veronika sent her appreciation for his wise decision.

She knew where Adrianna had gone when she walked away from the Sterlings.

But the Guardian's mark would lead Veronika to the second woman, who would hand over Adrianna for betraying Veronika's agreement with the Sterlings. Veronika would not bother with the Sterling leaders. They were nothing to her or her plan. Now that Adrianna had breached the contract, the Sterlings wouldn't lift a finger to prevent Veronika's going after Adrianna and combining her power with Ragan's.

In all honesty, the Sterlings wouldn't have interfered anyhow, but although Veronika had toyed with the idea of using Ragan to capture Adrianna, she'd not been willing to risk a battle that would have divided her attention and energy.

Not now when she was so close.

With Adrianna's power joined to Ragan's, Veronika's Witchlock powers would be greater than that of any KievRus coven leader in the past.

Veronika sent out soothing comfort to her family and thanked them for their love and support in guarding the host of the Witchlock power.

She sent them assurance that she would deal with this threat.

They rose to their feet, one at a time, and came to her with heads lowered in a show of confidence. Jafnan Mir had been formed with anticipation that one leader would rebuild the KievRus coven and make it so strong it would never fall again.

All of this had been created for the day a leader would rule over all others.

Veronika lifted the sphere, raising her hand high and pointing it toward Ragan. "Hear me now, Ragan of the Sterlings. You were traded in a fair deal. I have kept my word, and now you must fulfill your part."

. She pointed her index finger at Ragan, and a bolt of energy shot from the sphere in Veronika's hand to strike the center of Ragan's sphere. Power sparked inside around Ragan, and huge fissures fingered across the outside, spreading and emitting loud cracking sounds as the sphere hissed and came apart.

Ragan's screaming sounded far away, slipping through the cracks until a huge chunk of sphere fell away and her screams shook the forest.

Veronika focused her power on the small sphere she held, as it spun faster and faster until it was only a white blur.

The bolt of energy still connecting the two spheres roared with the flood of moving power.

White-hot streaks spewed through new breaks in the giant sphere and more chunks of the translucent white globe burst apart, falling from the sides.

The arc of energy exploded and a cloud of white-gold sparks shot through the air.

Power poured out of the giant sphere, gushing into a roaring wave that rolled toward Veronika.

Halfway to her, the power twisted and twisted, narrowing into a tiny, spinning tip the size of a fat needle by the time it reached the globe in Veronika's hand. The tip shot inside and energy funneled into the sphere. The globe sucked it in at a rapid pace.

When the last snap of energy had spun through the tiny opening, it smoothed over, sealing the sphere.

Energy hummed through Veronika's body. Yes. This would magnify a thousand times over when the time came for her to receive Witchlock.

When Veronika lowered her hand to eye level, she said, "Hello, Ragan."

A very small Ragan scooted and crawled around with her hands on the inside of the sphere, acting much like a trapped, blind rat in jar. Panic rode her face, a tiny version of Adrianna's. She banged on the inside of the sphere and opened her mouth, surprising Veronika when Ragan's voice came into her mind.

I hate you, Ragan screamed.

Veronika replied as a thought. *How are you in my mind?*

Ragan stopped hitting the wall of the sphere and sent a smug look up at her. *You didn't expect that, did you, bitch? I've heard your thoughts the entire time. I can tell where you are even though I'm blind.*

Veronika lifted a finger and tapped on the round surface.

Ragan cringed and backed away, hugging her arms around herself.

We are not done yet, Ragan. I had intended to leave you in the realm until the last minute, but your sister changed that plan. I can't risk her attempting a second time and being successful. Now you and I are going to take a trip across the ocean. You'd like to see your sister again once more, wouldn't you?

Ragan made no motion to agree or disagree.

But Veronika had managed to wipe that smug look off of Ragan's face.

Of course you want to see Adrianna again. I would not deny you the chance to watch as I burn her from the inside out.

CHAPTER 24

Evalle rushed from the elevator when it deposited her and Storm in her underground residence. Her hurry had nothing to do with wanting to see that rat bastard Sen or face a Tribunal of deities determined to make her life miserable, and everything to do with helping Tzader.

He'd sounded worried.

It took a lot to bother a man who dealt with monumental problems every day as the top Belador Maistir in the world.

Storm followed, as silent as he'd been on the way back from her and Adrianna's disastrous attempt at rescuing Ragan.

Fear and frustration coming off him had rushed across her skin the minute she regained consciousness after traveling back to this world.

Then he'd shut his emotions down faster than turning off a water faucet.

Was he shielding his anger, his worry or what?

After surviving Jafnan Mir and realizing what they may be up against with Veronika, worrying about where Storm lived shrank in comparison to facing a life on the run, hiding and trying to survive.

Still, until they could formulate a plan or got more information about Witchlock, they were here and she wanted everyone in her world happy, starting with Storm and Feenix.

They'd made headway earlier in the evening, but Storm was hiding his feelings from her now and Evalle had no experience with managing that. She had no experience with male-female relationships, period.

Nicole always gave Evalle good advice. Her witch friend had said to talk to Storm honestly. Evalle would do that just as soon as they had a quiet moment.

Normal couples had quiet moments. They walked on the beach and watched sunsets.

Would she never have a normal time with Storm?

She opened the door and took two steps inside to find Feenix on his beanbag, curled up with his stuffed alligator. She never came home and found him sitting still.

His abandoned toys were in the same pile they'd been this morning.

He looked up and smiled, rising from the beanbag.

Storm entered right behind her, pausing at her back with his hands settled on her shoulders.

Feenix took one look at Storm and dropped back into his chair, turning his gaze away.

Her heart sank to her feet. She didn't have time right now, but she couldn't leave him like this.

Storm leaned close to her ear and said, "Get cleaned up and give me a minute to talk to Feenix."

Good idea or bad idea?

She trusted this man with her life and her love. She had to trust him not to upset Feenix. Evalle nodded, but stepped over and leaned down to kiss Feenix's head between his horns. He cut his eyes at her and that wary look gripped her throat.

Feenix might not trust *her* with his love at this point.

She said, "I promise we'll spend time together as soon as I come back. But I have to go help Tzader right now. Okay?"

He lifted his pudgy fingers and patted her cheek, but his big orange eyes drooped with sadness. "K."

"Storm wants to visit with you. Is that okay, too?"

Those orange eyes turned a deep shade of suspicious. Feenix didn't have shrugging down, but he lifted his shoulders, which was as good an answer as she'd get for now.

With a quick look back at Storm, who smiled and winked at her, she raced away to clean up. She tossed his coat on the bed and dashed through a thirty-second shower, then pulled her wet hair into a slick ponytail and stepped into jeans and a spare set of boots. She finished buttoning a clean BDU shirt before walking back into the living room.

Feenix had left the beanbag and was playing with his toys, his back to Storm, who had squatted down to talk to him.

That didn't show much promise, but she had to look at the bright side. No one was yelling or squawking.

On the way out, Evalle said, "See you later, baby."

Feenix gave her his lifted hand goodbye that meant he was not in the mood to talk.

She stepped through the doorway and waited outside. Storm finally emerged and shut the door. He didn't say anything, so she shoved the Feenix and living together conversation to the back burner yet again.

She'd like to say it was because she wanted the perfect time to talk, but that would be a lie.

The longer she procrastinated, the longer she had with Storm before they faced that the only solution would be keeping separate residences. She'd been so happy at the idea of living together that the thought of him moving out now left her feeling as if she'd lost something before she had a chance to actually have it.

Much the way she'd felt after losing her ability to be in the sun almost immediately after gaining it.

The elevator spit them out into the dark area outside her apartment door, which was one level below today's street level. This area had been a gully back in 1869, then train tracks were laid and it became a new depot when Atlanta rebuilt after Sherman torched the city. The city gradually built bridges over the area to relieve congestion, and eventually the whole rail area turned into the famous Underground Atlanta.

Evalle started across weed-infested pavement that had once been a parking lot for the brick building above her home, and Storm stepped toward the passenger door of his truck. He always opened doors for her, and it made her heart flutter every time.

Tzader and Quinn were the only men before Storm who had ever treated her as anything but a weird anomaly.

She suggested, "Let's walk. That way you won't have to leave your truck up there. We're ten minutes away."

He fell into step with her and sent a sharp look her way. "What's wrong?"

She opened her mouth to say, "Nothing," but that lie would disappoint him. Instead she said, "I'm concerned about Feenix," which was true.

"Why?"

"It's clear he's unhappy. Maybe even depressed. I've never seen him like this."

Storm's jaw flexed then he said, "He's upset that I'm there."

Hadn't she just decided this was not the time to have this conversation? *So why'd you bring it up?*

"You're just new to him." That *could* be the truth.

"He likes Lanna. She told me Feenix knows Tzader and Quinn. You've left him with Nicole before. They were all new to him at one time. He knows who—and what—I am to you and doesn't like it."

"I can't do this right now, Storm. I know moving in with me has been difficult, but–"

Storm moved fast, swinging her into his arms. "Don't you dare apologize for anything. That's your home and I'm the reason there's an issue, but will you trust me to fix it?"

That sounded like Storm was asking for permission to work things out with Feenix on his own.

She knew she *could* trust him ... but *would* she be able to let go and let him handle Feenix?

She kissed him on the chin. "I love you. You know that, right?"

"I never doubt it and I don't want you to doubt *us*. I love you enough to do whatever it takes to make this work."

The tight muscles in her chest relaxed a little, and she hugged him. Just like everything else since she realized she wanted him in her life, she had to be able to meet him half way on this, or it was never going to work.

Tzader's voice came into her mind. *Sen will be at Woodruff in ten minutes.*

Evalle backed away and took Storm's hand. "Of course I trust you and whatever you do."

"Thank you," Storm said. His smile sent a thrill through her every time and now was no different. She hated to leave when they were finally talking, but forcing Sen to wait would probably end with being teleported the way Dorothy had traveled to Oz.

Plus Storm had never been to a Tribunal meeting and she needed time to give him pointers.

When they emerged on Marietta Street, Storm took her hand,

walking them at a fast clip. "Tell me about the Tribunal."

"Tribunals are made up of three deities. They could be all gods, all goddesses or a mix. I've only faced a mix. We'll be taken to a place in what's called the Nether Realm, where they're on a dais and we stand before them on...kind of a ground-like area that falls off at the edges is the best way I can explain it. The sky is dark, filled with stars and reaches all the way from side to side. It makes me feel like I'm inside a snow globe, sans snow."

"I've sensed your concern from the moment you told me Tzader requested my presence. What are you worried about?"

One of the deities zapping you into the ether. "The Medb are accusing the Beladors of killing their coven members without provocation."

He pulled her to the edge of the sidewalk, away from three guys huddled together against a building they passed.

She lifted her eyebrows at him. "They were human."

He huffed a noise of irritation, but he did it in jest. "You're gonna have to get used to it, sweetheart. It's a natural reaction for a man to protect a woman, even if she can take down Godzilla with a flick of her kinetic fingers." He grinned at her.

She shook her head at his teasing. She'd missed that during the six days he was gone.

He must have noticed how close they were to Woodruff Park, because he turned serious again. "Is there any chance a Belador would just kill a Medb without reason?"

"Only someone suicidal." She spoke quickly so they could finish before Sen saw them and popped in to ruin her moment alone with Storm. "We swear an oath to Macha that includes a code of honor with stiff penalties. And if we wrongly take a life or act without honor, everyone connected to that Belador, be it husband, wife, or any other family will suffer the same consequences, even death."

"Seriously?"

"Oh, yes. That's why Tzader needs help proving the Beladors are not killing warlocks or witches in the Medb coven, but above all you must tell the truth."

"What if I scent something that points at a Belador?"

"Doesn't matter. If you lie in a Tribunal, you'll light up as red as a signal flare and they'll hand you over to Sen—if they don't vaporize you on the spot. But handing anyone over to Sen would be as bad."

When Storm didn't reply, Evalle said, "Tzader and Macha want the truth. They'll deal with the fallout, but no one will blame you. I know Tzader. He'll request this be a closed meeting and that Sen be forbidden from sharing a word about it. If a Belador is at fault, they won't be able to retaliate against you or me."

He squeezed her hand as they crossed an intersection of five roads, which was the reason this area of downtown Atlanta was called Five Points.

The city had remodeled parts of Woodruff Park, adding planters along the short wall between the sidewalk and the park. With the temperature dropping into the forties, Evalle noted only two people meandering down the street away from the park.

Good thing, since the minute her foot touched the corner near the bronze sculpture of a woman releasing a bird, titled *Phoenix Rising From The Ashes*, Sen appeared.

Storm stepped up beside her and without a word of greeting, her world spun into a blur of colors.

Sen had some crazy abilities. Even if there were few people around, he still had to shield their blinking out of sight from Five Points. She had no idea how he managed that and didn't care.

Two trips to two different realms in a short span of time were playing worse havoc than normal with Evalle. Her stomach was doing a great imitation of a washing machine on spin cycle.

Storm's arms came around her from the back and the blurred colors receded. She inhaled deep breaths, fighting her nausea, and his scent flowed over her. When her feet touched down again, she couldn't have been more relaxed if she'd been in a spa on the way here.

If Sen had realized that Storm prevented her usual vertigo reaction, he'd have sent them separately.

A mist surrounding her and Storm dissipated, revealing just what she'd described to Storm. This Tribunal was mixed. The goddess wore a blindfold and held scales. Evalle guessed her to be Justitia. Then there was some guy wearing a wreath on his head and strumming a golden instrument. A lyre? Could that be Orpheus? Was he even a deity or had he been dragged in for entertainment and to show how little respect the deities had for Belador and Medb issues?

She recognized the last god immediately and held back her groan.

Loki. She'd thought he was on her side the first time she'd faced him in a Tribunal meeting, but she'd learned first hand how he'd earned one of his nicknames. Trickster. She'd landed in a South American jungle in the middle of an invisible, spelled cage that held another Alterant who wanted to kill her.

Good times.

Tzader stood four feet away and said under his breath, "Don't use telepathy."

She nodded. She'd used it with Brina during another Tribunal meeting, but everything felt tense here. Maybe Tzader wasn't allowed that leeway. She hoped like hell that Storm didn't pick up a Belador scent on whatever the Medb produced.

Sen appeared on the other side of Tzader and stood, looking bored, but he sent a cold look her way, then he smiled.

Her skin puckered with chill bumps. Good thing she'd picked a long-sleeved shirt so he couldn't see her reaction to his appearing happy. Sen happy could only equal bad news for her in this meeting.

The deities were speaking among themselves and glancing around every so often, which had Evalle thinking someone else was coming to this party.

Energy charged the air between Evalle's group and the dais.

A man materialized and announced, "I am here to represent the Medb."

Who was that?

Loki boomed, "Welcome Cathbad the Druid, representing the Medb."

Evalle glanced at Tzader for a sign that this was nothing unusual. The gut-punched look he sent her dashed those hopes.

CHAPTER 25

Evalle didn't show any reaction to Cathbad's presence, but she had no doubt Storm had picked up on her spike of anxiety.

She sent Storm a quick smile she hoped would convey that everything was okay so he'd think her emotional fluxuation was normal for facing a Tribunal. There was some truth to that, but she sensed the Medb had something up their sleeves that Tzader was not expecting, and that concerned her.

Loki stepped forward, playing with a feather. "We are here to settle grievances the Medb bring against the Beladors. Tzader Burke, Belador Maistir, will speak for the Beladors and should note that this Tribunal is displeased that Brina of Treoir is not present as expected."

Tzader spoke up loud and clear. "Our warrior queen is recovering from the ill affects of a Noirre attack. Macha appreciates the Tribunal's understanding."

Evalle mentally clapped at how smoothly Tzader pointed to Brina's absence being the fault of the Medb.

Loki ignored Tzader's subtle accusation and spoke to the man standing closer to the raised stage. "Cathbad the Druid, step to the side so that we may all face one another." Loki pointed to his right.

When Cathbad turned to place himself in full view of everyone, Evalle got her first look at the man who had supposedly been reincarnated along with Queen Maeve. Tall as Storm and with thick, dark, wavy hair, he was definitely not the Cathbad that Evalle had dealt with when she'd been taken to TÅµr Medb before the attack on Treoir. As deadly as that druid had been, this one had a look in his eyes that said he had indeed been around for more than one lifetime and he would not be outmaneuvered.

Orpheus strummed a lovely melody on his lyre, playing gentle background music and smiling like an idiot. Would someone serve hors d'oeuvres next?

Loki announced, "Let it be known that all the Tribunal groups are at the end of their collective patience with this constant conflict. We want it to cease. We agreed to do our part when the need arose, but this borders on frivolous use of our time."

Frivolous? Clearly a bloody war that had raged for eons was not worth their time. If a Tribunal hadn't accepted the Medb into the VIPER coalition, none of this would be happening, but good luck telling three powerful beings that they were the ones at fault.

Loki turned to Cathbad. "State your grievances and we will resolve them one at a time." Loki turned to Tzader and said, "Agreed?"

"Agreed."

Cathbad launched into his first issue. "Before we deal with the evidence of a Belador murdering a Medb—"

Evalle couldn't look at Tzader, who had to be seething.

"—I wish to revisit the fact that the Medb have delivered a reasonable offer on the gryphons and Macha has failed to accept it or make a counter offer. Why should she be keepin' them when 'tis common knowledge that these gryphons possess as much Medb blood as they do Belador blood?"

Evalle fought the urge to shout at him for all the wrongs the Medb had committed, but she would not speak until directed to do so by Tzader.

Loki sounded bored beyond tears. "What say you, Beladors?"

Tzader uncrossed his arms. "Macha submitted a petition that the Alterants, which evolve into gryphons, be recognized as a race and no Tribunal has acted upon that yet. She's provided sanctuary for the current gryphons until *all* Alterants and gryphons are granted the right to make their own choices. Macha has offered all Alterants and gryphons a chance to join her pantheon. Once a judgment on their petition is rendered, they'll be able to choose between remaining on Treoir or returning to this world where they'll be on their own."

Cathbad argued in a fierce voice, "The Medb are due half of the gryphons. Half that number of stock should be delivered immediately and the Medb will give them sanctuary until the petition is acted upon."

Evalle whispered, "Let me talk."

Tzader nodded and addressed the Tribunal. "I ask that Evalle Kincaid be allowed to speak."

Loki nodded and rolled his hand, telling her to get moving and say what she had to say.

She faced Cathbad who had a too-confident look in his eyes. The wrong people were happy right now. "Gryphons are not *stock* to be shared like cattle. We don't want to be in the middle of a tug-of-war any more than this Tribunal wants to hear about it. We are people, who should be granted the same rights as everyone else."

She felt Storm's admiration touch her and had to force herself not to smile.

Cathbad asked, "Ya aren't sayin' these beasts are people with families in the human world, are ya?"

His sarcastic tone grated on Evalle's frayed nerves. All the Alterants who had traveled to TÅµr Medb and been forced to fight for the Medb came to mind. Tristan and his sister. Bernie, who had a girlfriend in the human world. The list went on and on, including Evalle, who wanted a life with Storm.

She replied, "Yes, many of the gryphons have friends and family. We should be allowed to choose where we want to live and with whom we wish to associate." She hoped Macha had been treating the gryphons well on Treoir, in preparation for when the day to choose arrived.

Cathbad acted as if he hung on her every word. "I see. So, maybe you can tell me why these *people* are not livin' with their families and friends in the human world now?"

Loki grinned at the clever maneuver by Cathbad.

The druid had put Evalle on the spot.

If she didn't support bringing the gryphons back to the human world, it would look as though they were being held on Treoir against their will. If gryphons were sent to the human world before an agreement was reached on the petition, they would be vulnerable with no pantheon to support them. The Medb would come after them, regardless of what VIPER thought. If one of the Alterants shifted into a gryphon in the human realm, even for defense, he or she would face trial by a Tribunal.

She wanted full citizenship for those like her.

In fact, she wanted them to be free of *any* pantheon to make their own decisions, but until that happened, the gryphons were better off on Treoir where they played a role in the island and castle security in exchange for Macha's protection.

Everyone waited on Evalle to say something. "I agree that gryphons should be allowed to live with their families and friends. I am willing to ask each gryphon, and determine which ones, if any, wish to visit Táur Medb."

"No, it's half or nothing," Cathbad demanded.

Tzader said, "Evalle has made a reasonable offer. Where's the Medb's counter offer?" He'd thrown Cathbad's words back at the druid.

She loved that, but she was so tired of hearing yet one more person determined to run her life. She said, "Just once, I'd like to make a decision about my life. I've lived by my oath to the Beladors first and according to the laws of VIPER second. Beladors are held to a higher accountability than any other group. That alone should allow me some autonomy."

Loki actually grinned at her outburst, crazy deity that he was, and looked at the druid.

Cathbad stewed a moment then said, "We propose that Evalle put this offer to the gryphons *if* she accepts the role of liaison and swears to perform that duty to this Tribunal so we can trust her actions."

Tzader said, "No. Macha has already addressed this issue."

Evalle breathed out her relief.

Thank you, Macha. The goddess had saved Evalle from being stuck between Beladors and Medb, or even worse—having to visit TÅμr Medb to settle disputes. She never wanted to go back there.

Evalle told Cathbad, "I've been with the Beladors my entire adult life. I am sworn to serve Macha. That makes it difficult for me to be impartial."

"Your answer is no? Who's not being reasonable now, Belador?" Cathbad snarled.

Stars glowed brightly and lightning ripped across the black sky from side to side.

Loki shouted, "Silence." He sent his thunderous gaze at Evalle and said, "You admit ruling the gryphons. Ownership of these beasts is a thorn in our side. We will not rule on the petition until there is peace between Medb and the Beladors or the gryphons will continue to be a constant issue."

I'm not a damn beast. She remained silent, because Loki was going somewhere with this. He didn't make them wait long.

Eyes speared at Evalle, Loki said in the most magnanimous voice, "I will grant your wish to make a decision."

That sounded really similar to the last time Loki had set her up to fail.

Loki continued addressing Evalle. "Neither Macha nor Maeve may speak for you at this moment, yet a choice must be made. You decide if you will accept the liaison position or not, but be forewarned that refusing it means this Tribunal will decide the best place for the gryphons to be held until everything is resolved, which will very likely be in protective custody beneath the VIPER headquarters mountain."

She felt eyes on her and looked to see a twinkle in Sen's gaze. He'd known this was coming.

"You wanted a choice. Make your decision, leader of the gryphons," Loki said with a supreme look of pleasure in his face.

He'd done it to her again.

CHAPTER 26

Tzader couldn't believe how easily Cathbad had turned the tables on the Beladors.

Evalle hadn't responded to Loki's demands yet.

Her throat moved with a hard swallow and he wanted to kill someone, but from the look on Storm's face Tzader would have to stand in line behind the Skinwalker. If Storm went caveman in here, the Tribunal would lower the boom on both Evalle and Storm.

Evalle said, "I'd like a moment to speak with my Maistir as I am still a Belador and have sworn my oath to *them*." She finished that statement in Cathbad's direction.

The son of a bitch druid had a gleam of satisfaction in his eyes.

Thunder rolled, then Loki spoke. "Granted. One minute."

Evalle swung to Tzader as he turned to her and Storm joined them in the huddle. Tzader started, "I'm sorry—"

Evalle stopped him. "I know you and Macha tried to keep me out of this, but I am not going into protective custody."

"I'll take you somewhere safe," Storm interjected.

"You can't."

"You have no idea how many resources I have and I'll tap every one of them."

Tzader lifted an eyebrow at that, but wanted to let Evalle say what she had in mind before time was up.

She told Storm, "You're right, I don't know who you know, but it doesn't matter. The minute I refuse to give them a solution, they'll tell Sen to take me away. And not even Macha can stop that." Evalle looked to Tzader. "Can she?"

"Unfortunately, no. We need a plan for now that insures you leave here, then we'll fix this mess later." He shifted his attention to Storm. "We'll all make sure she isn't screwed on this deal."

Storm clearly didn't like it, but nodded. "What's next?"

Evalle said, "I accept the position of liaison to keep peace for now."

Loki called, "Time's up."

They broke the huddle and Evalle faced the dais with her shoulders squared. "I accept the position of liaison between the Beladors and the Medb."

"Well then," Cathbad announced. "I say we put you to work."

Tzader had been waiting for Cathbad to get down to the real reason for this Tribunal.

The goddess Justitia spoke up, lifting her ornately carved scales of justice. A gold blindfold kept her wavy brown hair off of what was an ordinary face for a goddess. Her simple gray gown wrapped around her feet and gave her the appearance of a living statue. She spoke with a rich vibrato that left no question as to her authority.

"The Medb have brought an accusation of murder against the Beladors."

Tzader stiffened at her opening foray, but silence worked better with this bunch.

Justitia stated, "During the last rotation of Earth, the Medb were ordered to deliver clear evidence of this or face sanctions. The Beladors will be given the same time to deliver their counter argument and proof of this being a false claim, if that is the case, or deliver the guilty party."

Tzader's palms never sweated, but the Medb would be fools to take that risk of sanctions without clear evidence. Cathbad and Queen Maeve did not sound like fools.

Tzader asked, "I request a chance to review the evidence."

"Granted," Justitia replied. "Sen, liaison of VIPER, deliver the evidence."

Sen stepped forward and lifted a hand, which he then lowered and pointed at the ground, adding to the drama.

A body took shape in the form of a man with his clothes half torn off. Gray skin covered the corpse's face and arms that had been ravaged from an attack or while in a battle, which could mean the death had occurred during self-defense.

There was no denying one piece of evidence.

Evalle's spelled blade had been buried in the man's forhead.

Cathbad launched into addressing the jury of deities. "Our warlocks have put their lives in danger for weeks to protect humans under the new rule of Queen Maeve. They've killed demons and caused no harm to others. But this poor warlock who had very little training only wanted a place to live and belong. He was no threat to someone as powerful as a Belador. His body was found in Stone Mountain Park the night she–" Cathbad pointed at Evalle and Storm's fury surged.

Thankfully, Evalle put a hand out, silently asking Storm to overlook a druid pointing a finger that could be considered a weapon. Immortal or not, Cathbad wouldn't survive an attack on her in a Tribunal.

The druid continued, "–claimed to have killed a demon on top of that mountain, but no evidence of such was found."

Evalle kept staring at the body. "I didn't kill a warlock, Tzader."

"I believe you."

Cathbad shouted, "Do you deny that is your dagger?"

Evalle lifted a stunned gaze to the gallery. "It is my dagger, but I killed a Réisc Dubh demon that night. The demon had a human glamour and was hunting humans when I first saw him. When I approached him and identified myself, he dropped his glamour and attacked me and I defended myself."

Cathbad asked, "What is your testimony, Sen?"

"I was called to the top of Stone Mountain two nights ago, specifically to the cable landing platform." Sen spoke as if he had been nothing more than a bystander to a terrible crime. The son of a bitch continued, "Evalle claimed she killed a demon. Her shirt was torn and bloody, but there was no sign of a demon inside the cable car she said contained a body." He shrugged.

That set off Cathbad. "Torn clothes and blood can be manufactured."

Tzader's trepidation rose at the scene unfolding. This was too fucking perfect. Sen played the role of the innocent VIPER liaison sent to clean up a mess and was now feeding Cathbad lines with the skill of a straight man in a dark comedy act.

Justitia called out, "How plead you, Evalle Kincaid?"

"I did not kill a warlock, goddess."

The goddess cocked her chin in the druid's direction. "What do you offer as conclusive evidence, Cathbad?"

"The dagger, goddess. No one has been able to remove the blade. I request the Skinwalker try to withdraw the dagger."

Oh. Shit. Tzader looked at Storm who was clearly torn over what to do. Evalle gave Storm a watery smile. "Go ahead. Do what they ask."

Storm sent the promise of death in the look that he swept around the room.

Loki, of course, found that amusing.

Storm dropped onto one knee and put his other knee on the corpse's chest to hold it down. He gripped the dagger handle with both hands and lifted. Muscles strained and bulged in his arms. Veins stood out on his neck.

The head moved up with each new yank.

After pulling for a full minute, Storm released the grip and dropped his head.

Cathbad was on a roll and said, "This Skinwalker was brought into VIPER because he is an exceptional majik tracker. I request that he give testimony of the energetic residue left on the body and reveal if it belongs to anyone in this meeting."

Storm's head snapped up and he jerked around, looking at Evalle.

She kept her hands at her sides, but Tzader could see the tremble in her fingers. She told Storm, "Do as they say."

Storm's gaze landed on Tzader with accusation burning. Storm had come here at Tzader's request and now he was forced to give testimony against Evalle, because Tzader and everyone else in here knew that dagger wasn't coming out unless she released the spell and removed the blade.

Loki asked, "Is there a problem?"

Tzader told Storm, "We'll handle whatever comes of all this." Then to appease Loki, Tzader explained, "This is Storm's first Tribunal appearance and I failed to inform him of how things work."

Storm sent one more gut-wrenching look at Evalle then turned and lowered his head, sniffing.

When he paused, hesitating to state what he'd discovered, Loki shouted, "You will immediately reveal what you have found or be banished from this world. No one defies a Tribunal."

Evalle whispered, "Please, Storm."

Storm stood and said, "There is a residue and it belongs to Evalle Kincaid."

Fuck. Tzader might be the one banished if he killed that druid.

"There you go, goddess," Cathbad called out, sounding as if he'd just rested his case.

Storm asked, "Where was the body found?"

Cathbad frowned at the question. "At the base of Stone Mountain. This warlock made a call for help and when one of our elite Scáth Force warlocks arrived, this one was dead and that dagger had been embedded so that it could not be removed."

"That is all," Loki said in Storm's direction.

Storm walked back to Tzader and Evalle with fury spilling from his pores.

She whispered, "It's okay," before Storm turned to stand as close to her as he could.

He whispered, "No it's not and I won't let them take you."

Tzader's sensitive hearing picked up Storm's soft words. He had to get those two out of here without upsetting the Tribunal. He'd risk pissing off deities if it was his own neck on the line, but not when Evalle's future was at risk and Storm stood ready to take on the universe to protect her.

Cathbad said, "Evalle is known to carry a dagger that holds a spell she controls. I request that Evalle now try to remove the blade."

Justitia called out, "Granted. If the dagger is being held in place by a spell, you will release the spell and remove your dagger, Evalle. Understood?"

"Yes, goddess."

Evalle wiped her hands on her pants as she stepped up to the corpse. She bent over the body, placing one hand on the grip, then whispered something and the blade pulled free without any resistance.

Not a surprised face anywhere in this meeting.

Standing up, Evalle said, "I've removed it, goddess, but on my honor as a Belador and on my life, I swear I did not kill a Medb warlock on top of Stone Mountain."

"Then explain that body," Cathbad yelled.

Tzader had had enough. He stepped forward. "We will. I request appropriate time to do so."

Sen spoke up. "I suggest the Alterant be put into VIPER custody in the meantime."

Tzader shouted, "*No!*" He turned to Sen. "Who are you to have any say in these proceedings? You're only a delivery person. Stick to your job."

For a moment, Tzader thought there might be some risk from the saying "if looks could kill," because murderous intent filled Sen's eyes.

Justitia announced, "All argument regarding this evidence and claim is to be delivered to this Tribunal only."

That was her reprimand of both Tzader and Sen.

Tzader quickly said, "I intend no disrespect toward the Tribunal, but as Maistir I have a responsibility to *every* Belador alive when I represent Macha. I require Evalle's aid in determining exactly what happened for her dagger to end up in this body."

Cathbad muttered, "We know what happened."

Tzader argued, "What we have is inconclusive evidence. Yes, that is Evalle's dagger and, yes, she would have had to be the one to order the dagger to stay put, but there is no evidence to prove that warlock was not in the form of a demon when she faced him."

Cathbad snarled, "There you go again, blaming the Medb for creating demons."

"That's not exactly news considering the history of the Medb, but we're here for one concern and the Tribunal does not want to listen to constant complaining about an *old* issue." Tzader caught the nods of the deities, letting him know he'd earned a few points. "Let's focus on this issue only and resolve it satisfactorily for both sides."

"You're just delaying the inevitable and wasting Tribunal time," Cathbad countered, picking up a few points of his own, dammit.

Tzader asked, "If you're so certain that Evalle killed your warlock, explain why she hasn't lit up red in this Tribunal every time she claimed not to have killed him?"

Silence answered Tzader's charge so he added, "Evalle has

been proven truthful in this Tribunal. For that reason alone, she has a right to bring proof that she did indeed kill what she believed was a demon. If that warlock was in demon form when she killed him, the Medb have no legitimate complaint, but should they take an interest, this Tribunal would certainly have the prerogative to question *why* a Medb warlock was disguised as a demon. Since Evalle must prove her innocence, I request that she be granted leave of absence from her duties as the Medb-Belador liaison until the question of her innocence is settled." Cathbad's jaw clenched at that. "I also ask for an additional day to gather evidence, so that I can fulfill my duties while I determine the truth behind this killing. Without that additional time, the lack of my availability to VIPER may create more imposition for the Tribunal."

The deities huddled and Cathbad scratched his chin.

Did I throw you a curve ball, druid?

Loki turned back around. "Agreed. You have forty-eight hours to deliver your counter argument with evidence."

Tzader blew out a breath. The argument about her not turning red should have been enough to clear her name, but at least she'd be going home with Storm.

Now he had to make sure Storm didn't grab her and run for the hills.

CHAPTER 27

Veronika watched two warlocks from her perch on top of a two-story building, where she was hidden by early morning dark and cloud cover from turbulent weather brewing.

Few vehicles moved in the hours beyond two in the morning here, but Atlanta would soon become a noisy place as human businesses started a new week.

Loud music blared from a lone car creeping by.

She missed the KievRus castle, where music never sounded like animals screaming in terror. Too many buildings and too much noise here for her, but she would change all of that once she held control.

The warlocks below were arguing. Why?

Veronika had located dark witches with deep purple auras walking everywhere in this city, which confirmed that the Medb really had been allowed to infiltrate the human world. Thanks to Ragan's power pulsing through Veronika, she'd had no trouble identifying the Medb auras, even if she hadn't been close enough to smell the Noirre majik around them.

These two warlocks had been the first to show any potential for what she needed.

The larger one had cornered a troll an hour ago, and while she gave him points for capturing the nasty beast, he hadn't shown any inclination toward killing it, even though she'd heard him mention using a troll to power a spell.

What was the warlock doing?

He did have the dark aura color, but he did not emit the repugnant smell of a Medb. She wanted a warlock capable of doing her bidding, and he seemed to fit her requirements for a minion. Having a powerful being to hunt Adrianna would allow Veronika to remain hidden as long as possible.

And once he found Adrianna, he would find the woman Ragan's twin had brought with her into the ancestral realm. The one who had shifted into something the Guardians called a gryphon. Why would a Sterling team up with a gryphon instead of a Medb, who might have been more helpful?

Veronika certainly appreciated Adrianna's poor planning, but it did make her wonder about the dark witch's intelligence.

The Medb were a deplorable coven, but a powerful one.

Once Veronika took control of both white and dark witchcraft, she'd weed out the weak and control the powerful leaders. Then she would teach them how to properly run a world.

KievRus had always watched over the people, but they'd wasted their talent on mere humans.

Veronika would follow in her ancestors' footsteps, taking control of the powerful of all races who governed, and they would keep the sheep in line.

Witchlock had changed the course of history more than once ... and would again.

She dropped silently to the narrow street that stretched between two buildings. Her robe floated gently around her until her booted feet touched the ground and she could walk.

The warlock who appeared in control raged at his companion.

She'd listened from above them, but down here it was even easier to hear the taller one say, "We *are* grabbing two more trolls tonight, and a warlock, then I can try a change in the spell."

"Bad idea, Donndubhán. Word is that VIPER's cracking down hard, looking for the troll killers. We get caught we got more problems than VIPER. We'll have to face Maeve and Cathbad, or have you forgotten what you told me they'd do to us?"

"I haven't forgotten a damn thing, Imar. We're in too deep at this point. You need to stop acting like a pussy and do whatever I tell you, especially after I saved both of our asses by handing that warlock's body over to Cathbad. That was brilliant on my part. You do as I say or you're gone, and I don't mean walking away kind of gone."

Imar mumbled something under his breath.

Donndubhán confirmed they were definitely Medb. He must be hiding his scent. Oh, yes, these two would be perfect.

Veronika wanted to test her powers now that she had Ragan close at hand. Her family would not be happy to find out she was testing her skills, but neither did they have her vision. Her family had spent years teaching her about world politics and how KievRus was the balance between dark witchcraft and light. She loved her family in spite of their limited points of view.

Every step Veronika made toward managing and wielding the power she'd gained thus far would shorten the learning curve for controlling Witchlock.

"Take your time learning how to handle Witchlock," one aunt constantly cautioned.

"Do not try to direct the power too soon or Witchlock may turn on you," her grandfather had warned.

"Concede your will to Witchlock," another had said.

Veronika's lips twisted with distaste. She would not concede anything to anyone, certainly not her own will to a power that would be *hers* to wield.

Pushing away distracting thoughts, Veronika eased toward the warlocks. They were just the resource she'd been searching for in this city.

Ghouls had been approaching her, offering deals for a handshake.

What was that about?

She'd given them a wide berth. Ghouls couldn't be trusted. They weren't worth the use of her power to control since they were so limited in abilities.

Continuing toward the pair of Medbs, she noticed movement to her left.

A human scavenger, based on his rough clothes and the way he tried to sneak up on the warlocks.

He thought he could mug a warlock?

Oh, right. Humans didn't know about the Medb or VIPER's corral of mercenaries. Veronika would enlighten humans when the time came, but since this human had no idea whom he thought to attack, he'd slow her down and create an unnecessary delay.

Veronika had kept her sphere hidden by tucking her hands into the opposite sleeves of her robe. She brought it out now.

She called up a small sample of power and felt it roll through her arm as she pointed, sending an arc of light shooting to the would-be mugger.

The man froze with a look of disbelief on his face.

At the whooshing noise and bright light splitting the early morning darkness, the warlocks whirled to see what went on behind them.

Veronika's beam of light struck the human, igniting him. He glowed red for a moment, then like an ember, blown upon to bring up the heat, he burst into a six-foot-tall tower of fire. The flames sucked into themselves and winked out of sight, leaving a chunk of black coal the size of her fist on the ground.

Hmm. That was expedient, and all the better that no one had seen it.

"Who are *you?*" the warlock called Donndubhán demanded.

Well ... no one except the warlocks had seen her little display. Which was exactly as she'd intended.

Donndubhán strode forward with Imar waddling quickly at his side.

She moved her hand so the sphere pointed at Imar and drew on the power again, but this time she directed the energy differently. White tendrils from the sphere covered her hand and shot a twisted bolt of white at Imar.

Donndubhán was quick.

He pointed at her, his power crossing her blast with one of his own, but hers knocked his aside as dust tossed by a strong wind. Her bolt streamed past him on its way to Imar.

When her twisted stream struck the shorter warlock, Imar lifted off the ground and his eyes rolled back in his head. He spoke in garbled murmurs for the next moment, then his feet touched the ground and he stared at Veronika.

She bent her finger, calling him to her.

He walked forward as Donndubhán watched, dumbfounded.

Taking control of Imar had gone better than she'd hoped, but he had not been much more challenge than the human. Disappointing.

When Imar reached her, he knelt on one knee and bowed his head. "I am yours, mistress."

"Yes, you are, and I have plans for you. Stand to the side and wait."

When he did as she ordered, she turned to Donndubhán, who threw up his hands. "Hold it. We can work out a deal."

She tsked. "I thought you were a Medb warrior, but warriors do not beg."

"I am a warrior and not just any kind. I'm Scáth Force, one of the most elite of the Medb coven. I do not beg, but if you attack me, you will waste the opportunity to gain a strong resource." He walked forward with an arrogant stride. Brown fuzzy hair had been cut short, probably for convenience, since she couldn't imagine how one would tame it otherwise. She'd seen bigger warriors than his decently muscled six feet, but she'd never known one to negotiate instead of retaliate.

He'd piqued her curiosity, but she should clear up his confusion as to where he stood on the power scale. "Attack? That sounds as though you think there would be question about the outcome if you were struck by my majik."

She admitted only to herself that she had no idea if she could control an elite Medb warrior—yet—especially one who showed no emotional vulnerability.

"Why put us both to the test when we could work together?"

"Are you so disloyal that you would leap away from the Medb without any thought?"

"Don't judge my actions until you know everything. I've spent my life locked away in TÅµr Medb, serving Queen Flaevynn in the past. As bad as that was, Queen Maeve has returned with Cathbad the Druid. I'm tired of being a slave. I'm an elite warrior, but I'm reduced to little more than errand boy most of the time. I want to use the skills I've honed to perfection, and I've been looking for someone powerful enough to utilize what I have to offer."

Interesting. "What have you been doing with trolls?"

He hesitated before speaking, but must have realized that she knew too much already. "Cathbad bestowed upon the the entire Scáth Force the ability to shield the Medb scent. We used that ability to take the life force of trolls, then use it to create demons that could never be traced to the Medb. Our warlocks have been disposing of demons and have thus won enough favor to gain access to VIPER."

"You're part of the coalition?"

"Yes, we are and we're here to stay."

"VIPER has changed significantly," she mused. "Do they *require* witches to join the coalition?"

"No. Not yet, anyhow. Queen Maeve and Cathbad have made a strategic move, which opened the door to resources they can use to destroy the Beladors."

"And *you* no longer wish to destroy your enemy, the Beladors?"

Donndubhán smiled with the confidence of a charmer. "I have but one goal. I want to be free to do as I wish. Given a position of authority and respect, I will serve a powerful witch whom the Medb cannot overpower. Are you Sterling?"

She laughed.

"What's funny?"

"I control the Sterling witches."

His dark eyes gleamed. "Are you as powerful as the Medb?"

"My people were *more* powerful than the Medb seven centuries ago."

"Who are you?"

It took him long enough to ask. "I am Veronika of the KievRus coven. I am chosen to wield Witchlock once again." This one would be simple enough to control even without her full powers.

"Witchlock? We had to study that. Everyone believes it's a myth."

"That's because my family *wished* for you to believe such. Until now. Witchlock has only been controlled by a KievRus witch born with the mark of our first leaders, Heide and Volkov." She extended the hand that held the sphere and pulled her sleeve back further to expose an ouroboros on her forearm. The emblem of a Celtic snake that swallowed its own tail was no tattoo created by a human hand. Veronika had been born with a circle birthmark the size of a quarter, with an eye and slash marks. It changed as she grew, forming into the final design when she reached the age of nineteen, two years ago.

Upon that birthday, she swore to bring her people to power again and set out to make the trade with the Sterling coven for Ragan. Her family had set a trade in motion when Veronika was born, but when Veronika was told of the most powerful Sterling to be born in seven generations, she knew that Ragan would be the first step in claiming Witchlock.

Donndubhán lifted his gaze to hers. "How do I know what you say is true?"

"Look into my eyes and you shall see the future." Then she lowered her shields to allow him to peer into her glowing eyes, where he'd see witches across the world falling to their knees in front of her, because she whispered a quiet spell that compelled him to believe what she projected.

His face lost color and he fell to one knee. "I will swear fealty to you. I ask only that you give me a position of significance. I want to be more than a servant."

She blinked, making her eyes normal again. "Do not swear fealty to me, because your word is meaningless. You stand here ready to break your oath to the Medb."

"Give me a chance to show you what I can do."

Should she take control of him now, or later when it would be so much simpler?

Later. He was a puppy anxious to please his master and he would serve her well.

If not, she would either take control of him or kill him trying.

Once she held the ability to take possession of his powers with no effort, she would *make* him completely loyal. "I'll give you a chance to prove yourself."

"You asked about the trolls. I will tell you all. I'm building an army of demons from Medb warlocks. Once this army is ready, I'll lead them for you."

"Where is this demon army?"

His eyebrows climbed high then dropped. "I ... have yet to produce a successful specimen, but I'm close."

"You're wasting your time and you will not waste mine. I have no use for a demon army. Once I have Witchlock, I will rule all witchcraft."

The warlock angled his head in compliance, then stood. "Then what do you want me to do?"

"First, I must find two women." Veronika knew Adrianna had come to the southeastern US, but still, she would have wasted time pinpointing the exact spot. The mark Veronika's ancestor had placed on the gryphon woman had provided the gryphon's location, leading Veronika straight to this city. She had not found the woman yet, but Adrianna couldn't be far if the two were friends.

He crossed his arms, looking pleased with himself. "Give me enough information and I can find anyone."

"One woman is a witch known as Adrianna of the Sterling coven and the other has dark brown, almost black, hair and kinetic ability, plus she can change into a gryphon."

He started laughing.

She prepared to teach him to never laugh at her, but he must have noticed the change in her expression, because he immediately explained.

"I'm not laughing at you, er, your highness?"

"You may call me Veronika." *For now,* she amended silently.

"Great." He rubbed his hands together, excited. "I like working on a first name basis. I was laughing because I already have what you need."

Was it possible? "What do you know of them?"

"Adrianna works with VIPER as a contractor."

So that is what she'd been doing since abandoning her coven. Veronika said, "Go on."

"The gryphon sounds like Evalle Kincaid, who I wouldn't have called a buddy of Adrianna's at one time, but those two *have* been seen together on occasion."

"What else can you tell me about this Evalle?"

"She isn't supposed to shift in this world. She's a gryphon, because she was born with Belador and Medb blood, which marked her as an Alterant. She's got wicked kinetics and communicates telepathically with other Beladors."

Evalle immediately moved up Veronika's list of powerful beings she needed in her stable of minions.

Donndubhán might not have been exaggerating when he claimed to be valuable. She told him, "Take Imar and bring me those two women."

"They won't come willingly."

"Do not kill them and leave no trail that leads back to me. If you require assistance, you will contact me, but tell no one I am in the city."

"Understood. I can handle this. Where do you want them delivered?"

She did like the confidence in his voice and told him where she'd meet him on the top of another roof. The open vantage point allowed her the best chance for escape if by some chance he betrayed her.

He would make that mistake only one time. She didn't need Witchlock to literally turn him inside out while still alive.

He nodded. "I know that building. It's in a good central place to watch over the city. Evalle only travels around at night. With daylight close, my best bet at catching her is this evening."

Wasn't he just a fount of information? "Does she function at night by choice?"

"No. She's has a deadly reaction to the sun."

Good information. "Find both and bring them tonight."

"Consider it done. Just to show you that I am holding nothing back on our arrangement, I'll tell you that Queen Maeve is very interested in another Belador known as Vladimir Quinn."

She thought on that. "I have heard this name. What is so special about him?"

"I don't know why Queen Maeve wants him, but she has one of her top people tracking him. Quinn has the ability to mindlock. He can take control of a mind and he can destroy one with his kinetics."

Mindlock. Energy rushed through her at considering the possibilities of controlling *that* power.

"What else do you know of him?"

"I saw him at Oakland Cemetery and I believe he's hiding someone in a tomb there."

Yes, Donndubhán was turning into quite the information source.

CHAPTER 28

Evalle gripped Storm's arms as they teleported from the Tribunal back to Atlanta. Just touching him gave her comfort, even though Storm was a churning mass of anger and frustration.

Storm couldn't blame Tzader. She wouldn't.

Tzader had been as blindsided as she'd been when Cathbad produced a warlock corpse with her dagger stuck in its head.

How had her dagger ended up there?

The only logical answer was that the dead warlock had to have been the demon she killed, but turning a Medb warlock into a demon would have required a lot of power. Why turn a warlock when changing something else that had less power would be simpler?

So who had changed a Medb warlock?

And for what reason?

The Tribunal would point at the Beladors for that and accuse them of some nefarious scheme to make it look as if Medb had created demons. But the Medb *had* created the earlier ones.

If the Medb weren't behind *this* demon creation, then who could be? And what would be the purpose of taking that kind of risk and facing getting caught by VIPER, the Beladors or the Medb?

The swirling colors in her peripheral vision cleared and she was standing on the top level of a parking deck near Woodruff Park.

Wrapped in Storm's arms was the only way to teleport.

A swift wind ahead of bad weather whipped hairs around her face. She stepped back and wiped the strands from her eyes.

Storm said, "Evidently dropping us on street level would have been too much of a strain on the prick."

"Wouldn't want to inconvenience the princess," Evalle

quipped.

That was enough to finally tug a smile from his lips.

Tzader materialized as Evalle turned to stand next to Storm, who draped an arm around her shoulder.

Tzader didn't waste any time. "I have no idea how we're going to find out how they framed you, Evalle, but I'll put everyone I have available on this."

"I want my dagger, Z." She nodded at where he'd hooked the weapon on his belt.

Looking apologetic, Tzader said, "I told them I'd hold it as evidence. I figured that was the only chance of you getting it back later."

"Damn." She stopped staring at the dagger with longing. "I appreciate you taking it though. I've just missed it."

Storm broke in. "We can't depend on the truth being revealed if the Medb are actively working to hide it, which you know they will be. Hell, I was with Evalle when she healed, but if a Tribunal wouldn't accept her statement of killing a demon as truth when she didn't glow red, I knew it would only agitate them for me to start defending her." He turned to her. "You aren't safe here."

Tzader said, "If you try to take Evalle somewhere to hide her, you'll hurt her without intending to. I promise you Sen can find her anywhere or I'd ship her off to Treoir right now. If he gets that kind of shot at her, none of us will be able to stop him and right about now Sen is close to begging for that chance."

Evalle asked Storm, "Were you thinking of trying that?"

Storm didn't even try to defend his position. He simply stated, "No one is taking you from me."

And she felt the same about being ripped away from him, but she would not stand by and give Sen reason to harm Storm or Tzader. In fact, Tzader looked worse every day and didn't need this crap. She asked Storm, "Let's not go up against Sen, please?"

Storm's determination showed no sign of changing, but he finally said, "I want to go back to the mountain and retrace everywhere Evalle went."

She had no intention of being left out of this. "I'll go with you."

Storm said, "No."

Tzader said, "I agree."

"What? You want to just lock me away? I'm no more interested in being stuck in my room underground than being imprisoned beneath VIPER headquarters."

Tzader frowned and Storm had the decency to look put in his place.

Storm wiped a hand over his face and let it fall to his side. "What do you want to do?"

"Find whoever is framing me."

Tzader asked, "We need to be asking *why* they're doing this if the Medb want gryphons."

With her guard dogs calming down, Evalle gave up her anger and scratched her head. "I don't know. It's not like the guy I tracked from Memorial Hall in Stone Mountain was trying to gain my attention. He seemed to be avoiding me. I went after him."

Storm quirked an eyebrow at that, but didn't comment on her running toward danger alone. He said, "The Medb have some plan in play and I'm betting it has to do with taking Evalle to TÅμr Medb."

Tzader grunted his agreement.

Evalle pointed out, "Why prove me a warlock killer when that would very likely end with Macha or the Tribunal vaporizing me?"

Storm snapped his fingers. "Cathbad wouldn't risk that, but that bastard *would* offer to take you as restitution for their loss."

"Crap."

"Storm's right," Tzader said, nodding. "We have to be smart about how we play this and hope that our people pick up intel or that Storm lucks into something."

"We have more than luck in our favor," Storm clarified. "I picked up a something besides just your energetic residue. I picked up a trace of majik."

Evalle and Tzader said, "You did?"

"Yes, but I didn't admit it because I wasn't specifically instructed to share that information."

Evalle laughed. *Take that, Loki.*

Storm added, "I can't tell what it is yet, because it's almost as if the majik was sanitized and that's what stood out about it."

This felt more like a team. Evalle smiled up at Storm and he curved his hand on her shoulder, pulling her a smidgeon closer.

Then he explained further, "The damage to the warlock's face was not consistent either. I think that clearly points to having changed shape, which is more than dropping a glamour. I'm going on the idea of what you and Evalle alluded to in the meeting, that the corpse was originally a warlock who was changed into a demon, then given a glamour."

She leaned into him, happy he agreed with her reasoning.

"Damn," Tzader said, scratching his chin. "That would actually explain how Evalle's dagger turned up in a warlock corpse. Now, we just have to deliver proof of someone changing that warlock."

"Another thing I didn't mention," Storm added. "That warlock barely had a scent of Medb. I doubt anyone standing back smelled it."

"I didn't," Evalle admitted.

"Me either," Tzader added.

"I think that adds to our theory," Storm continued. "While I was gone tracking the troll killer, I talked to Lucien, who said that last week when we had the first influx of demons along with the Medb, he got close enough to a Medb killing a demon that he should have been able to identify a scent, but there was none then either."

"Not even for the Medb?" Tzader asked. "I had reports that the warlocks doing the demon killing were part of the Medb's elite Scáth Force. They should have reeked of that lime scent."

"One would think," Evalle said.

Tzader's brown eyes narrowed. "Why didn't I hear about this, Storm?"

"I asked Lucien what happened when he reported that to VIPER and he said Sen dismissed it without a second thought because it was when all of you Beladors were having so many problems with your power while Brina was missing. Sen said he didn't care what the Medb smelled like as long as they kept killing demons."

"No one told me," Tzader snapped.

"Lucien was told not to repeat it, which makes me wonder if

Sen had a hand in any of this."

That floored Tzader based on the surprise in his face. "If that was ever proven, the Tribunal would take Sen apart one piece at a time for all this trouble they're going through."

"He tried to kill Storm once," Evalle interjected.

"There's no proof besides your word," Storm reminded her. "Sen would come up with some kind of defense to get around it, claiming that even if you believe that's what you saw you were too distraught to know what really happened. Or some shit like that."

"You've got a point, but I'd like to see Sen hung with abetting the person behind all this." Evalle looked over at Storm. "Lucien was told to say nothing, but he told you?"

"Lucien is a loner and he doesn't like Sen any more than I do. We talked. That's all."

"We need to get busy," Evalle said, ready to get out of there and do something while she still had a few hours of darkness left.

Tzader told Storm, "Sorry I had to put you on the spot in the Tribunal meeting, but I'm glad you were there."

Storm waved it off. "I'll go anywhere she goes."

But would he ever be able to stay with her anywhere she lived? He'd said he was glad about living with her, but she still had her doubts, and she needed to share those doubts with him, as Nicole had suggested. She stifled a sigh. That conversation would have to wait a little longer now.

Nodding at Storm, Tzader said, "I'll pull as many Beladors as we need off of any duty, other than guarding Brina, to help. You're about to see the full force of the Beladors when it's comes to protecting one of their own."

Tendrils of warmth swarmed through Evalle at Tzader's declaration of support from the entire tribe. She'd spent years trying to prove she belonged to the Belador tribe. She'd been called a Belador from the day a druid brought her into the fold, but saving Treoir from the Medb and bringing Storm to use his majik to return Brina to the castle had gone a long way to securing her position in the minds and hearts of some warriors who'd still been wary of her.

"Evalle?"

She looked up at Tzader calling to her and found both men

staring at her. "What?"

Storm almost smiled, but he managed to tuck it away and maintain a serious face in front of Tzader, who was scowling. "I asked if you could talk to Quinn."

"I told you I would."

"I need you to do it soon. I took Lanna to Treoir—"

"Good idea. Lanna may be able to help."

"We'll see, but I want to hand over the Maistir responsibilities for a few months once this is settled, and he's the only one I would put in my place. Maybe longer than a few months if it works out."

"You'd step down?"

Tzader and Quinn had been her rocks since the first time they'd met. They'd been captured in a Medb trap and all three had almost died. Tzader had always been the one in charge, because he was a leader of warriors.

But right now indecision warred with duty in his gaze and Evalle had never seen him so torn.

He said, "Brina isn't making progress. Macha said she believes Brina is losing more memories. I would never turn my back on the Beladors when they need me, but right now Brina needs me more."

He was breaking her heart. Evalle said, "Oh, Z. What do you need me to do?"

"Just help get Quinn's head in the right place so that if I have to ask him to take over for me, he can."

"How is his present state of mind?"

"I wanted him to tell you, but when Kizira was dying she told him they had a child, born of when they met thirteen years ago."

Evalle felt that punch to her stomach and she wasn't even Quinn. "He's going to want to find her."

"He's already started trying and I think he believed that Lanna was his best way to find Phoedra."

Finally, a bright spot in all this. "Lanna says she can find anyone by touching something that belongs to them."

"Right. Quinn has a narrow braid the size of a bracelet that Kizira made from his hair. She wove in strands of Phoedra's hair later. When Quinn handed the bracelet to Lanna it burned her hands severely."

"Is she okay?"

"I took her to Garwyli and left her there until I can go back and smooth the way with Macha to allow Lanna to stay with Brina. I think that will help her since Lanna was with Brina during the time she was gone and her memories corrupted."

All that sparked a thought. Evalle considered everything and decided maybe it was time she took care of her two best friends. "You bring up a good point about Quinn. I think he needs something to keep him from withdrawing and pulling inside himself. Hunting his daughter will do that if he doesn't lose hope."

Tzader's eyebrows drew tight in thought. "You're right. I hadn't wanted to bother him, but giving him more to do and keeping him close by so we can help him find Phoedra might be good for him."

"Right," Evalle agreed as if this was Tzader's idea. "Handing him some of your duties would be a good start, plus he'd have constant access to resources for hunting his daughter. Why don't you give him a push of motivation by telling him you need this time with Brina, which is the truth?"

Storm watched her with an assessing look. What was going on in his mind?

Evalle had never been much for touching, not even with Tzader and Quinn, but since Storm had changed all that, now she could offer her friend more than just words. She walked over and hugged Tzader, who put his arms around her, holding her close like the brother she never had. When she stepped back, she got a glimpse of the haunted soul Tzader kept stowed away from others.

She asked, "If I talk Quinn into taking over *now*, will you go to Treoir instead of waiting on the outcome of my trial?"

"No. Don't even start that."

"Then I won't help Quinn." She crossed her arms, letting her defiance fly in his face.

Storm looked at her as if she'd turned into a frog. "Why?"

She explained, "If Tzader thinks Quinn is capable of being Maistir, then he should trust him now. All of you are so damned determined to protect me. Let's give Quinn that job, too, if you think he needs something to do."

Tzader opened his mouth to argue and stopped.

"Right," Evalle said, pleased with herself. For once, she was giving directions. "You don't have an argument, Z. If you really believe Quinn can be the Maistir then give him all your trust.

Grumbling and pacing for a moment, Tzader said, "I don't like this."

"Welcome to my world." She smiled to soften her chiding. "You tell Quinn you're going to Treoir and you need him to take your place as Maistir. In all the time I've known you, you've asked nothing of me and I'll bet you've rarely asked anything of Quinn. It's your turn to let us do our part as friends. I have no problem trusting Quinn to stand by me with the Tribunal. If he calls to ask my opinion, I'll tell him that we need him now. And we do. This is me helping you on my terms the way you help me on yours. Get used to it."

Tzader gave her a sharp look but softened with amusement. "You do realize I'm still Maistir?"

"Yes and you're also one of my best friends. Do this for Quinn and Brina. Do something for yourself for once. Storm has the best chance of delivering the evidence we need. Let Quinn be a hero and help Storm."

"Damn," he said in a rush of exhale. "If Quinn's okay with it, then I'll go to Brina."

Evalle would make sure of it, because Quinn needed his friends now, too.

She swiped her hands over her hair. "Done." Now she had to go home to keep peace with Storm in an apartment that was starting to feel like a dungeon. Once this Tribunal trial was dealt with, she'd have to fulfill her new duties as liaison, but she was going to have that talk with Storm come hell or high water.

If she didn't end up in a real dungeon.

CHAPTER 29

Evalle watched Storm open the door of her apartment with his duffel in hand. He shrugged. "I'm sorry about this. My fault. I shouldn't have made you my mate without asking you first."

"It's okay. I love being bonded to you. I can make this work, but you're just walking away."

"You're not happy and it's my fault." Her chest hurt, but it couldn't be from her heart beating too hard, because she had nothing but an empty hole where her heart should be.

He stepped out and closed the door as a loud chiming started.

Nooo!

Evalle sat straight up, suddenly awake. The chiming was her phone ringing. Quinn's ringtone. Still trying to get back to the present, she reached for her phone and checked the clock.

Two ten.

In the afternoon?

"Hello?" She sounded drugged to her own ears. Or ... put into a deep majik sleep. Had Storm...?

He'd wakened her early this morning because she'd been crying in her sleep. The same dream she'd had again just now. He'd kissed her tears away, they'd ended up making love, and that's the last thing she remembered.

"Evalle? I tried calling you telepathically and didn't get an answer."

She sat up, rubbing her eyes, trying to focus on what Quinn was saying. "Sorry. I was ... up late."

"I can let you go."

"No, I'm good. What's going on?"

"I take it Tzader mentioned about passing off his Maistir position."

Hallelujah. Tzader had actually done what she'd asked. "Yes.

I know he doesn't want to impose on you but—"

"Frankly, I'm glad to have him not walking on eggshells around me."

Her heart whimpered every time she thought about what Quinn had suffered with losing Kizira. "I wish I could do something to take away your pain, Quinn."

"I know, but you can't. It's done and I'll have to live with it."

Guilt hung heavy in his words, but arguing right now would not change his mind. Evalle asked, "What did you do with ... Kizira?"

"She's in a mausoleum in Oakland Park Cemetery secured with one my triquetras." He paused, but his voice had gotten gruff sounding. He cleared his throat. "I doubt Macha knows or she'd have cardiac arrest if she found out that I didn't follow procedure for dealing with a deceased witch of Kizira's caliber."

"Macha wouldn't die, but she'd probably have a bad hair day."

"If that ever happens, I hope someone has a smart phone handy."

Evalle smiled, hearing the amusement in Quinn's voice. Might as well plow ahead. "Tzader told me about Phoedra."

That problem bombed Quinn's happy moment, but Evalle wanted to help him focus on something positive to do with Kizira. He admitted, "I couldn't talk about Phoedra before I left to go away."

"You didn't have to tell us then, but now that we know we'll all help you find her."

"I don't want anyone outside my closest circle to know about her. I have no idea if the Medb can find her, but you can bet if they could they'd try to take her."

"Good point. Let's hope they don't have a clue."

"The person who makes the mistake of touching Phoedra will find out just how powerful my mind is," he said in such a dark voice it raised the hair on Evalle's arms.

There was the grim Quinn that Tzader had been talking about.

Evalle said, "Agreed. We tell no one about this without clearing it through you first. Now, we need a plan."

"My plan burned the palms of Lanna's hands. Kizira must have placed a spell on it to protect someone with Lanna's gifts from finding Phoedra easily."

"I know that hurt Lanna, but Tzader told me Garwyli healed her hands immediately, and knowing Lanna she'd do it all over again if there was a chance to find Phoedra," Evalle said to soothe his remorse. "Adrianna might be able to help."

He asked with a hint of surprise, "The Sterling witch? I thought you didn't like her."

"She's okay. I've gotten to know her and she helped me find Storm. In fact, she's helped me several times now in one way or another. Traveling to Mitnal was freaky and Storm might complain about Adrianna sending me through the spirit world again, but I'm willing if she is and if you'll let her be in on finding Phoedra."

"I'm not interested in having you travel astrally, but I would be open to discussing this with Adrianna if you're sure we can trust her."

It hit Evalle hard that she did trust the witch. Funny how things changed. "We can trust her, which brings me to something I need to tell you now that you're Maistir. I didn't want to tell Tzader or he wouldn't have gone to Treoir."

"Oh?"

Adrianna might strangle Evalle, because she'd see any interference as putting Ragan at risk. But Adrianna was the one who said all would be lost anyhow if Veronika ended up with Witchlock. "Before I tell you, I need your promise not to do anything without telling me first, Quinn."

"That's a very broad promise."

"But you trust me," Evalle said quietly, not asking. Just reminding him.

"Of course."

She told him about traveling to Jafnan Mir and brought him up to speed about Veronika and Witchlock.

He murmured, "Holy hell."

"Yeah, but we have to stop Veronika, Quinn."

"What does she look like?"

"I don't know." Evalle sat up, thinking about that. "I hadn't planned on meeting up with Veronika, but I'll ask. Adrianna might be the only person in Atlanta who can recognize her at the moment, but we don't know for sure she'll follow us here, and

Adrianna says Veronika will for sure be avoiding *her* until after the eclipse, so the chances of her showing up in the city before that are pretty much zero."

"Get a description," he ordered, sounding every bit the Maistir in charge.

"Will do."

"What else do you have?"

"We only know that she'll come to this hemisphere for the eclipse. I'm concerned about putting word out through VIPER, because they aren't going to believe anything that comes from me and we risk the Medb finding out and getting involved in a bad way."

"I agree. Witchlock has been nothing more than a legend for so long I doubt anyone will take this threat seriously, especially with Adrianna having no support from her own coven. With this warlock mess hanging over your head, the Tribunal may think you're only trying to throw the attention off of yourself. On the other hand, the deities might believe you, and that would be bad."

"Why? What would they do?" Evalle asked.

"They would know the legend of Witchlock. Some of them would remember it of course. If they believed us, which would be a huge if, the deities would not stay to fight. They'd see this world as a lost cause and bail on VIPER and humans. They support the coalition for their own purposes. Those deities that are part of the coalition enjoy having the ability to keep an eye on other pantheons, preventing any single one from gaining an upper hand. Those who are not part of the coalition are fair game that no one will lift a finger to protect."

"Silly me to think there might be an ounce of honor among them."

Quinn said, "Some do possess honor, but the majority will always watch out for number one first. I see no value in telling the Tribunal until we have definitive proof of where Veronika is and what she's doing. That way, we can prevent any leaks to the Medb. Those bloody warmongers would find a way to use Witchlock against us."

"I have no idea what we do now, Quinn."

"You continue to stay safe."

"Don't start on me," she warned.

Quinn sounded as if he sat up straight and leaned forward when he spoke. "This is me speaking as your Maistir. And as such, I am ordering you to not put yourself in a position for the Medb to pile any new evidence against you."

She pulled the phone away and looked at it, then brought it back to her ear. "Yes, sir."

"Tzader and Storm are the overprotective ones. I know what you can do, Evalle. We will find a way to prove your innocence but it will do me no good to stand there with proof if you're dead or caught in one of their traps and forced to be under their control."

She grinned at his confidence in her. "Thank you. I'm so freaking tired of everyone suddenly treating me like I'll break."

"Not you." Quinn chuckled and it almost sounded like the man she'd known for a long time. "How's mated life?"

"I have no idea to be honest, but I can tell you cohabitating isn't as simple as I'd thought it would be. Of course, we had all of six hours together here the first day before Storm had to leave to track a troll killer." She shrugged and finally admitted, "Feenix and Storm are not hitting it off."

"What's the problem?"

"He's possessive and territorial."

"Which one?"

"Huh," she murmured. "Both, I guess."

Warmth came through when Quinn said, "They both love you."

"Yes."

"They have to learn to share."

That was easier said than done. "But it's more than that. I'm not sure I'm cut out to be a mate."

He laughed softly. "What do you think qualifies someone to be a mate?"

"For starters, I should be able to cook one freakin' edible meal. Anybody should be able to do that. Me? Evidently not. For another thing, I can't go outside in the daylight, which pretty much means the only time we can leave is in the dark. That's not normal. Who wants to live that way?" She was getting worked up, but for the first time she was spilling her guts and when she said it out loud this sounded even more like a plan that had no chance to succeed.

"Storm knew you were nocturnal when he met you, Evalle."

"I know."

"Has he ever asked if you could cook?"

"Not really, but my lack of skill will be obvious soon."

"I doubt it. I've spent enough time with Storm to have an idea of the type of man he is and I don't think any of that matters to him."

She considered Quinn's take on everything, then recalled the buckle incident. "I hear you, but I can't fix the tension between them."

"They'll work it out. There are some things *you* can't do." Quinn paused and asked, "What's the worst that can happen?"

"He'd leave me." She hated how vulnerable that sounded.

"Do you really think Storm would do that?"

"No, not walk away from me." She hated sounding so inflexible, but she admitted the truth, "I want Storm here. I want to live together."

"If it comes to separate places, you could make it work, couldn't you?" Quinn asked gently.

"Yes." But she'd been so happy at the idea of Storm being *with* her. Of being *with* him everyday. She loved Feenix, but she'd never realized how alone she'd been as a woman until Storm came into her life.

But Storm hadn't even mentioned bringing anything from his house to make this place more his home.

He probably didn't want to risk Feenix destroying his personal items.

She didn't want Feenix damaging Storm's things, but neither did she want to see Feenix sad. No-win situation. She had bigger things to worry about and turned the subject back to something productive.

"Storm is tracking every place I told him I'd seen the demon on Stone Mountain and around the base where the body of the warlock was found, but I haven't heard word from him yet."

"He texted me that he was following leads."

Storm hadn't texted *her*.

Because he didn't want to wake you, her harpy of a conscience said.

Determined to not make a mountain out of a molehill, she acted as if that was fine. "How do you want to handle this Veronika issue?"

"You and Adrianna keep me in the loop if you find out anything. I shouldn't have to tell you to stay out of Veronika's reach."

"Nope. I'm following my Maistir's orders," she said in a teasing tone, but meant every word. "If we can determine where Veronika is going to observe the eclipse and do her woo-woo when it happens, we may have to call in Sen to stop her. She's that powerful. I'd be concerned about having Beladors go up against her and especially if they linked."

"Point taken. We keep this on a need to know basis and I'll deal with bringing in Sen if it comes to that. I don't trust that bastard any further than I could toss him."

She didn't either, but for once, Evalle hoped Sen was as deadly as he seemed.

She hung up with Quinn and texted Adrianna: *Have you heard or seen anything?*

Adrianna sent back: *R u just now rolling, Sleeping Beauty?*

Evalle's face heated at the dig, but she texted: *I told Quinn about V and the realm. He's the new Belador Maistir. Won't share what he knows on this. Text/call him if you find out anything before I do.*

The phone hummed with an incoming call. Adrianna

Evalle answered, getting in the first shot. "Don't bitch at me about telling Quinn. I have a duty to protect the Beladors, too."

"I understand and I'm trying to keep the greater good in perspective," Adrianna said. "But if Quinn or anyone else interferes and costs me my sister, they'll regret it."

Evalle looked up, where no answers majikally appeared on the ceiling and said, "If you trust me, you trust Quinn. Just so you know, he isn't telling anyone at VIPER about this and he won't send out some blanket order to Beladors, because it would be suicidal to send them in with no idea what they were up against. But if Veronika shows up, we'll have every Belador we need stepping up to help."

"I hear you, but I'm telling you the fewer people involved, the better, because I am the only one who can break that chain of power and that's only if I can open the bond with Ragan. She and I have to open the bond at the same time."

"Do we have any reason to believe Veronika will be anywhere near Atlanta for the eclipse?"

"No, and in fact I expect her to stay away because she knows I'm here," Adrianna explained. "If she's smart, she isn't going to risk me interfering again without the realm to drain my power. Even if she does come here, I don't expect her to show up until the last minute, so I'm guessing that we have until right before the eclipse tomorrow to find her."

Not much time. Evalle asked, "Shouldn't we warn people?"

"What would you tell them? Run for the hills?" Adrianna was silent for a moment, as if thinking. "No. There will be no hiding from her if she gains Witchlock. A deity might have a chance against her, but they aren't going to put their pantheons on the line for anyone."

"That's what Quinn said."

"He's right."

Evalle started digging out fresh clothes. "Have you found out anything?"

"No, and I consider that good news. I've been searching out Nightstalkers for hours, but coming up empty. What about your guy?"

"Grady? I'll catch up with him later and ask if he's got anything. He hears news from all over the country sometimes, so I'll get him to put out feelers. That reminds me, what does Veronika look like?"

"I saw her only the one time seventeen months back. She's five-seven, busty, sort of like Madonna, the singer, if she were taller and had black hair streaked with white, blue eyes, a narrow chin."

"Got it. I'll pass that on to Quinn."

"Okay, but I'm telling you that I'll share with Quinn only if he shares with me."

"Understood."

She finished the call and sent a text to Quinn, then dove through the shower, dressed and grabbed a power bar from the kitchen. She was starting to unwrap it when her phone buzzed with an incoming text message from Rowan.

Crud. *Could somebody please kill the faerie who decided to whack me with a popularity wand today?*

Thumbing keys, Evalle asked what Rowan needed.

Rowan sent back: *I need to talk to you about a problem brewing within the covens. I hate to ask you to come out in daylight, but we don't have much time and I need your help.*

Evalle wanted to find out if Rowan knew anything about Witchlock, too. She replied: *I'll put on my protective gear and head your way. Why the urgency?*

Rowan sent: *I'm trying to prevent a war among the witches.*

Evalle rushed through the living room and slid to a stop when something the size of a tennis ball flew across the room, with Feenix leaping for it. She watched him flutter up and down after the buzzing toy, his eyes lit up with excitement.

Stepping closer, Evalle asked, "Where'd you get that, baby?"

Feenix jerked around and looked guilty, but he hadn't been doing anything wrong. "Uh..."

"Did Lanna leave that?"

He shook his head, ignoring the buzzing ... what was that thing?

A flying alligator that opened and closed its jaws every few seconds. That was new.

She squatted down. "Who made that?"

He shrugged and turned back to his stack of toys.

She was so glad to see him not moping around she let it go, but when she reached the door, Feenix spoke in a voice so small a human might have missed it. "Thorm."

Looking back at Feenix's little shoulders hunched over his building blocks, she started to ask what Feenix thought of Storm being around to make more things fly.

But her little gargoyle was now ignoring the buzzing alligator. One step at a time.

She'd watch him and Storm together later and see if ... maybe those two could work things out.

Hope settled into her chest as she left.

CHAPTER 30

Quinn walked along the sidewalk where Marietta Street separated the CNN Center, which took up the entire block on his left, from Centennial Park on the other side of the street. He welcomed the drizzle that hid any slip in his emotions.

He had to make good on the argument he'd just won with Tzader and stop thinking only about himself.

As two couples passed Quinn, one of the men called over to his buddy, "Never say never, bro." They laughed and moved on.

Never.

Quinn knew that word intimately. Just forming those five letters in his mind brought Kizira's image into focus and all that he'd missed with her because she was Medb, and all he would now miss, because she was gone.

He'd never fold her hand inside his to walk along a street. He'd never hold her in his arms again.

And Phoedra would never see her mother again.

He sucked in a breath, and then another.

Where are you, Quinn? Tzader asked, his voice filtering into Quinn's mind and snatching him from yet another drop into a bottomless chasm of self-pity.

Clearing his thoughts to sound like the leader he was expected to be, Quinn sent back, *Walking a section of downtown. I've assigned Beladors specific zones that overlap. Why are you still here?*

Just making sure you're good with taking over as Maistir.

I wouldn't have called you if I hadn't thought it through. You need to be with Brina and ... I need this duty.

I owe you big time, bro.

No, you don't, Tzader. If you do, then I owe you many times more. Let me know how it goes and you can send Lanna back if she becomes a problem.

I'm glad Lanna is there. I think Brina will be happy to see her once I clear it with Macha. We'll be good. Let me know if you need me to come back for Evalle.

We won't. Between all of us and Storm, she'll be fine. Quinn wasn't as certain as he tried to sound, but Tzader could do nothing beyond the combined efforts of everyone he'd just listed.

Just promise you'll have Sen call for me if anything goes bad in the Tribunal. I'll drag Macha in there and damn the rules.

I will definitely alert you if anything goes askew with the bloody Tribunal.

Roger that. Then Tzader was gone and Quinn was now Maistir over all of the North American Beladors. The only reason Macha probably went along with it was for Brina's sake. At least, Quinn assumed Tzader had cleared this with the goddess.

Quinn just hoped Tzader had a chance to be with the woman he loved.

Black clouds that had hung over the city for the last hour, spitting out a drizzle, finally dumped their load of rain.

Quinn pulled his wool coat up around his neck and hunched his shoulders. He'd worn a cap, and now pulled the bill down to block water from his eyes. Reminded him of school in England after having grown up in Russia.

That had been one damned cold country. He didn't miss it.

The one fond memory he held from the region was the two weeks he'd spent with Kizira in Chechnya. They'd hidden in a cabin with snow piled around the windows and a fire flickering.

Moisture stung his eyes and he blinked it away.

His heart could grieve all it wanted, but on the outside he had to pull it together.

A Maistir could show no weakness.

For four years, Tzader had kept his emotions hidden from all while he watched Brina slide from his grasp.

Quinn could do no less.

He reached the end of the block and continued his constant visual sweep of the area, but everyone was running to shelter now that lightning crackled and a major water dump was happening.

Quinn moved down the empty sidewalk as cars splashed by. He passed a street on his left that went to an industrial area with a rail line running to it. Between the rain and dark skies, the place had a gloomy shroud, but it was empty so he walked on across the narrow intersection.

Something pulled his attention for a second look.

He backed up and turned to his left again.

A woman stood a half block away in a red robe that billowed around her. No umbrella, but neither was she getting wet.

Quinn's instincts kicked in and put him on alert. An arched corridor between him and the woman formed an invisible shield against the rain.

Very likely a witch and no one that Quinn recognized, which made him think Medb.

Could this be Veronika? Almost certainly not. According to Evalle and Adrianna, she shouldn't be anywhere near the city. That said, he had a description. If he could get a look at her face, he'd know.

He eased forward and the alley grew darker except where light glowed around her. Yep, he was dealing with something unnatural, and powerful.

He couldn't ignore an unknown witch in the area when she could be Medb. The whole point of this search was to glean information about the warlock-turned-demon.

He needed to get a look at her face, but she kept it hidden in the shadow of her robe. She had her head bent forward and her hands tucked into each bell-shaped sleeve.

When he was twenty feet away, he stopped. That was close enough. "What business do you have in Atlanta?"

"Quinn?" whispered and echoed around him.

What? Pain clutched his chest at that feminine voice.

Kizira?

His heart screamed *yes* and his mind trembled at the possibility. This was ridiculous. Kizira was dead.

He cursed himself for allowing his mind to go there with a potential threat in front of him.

The world closed down to him and this witch.

As she came within two steps of him, he said, "Stop there."

She did.

He ordered, "Reveal yourself and explain your presence."

She lowered her hood with one hand and held a white sphere the size of a cantaloupe in the other. His gaze latched onto the spinning sphere. White-hot vapors smoked away from the ball and it almost looked as though a tiny figure was silhouetted inside.

"Quinn?"

He jerked at the sound of his name said in Kizira's voice.

When he stared into Kizira's face, a fist gripped his heart. That couldn't be.

All the blood rushed from his head and he swayed where he stood. He whispered a desperate plea. "Kizira?"

Please be Kizira.

You can't be Kizira.

Her beautiful lips lifted in that heart-shaped smile that sent his world somersaulting out of control. She said, "I'm here. I miss you."

Her voice echoed around in his head. "How can you be alive?" *Lie to me, but just be real.*

"Because you need me."

Tears burned his eyes. He shook his head, cursing himself for climbing into his grief so deeply that he believed Kizira was alive. "This isn't real. You're a ghost."

The most alive-looking one he'd ever encountered. His heart hammered in his chest.

She extended a hand, palm down. "Touch me with one finger only."

Damn his soul, that's all it took for hope to explode in his chest. He'd do anything for one more minute with Kizira. He crossed the space between them.

His hand moved toward her smooth skin. He was breathing as hard as a racehorse at the finish line. He could do this.

His finger trembled as he placed it upon her cool skin.

She *was* real.

He had to know what was happening. Standing this close to her and not holding her was torment. Was he losing his mind?

"If you're Kizira, tell me the truth. What's going on?"

"I am here for you, Quinn, but I can't remain."

He cried out, "Don't go. Please don't go."

"I came only to help you. What do you need from me?"

"You. I need you to be alive and in my life." His heart wrenched in his chest, hurting more than he'd thought possible after watching her die.

"I can't stay, Quinn. I have to go. Open up and show me what you need."

Pressure gripped his mind and tightened around his skull from all sides. He grabbed his head with one hand, too terrified to move his finger from her skin. "No, Kizira. We don't need telepathy."

The pressure eased immediately.

She sounded disappointed when she said, "The only way I can talk to you when I leave is through our minds."

He was dying inside all over again. Tears streamed down his face. The finger he had on her skin was shaking hard, but he couldn't move it for fear that she'd vanish. "Don't leave me again. I can't live without you. I keep failing you and I have to find Phoedra."

Kizira's face brightened at that. "How is Phoedra?"

"I don't know!" he groaned. "I haven't found our daughter. I'm failing her too. The bracelet isn't helping. Tell me where she is—"

Kizira floated back, breaking the connection. "I have to leave."

Quinn lunged for her. "Noooo."

Her voice whispered all around him. "I'll be back, but don't tell anyone or I won't be able to return. They'll stop me."

"Who will stop you?" He fell to his knees, holding his head, but nothing would quelch the agony shredding his insides. He'd had her so close. So close and now she was gone again.

Rain crashed down on him.

He didn't care. He wished he hadn't agreed to take Tzader's place, because now Quinn could let go and fall all the way into the chasm of insanity he'd been so close to last week while he was gone.

He'd gone away to mourn in private and to determine if he was still mentally strong, a deep concern since he possessed mindlock ability. The monks had healed his fratured mind once before in the past.

When he lost Kizira, he'd had doubts about his mental control, but the monks patched him up again.

He'd walked away from everything. Losing Kizira had stripped him bare and left his mind raw. With his level of power and the gift of mindlock, he couldn't stay when he was more of a dangerous liability than an asset.

The monks he'd gone to earlier for rehabilitation had given him sanctuary while he mourned, but they'd warned him that while his mindlock was strong and was truly healed, now his *soul* had suffered great damage, and he was far from whole.

He staggered to his feet with rain beating down on him, seeing now how arrogant he'd sounded when he told the monks, "No one wants to test me any time soon. They'll wish they'd stepped into boiling oil instead."

The monks had watched him with worried eyes.

He finally understood what they had been trying to say. His mind was as strong as ever, but his soul and heart could not withstand seeing Kizira again. Had she taken his hand and led him off a cliff just now, he'd have gone willingly.

The monks had warned Quinn he'd be vulnerable to attack.

He turned and trudged back to the street, putting one foot ahead of the next to finish his rounds. He had no explanation for what had just happened, but he could not allow it to happen again.

Should he tell anyone?

What would he say? He suffered hallucinations of Kizira? Or should he admit that he'd failed to insure she didn't return to this world by burning and salting the body?

I'll be back, but don't tell anyone or I won't be able to return. They'll stop me.

Who had Kizira been talking about?

The Medb.

Quinn gripped his head where pain now drummed his temples with each pump of his heart. He'd give Tzader a week and hope his friend brought Brina back, because Quinn could not be Maistir if he was the weak link in the Beladors.

With his mindlock ability and now his position as Maistir, he had control of every North American Belador warrior, who would act upon his word. He would not put them at risk. He would buck up and do the job Tzader and Evalle believed he could do.

For now.

CHAPTER 31

Evalle rode up to Rowan's Midtown house in a downpour, glad to be off the roads with it raining so hard, even if the bad weather did shield her from the sun.

Of course, the rain eased off as soon as she was out of traffic.

She parked her bike behind three cars at the curb in front of the witch's house.

Who else was here?

"What your skinny ass doin' here?"

She swung around, hand going to her hip for her dagger ... that wasn't there.

Rain still fell in a mild drizzle, but it had no affect on Grady, her favorite Nightstalker *if* he wasn't in some kind of trouble. He had coffee brown skin, but since he was a Nightstalker, it was translucent like a weak brew. Nightstalkers were ghouls who'd died as homeless people, and who gathered gossip and intelligence which they would trade for a handshake with a powerful being, gaining them ten minutes of solid form.

Most of them used that ten minutes to guzzle whatever they'd been addicted to when they were alive.

Grady could be ornery as an old goat, but his whisker-riddled face and wrinkled, brown eyes warmed her heart.

She'd missed him.

But that didn't explain why he was two miles from Grady Hospital, his namesake in downtown Atlanta. Until recently, she'd *always* found the old ghoul near the hospital she'd named him after because he wouldn't share his true name.

"I'm not the one who shouldn't be here, you old coot," she told him in good-natured ribbing.

"I thought you'd partnered with that Injun'."

He did that just get to her. "That's politically incorrect."

"Not when I was alive." He grinned and lifted his hands.

She looked around. Humans normally couldn't see him, but witches could. Rowan had stepped out on the wide front porch wrapping a frame house that had been built in the early 1900s.

Evalle gave a thumbs-up to let Rowan know she was fine and coming soon, then she turned back to Grady. "I have to hurry. What's going on?"

His eyebrows jumped. "You think I'm givin' you intel without a handshake?"

"I didn't come here looking for you."

"Then you won't be disappointed when I don't tell you nothin'." He grinned at that logic.

She'd threaten to strangle him, but that would do no good since he was already dead, and had *been* dead since the 80's. "Fine. I'll shake, but I don't want to hear a word about Old Forrester, Mickey-D meals or anything else. I have to get inside for a meeting."

"You sure are cranky these days. You got problems in your love life?"

She was not discussing Storm with Grady. "Shake or not. Make up your mind." She could be just as ornery.

"Fine. You ain't no fun today anyhow."

She looked around and found a place where she could step between two tall hedges so no human would see Grady take solid form.

Once there, she pulled off her glove, eyes turned up to check the sky.

"Don't worry. That sun ain't poppin' out for a while," Grady said.

He was right. She held her hand out and his shimmering hand reached for hers. The minute they touched, power rolled down her arm and passed to him, fueling his corporeal form.

Grady's solid form filled his flannel shirt and loose trousers, looking so alive it hurt to know he could only hold that form for ten minutes. He'd been solid longer, one time when she'd broken the rules, big-time. Evalle and Grady had hidden in the church balcony, and she'd held his hand so he could watch his granddaughter get married.

She released him and he left his arm outstretched for a

moment, but didn't berate her for only giving the minimum this time. Grady could be a roaring pain, but he'd been her friend since she came to Atlanta.

"Okay, Grady, spill whatever you have."

"A new power has entered the city."

"That's it? Grady, we have Medb warlocks coming and going. Queen Maeve and Cathbad can visit when they want. Plus something is killing trolls. Does it have anything to do with any of those?"

"Maybe."

"So what is it?"

"I saw it being used on a Medb warlock."

Evalle felt her pulse pick up. Could Grady be key to finding out who had turned a Medb into a demon? "What did you see?"

"Two warlocks wuz stalkin' a troll, then they caught it and locked it in their van. Must have knocked it out, 'cause nothing in that van made a sound, then the two warlocks walked off arguin'. All I heard was the big one say they had to get another troll. Little one, he ain't happy at all but the big one threatened him."

"Did you get names?"

"No. Big guy had a scar down the side of his cheek like this." Grady drew a line from his left eyebrow straight to his jaw. "Some woman showed up and she must be one hell of a witch. She called the little one to her like a damn puppy and made him heel to the side. Then she and the big one had a talk. I tried to get close but she was puttin' some kind of whammy majik up to prevent anything from comin' around. She won't talk to no Nightstalkers either."

A powerful witch? Veronika?

But why would she be anywhere around the Medb before she possessed her full power, and wouldn't Adrianna have heard something?

Wait. Evalle considered a more realistic possibility. "Do you know what Queen Maeve looks like?"

"Nah. Do you?"

"No. That might have been her. The Medb are accusing me of murdering one of their people without provocation."

"That shows those fools don't know you."

There was her Grady, always in her corner. "The problem is that I killed a demon when it dropped its glamour in Stone Mountain Park. I shoved my dagger into its head and told the dagger to stay. That body disappeared. Then Cathbad showed up at a Tribunal with a corpse and my dagger stuck in it. I was the only one who could release the dagger."

Grady growled and stomped around, then told her, "I'll try to find that bunch again. Wish I'd had a way to follow their van. I'll put word out what I'm lookin' for among the Nightstalkers. They won't tell me nothing, but they'll let me know when they have somethin' to trade with you for a handshake."

"Thanks. That would be a lot of help."

"Go on and git to your hen party."

She hugged him and she could tell it surprised him. He patted her on the back. "Don't worry. I'll find somethin'."

When she stepped away, he said, "You never said why you're not workin' with that Injun."

She shook her head at him. "His name is Storm and he's busy following a scent up and down Stone Mountain Park."

"Oh, I just seen him downtown for the last hour before I came here."

She had no answer for that. Storm had been back in the city and hadn't called or stopped by the apartment? That hurt and she couldn't put her finger on why, which meant she was making too much of it again.

Acting happy to hear that news, she said, "Glad to know he's back, then. He has some business he's taking care of in town."

It dawned on her that Grady hadn't explained why he left downtown. "What are you doing here, Grady?"

"I was followin' that witch in the robe. Minute she showed up, everything about her blurred into one bright ball of red. I wanted to git a look at her face. Don't like people in my territory I don't know. Especially one bringin' a load of power with her, but she just whooshed away, poofed out of sight, about a mile from here. So I came over to see if she was on her way to see this witch."

"No. Rowan is a white witch."

"That one I followed is keeping a whole lotta power shielded, so don't you mess with her. She's not like the others."

"I'll keep that in mind." But Evalle would like a look at her, too. "What could you see?"

"Nothin' but her red robe. Had a hood. That's all." He laughed. "Little Red Ridin' Hood witch, 'cept this one's robe goes to the ground and it's got big ol' sleeves, and she wouldn't have no problem smokin'the Big Bad Wolf."

A flowing red robe? Could the witch get anymore dramatic?

If the new Medb queen was anything like Flaevynn, the drama totally fit.

"Thanks." Evalle nodded and made her way to the porch.

Rowan met her at the door. "Thanks for coming, Evalle."

"Nice to see you." She peeled out of her gear down to her shirt and jeans, then followed Rowan into the living room where Sasha McCree played with her new baby, rocking it in a bassinet. That baby was the reason Trey had been looking worn out all the time lately.

She said hello to Sashsa then looked around to find Lucien Solis, the mysterious Castilian contractor for VIPER. He'd been on the hunt with Storm last week when they tracked the troll killer.

Taking in the room, she asked, "Is this VIPER business?"

Both women looked to Lucien, who said, "No."

Evalle grinned and took a spot on the sofa next to Rowan. "Works for me."

"Do you know anything about Witchlock, Evalle?" Rowan said, diving into a hot topic.

"Some." After that conversation with Adrianna, Evalle had to be careful what she said around Lucien. He'd shared information with Storm that he'd been told not to and Evalle wanted to high-five Lucien for ignoring what Sen had said. But she had no idea where his allegiance lay and until she did, she'd err on the side of caution.

Back to Rowan's question. Evalle asked, "What do *you* know about it?"

Lucien addressed Evalle, "In the interest of time, let's put our cards on the table. I'm not here in any capacity for VIPER. I couldn't care less if an asteroid took out Sen tomorrow. I'm also not a fan of witches."

Rowan's sly smile called him a liar.

Lucien narrowed his eyes at her and she merely arched an eyebrow at him, sending enough sexual undertones zipping around to scare the flying monkeys from *The Wizard of Oz.*

Lucien told Rowan, "You know she's empathic, right?"

Rowan's cheeks pinked, but she still laughed. "I know Evalle." After her moment of amusement, she sobered and told Evalle, "We have problems in the witch community with trying to create this council."

"Is there anything I can do to help?"

"That's not why I asked you here. I've been trying to take my time to coax the witches into making the right choice. As individual covens, we're vulnerable to the Medb."

Sasha snorted. "The other covens might be, but the Medb would have a rude awakening if they came after ours."

Rowan said, "Be that as it may, unifying us under a council will solve a lot of issues, such as self-policing any who fail to support our doctrine to harm none—at least for the white witches—and protect those who might be vulnerable to more powerful covens, white *or* dark."

Evalle frowned at that doctrine clarification. "Will your council have anyone who isn't a white witch?"

"Not at first, but I'm looking down the road," Rowan explained. "Now that the members of the Medb coven are living among us, it's just a matter of time before there's a major conflict between one of ours and the Medb. If that happens and we have no ruling body, VIPER will try to force us under the coalition rule. We won't have it."

"Makes sense to me," Evalle said. "I'm behind all of you, but I'm not sure why you're telling me this?"

"I need security that I can trust. You top that list for me."

"I'm flattered, but what do you think is going to happen?"

"We have to move up our timeline for the vote on the council leadership to have it tomorrow well ahead of the eclipse."

Cold fingers of warning climbed up Evalle's spine. "Why?"

"We have to finalize the decision before Witchlock. That's why I asked what you know about it."

Evalle avoided eye contact. *What would Adrianna do if she were here?*

Lucien interjected, "Adrianna's from the same part of the

world as the KievRus. She has to have told you about
Witchlock."

Evalle glanced at him and, yes, he was talking to her.
Adrianna trusted Evalle's judgment, but she'd made a promise to
tell as few people as possible, and this little group had caught
Evalle off guard.

She glanced at Sasha. Even if Lucien swore to say nothing,
Sasha was married to a Belador.

Sasha obviously caught on. "Trey doesn't tell me about secret
Belador business, and I don't share priviledged information from
the coven. You can speak freely."

Evalle held up a finger. She texted Adrianna and laid out what
was going on then asked if she wanted to attend. Adrianna
declined. When Evalle pointed out that this was an opportunity
for some support, Adrianna sent back: *I will not be responsible
for their deaths. If they try to make a stand against Veronika and
I see a chance to save Ragan, there will be casualties.*

After sending back a confirmation, Evalle felt better about
continuing this conversation. She said to everyone in the room,
"I'll make you a deal. Tell me what all of you know and I'll tell
you what I know, as long as you agree to help Adrianna if you
can."

Lucien started to speak and Rowan cut him off. "Yes. If
Adrianna is trying to prevent that power from spreading to our
country, then I will help her." Rowan turned to Lucien who
scowled silently. "You don't know Adrianna."

"She's a Sterling witch," Lucien replied. "What else is there
to know?"

Evalle groaned and covered her face then dropped her hands
to find Lucien staring at her with a look of confusion. "Is that
how I sounded back when I first met Adrianna?"

"Pretty much," he confirmed.

"I've gotten to know her and I'm no longer being a jerk
around her."

Rowan chuckled at Lucien's face. "She didn't insult you, but
you are judging Adrianna without knowing her."

"Would you two be as open-minded if we were talking about
a Medb warlock?" Lucien asked.

Evalle gave up. "You win when it comes to the Medb, but I'm

here to tell you I've already witnessed Adrianna trying to sacrifice herself to destroy Witchlock."

Stunned silence answered her so Evalle continued, "I'm still not sure I did the right thing by stopping her, but that's in the past and my first thought was to keep her alive. It's up to Adrianna who she decides to be friends with, because she's got reasons to avoid both light and dark covens. Reasons that are bigger than all of us here. So what do you know about Witchlock?"

Rowan spoke up. "Lucien and I have been researching it for a while, because he'd heard rumors that the original coven still exists."

Evalle nodded, "It does, but how did you find out? And, Lucien, just where do you come from anyhow?"

He gave her a devastating smile that would have melted her on the spot if not for loving Storm. Good grief. How did any woman refuse him?

Then she caught the way Rowan watched him. Now the tension between those two made sense, but in a fascinating way since the rumors were that Lucien had refused to work with Adrianna just because she was a witch.

Lucien relented by explaining, "I go home to Spain when I can, and when I don't, my associates keep me informed of any new activity on that side of the world. The KievRus coven is active and they have a chosen one they're grooming who can take possession of Witchlock. It's a power that can control all witchcraft."

"That's what I've learned," Evalle said. "The chosen one is called Veronika."

"That's good information, but did you know that she will also be able to take control of the power of other beings?"

Adrianna had warned the same thing. Evalle admitted, "Yes."

"The only hope we have is of finding Veronika's power source and destroying it."

"Been there. Tried that. Got the burn mark," Evalle chirped. When every face in the room ranged from shock to disbelief, she explained what she and Adrianna had attempted. "We barely made it out. Adrianna said there's no second chance and she's right. The realm Guardians would never let us get that close again, and the realm takes too much power."

Sasha's baby had fallen asleep. She said, "So what's going to happen to Adrianna's sister?"

"I don't know. Adrianna thinks Veronika is so close to gaining the power that she'll come to this country at the last minute and grab it when the eclipse hits. If that happens, we'll have no chance to rescue Ragan."

"That sucks."

"Yep."

Rowan had grown quiet, deep in thought. She said, "This is why we have to push up the timeline on the council vote, because we can unite a powerful force to combat Veronika."

Evalle looked around. "Then what's the problem and why do you need me for security?"

"There's a rogue group of witches who are with no coven. They're young and many of them are untrained, which opens the door to mistakes or misuse."

Evalle nodded. "Nicole mentioned that you were having an issue like that with solitary witches."

"It's worse than it was. Now they've banded together and are demanding the vote be determined by majority of individual witches instead of one vote from each coven. That sounds good on paper, but many people, witch or otherwise, will not take the time to become informed on any issue. That's why I'm pushing for a five-member council who will be held accountable to stay informed and make decisions in an unbiased manner. We'll have a checks and balances system with severe penalties for anyone who does not respect the gravity of their position."

"The solitary witches don't like that idea?" Evalle asked.

"I don't want to say they're being scammed, but they are being herded by one person. If the rogue witches have their way, they have the numbers to put one of their own at the head of the council, which would be disastrous. The one stirring them up needs to mature and be trained or she'll be easy prey, or damn us all by making a huge mistake."

"Can you talk them into forming a coven?" Evalle asked.

"Most covens are thirteen or smaller. This group boasts over two hundred and with no real organization. There are reports of some dabbling in the dark arts, but no one is sanctioning it.

VIPER will not respect our right to govern ourselves if we fail to form a legitimate council."

Sasha interjected, "Witchlock would thrive on witch wars. As a community of witches, we have a fighting chance against Witchlock, but only if all the covens unite to focus power. Not just here but nationally and internationally. The other cities are making headway by forming councils, but the council here, if it ever happens, will be the most powerful."

"It *will* happen," Rowan said with enough power the windows rattled.

Sasha hissed, "Don't wake her."

"Sorry, sis."

Lucien muttered something.

Rowan said, "I resent that."

Evalle asked, "What'd he say?"

Rowan sent him a censuring look that had no effect on the Castilian. He addressed Evalle. "I said that's what happens when you deal with witches."

"We're not all alike," Rowan argued.

"But you're all witches," Lucien countered. "White, dark, gray, your power comes with a load of trouble. But before you snarl at me, I agreed to work security for your council vote as long as this meeting doesn't turned into a cluster—"

"Thank you, Lucien," Rowan said, smoothly cutting off his curse.

"If we don't have a lead on Veronika's location by the time of your vote, Storm and I will help," Evalle offered, sure that Storm would do this. "But if we do find Veronika, we'll have to go with Adrianna."

Rowan stood. "Understood and as soon as the council is finalized, I will come to help with Veronika, too."

If things went badly with Veronika, Evalle might not have to worry about meeting the Tribunal after the eclipse, but she had to keep hunting for information. Evalle added, "I have an issue with the Tribunal–"

"Again?" Lucien asked.

"What can I say? I'm their favorite ex-con." Evalle brushed it off so no one would know how much it had bothered her when she'd been locked beneath VIPER a few months back. She explained what was going on with the demon killing and said, "Any help you can offer with proving they turned a warlock into a demon and glamoured him to then look human would be great."

"I'll check my contacts," Lucien said.

"Thanks." Evalle's phone buzzed. That had to be Storm.

She grabbed it out of her pocket and ... it was Isak.

CHAPTER 32

Maeve studied the mausoleum that held Kizira while Cathbad ran his hands over the heavy metal doors. She asked, "Feel anything?"

"Not out here, which is what bothers me. I would have expected a blood ward if he didna want anyone to enter."

"You think the security is on the inside of this vault?"

"I do and I've not had enough time around the Beladors in this century to learn everythin' of their powers. This Quinn is highly respected for his mindlock. That alone tells me his kinetics and telepathic abilities may be enhanced by that power. It would not be difficult for him to place something inside and activate it once he was out here."

"I want someone on Quinn all the time. We have to know when he comes here."

Cathbad studied the vault. "Agreed, although it may not be so simple to keep track of him. Our man Ossian is making headway as a new contractor with VIPER. I changed his orders from capturing Quinn to gaining the Beladors' trust. Once Ossian manages that, we'll be on our way into this mausoleum unless we find a way sooner."

"If we could just hear what Kizira said to Quinn as she died in Treoir," Maeve grumbled. What was the use of having a scrying wall that could replay past events if all the sounds didn't come through?

"I've tried everything I can to improve the audio, Maeve. I'm thinking Kizira somehow shielded her words so no one would hear except Quinn."

"That alone means whatever she said is of great value to me."

"Ossian's strength is in studying a person and figuring out the weak point for getting past walls. With Quinn just appointed as the new Maistir, he is the key to breaking the Beladors one at a time. Gain control of him and we will have unlimited access to the Beladors."

Maeve liked the sound of that. "It won't be long before we'll accomplish what that fool Flaevynn never could–seizing control of Treoir Island and the castle Macha stole from me." She took one last look at the mausoleum.

No one denied the goddess Maeve answers.

Not even the dead.

If they didn't get answers from Quinn, then Maeve would ask them of Kizira and she would answer.

She told Cathbad, "For now, weave a spell around this place so that we're alerted when anyone with power visits the chamber. It's been a long time since I've raised the dead, but I still have the touch."

CHAPTER 33

Six Feet Under was doing its normal booming business in spite of a rainy Monday night.

Evalle hooked her helmet on the mirror of her Gixxer and shook out her hair, then pulled it back into a ponytail.

Veronika was coming to the US tomorrow for that eclipse.

I should be out hunting for intel instead of on a date.

Okay, this was *not* a date.

Besides, if there was intel to be had, Adrianna would have found it by now. If not, Grady, Storm or Quinn would have flushed out something.

Evalle had given her agreement to Quinn that she'd stay out of the Medb's way. If she wanted everyone to respect her reasonable requests, then she had to give the same. Since she couldn't run the streets with the Beladors tonight, she could at least accomplish one simple thing, which was to settle her debt with Isak and convince him that she was not the woman for him.

And remain friends.

She wiped the water spots off her phone and sent a text to Storm asking where he was since Grady had seen him downtown. She'd thought Storm would at least swing by here to see her before she went inside to eat, but she took his lack of presence as respecting her space to handle this dinner thing with Isak.

Her phone rang.

Storm.

She hurried to answer and almost dropped it. "Hey."

"Hi, sweetheart. Where are you?"

After the first two words, she wished to be meeting *him* for dinner. She said, "Six Feet Under."

"Okay." That had sounded resigned and not happy about it.

She wanted to snap her fingers and make him happy, but that wasn't happening so she offered, "This is just dinner and then we're done. You can go with me when I pick up the twins, okay?"

"Sure. No problem."

She changed the subject. "Where are you?"

There was a brief silence that bothered her, then he said, "Taking care of some business in town."

"How'd the tracking go?"

"Not bad. I followed a trail from the mountain and I've got a few ideas, but nothing firm yet. Don't worry, we'll get to the truth."

She tried to sound like she had his faith. "I know. I talked to Grady." She shared what Grady had told her. "He's doing some snooping around too."

"I wish you weren't out tonight."

"Are you on the way to the apartment?" she asked, thinking she might be able to beg one more day out of Isak if it meant she'd get to spend time with Storm.

"Uhm, not yet. I've got a few more things to do. I'll be there before daylight."

She wasn't planning on staying out more than a couple of hours. What was keeping Storm out so late? "I should be home in two hours, tops. Can you be there by then?"

"I'll try. I've still got to deal with my house."

"We could go together."

"I've got it handled. I don't want you around that place after what happened because of ... her."

He meant Nadina, but Storm wouldn't say the witch doctor's name. They'd slept outside the last night there because he didn't want to take Evalle back inside where the witch doctor had been.

She should appreciate that and roll with it. He accepted her nocturnal life. She'd accept his hours, whatever they were. "Okay, that's fine. I'll see you when you get there."

"Great." Now he sounded relieved so she must have given him the right answer. *Points to me!*

Isak pulled up in his black hummer and Evalle lifted her hand to let him know she saw him. "I've got to go, Storm."

"I know. Tell him if he touches you, he'll lose that hand."

"That's not going to happen." But she did smile at the threat. "Love you."

"Love you more. Be careful going home."

Isak got out and left his truck running as Evalle hung up.

She said, "Don't think they'll let you park there all night."

"We're not staying long."

"That was not the agreement."

"Yes it was," he argued. "You said to meet you here, not that we had to eat here."

She crossed her arms. "I plan to eat here."

Isak's tone changed to a more conciliatory one, with a dash of charm thrown in. "I've got a nice quiet place to have—"

He stopped talking and looked past Evalle.

She turned to find Adrianna strolling up in a snug red dress with a short furry jacket over a scoop neck that showed off her assets.

Evalle looked back at Isak. He had his laser gaze locked on the witch.

Adrianna stepped up and said, "Where are we going for dinner?"

Isak pulled himself together and said, "You weren't invited."

Adrianna looked at Evalle who gave her an I-don't-care look so the witch flashed a brilliant white smile. "You didn't say I couldn't join you, either."

Ha. Adrianna had turned Isak's tactical use of omission right back on him. She owed the witch, even if said witch didn't know it. Relieved to not be alone with Isak, which should make Storm happy, Evalle said, "The more the merrier."

Then Adrianna lost all her friend points when she said, "I ate here last night."

Isak piped up. "I was just telling Evalle I have reservations at a nice quiet place. For two."

Adrianna smiled. "I'm sure changing that to three will be no issue for a man with your... resources." She sashayed toward his truck.

Isak growled and strode over behind her.

Evalle saw her window and all but flew past both of them so she could jump in the back and force Adrianna to sit up front.

He ended up lifting Adrianna into the Hummer by her waist.

It was either that or produce a set of steps.

Once Isak had them on the road and cruising through the city, Adrianna said, "This dashboard looks like an aircraft cockpit. What is all this?"

Even though Isak hadn't been happy about her presence, in spite of his first refusal to bring her, he behaved like the gentleman Kit had raised. He pointed at various controls. "Access to computers at Nyght headquarters. I can reach any teams on surveillance and link their video, traffic cams, whatever is needed."

Evalle asked, "Is that how you can always find me so easily."

His gaze filled the rearview mirror. "I have special equipment dedicated *just* to keeping up with *you*."

Adrianna half turned and looked at Evalle, who held her head in frustration. Adrianna winked and asked Isak, "So you can find anyone you want right now?"

"Pretty much."

"What about Storm? Can you find him?" Adrianna flashed the smile of an imp.

Evalle warmed to the idea. Put the focus on Storm and not her, because she seriously doubted Isak could locate Storm so easily. "Really, Isak. You could find Storm?"

Isak rose to the challenge and punched a number on his dash that connected him to a male voice who answered, "What can I do for you, sir?"

Isak said, "Give me a ten-twenty on nine-seven-seven."

"You have a number for Storm?" Evalle asked.

"I have a file on every nonhuman." Isak looked over at Adrianna and added, "Including witches."

Amused, Adrianna asked, "What's my number?"

"Six-six-six."

Evalle burst out laughing and Adrianna chuckled.

After a moment, even Isak saw the humor in his attempt to take a dig at Adrianna. Then he said, "Here comes the report."

Adrianna said, "There's like eight listings for Stone Mountain."

"They do an update every fifteen minutes on a sighting."

Evalle did the math. Storm had only been in Stone Mountain Park for two hours. The rest of the addresses were primarily downtown and one had been two blocks from the apartment.

Two blocks and he hadn't even called.

She squinted at the list. "What's the last one on that list?"

"His current location as of nine minutes ago. Want to see it?"

Of course she did. She had a moment of feeling like a snoop, but Storm had said he was taking care of business. If he was on a traffic cam, it was public knowledge.

See? Didn't take much to talk herself into this. "Sure. What the heck?"

Isak tapped the screen and the text went away. An image appeared from the street cam, but the street was empty.

She was glad. All of a sudden, she felt bad about snooping on Storm after all, since ...

Two people stepped into view and Evalle couldn't have looked away if her life depended upon it.

One person was definitely Storm. She'd know that strong profile anywhere.

The other person turned at an angle that showed her attractive face, her blond hair in a chic, swept-up hairdo and the frilly while blouse and trim slacks in a style more suited to Adrianna than Evalle.

Storm reached over and opened the door, smiling and holding it for her to walk through, then he followed her inside.

Evalle thought her stomach was going to come up her throat.

Adrianna gave her a guarded look and asked Isak, "What's in that building?"

"It's empty." He tapped buttons. "Zoned for ... light commercial, uh, no that's not right." He tapped some more. "Looks to be plans for condos or apartments and offices, but there's no certificate of occupancy on file yet so no one has moved in."

Adrianna gave her a look and a tiny lift of her shoulders as if she didn't understand either, but Evalle had it figured out.

She was not going to insult Storm by thinking he was seeing that woman. He'd earned Evalle's trust, but Storm *was* looking for a place to live and probably wanted his apartment finished before he told her. She should be glad he at least wanted to move closer to her, but it was hard to swallow past the ball of hurt lodged in her throat.

They'd never have a life together. Not like other people lived together.

Was it asking too much to have one part of her life feel normal?

Evalle wanted to get out and just leave. Walk home.

Isak flipped off the video as he found a three-story parking garage on the north side of downtown. He pulled into a second-level spot in front of a short wall that allowed a view of the night blanketing Atlanta.

"This place is dead for a downtown parking deck," Adrianna muttered, looking around.

Isak parked and turned off the engine. "There are never many cars here at night. These are all purchased spots. I own this space."

Evalle didn't care. She'd do what she promised, but she needed some time to get her head straight.

Isak got out and walked around the front of the Hummer.

Adrianna turned quickly to Evalle. "Storm is the one who asked me to join you tonight, so give him a chance to explain. As soon as we have time, I need to tell you what I found out after we talked today."

Her door opened and Isak was there before Evalle could answer her. She had things to tell Adrianna, too. Evalle jumped out quickly. She wasn't up for Isak touching her right now, even if Storm couldn't see it and there wouldn't be a fight about it.

She didn't want to be around anyone at the moment.

Cool night air swirled, but it brought a hint of warning. Evalle paused and opened her senses to assess the area for a threat.

Adrianna came around first and stopped next to Evalle, obviously also on alert, then Isak strolled up behind the witch as the lights went out in the garage.

A whip of energy buzzed and circled Evalle, pulling tight like an invisible lasso that tied her arms to her body.

Isak and Adrianna were in the same fix except whatever looped around them had bound the two together with Adrianna's back to Isak's front.

CHAPTER 34

Evalle realized Isak was trying to lift his hand that held a phone, but the lasso of energy had his arm pinned so tightly he couldn't move his hand and turn the phone, and couldn't touch the screen with his fingers.

Adrianna was sandwiched tight against his chest, but she stared forward, ready to face whatever had captured them.

A man who had to be a warlock stepped into Evalle's line of sight. She could see just fine in here, but Adrianna and Isak would be at a disadvantage.

Evalle started with simple questions. "Who are you?"

"I am Imar."

Adrianna spoke up. "What do you want? I don't normally grant a last wish before executing a criminal, but I'll make an exception in your case."

Go Adrianna.

Isak stared down at the top of Adrianna's head with a look of surprise and muttered, "Damn, that's hot."

"I am here for my mistress. You will come with me." The warlock talked like a robot and had the unfocused gaze of a zombie.

Evalle worked her fingers loose. The binding went from her elbows to her hands, but with some effort that had her gritting her teeth, she managed to bend her wrist on the side of her body Imar wouldn't see.

Imar lifted his hand to reach for Adrianna, who bit off a fast series of words. Imar's arm wrapped around his neck to grab his own chin.

Fury seethed in Adrianna's eyes and she ordered, *"Cuir gu bàs!"*

Imar yanked his hand and the snap of his neck breaking away from the rest of his spine cracked the quiet.

"Holy shit," Isak said. "Remind me to never piss you off."

Adrianna smiled at the compliment.

Evalle said, "What language was that?"

"One of the Gaelic languages. He has a Medb aura, which means he's of Celtic descent. I spoke in a language his blood would recognize, but he likely would not." Then Adrianna pointed out, "We're still stuck."

Evalle searched the dark space. "That's because there's more than one warlock here and Imar was sent as a sacrificial fool."

Isak said softly, "Can you touch my phone if I turn it toward your hands, Adrianna?"

"Maybe." She wiggled the fingers on one hand, inching them around her hip toward him.

"Listen you two," Evalle whispered. "I need whoever is in charge alive."

"Are you serious?" Isak groused.

"Yes. Do not kill the head guy once he shows his face. It's important."

"We won't kill him ... unless we have no choice," Adrianna clarified. "But no one is taking me captive."

"Agreed." Evalle would never put Adrianna and Isak's safety second to her need to deliver evidence to a Tribunal, but anything out of the ordinary could lead to that evidence.

Energy sizzled from the entrance where another man walked in, but intelligence slashed through this one's gaze.

Adrianna whispered, "Medb."

And a scar that sliced straight down his left cheek.

This was the guy Grady had seen.

"Poor Imar can't handle anything by himself and now I'm going to have to replace him plus explain his death." The warlock took in all three captives and paused at Evalle, withdrawing his knife and touching the tip. "Not so deadly without your dagger, are you?"

Had he heard about the dead warlock and her dagger ... or did this guy know something?

Replacing the knife, he lifted a radio and said, "Bring the truck."

Adrianna opened her mouth and the warlock pointed a finger at her. "That crap you spewed won't work on me. I was told to deliver you two kicking, but that doesn't mean I can't rough you up some. Try that spell on me and you'll find out I'm not your average warlock."

Adrianna closed her mouth and gave him the attention one would a slug.

He might think he'd shut her down, but Evalle knew enough about Adrianna now to know the witch was merely thinking, not beaten.

Evalle asked this warlock the same question. "Who are you?"

"We're not going to be friends, but you can call me Don since we'll be intimate soon." He leered at her.

Evalle shook her head. "Forget I asked. No point in remembering the name of a dead warlock walking."

"You got a smart mouth for someone with trouble hanging over your head."

She hadn't smelled the Medb scent, but Adrianna called these guys Medb and he just confirmed it for Evalle because no other warlock should know about her dagger right now. Plus, she couldn't think of any other kind of warlock around who would be arrogant or stupid enough to attack her, much less her and Adrianna together, even if they knew nothing of Isak's reputation.

While killing a Medb warlock would be a great stress relief right now, explaining a second Medb death might not go well with the Tribunal in their current frame of mind.

Adrianna was still working her fingers behind her, but staring calmly at this Medb, who kept his eyes on her and the cleavage the witch intentionally lifted with deep sighs of boredom.

Don clearly dismissed Isak as a threat because he was human.

To pull the Medb's gaze to her and confirm a guess, Evalle said, "I bet someone thought that was a slick trick, changing one of your warlocks into a demon then sticking a glamour on him, but it didn't work."

"Looks like it did from where I'm standing." Don found that highly amusing.

Damn. She had the guy she needed right in front of her.

Adrianna and Isak had no idea what this Don would mean for

clearing Evalle's name. She scoffed. "You don't really expect me to believe that you could have done that? If you were that powerful, Queen Maeve wouldn't have you out here doing grunt work."

That pissed off the warlock. Perfect.

Don stepped over and got in Evalle's face. "Believe it, bitch. I'm the one who handed the corpse to Cathbad. I saw you kill my demon up on Stone Mountain."

"Why change a Medb warlock into a demon? That makes no sense at all." She tried to sound so unimpressed.

Adrianna helped out by chuckling.

"I was building an army, but I won't need one now."

Evalle said in all honesty, "Once the Tribunal finds out what you did, you'll be lucky if Queen Maeve and Cathbad only kill you."

"That's never going to happen and those two are no longer my problem. I don't answer to that witch or Cathbad."

He was serious.

When he turned away, looking for his truck, Evalle twisted fingers on her left hand that was on the side angled away from the warlock. She fed her kinetics into the fingers and pushed at the invisible wrap around the middle of her body, feeding more power and straining to keep it isolated while she experimented.

She felt it stretch then give. Her finger poked through.

After all that, she'd only managed to punch a hole.

The sound of a large truck engine slowing meant Evalle and her friends were out of time.

The warlock standing with them waved his truck in.

Twisting her wrist into a painful angle, Evalle called up her warrior form where muscles expanded and cartilage popped up under the skin.

That upped her kinetic power, but more than that, her expanded body size stretched her binding until she could move her wrist. She whipped her fingers fast at the warlock and slapped him in the back of the head.

The blow knocked him off his feet and facedown on the floor.

Evalle gave Adrianna and Isak a look. "Time to make our move." Using her kinetics, she called his knife to her.

The blade flew from his sheath to her hand, grip first.

She pushed the blade between her and the binding, hoping a Medb knife would cut Medb majik. She sawed through an inch.

It was working. Not fast enough.

Isak shouted, *"Code Nine! Code Nine!"*

What did that mean?

Adrianna leaned her head forward and chanted, *"Black clouds of night and lightning strikes, heed my will...*

The sky exploded with thunder and lightning drowing out her words.

The truck pulled into the garage and stopped.

Thunder boomed and boomed and boomed.

Vicious electrical strikes slashed all around the building, coming closer, then merging into one that struck at the side of Adrianna and Isak.

He cursed a blue streak, but they broke free.

Evalle got enough leverage to shove the knife blade up and rip out of her bindings.

Isak stepped in front of Adrianna, pushing her behind him.

Evalle did a double take at Adrianna, who rolled her eyes at Isak's protective move, but then with a shrug and a smile, she crossed her arms.

Was she mental? This wasn't done.

A warlock jumped from the truck. In his former life, he must have been a sumo wrestler. Don was on his hands and knees, getting back up from when he'd had his bell rung by Evalle's kinetic slap. That was nothing compared to what she planned to do next, but Isak produce a handgun that looked nothing like his demon blasters.

She asked, "Is that set on stun?"

"I'm sure they'll get a shock when a hollowpoint hits them in the chest."

"I need that guy Don alive, Isak."

"You take all the fun out of fighting nonhumans."

Isak might just be mental, too.

Don and his sidekick stood back, waiting. What were they waiting on? Coalescing from the darkness outside, where Adrianna's weather display had finally diminished, came a person wearing a long red robe with a wide hood that left the face hidden in darkness.

Isak looked over at Evalle and asked, "What happened to your arms and upper body? Looks like you just did a steroid highball."

"It's Belador battle form. Increases my power."

"Hmm."

She couldn't tell if Isak was impressed or disgusted, because she couldn't afford the distraction of using her empathic gift. The funny thing was that she'd never wanted him to see her this way before, but she no longer cared what Isak thought. Storm had seen her at her absolute worst, broken and bleeding and in full beast form, and he still loved her.

She'd hold onto that and worry about anything else later.

Adrianna had stepped up between Evalle and Isak. "That's what I wanted to tell you, Evalle. *She's* here."

There was only one person who could be the reason for the sick sound in Adrianna's usually snarky voice.

Veronika.

Isak asked, "Who is she? Friend or foe?"

"Definitely an enemy, but don't make any sudden moves, Isak," Adrianna warned. "Remember containing that witch doctor with me and Evalle?"

"Hard to forget some crazy bitch who pinned me and my weapon to a wall without touching me," he growled with menace from the memory.

"She was nothing compared to this witch, and this one is carrying the equivalent of a nuclear warhead in her hand."

Veronika's hand held a small version of what Evalle had seen in the other realm, but it appeared dense with so much white energy churning inside.

As the witch covered the hundred feet between Evalle's group and the warlocks, Isak asked, "What makes her so powerful?"

"My sister," Adrianna answered. "We'll tell you more later, but first we have to get out of here and as deadly as you are with a weapon, shooting her would be like throwing a dart at a balloon full of acid hanging over your head. You won't like the outcome."

Veronika stopped fifty feet away. "I have no use for the human, but I will kill him if he gets in my way or if you create any more problems for me."

"Are we supposed to be shaking in our boots, Veronika?"

Evalle asked.

Adrianna picked up the thread of antagonism and added, "I think we proved we can take care of ourselves. We made it in and out of your ancestors' realm."

"You failed to accomplish what you went there for and I now have Ragan right where I want her." Veronika lifted her sphere and Evalle finally figured out why it seemed so dense. Ragan was captured inside that small globe of energy. Tendrils of white snaked up Veronika's arm and disappeared inside the sleeve.

Evalle glanced at Adrianna, whose face had lost color, but she had a death glare building in her gaze.

Adrianna warned, "You should never have taken my sister. You have no idea of the connection we hold."

"Oh, I think I do. You've proven to be trouble once before, but you will not do so again."

"We will stop you," Adrianna warned.

"Oh, I am sure you'd like to, but first you'd have to find out the location I have in mind for taking possession of Witchlock. I've told no one and you'll be contained. I'll tell you all about it afterwards ... when I come for you. Once Witchlock completely manifests throughout my body at the end of the eclipse, I will take your power and you will serve me. Then I'll go through the entire Sterling coven because I'll hold the knowledge of all that you and your sister knew about your people."

Isak still pointed a gun at the witch.

A sound escaped from the dark shadow inside Veronika's hood, and she lifted the empty hand and whispered a chant.

Isak scowled and dropped the weapon, which glowed red. He held up his hand, and she saw a burn imprint where the metal had touched his skin.

Evalle had to get them out of here. She called over to Veronika, "I know juvenile witches who are more impressive, but they don't pick on humans."

Adrianna hissed, "Careful or we'll all go up in flames."

Evalle answered under her breath, "She needs us or she'd have sent them to kill us first thing."

Isak gritted out. "Evalle's right."

When Veronika didn't rise to Evalle's bait, it was time to up the game. Evalle said, "This has been fun, but you're interruping our dinner plans. Have your people get in touch with my people if you want to talk again."

Veronika said, "I had planned on taking control of Adrianna first, but I would enjoy watching you move as my puppet even more." The witch lifted her hand with the sphere and power burst from it, shooting at Evalle, who threw up a kinetic field.

The power smacked her invisible field hard and knocked her back a step. Evalle muttered, "If this is only a taste of her future power, we're all in trouble. You two get out of here and I'll follow."

Adrianna and Isak both yelled, "*No!*"

Lifting her arms and spreading her fingers, Adrianna spoke in yet another language Evalle didn't recognize. Maybe she should take one of those Rosetta courses.

The weather outside boomed again.

Atlanta forecasters had to be going crazy about now.

Veronika's sphere energy intensified, burning against Evalle's kinetics and sliding along her power to reach her body. Heat scorched her muscles, and they quivered from the strain.

Isak had run to his truck and returned with one of his Nyght megablasters. "Drop your shield and I'll hit them."

Evalle's body shook and her voice sounded like she was riding her bike over a rutted road. "No. Might backfire. Her sphere is too strong."

Adrianna called up the elements and a powerful wind shear blasted through the open wall, bringing rocks and debris inside the deck behind Veronika.

Her warlocks dove under the truck and a barrier of red appeared, glowing beneath the truck's frame. The mini hurricane slammed the side of the truck. Metal peeled off the bed and the truck body rocked.

Veronika stood firm, holding up her free hand to ward off the wind and rocks that were shredding metal, but not harming her.

Should I call in more Beladors? Evalle dismissed that idea as quickly as it came to mind. She had to fill them in first, on who and what Veronika was, so they wouldn't link to fight. This bitch would love that. Kill one Belador linked and everyone connected suffered the same fate.

That would be easier than knocking down bowling pins for

Veronika.

Isak shouted, "I can take her. This is a Nyght 757 Stinger."

"No," Evalle told him but she was losing ground, sliding back six inches at a time, and her arms were getting weaker. Sweat drenched her clothes and her head was on fire. Her blood might be boiling.

Adrianna started forward, arms still raised and a mad look in her eyes.

Evalle yelled at Isak, "Stop *her*!"

He cursed and grabbed Adrianna around her waist, lifting her off the floor.

She screamed, "Let me down. I'm killing that bitch."

Evalle wished she'd get on with it then.

Boom, boom, boom shook the air and ground.

Don's truck burst into a thousand pieces.

Veronika took one look at the source of the attack—a silver Hummer covered in armor plates with a long barrel sticking out the front like a military tank—and she swept her sphere in a circle, filling the parking deck with a cloud of red.

The pressure against Evalle's kinetics disappeared.

She dropped her arms, groaning. A bath of icewater would feel seriously good right now.

Isak held his blaster propped in one arm still pointed at the last place they'd seen Veronika, with Adrianna locked in his other arm.

She'd quieted, and the devastation that was left behind her earlier anger actually hurt to see.

Adrianna said, "She's got Ragan in that sphere. Getting her out is going to be ..."

"A *challenge*," Evalle finished, to prevent Adrianna from drowning in the depressing odds.

The red haze slowly dissipated.

Veronika and her warlocks were gone, but Evalle now had something to hand the Tribunal.

She had Adrianna to testify that a Medb warlock admitted to setting up Evalle, but she would not ask Adrianna until after the eclipse.

"You can put me down, Isak," Adrianna announced.

"I could."

Evalle choked back a laugh at the incredulous look on Adrianna's face. Isak didn't appear to be finished protecting the witch, and wasn't *that* interesting?

"Don't make me hurt you," the witch warned.

Isak grinned. "You won't."

"I hate you," Adrianna muttered.

"That's not an unsurmountable problem."

Evalle sat down hard and laughed out loud as Isak's men spilled out of the Hummer-tank, locked and loaded as they searched the parking deck for any remaining threat.

Nope. The threat had taken off, but Evalle now knew what they were up against. A sobering thought.

Veronika hadn't been bragging.

She'd merely stated the facts and the facts were daunting.

One of Isak's men hurried over. Evalle recognized the super-sized operator as Laredo Jones, who had led a team to kidnap her for dinner with Isak one night. "Hi, Laredo."

"Evalle." Then he turned to Isak. "None of what went on up here was obvious on street level. Just a bad storm that kept coming and going."

Adrianna shoved an elbow into Isak's chest.

He barely grunted, but he did finally lower the witch to stand on her own and Adrianna glared her appreciation at him.

Isak's lips twitched. "I'll be back in a minute. Stay here until I know it's safe to leave." Then he walked off with his man.

Adrianna grabbed her hair with both hands. "I really might have to kill that one."

"Welcome to the world of Isak Nyght, where his opinion is the only one that counts." Evalle sighed and rubbed her arms. They felt singed from the inside out. She'd call up her healing powers as soon as she caught her breath. "Can Veronika do what she claims?"

"Yes."

"Could Queen Maeve and Cathbad stop her?"

"Maybe and that's a slim maybe, but those two would join ranks with her before fighting her. Any way you look at it spells disaster for humans and everyone in VIPER."

"Can we get Ragan away from her?"

Adrianna lowered her hands to cross in front of her stomach.

"I don't know. If I could talk to Ragan, the two of us might be able to use our power together, but I don't see a way to get close enough to do that. I'd have to have my hands on the sphere."

That would happen over Veronika's cold, dead body, and Evalle would be the first to admit Veronika was shaping up to be unstoppable.

Could VIPER talk the deities in the coalition into joining forces to take down Veronika?

Based on what Quinn and Adrianna had said, Evalle had a better chance of Sen throwing a party in her honor than deities sticking their necks out to take on an unknown power that had disappeared in the thirteenth century.

She had to go find Quinn to tell him what had happened and warn him about the Beladors linking.

How were they going to find the location where Veronika would set up to watch the eclipse?

CHAPTER 35

Storm walked out the delivery entrance of the five-story building, surprised to see the weather cleared up after all that noise for the last half hour. He waited for Cadee Ahearn to exit behind him, then he hit the button for the overhead door to lower.

He stepped back and let his gaze climb the brick walls. This had once been a textile plant, and he liked the changes happening.

Cadee read her notes. "You want to be able to sleep and eat here as soon as possible. I can't complete all the final decorating that quickly, but your bedroom, bathroom and kitchen will be usable in two days," Cadee said, drawing his attention to her. She frowned. "I wish I could pull this together as fast as I did your Midtown house, but I'm starting with nothing but open space here."

"I understand and I know I changed my plans for this building in midstream, but anything you can do will be fine. I only need the basics for now." Just enough living space to take the pressure off of Evalle. "You'll have all the time you need for finishing the rest of the living area, then we'll start on the office space."

"Even with that, you may not get your money back out of this investment."

"I'm not worried about that." He shook hands with Cadee and started for his truck. He started to call Evalle and realized it was close to daylight.

He opened his phone and found a text he hadn't heard over all the noise of the booming thunder outside and the construction racket going on inside.

Evalle had sent: *Guess you're still in town taking care of business. We need to talk ... about a lot of things, but mainly Veronika. She's in the city.*

His heart did a double pump as he finished reading the text.

Don't panic. I'm home in my underground bunker. She's going into hiding until the eclipse is done. We have no plan. Oh, there is good news. I found the evidence I needed for the Tribunal tonight.

How had she done that after he'd covered over a hundred and fifty miles today trying to pin something down?

Storm paused, leaned back against the brick wall and stared up at the sky, searching for a star, but nothing shined through the clouds hanging over the city.

He had to tell her what he'd been doing with this building.

Would he and Evalle be alive tomorrow at this time for him to confess his plan?

Would she hate his idea?

Would life ever go on in a way that was normal?

Normal. He had no idea what that word meant for regular people, but he wanted his and Evalle's version of normal ... and forever.

There was still the issue with Feenix.

Storm had left Feenix a toy, but it didn't appear as though the little gargoyle had even touched it the last time Storm had swung by. When Storm had tried to talk with Feenix, the gargoyle had ignored him. Was Feenix so determined to stake a claim on his territory that he'd never be willing to share Evalle?

Storm ran a hand over his face, so exhausted he could sleep on a bed of rocks. He wanted to think positive and believe that he'd still be able to hold Evalle tomorrow and their world would continue, but he was heading home now and would spend what time he could with her in his arms.

CHAPTER 36

Having located Lanna and Garwyli, Tzader now guided the girl through Treoir Castle. This place had been home to Brina's ancestors for millennia and was filled with memories both tender and traumatic.

He had to find a way to return Brina's memories of him, of them, or ... he couldn't face the idea of failure.

Or of her married to someone else.

Lanna cupped one of her tender hands against her chest. Lanna said Garwyli had cooed to her, smiling and talking as he'd healed her damaged skin. She thought he was amazing and Garwyli was taken with the young woman.

Garwyli also warned Tzader that Macha was on a tear, as if that was news.

"When did you return, Tzader?" Macha asked from behind him.

His neck muscles tightened at her annoyed tone and Lanna froze, but he gave Lanna's shoulder a squeeze and whispered, "You're fine."

When he turned around, Lanna did, too, folding her hands together in front her. The young woman acted as if meeting Macha in Treoir Castle were part of her normal day. "Hello, goddess."

Tzader thanked all the stars that Lanna had addressed Macha properly.

Macha scowled, but managed a curt, "Hello. What are you *both* doing here?"

Tzader had wanted to talk to Macha once he had Lanna settled, but wishing to have your way around Macha would result in leaving empty handed. He launched into what had to be said.

"I brought Lanna with me for Garwyli to heal her hands–"

"Why couldn't someone at VIPER take care of that?"

Tzader bit back his sharp retort. If he wanted to remain here, he had to appease Macha and get her on his side. "I could have gone that route, but I think Lanna might be able to help Brina. I'd like for you to allow her to spend some time with Brina ... and I'm here to do the same."

Macha's eyes almost ran out on stems. "What about your duties?"

"I've put Quinn in place as Maistir while I'm on leave."

Three, two, one... Macha snarled, "Who gave you the authority to make that decision?"

Tzader turned to Lanna. "Do you remember where Brina's solarium is?"

"Yes."

"Wait for me there."

Her expression held sympathy, but as she turned, she said, "Win this battle for Brina."

Once Lanna left, Macha said, "Now that we have privacy, explain yourself."

He considered Lanna's words. She had reminded him what the war was all about–bringing Brina's memories back–and he couldn't do that unless he convinced Macha that they had the same goal. He kept his arms uncrossed, showing he was open to discussion, but he was not accepting anything but a win.

"Is Brina's condition improving, Macha?"

The goddess quirked her head. "No."

"Is it getting worse?" *Say no.*

"Yes."

He had to put this in a context that would matter to Macha. "If Brina continues to lose her memories, where does that leave the future of the Beladors?"

Macha didn't answer, so Tzader suggested, "If Brina forgets entirely about what we had, she might choose Allyn, but I doubt that based on her reaction to him." Good thing. Tzader would rather not kill a castle guard. "Then what? Will you parade men in front of her until she chooses one? Can you insure her happiness for the rest of her life and guarantee the man she marries will be happy as a prisoner on this island?"

Macha actually flinched at that but they both knew she had no argument.

Tzader pressed on. "Will Brina and this unknown man's children care about continuing the Treoir dynasty and maintaining the Belador power base?" He paused, allowing that to sink in. "I have lived in the human world long enough to know what's out there. I have no oats to sow, because my world is here, with Brina. I will be content to live on this island and raise our children here. I will teach them about duty and honor, then once they're old enough, Brina and I will show them the world one at a time so that a Treoir is always here and the Belador power will continue to be strong. Tell me you can find a man to Brina's liking who will be that husband, and stand beside her to rule over the Beladors."

The goddess remained silent and thoughtful longer than at any time Tzader could recall in the past.

When she answered him, it was with resignation. "I shall allow Quinn to take your place until Brina's memories either return fully and she accepts you for marriage or she is incapable of recognizing you. If the day comes that she no longer knows you, then I expect you to step aside while she chooses a husband, because her duty is to procreate and my duty is to insure the future of the Beladors. Do you agree to those terms?"

Did he have a choice? "I'll agree as long as you don't interfere."

She huffed a sarcastic chuckle. "As much as you may believe differently, I do not interfere to amuse myself. I have enough to do with watching over our Beladors worldwide. I have interfered only for the greater good and I will do so again if I feel that cause is at risk."

Clearly, Brina's happiness was not part of the greater good, but Tzader had gained Macha's consent to stay here, which was the first step in his plan. He asked, "Will you allow Lanna to remain?"

"As long as she does not become a problem."

"She won't."

"You say that as if you have any control over someone with her level of powers who is also untrained. She will create havoc for you, which is fine as long as it doesn't disrupt my castle." With that parting warning, Macha vanished.

Tzader continued to the solarium, anxious to see Brina again. He'd spent four years standing on one side of an invisible wall, with her on the other.

Only one wall separated them now.

Brina's lack of memories.

When he strode into the room, Lanna sat next to Brina on the window seat where light filtered in through the leaded glass.

Lanna smiled and Brina seemed pleased to see her.

Tzader enjoyed a moment of pride over doing something that made Brina happy.

As he approached, Lanna looked up and her eyes turned wary. What was that all about?"

Brina lifted her head and studied his face with mild interest.

He'd never been nervous, but seeing Brina now took him back to the first time he'd met her and lost his heart when she smiled at him. He'd out-fought men older and more experienced than he was, and had spent time in the human world with his father for years, but nothing had struck him mute like Brina's smile.

She stood and Lanna jumped up, saying, "It's good to see you, Tzader."

Why was Lanna acting as if she'd just realized he was here, when they'd walked over from Garwyli's private quarters together?

Brina's lips curved up and the tight muscles in Tzader's chest relaxed until she extended her hand and said, "It's nice to meet you."

CHAPTER 37

Evalle rolled over to answer as the phone played the loud, obnoxious default tune from an unknown number. She reached for her cell phone, but her attention snagged on the empty spot beside her where Storm should be.

She answered, "What?"

"This is Rowan. I need help."

Evalle sat up, shoving hair out of her eyes. Why had she slept so hard again?

Storm must have used majik to influence her sleep. That had to be the only answer. She'd felt him crawl into bed and curl his body around hers.

"Are you there, Evalle?"

Shaking off the grogginess, Evalle said, "Yes, I'm just trying to wake up. What time is it?"

"Half past two."

"What?" That had to be two in the afternoon *again.* "We found Veronika last night."

"Adrianna called and told me."

Since Rowan knew the details, Evalle moved on. "Veronika says she's going to some secret place for the eclipse so we have no way to find her or stop her."

"You're right. All we can do is prepare for the battle once she shows up with her new powers. That's why I called you. I just heard that Coven Nikoleta—that's the band of solitary witches— has rallied their supporters and told them to meet in Newnan to decide who will lead all witches."

"They have a right to meet, don't they?" Evalle walked to the bathroom and washed her face with her free hand to clear out the cobwebs.

"Of course they do, but their meeting is set to coincide with the eclipse. Hermia has waited until the last minute to send out a message that Witchlock will be their salvation."

Now Evalle got the panic in Rowan's voice. "Oh, crap."

"Exactly. This can't be a coincidence with Veronika in Atlanta."

"I've seen someone she turned into one of her robotic minions, Rowan. Veronika might have done that to Hermia."

"If Veronika is behind this, Hermia and her coven of over two hundred will be her first victory, because Hermia is calling them all into one spot. It will be a slaughter. Hermia is young and mouthy, but she's got raw, impressive power that will be dangerous in the wrong hands. I'd hoped to create the council first then bring Hermia in to discuss a position on the council as my intern so I could show her the benefit of encouraging her followers to break into normal sized covens that would have their own leadership, then have them each send a representative when it was time for a new vote, but she's power hungry. She's taking advantage of so many young witches by turning them against what she calls the outdated old order."

Evalle estimated Rowan as being in her early thirties at the oldest. If so, Rowan was far from old, but she had a point.

"What do you want to do?" Evalle hunted for her shirt and jeans, tossing them on the bed.

"I called off the council meeting, because there is no time for that right now. I've asked the ruling witches of all the other covens supporting the council to join me in trying to disperse Hermia's group. We have no idea how far away Veronika will be, but if Hermia is already in league with Veronika, then she will hold them until Veronika arrives. Our best bet is to break up the gathering and get as many of them out of that valley as possible."

Evalle kept getting dressed with the phone under her chin, hopping on one foot, pulling on her jeans. "I can call Quinn and have him—"

"No. If you bring in the Beladors, you open the door for Sen to join us because it involves witches, which means it's not a purely Belador issue. You don't want to give Veronika a chance to get her hands on Quinn, especially."

"I told Quinn about finding Veronika last night."

"That's fine, because he needs to know, but knowing and facing her are two different things. Plus, as the Belador Maistir, Quinn must uphold the Belador agreement with VIPER, which would involve alerting Sen about Hermia's meeting. Sen's so unpredictable that he's the last person we want anywhere around this bunch. I don't trust him and I'm not sure he isn't in league with the Medb after what happened with you and the Tribunal over that demon body."

She had a point, but it limited Evalle's choices. "Can we bring in Lucien?"

"No. He only agreed to be security at the council meeting because I would have been in charge and there would have been fewer than twenty people there. He wouldn't have had to interact with any of them, because he knows I'm more powerful. Having him close by was to prevent Hermia from crashing our vote, but hundreds of witches? Lucien hates witches in a way that even I don't understand."

"He doesn't hate you." The words were out before Evalle could stop them.

"Uhm, Lucien and I have an understanding, but he really avoids anything to do with witches as a rule, and if one provokes him I'm not sure how he'd react. He's a lot more powerful than any of you realize."

That didn't surprise Evalle. She'd wondered about Lucien for a long time and respected Rowan's opinion enough to let that go. "Can Trey help?"

"Yes. He understands why he can't get near Veronika and why it would be disastrous for the Beladors if Quinn and the others showed up. You can't get near her either," Rowan warned.

Evalle had no interest in being turned into a winged pet for Veronika. "I'll get in touch with Storm and see if—"

"Trey moved Sasha and their baby to a bunker I warded in advance just in case this happened. I can't stop Trey from coming, because he's family, but he won't call in other Beladors. There's no way they can fight this unless Macha shows, and Quinn said Macha will not leave Brina unprotected."

That was true. If Macha left Treoir and Brina was taken again or killed, that would destroy the Belador power base.

Rowan continued, "Trey told me that Quinn asked Storm to

help them scout areas that Veronika might be using close to the city. Storm said he consulted a shaman in town who told Storm that he would receive a sign of where to find Veronika."

Evalle had just sat down to pull on her socks when a piece of paper caught her eye. "Hold on a sec."

She lifted a note off the nightstand that repeated what Rowan had just said, plus: *I didn't want to wake you. Call me when you get up. I know it's been strained between us, but for today, please be careful. I need to know you're safe. I need your love. I need you.*

Her heart did a crazy gymnastics workout in her chest.

Evalle clutched the paper in one hand and the phone in her other. "I'll meet you, plus I'll call Storm, but what about Adrianna being there?"

"I'm good with Adrianna, but keep her out of view because the rest of our covens want nothing to do with a Sterling witch. If she'd agreed to meet with us, I had hoped to change their opinion of her, but she didn't."

Evalle understood Rowan's frustration, but had to hang up soon and get dressed. "Okay, that gives us Trey, maybe Adrianna, Storm and me." If she could find Storm *and* convince Adrianna. "Give me the address and I'll be on the way as soon as I can."

"Thanks."

Clothes on, hair brushed into a ponytail and backup boots buckled, Evalle picked up her phone and texted Storm: *Where are you?*

Storm: *At Kennesaw National Battlefield with a shaman who's trying to help us find Veronika.*

Evalle: *Rowan needs help with a coven meeting. Can you meet me there?*

The phone rang and she hit the talk button. "What, Storm?"

"Why do you have to go?"

"Because they need help in case it gets out of hand. Rowan has a rogue group of two hundred witches claiming they're all in one coven. They'll be sitting ducks for Veronika the minute the eclipse is finished and she shows up to start collecting minions."

"That's what I figured. Stay home and let me–"

"No." She didn't snap or yell. She calmly drew her line for

this relationship. "I'm never going to be the person who stands on the sidelines to cheer the team. I have to be on the team and playing. I don't want anything to happen to you either, but I could never stop you from doing what you believe is right. That's just one thing I love about you. I have to do what *I* believe is right. I just told Rowan I was going, Storm. Now I'm telling you I'm going. I only called to see if you could help."

His silence televised his frustration. Finally he said, "I'll pick you up."

"You're twenty miles northwest of the city and the address is southwest in Newnan. It'll be faster for you to go straight there and for me to meet you."

More silence.

She had her own share of frustration. "What time did you come home?" She slapped her head. She had to get a grip on her mouth.

"Just after four."

She'd opened this Pandora's box, so ... "When'd you leave?"

"Six."

"Did you use majik on me?"

"You were exhausted and you haven't slept well or for more than an hour or two at a time unless..." He stopped and asked, "Did you get my note?"

"Yes. I loved your note. I just feel like my life is out of control right now and I ... want that life with you."

"I want that, too, sweetheart. I've been doing this all wrong. There's so much I want to tell you and I will once we finish with Rowan. I don't care if the Kraken crawls out of the swamp. Once we're out of this meeting, they'll have to fight it without us."

"Deal." Then she remembered to tell him, "I haven't had a chance to tell you what happened last night."

"Quinn gave me bullet points and that's why I hope this works with the shaman."

"What's he doing?"

"Right now? Staring at the sky."

Oh, boy. "I was hoping for something a little more active and deadly-sounding."

Storm huffed in amusement. "Doesn't always work like that. He told me I'd have a sign that would point me to Veronika. I'm leaving one of Quinn's Beladors with him. They'll call me with any updates."

"He can't do any worse than the rest of us and we're having as much luck as asking a Magic 8-Ball."

"I'll meet you and we'll help Rowan disperse her witches. Let's get through that and we'll figure the rest out from there. Okay?"

He was trying to reassure her. She stood. "Okay. I'll text you the address when I hang up and then I'm heading out."

"Be careful. I love you, sweetheart."

Her throat constricted. She knew he loved her, but she hadn't been doing a very good job of loving him back. "I love you, too," she whispered.

"Please don't try to get yourself killed."

"I won't." Evalle hung up, typed the address for Storm and had just hit send when a new text popped up from Adrianna: *I heard about the Idiot Convention in Newnan. I'm going.*

Evalle: *I was about to text you. Rowan wants to disperse the crowd and needs help, but why are you going?*

Adrianna: *V will show for that chum line of power. If it's too late to stop her before she takes on W, then we have one last chance if we catch her during the first hours of having Witchlock. If she's arrogant enough to show that soon, we'll have to try to stop her. Every day she'll get stronger.*

Evalle: *I wonder if Isak could get a fix on her location.*

Adrianna: *No. Just talked to him. He's not happy he can't find her.*

No one had sighted Veronika after last night's encounter. If Isak couldn't pin her down with his CIA level surveillance, it was a fair bet that nobody could.

Evalle: *I'm heading out now.*

Adrianna: *I'm at Colony Square. Want to ride shotgun?*

Air conditioning? Sold.

Evalle: *Pick me up at Five Points in ten.*

She shoved the phone in her pocket and grabbed her full-body riding suit, then hesitated.

With Quinn coordinating the search effort, he'd be doing it from the center of town, which would keep him away from Newnan.

If this went badly, surely Macha would pull Quinn into Treoir with her most prized Beladors.

Quinn and Tzader would take care of Feenix.

CHAPTER 38

Quinn searched the lawn at Piedmont Park for any sign of Medb, but all he found were runners, dogs playing catch, a toddler practicing a wobbly walk and lots of sunbathing on an unusually warm day for November.

This was a prime spot for watching the eclipse, but if Veronika wanted a secret place, this massive in-town park was not it. Still, he'd rather walk a section of the grid he'd laid out for his warriors than sit somewhere and wait for reports.

A woman in her late twenties sat cross-legged on a blanket with a little girl of seven or eight, along with bottled water and snacks. The mother held two sheets of letter-size paper, one above the other, and explained something.

He'd bet she had a hole in one sheet and was showing her child how they'd watch the solar eclipse expected in about ninety minutes.

Watching them together sent his thoughts to Phoedra.

Had someone shown his daughter how to watch an eclipse?

Swallowing hard, he kept moving when he should be home in bed, but sleep brought on nightmares. He rubbed his head, which now ached constantly. This bloody headache had started yesterday and he was ready to cut his own head off.

When he handed off this route to another Belador in thirty minutes, he'd go see the druids at headquarters. One of them could ease the pain, then they'd chew on him about getting decent rest, which he'd promise.

Maybe he could convince one of them to put him into deep sleep for ten minutes and then pull him out.

He kept rubbing his head and stumbled over a rise in the ground. He blinked to clear his vision. What was he doing on this side of the field and not back over on the sidewalk?

Quinn turned slowly, taking in the drop-off that led to the underpass beneath a bridge on the north side of the park

Red flashed into view.

There and gone, disappearing behind tall evergreens.

Evalle had told him about Veronika's red robe, and he'd known immediately that the woman in red he'd seen the other night was the KievRus witch. Not Kizira.

His pain had made him vulnerable, and he'd almost succumbed to Veronika's impressive powers of illusion, but according to all intel, Veronika should not have been in Atlanta at that point. He'd dismissed the possibility, and that was his failing. He'd had no idea who he'd been facing.

If he'd thought sharing that debacle with anyone would help this hunt, he'd have laid his soul bare for being vulnerable to that illusion of Kizira, but that would almost certainly remove him from the position of Maistir and force Tzader back home, for no good reason, when all the Beladors needed Tzader there with the Warrior Queen.

He'd seen flashes of a red robe a few times since then, but when he'd raised his energy shields and gone to check, Veronika hadn't been there. Of all people, Quinn knew the power of majik residue and the tricks it could play on the mind. He walked forward just to prove to himself there was no red robe here this time either. Veronika would not make it that easy to find her.

If she was here, Quinn would take control of that evil mind and show her the mistake of threatening his people and this city. He would hold her until Sen arrived and let Sen deal with her. He'd put Sen on notice that a deadly power had entered the city and Quinn expected Sen to come the minute he was called.

If Veronika gained Witchlock, there might be no stopping her. But Quinn had the power to reach out and grasp a mind. He'd never failed when he'd made an attempt and the most powerful monks in the world had said his mind was strong.

She'd shown her hand and played her trump card too soon when she'd fooled him by pretending to be Kizira. He was no longer vulnerable.

The further he walked, the more it was obvious that this area was a perfect spot for a private rendezvous. If there was, indeed, a red dress, it was a woman likely meeting her boyfriend.

When he entered the graffiti-covered underpass, the air warmed considerably, which seemed odd in the shade where it should be cooler. He paused in the center of the shade and opened his Belador senses.

Energy buzzed and he pivoted, searching for the source.

She stood with her side to him, the red robe flowing to the ground.

This is it. His heartbeat picked up speed as adrenaline surged through him. He sent power to his energetic shields, preparing his mind for battle.

She turned toward him, her robe billowing gently around her and she extended her hand with the glowing sphere in her palm. The energy around him buzzed even louder.

He reached out with his mind and ... his power tangled up.

Bloody hell.

He withdrew and reinforced his effort. He had to ...

He couldn't finish the thought. He took a step back as his head pounded harder and the pressure built until he wanted to wrench his own head off and throw it against the stone underpass.

That damned buzzing swept over his skin.

She pushed her hood off and there was Kizira again.

No! screamed inside his head. Kizira was dead. He gritted his teeth and forced that thought through the bees humming in his brain.

I won't let her do this to me.

"I miss you, Quinn," she whispered, the sound echoing again all around him.

Pressure built in his head.

Dear goddess. *That. Is. Not. Her!*

He grabbed his head and backed up farther. "You're not Kizira." That didn't stop him from drinking up every second of the vision.

She extended an arm, reaching for him.

No. No. No! Grab her mind now!

Forcing himself backward to avoid her touch caused him to physically hurt, but that was not Kizira. The monks had never been wrong in the past. *Why can't I grasp her mind?*

"Come to me, Quinn. I want you."

But her lips weren't moving.

His mind battled through the confusion.

He roared in his head, *That vision is not Kizira!*

He wiped at moisture trickling from his nose and it was blood. He grabbed his head. He had to use his mindlock and stop whatever was happening.

Gathering power and opening his mind, he mentally lunged out for her.

Blinding light burst inside his head. His knees buckled and he hit the ground. The world dimmed ... and disappeared.

He was on his way to join Kizira.

CHAPTER 39

"Next time we take my Gixxer," Evalle grumbled, one hand on the doorframe and the other clutching the center console. "Or your Lexus. What happened to that?"

Adrianna fishtailed on the dirt road, kicking up a dust storm behind her fire-red Ferrari. She smirked and cut her eyes at Evalle. "I was already in this one when I called. I trained in a 430 Scuderia just like this one with a professional instructor at Atlanta Speedway."

That didn't mean Evalle trusted the crazy witch out here, where if they hit one bad rut, this thing might go airborne.

"Pretty land," Adrianna mentioned, glancing around while handling the car. "So Grady had the same intel as the Nightstalker I found?"

In spite of Evalle expecting to get a mouthful of airbag any minute, she rewound her conversation with Grady at Five Points before Adrianna had arrived. She could not recall another time he'd been so agitated that he'd told Evalle his intel without asking for a shake. She couldn't have given him one right then anyway, because they were out in the open.

Evalle rubbed her neck, thinking out loud. "Pretty much. He heard a thirtyish woman, presumably a witch, trying to talk two other younger women into making this meeting. Sounded like what Rowan told me about Hermia. This woman kept telling the other two that this was a one-time opportunity."

Adrianna snorted. "Ignorance will get you killed."

True. Evalle continued, "Grady said the two women seemed hesitant until the one doing all the talking said they wouldn't have to answer to Rowan and a council. That the witch who would lead their coven liked the idea of the large number and that they would be more powerful than Rowan and her council put together. Grady also said he followed that same woman who said those exact words again to another female, like someone had hit a replay button on her."

Adrianna slowed for a deep dip in the road, then motored into a dense forest. "That's a bad sign. Sounds like Veronika has been testing her abilities and now that I think about it, Imar sounded like a robot."

"Yep. But we don't know if that woman going around with the sales pitch is a witch or just someone trying to be a witch."

"True. But the closer Veronika gets to the zenith of the eclipse, the stronger her power will be. The one thing I got from her when we met is that she's got a huge ego. She might be getting impatient. The difference is that it *should* take major effort to claim a powerful person now, but after she fully takes possession of Witchlock, she'll do the same thing with little effort. Still, even without Witchlock, between her KievRus majik and Ragan's power, she could get ahold of anyone if she finds a way past that person's shields. Without Witchlock, though, she doesn't completely own that woman yet, which means the connection can be broken before the eclipse."

"How would we do that when we don't know where Veronika is?" Evalle asked.

Adrianna puttered slowly now, on what had turned into a trail instead of a road. "There's a chance she'll come for me to bind my power to my sister's *before* she takes possession of Witchlock."

"Why would she do that?"

"With Ragan's power fueling Witchlock, Veronika would need about ten years to take over this world and maybe even a pantheon. If she combined my power with my sister's, she might only need a year."

"You really think no one could kill her?"

"Only because pantheons won't work together. They'll barely support the Tribunals. They'll never show each other their entire strengths or weaknesses, so while Veronika is stripping this world of every ounce of power, the deities will shut the gates to their own personal kingdoms and wait for someone else to deal with her."

"If Veronika does come looking for you, we might still have a chance to save Ragan."

"I can only hope."

Evalle added, "That's *if* Veronika doesn't kill you first."

"If she does and takes my power, you should pack up Feenix and leave with Storm. If anyone could hide all three of you, it would be Storm, because I meant what I said. Deities with enough sense will pull up stakes and prevent any opening Veronika could use to enter their pantheons."

"I thought deities needed worshippers to fuel their power."

"True, but non-deities have found ways into the secret worlds of pantheons before, and caused all kinds of problems. I'm telling you they won't risk it. Gullveig was never really known as a deity, but she had power, and she found her way in, then she wreaked havoc among the Æsir until someone finally figured out how to kill her. No pantheon will risk that Veronika could really be a descendant of Gullveig, because she could possibly enter their world in disguise and bring a god-killer power with her. The deities will pack up shop until they find a way to kill her."

Evalle tapped the doorframe. "That would solve our problem."

"Oh, sure, if not for the fact that a hundred years is nothing to an immortal, so they may not deal with her for centuries."

Adrianna stopped the car and shoved it into park. She must have caught Evalle's thoughts, because she said. "Macha and the other immortals haven't made it this long by putting themselves in jeopardy for lesser beings. I'll make a wild guess that Macha doesn't have enough room for all the Beladors and their families on her island."

"No."

"Fair or not, there's your answer. Let's go break up a party." Adrianna got out and had no trouble traversing the rough terrain in black jeans, short boots with low heels for once, and a lightweight black jacket over a black sweater.

Evalle pulled on the leather head covering she'd had made that hid all of her face, including eye holes shielded with the same dark lenses she had in her sunglasses, specially created for her unusual vision.

When she reached Adrianna, the witch gave Evalle a once-over and joked, "Is that your ninja outfit?"

"Hey, I'm not running around in an FBI jacket missing three yellow letters on the back."

Adrianna muttered, "Should have made you ride your bike."

Evalle heard voices and motioned for Adrianna to come her way. They stepped through the trees to the edge of a ridge overlooking a bowl-shaped clearing that was wider than a football field once it leveled out at the bottom. The sides stretching down from the ridge were gentle slopes covered in knee-deep grass, now turning brown for the winter.

This place would make a nice amphitheater.

Adrianna whispered, "I didn't believe Hermia could pull together that many witches."

"You don't have to whisper. There must be close to three hundred down there and they're all yammering." Evalle swung to Adrianna. "You know about Hermia?"

"I've known about her for a long time, well before Rowan did."

"Why wouldn't you meet with Rowan when she asked? Why is it you don't choose a side?"

Adrianna's expression iced over. "You really want to know?"

"Yes."

"White witches have been no better to me than Sterlings. My mother was the youngest of three ruling Sterling witches and the one slated to take over once the others stepped down. For that reason, her future husband had been chosen from the Medb coven."

"Seriously?" Evalle's jaw dropped. "The Medb intermarry with other covens?"

"Not as a practice, but this was a very special arrangement that would be advantageous to the Medb. The Sterlings intended to use my mother to gain a foothold in the Medb coven and insure Sterlings would continue as a dynasty. My mother, however, fell in love with the only son of the Spanish witch who ruled the Viaje de la Luz coven. You already know they're white witches. The name translates into Journey of Light, and that should tell you how well her choice in men went over with the Sterlings."

"Lead balloon?"

"Pretty much."

Evalle cringed over the fallout *that* must have caused and kept an eye on the field, where a trickle of new arrivals continued to join the crowd via what must be the front entrance to the property through a break in the trees on the far side. Adrianna had bypassed that entrance and opted for the dirt road. Not exactly the kind of racetrack a Ferrari was built to traverse.

Adrianna kept scanning the group as she finished explaining. "When the Sterlings realized my mother carried their future leaders, they put her inside the coven compound for her *protection*, as they called it." Adrianna made quote marks with her fingers in the air, and her mouth twisted in a mean smile.

"Sounds like the kind of protective facility Sen would put me in if he could."

"Almost that bad. When they realized she carried twins, they were even more determined to keep us out of the hands of a white coven. My father had the same battle on his end and walked away to get back to my mother, but he was found dead one mile from the Sterling compound. No one ever admitted what happened, but I've been around Sterlings long enough to know. They sent out witches who led him to his death. His mother wanted to start a war until she realized his two children would be at risk and backed off."

"When you left the Sterlings, why didn't you go to your father's coven for help in saving Ragan?"

"Because his mother made the same deal with Veronika as the Sterlings."

"You've got to be kidding. The white witches agreed to that?"

"Yep. They didn't have to turn over another witch, but she agreed that even though we were half Viaje de la Luz, she wouldn't lift a finger to stop Veronika from taking Ragan as long as Veronika left *her* coven alone. I don't trust either side. No matter who runs a coven, they'll only watch after their own and none would lift a finger to help me save Ragan."

Evalle wanted to tell Adrianna that Rowan *would* help her, but mere words would not erase the betrayal the witch had experienced on both sides. Evalle knew that first hand.

Shouting erupted in the center of the field.

Evalle and Adrianna moved as close as they could to the edge of the tree line and still remain out of sight.

Rowan stepped from the woods on the far side of the ridge. Guess there must be a third access into this property, but with over two hundred acres surrounded by residential developments, that made sense.

Fifteen women followed Rowan down the hill.

Rowan had brought the leaders of the covens that had been discussing joining the council. Evalle asked, "Why don't I see any male witches out here?"

Adrianna made a *humph* sound. "Those particular covens are all matriarchal. They have male witches as members, but the males are never put in positions of leadership. My father wouldn't have been either, but you can be sure his mother *still* expected him to marry a witch born to leadership—someone who would strengthen her coven."

"That's too weird in today's world," Evalle murmured.

"Some of the very old covens hold true to the traditions of their ancestors. Rowan may not act like it, or speak about those old covens, but her bloodline goes back a long way. You're getting ready to see the old clash with the new when they reach the bottom of that hill and Rowan tries to bring sanity to an insane situation."

Evalle needed to get down there and back up Rowan.

She'd promised Storm she wouldn't try to get killed.

She searched the tree line for Trey, but with his military background he'd know how to blend in. Where was Storm? He wouldn't know where she hid, but neither had he texted to say he'd arrived. She debated on texting him but he'd been unhappy that she hadn't ridden up here with him.

She was trying to give him space, especially since she knew he was checking out a new apartment, and *Where are you?* sounded ...needy.

She was not needy, dammit.

And now she was talking like Feenix.

But she did not want to place demands on Storm that would make him think twice about trying to make their relationship work.

Adrianna leaned forward. "I need to hear what's being said. The minute I hear Hermia's voice, I'll know if she's being controlled by Veronika. If not, then getting these witches out of here will be a whole lot simpler."

"I can power up my ability to hear but it won't help you."

"We have to get down there." Adrianna turned to Evalle. "If Veronika *is* pulling the strings on Hermia, you need to choose who you want to save and get them out of there."

"Can you cloak us?"

Adrianna chewed on the edge of her lip. "I can shield us with a no-see spell, but I don't have time or materials to create one that can protect you from the sun, and you can't use your kinetic powers while you're inside this cloaking."

"Can I get *out* of the cloaking to use my powers if I have to?"

"Yes. I'll make it so that if you step outside the protected area you're free to do what you want, but you'd be exposed at that point, too."

That sounded as safe as it was going to get. "Let's do it."

Adrianna turned to Evalle and took three steps back, then raised both hands, chanting quickly.

Just like the time a witch doctor had cloaked Evalle, the world around her appeared as though she viewed it through a glass wall.

Adrianna said, "You're good as long as you stay about this same distance from me. Get too far away and you're exposed."

That was actually better than the last cloaking, where Evalle had to pry her way out of the spell to use her powers. "Take off and I'll be right behind you."

To Adrianna's credit, she covered ground quickly, running downhill, and they reached the fringe of the crowd in time for Evalle to hear Rowan shout, "You have been brought here as sacrificial lambs for Veronika. She will not care for you. She will not protect you. She will take all of your powers and use them to rule you and to destroy all that you care for. The best chance you have to live a life of freedom is by walking out of here now. Do not follow Hermia to her death."

Hermia lifted her hands and called out a string of words.

Before Evalle could ask Adrianna if she understood them, Adrianna spun around and said, "That's a KievRus spell. See how blurry the grass and trees beyond this area look now? Hermia's chant has just flipped the switch on a spell that was already in place to enclose everyone here. She literally just shut the doors on Veronika's trap."

CHAPTER 40

Storm moved as quickly as possible through the dense forest, watching around him for any sign of nonhumans. The woods began to thin as he reached the ridge indicated on the map for the valley site of the gathering Rowan needed to disperse.

Now, where was Evalle?

He checked his phone, but still no reply to the text he'd sent two minutes ago.

She had to be here. Evalle was mule-headed stubborn when it came to protecting those she cared about.

Storm passed a bush and caught a whiff of ... a Belador. One he knew, and who'd been in this spot recently. He might not have recognized it if he hadn't been working so closely with Tzader's team for the past week. He moved with stealth, tracking the scent that lead him closer to the tree line where he could see the crowd responsible for all the shouting going on.

That was one heck of a witch bitchfest.

He didn't see Evalle. Even with the throng of hooded robes down there, because of her height she'd stand out in her full protective gear, which was all black. He'd have to look into having full body protection custom made of something lightweight. Maybe Mylar just for walking around.

Stick that on the mental list of things she needs that will allow her more of a real life.

First he'd have to talk to her about Feenix and that underground apartment, which he could have discussed on the way here, but she'd been right about him losing too much time going back into the city to pick her up.

Besides, riding out on her Gixxer might have given her a chance to unwind and feel free.

Tough to feel free when she was boxed in between duties to

the Beladors, duties to VIPER, a forced nocturnal life and now adjusting to a full-time relationship. And oh yeah...trying to clear herself from a murder rap.

Evalle needed a break.

He'd wanted to finish his downtown project before broaching the subject of ... everything, but waiting was only causing her more grief.

Trey stepped out from behind an old oak tree two feet in diameter. It grew right on the edge of the ridge where they stood. He wore dark aviator sunglasses.

Storm had on a pair of Oakley wrap arounds. "You couldn't have heard me."

"I could feel your energy."

Note to self: *Keep your mind off Evalle while in a potentially hostile environment.*

Easier said than done when she was foremost in his thoughts all day and night.

Storm angled his head toward the open field. "Evalle asked me to come help Rowan. What's going on?"

Trey scratched his scruffy hair, his signature bed-head look that actually made sense now that he had a new baby. "Hermia was here when I arrived. She had about a hundred and fifty at that point, but at least another hundred have shown up, maybe more, and Hermia has talked nonstop like a broken record. Sounds like a robot. I'd have stuck a sock in her mouth by now for no other reason than not hearing the same message repeated over and over."

"Have you seen Evalle or Adrianna?"

"Nope. Not a sign of them. Rowan just arrived and marched into Hermia's arena leading the ruling witches of fifteen other covens. All of them support the idea of a council. Rowan just gave Hermia's bunch a smackdown talking-to, then everything went quiet. I was moving forward when I felt your energy. I can't hear anything now and that's not right. I should be able to pick up any normal conversation by using my Belador hearing."

"Let me give it a try." Storm dropped onto his stomach and crawled to the edge while Trey mimicked his motion six feet to his left.

When he stopped, Storm's sharp jaguar vision could see

mouths moving, but not a word reached him. He told Trey, "Someone has dropped a privacy shield around the group."

"That'd be a hell of a shield to power. Maybe Rowan did that, but it would have taken a while for her and few more of the witches she brought to cast a spell that would wrap that crowd."

Storm agreed. "Even so, why would she do that knowing you're up here and expecting Evalle to show?"

"I don't know."

Storm checked his watch. The eclipse would start soon. He didn't like anything about this. "Can you reach Rowan by text and find out if she's behind the spell? If she is, why shut down the sound and not the visual?"

But Storm was glad to have eyes on them. If Veronika showed up here, this would look like an all-you-can-eat buffet for a shark.

Trey grumbled. "Not getting a reply."

"Maybe she's ignoring it."

"Nope. I sent a triple six code. We agreed on that. It means to respond immediately."

Storm looked at his phone. "Evalle hasn't responded either. He sent another text, telling Trey, "I sent you a test."

Trey checked his phone. "Got it."

"Shit."

"What?"

"If Rowan isn't getting a text and Evalle isn't getting a text, that means they're both inside that invisible barrier."

Storm shoved to his feet, not giving a damn who saw him.

Trey popped up next to him. "Where is she? Evalle's hard to miss since she's taller than most of those women and has to be covered from head to toe. And she's with Adrianna so we ought to be able to see a tall woman clad in black next to all that screaming blond hair."

Storm wheeled on Trey. "Evalle is with Adrianna?"

"Yep. Adrianna texted Rowan earlier. Said she'd be here, but that if Veronika showed, not to count on her for anything."

"Shit."

Storm sent a text to Adrianna, and a minute later had no answer. "Evalle's with Adrianna, and she's cloaked them with shielding."

"You're sure?"

"As sure as I can be. I can see Evalle and Adrianna deciding to move in close to be in the middle of things. Dammit, she promised me she'd stay safe."

Trey chuckled. "Evalle wouldn't lie to you, but she isn't going to stand back and just watch anyone she cares about if they're in trouble."

"Tell me about it."

"What's the plan? I can't watch Rowan's back from up here."

Storm's watch vibrated. He turned off the timer. "The eclipse starts in four minutes and lasts just over seven minutes. We have to—"

Veronika appeared in her red robe at the far side of the outdoor arena. She had two men with her.

"Fuck!" Trey's tension burst from him so fast it slapped Storm's empathic senses hard.

Storm snapped, "What?"

"That's gotta be Veronika. The crazy bitch has a Medb warlock with her *and* Quinn."

Storm looked more closely and identified one of the men Evalle considered a brother.

What the hell was Quinn doing with Veronika?

CHAPTER 41

Evalle whispered, "*Quinn?* That can't be him. And what's Veronika doing here before the eclipse?"

Adrianna stopped short in front of her. "It is Quinn. Veronika has him under her control. Her pet Medb warlock, Don, is here too, but he's probably more gopher than protection. She's insanely confident."

Evalle had directed Adrianna to move closer to Rowan, who'd positioned herself at the front of the crowd. Now Evalle and Adrianna stood between Veronika, who approached from the front entrance, and everyone else. "What do you mean she has Quinn under control? What has Veronika done to him? I'll kill her."

"Don't kill her until I get Ragan out of her hands. Veronika wouldn't have the ability to take full control of Quinn yet. She found a vulnerable spot."

"But how? Quinn has mindlock."

"I'm guessing she approached him and he reached out with his power. If he did, she latched on to that power long enough to find a weakness and take control of him."

Evalle's blood chilled. "If Veronika can do that to someone as strong as Quinn *before* she comes into her full power ... she's unstoppable."

Adrianna shook her head. "All she has at this point is a temporary leash on Quinn. It can be broken *if* we break it before the eclipse ends."

Evalle cast a look up to see the moon moving closer to the sun. "We still have like three minutes until it starts. Back to my original question. Why is Veronika here before the eclipse? It takes seven minutes to complete."

"My guess is that she found Hermia and arranged all this so

she could have a throwdown with Rowan *before* the eclipse, and before the witches here take their vote, to show how powerful she is in front of them all."

"Why?"

"Knock down the most powerful leader in view and the others will bow to Veronika without a fight. I knew she was arrogant, but I didn't expect this."

"Okay, but why Rowan?"

"I told you, Rowan is from a very old line, and is quite possibly the most powerful witch here other than me, if you count raw power combined with skill based on years of training."

Anger vibrated in Evalle's voice. "I will not let her have Quinn."

Adrianna looked at Evalle's gloved hands. "Can you use your kinetics if you step outside the boundaries of the spell?"

"Not while the sun is out. I need to have my hands uncovered to use my power, but Quinn would walk into a fight with one arm if it meant my life. I would do the same for him."

Adrianna froze for a second, then she met Evalle's gaze. "I've never had anyone willing to lift a finger for me except my sister."

"Then let's take her back from that bitch and save Quinn. As soon as the moon covers the sun, I'll use my kinetics and try to break Quinn free or distract Veronika as a minimum. Pull out your baddest mojo and lay it on her. Make her fight more than one of us at a time. I promise you Rowan will step up to the plate. She'll do whatever she can to help."

Adrianna nodded, eyeing Evalle with a glimmer of admiration and appreciation. "Thanks."

"We haven't survived this yet."

"That's why I'm thanking you now in case I don't have a chance later. You're here when I have no family or anyone else who would put their life on the line for my sister and me. I never forget a favor ... or a betrayal."

Evalle knew exactly what that felt like. She'd been there, and not very long ago. But now she had so many people in her world to love. She couldn't imagine life now without Storm, Feenix, Tzader, Quinn, Nicole and Lanna in it. She wouldn't give up even one of them. *Guess I'll have to add one annoying Sterling witch to that list if we live through this.*

Her heart ached. She could die without the chance to say goodbye to Storm. She'd put off their talk for too long.

If she got out of this mess alive, she'd never let anger or fear stop her from talking to him when it was important.

Rowan turned to face Veronika, who continued moving forward with her entourage.

Evalle stood two steps to the side of Rowan, but the witch had no idea she was there, which was a weird feeling. And it was also evidence that Adrianna had some seriously awesome mojo.

Rowan held up a hand, but did not point a finger at Veronika, which could be taken as an act of aggression since witches used fingers to throw all kinds of power. She shouted, "You are not welcome in our land, Veronika. Withdraw from here, with your minions and your majik, and return to the realm from whence you came."

Rowan's words sounded as though she weren't just from a very old line of witches, but that she was a much older witch than the contemporary woman Evalle knew.

Veronika didn't even slow until she was fifty feet away. She lifted her hand where the sphere burned bright in her palm and warned, "This is my coven and my people. The have come to witness the return of Witchlock. Bow to me now or suffer the consequences."

Rowan roared, "Never!" Then she raised both hands and called out, "Earth to sun, wind to—"

Veronika boomed a word in the same language Hermia had used, and Rowan went flying backwards, knocking down twenty women like bowling pins.

Evalle's hope did a nosedive. "Get ready."

Adrianna replied, "Waiting on you."

Veronika kept her other hand outstretched toward Quinn, who moved forward with her, but had a dazed look on his face. In fact, he hardly appeared to breath. Evalle put her hand on Adrianna's shoulder. "Quinn *is* still alive, right?"

"Yes. He's in the early stages of stasis. That's how she started with my sister. She will bleed Quinn of his power once she has Witchlock, and take control of his gifts."

Oh, *crap.* Evalle said, "If she gains control of Quinn, she'll have access to every North American Belador and secret information about Treoir. I have to get him out of that hold *now*."

"Wait until we get close enough for you to go for Quinn and me to reach Ragan," Adrianna said, working her way closer without bumping into the Medb warlock on this side of Veronika.

"What do I do? How do I break her hold on Quinn?"

"Get between her and Quinn. Your power will interrupt her connection to him. Other than that, you're on your own. Remember, once we separate, your cloaking will fail."

"Will yours hold?"

"I have no idea."

Lovely. *How come I always end up going in blind?* At least she was part of a blind *team* this time, and that felt good.

"In for a penny, in for a pound," Evalle said. "Time to kick some witch ass."

Adrianna raised one eyebrow, but Veronika addressed the crowd. "You must heed all that Hermia has told you. I have come to deliver you from the persecution of VIPER and—" She bent her finger in Quinn's direction and he walked forward. "—from under the thumb of Beladors. You will never fear for your safety or your freedom again."

Rowan gained her feet and turned to the crowd. "Lies! Run now, or she will take you all as slaves."

Veronika spit out something that sounded like a curse and a spike of energy arced from the sphere she held to strike Rowan, bursting into a ball of flames.

Adrianna yelled, "Now!"

Evalle broke away from the cloaking, shoved warlock Don aside, and lunged between Veronika and Quinn, which put her in the line of whatever hold Veronika had over Quinn. In that moment, as Evalle flew sideways, Veronika's majik stabbed through her.

The force of power held Evalle in mid-air for a second. She saw Kizira staring back and calling, "Quinn, stay with me."

Evalle blinked and Storm stood there, bleeding all over his body. He held out his hand. "I will always love you."

Everything vanished except the two of them.

Storm's eyes rolled back in his head.

No! She couldn't lose him. Evalle leaned forward, reaching for Storm, but the Medb warlock she'd shoved aside rammed her with his body, knocking her down and breaking the hold on her mind.

The chaos going on around her came flooding back into focus. Crud, no wonder this bitch could control people. She rolled away and jumped up, stomping her boots hard.

Blades flipped out around the edges of her soles.

The warlock came at her.

She stepped into a scissor kick that missed him by a hair when he flipped away. He called out words that were guttural and vicious sounding, then wound up his arm and threw a glowing red curve ball at her, which she dodged. She couldn't use her kinetics yet, because she still had her gloves on, but she had Belador speed. She somersaulted away, twisting to land on her feet.

A shadow moved over the grass from the eclipse.

Warlock Don came at her with an unholy look in his eyes and fire blazing from both hands.

What had Veronika done to him to rev him up this way?

All that fighting had taken Evalle away from Quinn, who was back under Veronika's control, following her as if a tether ran between Veronika's free hand and his neck.

Adrianna pushed against the power from Veronika's sphere, but it held her thirty feet back.

The crowd cleared a path for Veronika and no one interfered.

Correction.

Rowan struggled to her feet, singed from head to toe, but still alive. She started toward Veronika, saying in a raw voice, "You can't fight us all."

Evalle was starting to question her own statement to that effect.

She ran straight at Don, zigzagging at blinding speed to avoid his fireballs, and slid under the next one, slamming into his legs. He went down on his face. She came to her feet as he pushed up again. Evalle stepped forward and booted him in the head as hard as she could.

His head snapped back and he went flying ten feet, then stayed down with his head at an unnatural angle.

Veronika laughed at Rowan and whipped her sphere hand away from Adrianna for a second, to toss Rowan up and over Veronika's head and so far away that Rowan had to have landed outside the spelled enclosure.

That interruption gained Adrianna only ten feet.

But she had her hands up, yelling in what sounded like Russian to Evalle. Two dark bodies with solid white eyes, open jaws and red, glowing teeth shot up from the ground next to Adrianna, towering over her and turning their pointy claws toward Veronika.

Veronika split the power from the sphere she held to blow up those creatures.

Shock filled Adrianna's face.

Storm and Trey ran up to Rowan outside the invisible field. Where had they come from? Could they get inside? Storm turned and ran at the invisible field. He slapped his hands on it and was yelling something so loud, the veins in his neck stuck out. His hand glowed and his eyes turned red.

No, not the demon. Evalle would not be the reason Storm's demon blood rose to the surface again.

She needed her kinetics to break Veronika's hold on Quinn.

The sun was almost completely covered.

Any second now Evalle could peel off her gloves and ...

Veronika called to Adrianna, "Your power will join your sister's and we three will become one."

Power racing from the sphere in Veronika's hand shifted from pushing Adrianna back to flooding over her.

Evalle couldn't save Quinn and Adrianna too. In that moment, Adrianna looked at Evalle and mouthed, *Save Quinn.*

Then Adrianna's body shot up in the air, jerked left and right like a rag doll in strong wind. The arc of power spewing from the sphere to Adrianna brightened, but this one did not toss her the way it had Rowan.

The power engulfed Adrianna. She screamed in agony and arched backwards.

CHAPTER 42

Adrianna fought the pain that spiked through every inch of her body. She would not give that witch her power.

The moon sealed off the sun overhead.

No. Veronika can't win.

Ragan's voice spoke in Adrianna's head. *Now is the moment, sister. Veronika is greedy and wants to bind our powers before Witchlock takes over. Kill her now.*

Adrianna cried out, *I can't. I'm sorry. I have to save you.* Her body spun two rotations, then she still floated above the ground, flailing her arms and feeling her body being sucked dry.

When she could focus again, Adrianna saw the fight below. Evalle snatched off her gloves and took off running straight for Quinn and Veronika. She tossed a hand at Quinn, hitting him with kinetics that sent him flying twenty feet, then Evalle stepped into a kick, booting Veronika's hand hard and knocking the sphere flying.

Adrianna watched in shock as the sphere flew up in the air, straight for her. Ragan's panicked face came into focus, white eyes glowing. Adrianna reached out and grabbed the sphere as it passed her, laughing and crying at catching it until she realized her horizontal body still hung suspended in the air.

Ragan's voice shouted, "Stop her, Adrianna. Stop her now! I'll give you my power."

"No. I'm getting you out of there."

"You *can* stop Veronika. *Take my power!*"

Adrianna shook her head. "You'll die!"

"I'm already dead, sister. She fed my power into this sphere. The sphere and I are one. I will never have a life or a death as long as she controls Witchlock."

Evalle was pushing a kinetic wall at Veronika, whose hood had fallen away to show the vicious gaze that would kill a thousand as easily as it would step on an ant. But she wasn't looking at Evalle. She stared up, speechless at sight of the sphere in Adrianna's hands.

Then Veronika screeched in a blood curdling cry, "*Mine!*"

A black tornado of smoke spiraled down from the eclipse, spinning faster the closer it came to the ground.

Ragan begged, "Open our bond, Adrianna, and I will send you my power. Take it and kill her. Free me, please. Don't leave me to suffer any more. Open the bond on your side."

Adrianna's eyes flooded and the tears poured. She stared at Ragan and tried to breathe. After all this time she'd thought she could do the right thing to free Ragan, but she didn't have it in her to kill the one person she loved in this world.

Ragan looked up. "Veronika rushed the process bringing me from the realm. She made a mistake and opened herself up. I've gained Veronika's innermost thoughts. The second that tornado touches down, someone has to take control of Witchlock or it will kill everyone here."

Storm still hadn't broken through Hermia and Veronika's spelled wall.

Rowan wasn't moving.

Evalle continued to shove her kinetics at Veronika, but Evalle slid another foot backwards. She was losing ground and the sun would come out any second and burn her to a crisp.

Ragan sobbed and begged, "Please. You can do this."

Adrianna had no choices left. She looked at her sister and said, "I'm sorry. I love you."

"I love you and I know you love me. Stop Veronika. Do it for me."

Squeezing her eyes shut, Adrianna opened the bond they'd had from birth and Ragan's power flooded her. The burst of power washed across her skin and soaked into her body.

She opened her eyes and the sphere expanded until it engulfed both Adrianna and her sister. She reached for Ragan, whose fingers extended to hers.

The second they touched, Ragan gasped and began shrinking.

"Ragaaan!"

Ragan turned into a tiny spark that blinked out.

Adrianna's heart tried to climb out of her chest and grab her sister.

The sphere had vanished but Adrianna's prone body was still suspended thirty feet above the ground.

The tornado tip spun tighter into a narrow, twisting funnel, heading for Veronika.

Adrianna stared in horror. Veronika would gain both her and her sister's power. *What do I do?*

Storm crashed through the invisible wall, leaving it smoking. His eyes glowed demon red.

Ragan's voice whispered in Adrianna's mind. *Call Witchlock to you. That's all you have to do. Now!*

As if on autopilot, Adrianna's mouth opened and her voice called out, *"I command Witchlock to obey me!"*

Veronika's eyes rounded. She shook her head, reached toward the tornado and screamed, *"Noooo!"*

The tornado tip hovered ten feet above the ground, just out of Veronika's reach.

CHAPTER 43

Evalle's body shook. She wouldn't be able to hold this kinetic field against Veronika's power much longer.

A freakin' tornado had spun down from the eclipsed sun.

And headed straight for Veronika.

No, no, *no*.

As Evalle watched, the tornado paused, then curled away from Veronika, leaving the dark-haired witch slack-jawed as the spinning tip turned up at an angle ... toward Adrianna, who was glowing bright gold.

A blur flew by Evalle, and Storm hit Veronika so hard, he knocked her fifty feet, where she landed and slid across the ground in a pile of billowing red.

The pressure from Veronika's majik evaporated and Evalle fell forward on her face. Grace be to Macha, her arms were shot from muscle fatigue.

Someone rolled her over, and she tensed, ready to slam a power shot into whoever was touching her, but then she heard Storm's voice. "Are you okay, sweetheart?"

She looked up smiling even though he couldn't see her face beneath the ninja head covering.

Then she saw the full eclipse. *"Sun! Gloves!"*

He grabbed her hands and shoved them inside his coat as the first rays of sunshine struck the ground around them. He had her hands against his chest and she could feel his heart slamming like an engine in overdrive.

Hers was no calmer.

All of a sudden the air cooled around them. Adrianna dropped to her knees next to Evalle, with the gloves in her hands. She told Storm, "I've got you both shielded from the sun right now. It's safe to let her move her hands."

That would explain the temperature drop, even with the late-day sun coming back to full force.

Storm said to Evalle, "You haven't answered my question."

"I'm good. Help me sit up." Once she was upright, she carefully pulled her hands out and, when they didn't fry, she lifted her ninja headgear.

Storm kissed her.

She was alive. The people she cared about were alive and well. She was kissing the man she loved. Living arrangements were small bubbles.

"You two are nauseating," Adrianna chided, trying to sound light, but her voice held so much pain it hurt Evalle's heart, hearing her try to be chipper.

People were in chaos, running all around them.

Wannabe witches had changed their minds—imagine that—and ran for the exit path. Rowan looked like she'd been fighting a wildfire, covered in black soot from head to toe, but she had Hermia off to one side, unloading on her. Hermia had crossed the wrong witch, because after today there was no question that there would be a council of five or that Rowan would lead it.

Storm sat down with his arm around Evalle's shoulders. His eyes were their normal brown again.

Adrianna stared off into the distance.

Evalle said, "We didn't save Ragan, did we?"

"No."

"I'm sorry, Adrianna."

Adrianna swallowed and took a moment, clearly gathering herself back to the contained woman she always presented to the world. "It's okay. She's free. She asked to be ... released."

Evalle had to take some deep breaths to keep tears back. Adrianna had lost everything. "What happened with the sphere and ... Witchlock?"

Turning an intense blue gaze on Evalle, Adrianna said, "We thought we failed when we went to Jafnan Mir, but when Veronika found out we'd been there trying rescue Ragan, she rushed the process, taking my sister out of the realm too soon. She assumed Ragan would still be absorbed into Witchlock as planned, so Veronika didn't expend the energy to shield her mind from Ragan. But because she was taken out too soon,

Ragan had access to everything Veronika knew. Ragan knew that if no one took possession of Witchlock, it would destroy this world."

Evalle said, "Did you really ... call it to you?"

Adrianna nodded, eyes haunted.

"Is that how you could make a sun shield for me so fast?"

The witch nodded again. Pulling a hand from where it had been tucked against her body, Adrianna's fingers unfolded and a golf-ball sized, spinning sphere appeared in her palm.

Storm leaned in. "You *have it*?"

"Or it has me. Only time will tell." Adrianna looked at Evalle with a sad smile. "But as far as I know, I now possess the most powerful witchcraft on this planet."

Evalle cocked her head, staring at the spinning ball. "I thought only a marked KievRus witch could wield Witchlock. How can you..."

"I don't know. Ragan and I have—we had—exactly the same powers. She was stronger, but whatever one of us could do, the other could do. All I can figure is that Veronika set up a screaming-strong link to Ragan so she could draw on Ragan's power, and through that, Ragan somehow gained Veronika's ability to call Witchlock to her. Then when Ragan and I opened our bond, I guess I gained that ability too. And the ability to at least *hold* Witchlock. Whether or not I can actually wield it remains to be seen."

The responsibility of what she'd taken on showed in Adrianna's eyes. And alongside it, the fact that she'd trade all that power for her sister without question.

Evalle had no idea what this meant for the future, and she had no idea whether her concern would be welcome, but she took a deep breath and said, "I know you didn't want it, but you'll make the right choices with that power."

Adrianna folded her fingers closed and the ball of light vanished. She glanced over to where Quinn and Trey had Veronika bound and under control. Twenty Beladors had arrived, probably at Trey's call, and were dealing with the crowd.

Lucien was there, too, and the look he was giving Hermia threatened far worse than Rowan's scolding, but when his gaze shifted to Rowan, she looked up and smiled at him.

Hermia would be safe from Lucien's wrath only because Rowan had her hand on Hermia's shoulder in a clear sign she was now under Rowan's protection.

Evalle's gaze strayed back to the Beladors. She was glad to see that Quinn looked like Quinn. She turned back to Adrianna. "Are you sorry we didn't kill Veronika?"

Adrianna sighed. "I could have killed Veronika the minute I took Witchlock, but my sister and I swore to never follow the dark witch—or the white witch—ways. My sister died to keep dark power from wreaking devastation on this world. It would be a travesty to use that power only to take a life, even Veronika's, because yes, Veronika has some juice, but once she lost Ragan's power, she was no longer a threat. At least as long as witches like Rowan are around."

And you, Evalle amended silently.

Storm added, "And as long as VIPER keeps her locked up."

Quinn walked up. "Evalle, I..."

She jumped up and hugged him. "I'm so sorry she used Kizira to get into your head."

Quinn hugged her back. "I screwed up. I believed I could take control of her mind and bring in Sen to lock her up. I'm ... not fit to be Maistir. I should—"

She pulled back and finished his sentence. "Accept that you're human." She gave him a soft smile. "Okay, not really, but sort of. As much as any of us are, because we're *all* vulnerable one way or another, and please realize we need you. This shows how *much* we need you. She'd have gained full control of anyone weaker than you."

"Maybe you're right." He pulled his hands back and raked them both through his hair. "It was so ... real. I tried to use mindlock to fight her, but—"

Adrianna interjected, "That was her gift, Quinn. She could draw an image from any thought. She didn't even need to get past your shields. Once you reached out with your mind, she only had to pull up enough visual to attack your most vulnerable point. I'm just starting to figure out some of the other gifts she had, and intended to abuse."

"What do you mean?" Quinn asked as Storm stood and pulled Evalle next to him again.

The men in Evalle's life were protective and possessive. She'd just have to accept that.

Adrianna stood, too. She looked around and leaned in, keeping her voice down. "I think Ragan's power brought me a mirror of Veronika's consciousness."

"Like a backup hard drive?" Storm asked.

"Something like that." Adrianna looked around again and added, "Veronika had some truly ambitious goals."

"What else did the egomaniac want?" Evalle asked.

"I told you she'd need maybe ten years to take over this world unless she gained my power, but she planned to go up against Queen Maeve first thing."

"Wow. She was more mental than I'd have thought possible."

Quinn shook his head and said, "Evalle, I hate to bring this up, but we have to meet the Tribunal in eight hours."

Storm's arm tightened. "See if you can get an extension."

Adrianna broke in. "He doesn't have to, because we found out the truth last night."

Storm stopped. "You said a warlock confessed last night. Who is he?"

Evalle supplied the answer. "Over there on the ground with his head hanging at the wrong angle. While we were on our way to dinner, Veronika and that Medb warlock, Don—" She tossed her thumb in the direction of the dead one. "—admitted making the demon from another warlock, and adding the glamour. Don is the one who took the body and gave it to Cathbad. But then our enterprising warlock, Don, moved up to the big leagues with Veronika. Whatever he'd been up to sounded as if it hadn't been sanctioned by the Medb, believe it or not."

"Too bad he's dead. What are we giving the Tribunal for evidence?" Quinn asked.

Adrianna answered, "Me. I'll testify and they'll accept that since I can't lie in a Tribunal."

Evalle thought on that. They wouldn't accept *her* not lighting up red as evidence, but the Tribunal wanted an end to the Medb and Belador issues. When Adrianna didn't light up, they should take that testimony as truth. Evalle recalled Tzader's comments at the Tribunal and asked, "You think Cathbad will end up sanctioned?"

Quinn sighed. "Probably not. The Medb will find some way to prove their warlock was either rogue or coerced into doing this, and testify that Cathbad knew nothing. As long as he doesn't light up, he'll get away with it by offering to call it all done." Quinn glanced around. "I've been through a few legal battles in my time. You have to think like your opponent."

Stepping back, Quinn said, "Please excuse me. I need to speak with my Beladors."

"Wait, how did the Beladors know about this? Did Trey call them?"

"Yes. When he and Storm determined that the shielding around this gathering was of hostile origin, Trey called for any Beladors who could get here, and told them not to link."

Evalle nodded, and when Quinn walked away, she asked Adrianna, "Why would Veronika go after Maeve first?"

"I'm not sure. All I've picked up was an obsession with a dragon that belongs to the Medb."

Storm said, "That's new. Why would Veronika want a dragon?"

Adrianna tapped a long red nail against her chin. "I don't know, but I intend to find out. I know Ragan wants me to..." She paused. "I can't explain it, but I can feel when she's gently pushing on a thought." She drew a deep breath and her voice lost the thickness when she spoke this time. "I suppose since Storm is here, you don't need a ride home."

"Thanks, but no," Evalle replied. "I've had all the terror I can take for one day."

"This from the maniac on a Gixxer."

Evalle narrowed her eyes at Adrianna. "Let me know when you want to see what it's like to take curves laid over close enough to touch the ground."

"Pass." Adrianna told Storm, "Her sun shield will follow her to your truck, but you only have about ninety minutes left to worry about." Then she gave Storm the words he'd need to break the spell.

"We'll be home in half that time," Evalle said, then extended her hand to Adrianna, something she'd done only once before. That first time had surprised the witch because you didn't touch a witch unless you had no choice. When Adrianna took her hand,

Evalle said, "Thanks for taking Witchlock and ...you know if you
need me..."

Adrianna glanced at Storm, then back at Evalle. "I know."

"I hope Ragan's at peace."

Adrianna nodded, then walked away.

Evalle searched the area for Rowan, who wasn't hard to find
since only Rowan, Hermia, Veronika and the Beladors were left.

"I don't know how Rowan didn't turn into charcoal after
Veronika torched her."

Storm explained, "I'm thinking she saw it coming and called
up a protection spell that minimized the damage."

Evalle called over, "Rowan? Are you okay? Your clothes are
smoking."

Rowan met Evalle's gaze and answered, "I'll be fine. Come
by this week and we'll talk about the council."

"I will."

"Thanks for being here."

Evalle smiled and shrugged then Rowan's sweet look
vanished and her don't-piss-off-Rowan face returned when she
started in on a humble-looking Hermia again.

Storm turned Evalle around to face him. He stared at her so
long she fidgeted and started talking.

"I didn't get a chance to tell you about last night because you
didn't wake me up and I know we could have talked on the way
here, but–"

"Stop."

She didn't. "I want you to be happy and I want Feenix to be
happy and I want–"

He shook his head and sighed then he kissed her, and kissed
her again until she forgot about talking.

CHAPTER 44

"Wake up, sweetheart."

Evalle blinked and shook off the dregs of deep sleep. She looked around, orienting herself.

She was inside Storm's truck.

With Storm.

All was good in her world.

She sat up and looked around as Storm drove north on the interstate toward downtown Atlanta. She stretched and ran her fingers through her hair that had to be scary by now. "Did I sleep the whole way?"

"Yes. For the first time this week, you slept without nightmares ... or majik," he said, mouth tight from some unhappy thought. "You can be angry with me for using my majik, but I can't watch you struggle even in your sleep."

"I'm okay with that. I've just been..." A bitch? "Grumpy."

"Stressed and worried is more like it," he amended. Then he changed the subject. "Tell me all of what happened last night with Isak."

Might as well get this done. "I met him at Six Feet Under, but he didn't want to eat there."

"Of course not," Storm growled.

"It was fine. Adrianna showed up." Evalle smiled at him. "She said you sent her."

"I told you I wouldn't leave you alone with Isak. I don't trust that bastard."

She shouldn't be smiling even bigger over that, but she could admit that Storm's possessive side sometimes warmed her heart. Sometimes it made her want to pull her hair out, but she could live with that, too. She had to put this whole Isak issue behind them, because she doubted Isak was going away completely.

And to be honest, she wanted him in her life, just not between her and Storm.

Evalle cared about Isak and Kit, and she still wanted their friendship. "I don't think Isak is focused on me anymore."

Storm glanced at her, but she saw no sign of his being convinced, so she explained, "We fought Veronika and her Medb minions." Evalle lifted a hand to dismiss it. "I'll tell you more about that later." When Storm gave her a nod, she said, "When Isak stepped in to help, he shoved Adrianna behind his back to protect *her*."

The look of amusement on Storm's face brought a chuckle from Evalle. "Yeah, I know. Adrianna found it hilarious, but didn't let Isak know."

"I don't care who he goes after as long as he stays away from you, but that sounds like an unlikely pair."

"Don't discount Adrianna. She's more likely to make it work with Isak than I ever could." Evalle snapped her lips shut. That had sounded better in her head. She'd just given Storm a reason to continue questioning her relationship with Isak, when that had been meant as a statement of her own lack.

After an uncomfortable silence, Storm asked, "Does the possibility of those two together bother you?"

Evalle turned quickly to face him. "No. Not even a little. I never wanted Isak. Only you."

"You don't regret being my mate?"

"Me? I got the best end of this deal. I can't cook or do anything like other women. Or look like a normal woman. You're the one who ended up with a—"

"—beautiful, sincere, amazing woman I thought I'd never find. I don't care if you can cook, because I like to cook."

"You're kidding." She stared, open-mouthed for a minute, until he raised one eyebrow. He *wasn't* kidding. She muttered, "Good thing or we'd starve, since no one can deliver to a basement apartment with no public access."

"Speaking of Adrianna and working together," Storm said. His tone was smooth and even, but she could feel his tension jack up a notch. "She told me she tried to go with you when you followed the glamoured demon at Stone Mountain Park. You made her wait behind. Why didn't you take her with you?"

Oh, shit. *Busted.*

She clenched her jaw to keep from yelling at him to back off, that it was none of his business. When she sat there, silent and grinding her teeth, Storm took her hand, circling his thumb over her skin in soothing circles. "It's okay. Just say it, sweetheart."

"I work alone. I don't need anybo–"

She couldn't finish the sentence. It sounded hollow. Stupid. She stared out the window as her heart pounded.

He said, "I promise I'm not trying to force you into a corner, but Adrianna was your backup. I can't help thinking that if she'd been with you, things might have gone very differently."

Evalle hated the knot of shame that clogged her throat. "And I would've had a witness for the Tribunal in the first place."

"That too."

Talk about a double standard. She'd been worried sick about Storm all last week while he hunted the troll killer, and he'd had Trey and a Belador team with him.

Evalle could feel the tension in Storm, but she also felt it wrapped in a deep need for her. He was protective, but she knew what fueled it. Love and the fear of losing her. He was trying to lighten up on her, and she needed to suck it up and meet him half way. "I don't know. Old habits die hard I guess. Having people I can trust to watch my back—I'm not used to it."

"I know. It's okay."

Storm tightened his grip on her hand, but said nothing for a while and she wondered what he was thinking as he drove through downtown. As for her, if she wanted to make this work, she needed to figure out why she'd dumped Adrianna at the park when they both knew she might be going after a demon.

She sat up. "You missed our exit."

"I know. I have somewhere to stop first."

Sighing, she reached down to the floorboard for her gloves since she still had just over a half hour until the evil sun disappeared.

Storm caught her arm. "You won't need them."

That meant wherever they were going, she'd have to stay in the car like a kid who couldn't be out where it wasn't safe. A simple stop on the way home and she couldn't even step out to go with him without looking like some ninja from hell.

Then they'd have to go home to a place that didn't feel like a real home.

She had to ask, "Do you miss your house?"

"No."

He didn't say anything else so she hit the topic straight on. "Living underground will get old. I'm used to it. I know I have to be there, but even I have a limit to how much I can stand being there. I've been finding it confining lately."

"You wouldn't have to stay hidden during the day if–"

She lifted a finger to his lips before he apologized again. "I do not regret losing my ability to walk in the sun, only that I'll never be able to do normal things other women can do with the men in their lives." She blinked back the sting in her eyes. Tears would only make him feel worse.

He kissed her finger and took her hand in his, moving their hands to the console. "I'm sorry for being an ass lately, but I'll make it up to you."

Evalle couldn't believe he was apologizing. Sure, he'd been testy, but he never complained. She said, "The friction is not your fault. I asked you to move into a basement with a territorial gargoyle and live in the dark."

Holding tight to her hand, which prevented her from stopping his words this time, he said, "Not just about that, but I told you I'd live anywhere as long as you're there and it *is* my fault you can't walk in the sun."

"Not true. I was born this way. That only changed when I evolved into a gryphon. I only had the ability to be in sunlight for a day, so I didn't lose something I'd had a long time." Not like Storm, who had grown up in a world filled with daylight. She'd started on this and now the truth pushed its way out. "It's not that I need to spend every day in the sun, but ... "

"What?"

"Nothing. It's silly."

"Tell me." He rubbed his fingers over her hand. He'd pulled off the interstate and was still driving one-handed, weaving his way through the city. Where was he going?

When he squeezed her fingers, she got the message that he wanted her to finish. Baring her soul this way felt risky, but it was looking like Nicole was right. That came along with the whole relationship package. Storm was the only one she'd allow to see her vulnerable.

"I can watch the sunset from inside this warded truck, but with the heavy tinting on the glass it just isn't the same as watching the sun set for real through a clear window. I just want to share little things like that with you."

He lifted her hand and kissed her palm. "I understand and it's not silly to want to experience the world like any other woman."

But she'd never be just like any other woman and the sooner she accepted that, the sooner she'd figure out how to be a better mate.

He made a couple of turns that circled closer to her apartment. They entered an area of Atlanta being reclaimed from years of neglect after industry and businesses had moved to new locations.

Reaching up, Storm pressed the button on a small remote clipped to his visor. She hadn't noticed it before.

She took in the building and her pulse tripped into high gear.

This was the building she'd seen Storm visiting with some woman when she'd watched the video display in Isak's Hummer.

Storm had said he would make everything better.

She prepared herself to pretend this was a great idea. She could do this for Storm. He'd clearly gone to trouble to find a place to live near her.

She would not let this come between them.

Storm pulled his truck inside the dark space lit only by the late-day sun. It covered half a city block in both directions. Construction for the commercial area on the street level had begun. He'd originally planned offices for every floor but the top level.

He'd changed his mind about that a week ago.

Evalle had grown quiet the minute he drove through the garage door opening. He clicked the button, closing the overhead door so that no sunlight reached inside.

He gave her fingers a little squeeze. "Wait for me to open your door?"

"Sure."

She said that with a perky look, but she was not happy.

He started to reconsider this stop as premature, but the tension would not ease for Evalle until he showed her what he had in mind.

When he reached her door, she'd pulled off her jacket and was down to her shirt, black jeans and boots. She stepped out and looked around at where old walls had been ripped out and new ones were now being constructed.

She said, "I know you were here with ... that blonde."

Storm's only thought jumped from his lips. "How?" *Way to go, moron.* That sounded guilty as hell and he hadn't done anything wrong.

"Isak has elaborate surveillance equipment and tapped into the traffic cam that must be on a pole outside this building. It filmed in real time last night."

Isak would be lucky to see his next birthday if he didn't stop interfering in Storm and Evalle's life. "Did you think ... what did you think?"

Evalle took a moment. "I do not think you're seeing someone else. Give me more credit than that. I trust you and I trust your love."

He reached for her and she came to him, returning his kiss with the passion that always simmered just beneath the surface with her. This woman owned him inside and out.

And if he let this kiss go any further, he'd forget about why he'd brought her here now. He paused, then kissed her cheeks and nose.

She laughed. "What brought that on? Not that I'm complaining."

"I've known you trust me, but I had a sick moment of panic when you told me you'd seen me here with another woman and I hadn't told you about this place. Do you have any idea how amazing it is to have your unconditional trust like that?" Just another Evalle gift he would always cherish.

"Then tell me next time so I'm not blindsided in front of people, especially Isak."

"That guy needs to go away."

Her body went rigid. "He's not going away, Storm. And I'll be honest. I don't want to lose him as a friend. I don't have a lot of friends. Each one is important to me."

Storm looked away, thinking then brought his gaze back to her. "You're right. I've never had to deal with jealousy before because I never wanted anyone the way I do you."

She smiled, but he had to man up and make this right. "Isak and I will never become chums, but he did help you when I couldn't be here. I'm glad you had friends then and I will support any friend of yours. Even Isak. I owe him my respect if nothing else. And I know I have to respect *your* choices and decisions. I've been letting this unholy fear of losing you screw with my thinking."

That brought out an Evalle smile capable of stopping his heart. She lifted her fingers to his cheek. "Nothing in the world is more important to me than you are ... except being free. I spent the first eighteen years of my life imprisoned and with someone controlling everything I did. I spent the following years walking a tightrope and dancing between remaining free and facing being locked in a box just because I'm an Alterant."

His jaguar wanted out to punish the people who'd rained those injustices down on her, but he forced the animal back down. Evalle had fought her own battles back then. Storm would be there to back her up in future battles, but he had to let her live her life and decide when to fight and when to stand down.

She said, "I'm done with going along to get along when it comes to Macha, VIPER ... anyone. I know your actions come from your heart and you'd do anything for me, but all I need is to feel free and loved."

He cupped her face. "You are so loved, you have no idea."

"I think I do." She smiled then turned serious again. "I love you, but I can't allow anyone to control me. Not even you, and not even when you have my best interests at heart."

"I'm thick headed sometimes, but I get that and never want to make you feel as if I'm trying to control you. There is no controlling a force of nature." He kissed her.

"Now, tell me about your secret building."

Storm's guilt came back with a double hit. He'd been putting off talking about this until Evalle was ready and he'd unintentionally embarrassed her. "I wasn't hiding this from you." The pain that shot through his chest at that lie brought a groan.

"Want to rephrase that?" Evalle suggested with a smirk.

He rubbed his chest. "I *was* hiding this from you, but as a surprise for you. I wanted to wait until the right moment. Things were so hectic and I didn't want to add to the stress you've been under."

She sobered at that, but drew herself up and stuck a smile on her face again that he didn't believe. She glanced around, "So. What *were* you doing here?"

"I've been buying and selling real estate in Atlanta since I got into town. Cadee Ahearn, the blonde you saw, is my realtor. She's also a designer and a Belador."

"A Belador? You're kidding."

"Nope. I've been watching this building for a while. It's prime commercial real estate and the old man who owned the restaurant on the ground floor passed away. His heirs closed the business. When I first told Cadee that I'd buy the building, I told her the old guy could stay as long as he wanted and we'd keep the leases low, but when he died I just let his family out of the lease, which they were happy about." He waited for Evalle's reaction.

She still had that phony grin in place. "Nice."

Storm would get to the bottom of this pseudo-enthusiasm later. He had to show her why he'd brought her here. "Want to see it?"

"Sure."

He sighed at how hard she seemed to be trying and took her hand, leading her to the stairwell. "The elevator has to be remodeled and certified."

"I'd like to know more about what you do with investing and ... just more." She followed him up, still talking as if they were on a first date and she was determined to impress him.

When had Evalle ever thought she had to do that?

Just watching her wake up in the mornings took his breath away.

On each floor, Storm explained what the crews were doing. On the third floor, he bypassed the door, explaining, "That's not ready to be seen yet."

She didn't comment until they entered the top floor where plumbing had been completed and many of the walls were up. Furniture had been delivered that was stored on one side and the kitchen was underway.

Evalle froze.

She stared at the furniture, her throat moving, but not saying a word.

Storm caught her hand. "Are you okay?"

"Oh. Sorry." She looked around, eyes hunting for something. "The windows. I was glad to see they're covered with black tarp since sunset isn't for another twenty minutes."

She tried to sound lighthearted, but she was breaking his. There came that empty smile again when she asked, "Is this one apartment?"

"Yes." He tugged her over to a wide spiral staircase a few feet away. "Want to see the last floor?"

"I thought this building had four floors."

"It sort of does. I've had work being done on the roof that I want you to see."

Evalle couldn't keep up this level of happy much longer. She needed to go out tonight and find a demon to kill.

Storm's excitement and trepidation kept brushing her empathic sense.

The conflict had to be due to him picking up her emotions, which she figured weren't matching her expressions at all. She could smack-talk a troll, but trolls were stupid. Truth was, she had a lousy poker face and Storm was not fooled.

She tried to envision what he'd built on the roof and it must be some four-walled room since the sun was still out and he wouldn't risk frying her to a crisp.

When he opened a door at the top landing area, she stared at the bright glow outside and snatched her hand back. "Storm ... this is a bad idea."

"Trust me?"

"Of course."

"Then take my hand."

She pulled in a deep breath, heart hammering away, and

accepted his hand the way she'd accepted his love, scared as hell but determined. As she stepped through the door, she flinched at the first thing she saw.

The sun still hovered just above the horizon.

Nothing burned her skin.

She looked around where every wall had a wide view of the city in all directions.

Words weren't possible.

How was she standing in the center of a room filled with sunlight? Tears burned her eyes and she stood awestruck as the sun slowly dropped toward the horizon.

Storm nudged her forward until they stood in the center of the room, then he wrapped his arms around her, pulling her back to his chest.

She kept waiting for the sun to burn a hole through her.

He held her quietly as she soaked it in.

When she could speak, her throat was raw with emotion. "How? How can I be standing here?"

He kissed her hair and his deep voice rasped across her senses. "I chose this property right after I met you to put me closer to you than my Midtown house, and the construction started the day I went with you to your apartment for the first time." He hugged her to him again. "It's not that I don't like it or that I won't live down there. I'll live in a hut if it makes you happy. But being in that apartment reminds me of how much you've given up for everyone... especially for me."

She swallowed hard, fighting tears.

"I offered an incentive to the construction company last week and they've been running crews around the clock. Cadee helped me get the roof enclosed with a material that's similar to a bulletproof, one-way Plexiglas with no more tinting than a standard window that looks clear. I brought in a shaman from my father's tribe and told him what I wanted."

"The one who went to Kennesaw with you?"

"Yes. He said I'd receive a sign when it was time to find Veronika. Now I realize that you calling me to meet you was the sign. I wouldn't have left his side for any reason other than you."

She said nothing, but she felt his love wrap around her like a safe blanket.

He continued explaining. "The shaman had spent the last two days and nights performing an ancient ritual that basically wards this area on the inside so that you can see the sun, but it can't touch you. And he blessed it for us."

"Us?"

"I told you I go where you go. You can watch all the sunrises and sunsets you want."

Tears streamed down her face. Storm had brought the world to her. "Thank you."

"The first floor of the building beneath us will be our living quarters with the same kind of windows, and it's being finished out for me, you and Feenix."

"He'll be better and I promise ... "

Storm pulled her around and kissed her. She could give up everything in life to feel his kiss. When he stopped, he said, "Feenix is fine."

"But he ate your buckle."

"I'll get another one."

"That one was from your dad."

"There's enough left for me to have it remade." He used his thumbs to wipe away her tears. "I spent some time with Feenix. He knows I'm not taking you away from him."

She thought she loved Storm. What she'd felt for him had been nothing compared to this moment. "We'll get him more toys and lug nuts."

Storm continued explaining, "I've got plenty of things planned for Feenix's entertainment. He needs company when we're away and more room, too."

"You'll spoil him."

"Not as much as I plan to spoil you." He hugged her tight to him. "I'm so sorry for making you unhappy. I just ... " He swallowed. "Never expected to find someone I couldn't survive losing, but I have nothing in this world without you. Living together will work out and I need you to accept that you are everything I could ever want in a mate."

She looked around as the sun sank lower, then back at him. She brushed black hair off his forehead. "What can I ever do to make you happy the way I am right now?"

He dipped his head and almost kissed her, pausing to say,

"I've never made love with you as the sun set. That would make me very happy."

"Then prepare to be euphoric."

The End

MORE BOOKS FROM DIANNA LOVE

Rogue Belador
Book 7 – April 2016

Tzader Burke uncovers a secret within the Medb coven that threatens to trigger an apocalyptic war plus cost him the only woman he loves – Brina Treoir, the Belador warrior queen. Unfortunately, his only battle plan means going into the heart of his enemy's stronghold—*TÅµr Medb*. As leader of all North American Belador warriors, he's willing to die to protect those he loves, but his close friend Evalle Kincaid, her mate Storm and a tight circle of friends will not stand by and allow him to face that battle alone. With their lives also on the line and a tenuous peace at stake, Tzader has never had more at risk with so little chance to survive.

BELADOR URBAN FANTASY SERIES

Blood Trinity
Alterant
The Curse
Rise Of The Gryphon
Demon Storm
Witchlock
Rogue Belador (April 2016)

Slye Temp romantic thriller series
Last Chance To Run
Nowhere Safe
Honeymoon To Die For
Kiss The Enemy
Deceptive Treasures
Stolen Vengeance
Fatal Promise (2016)

Micah Caida young adult Trilogy
Time Trap
Time Return
Time Lock
To read excerpts, go to http://www.MicahCaida.com

NOTE FROM DIANNA:

Thank you for reading this series. I'd like to do a little something extra for those of you who have taken the time to write a review. Posting a review is the easiest way to help an author and something we all appreciate, me especially!

This offer is for a limited time:

If you'll email a copy of your review on Amazon for Witchlock along with the date posted and the name you posted under to my assistant - Cassondra@authordiannalove.com - I will send you a set of the first 6 Belador cover cards (4" x 6" each, printed on both sides), all signed by me, plus a Belador temporary tattoo as a thank you. ☺

If you'd like to keep up with my new book releases and to find out about events I'll be attending, please join my newsletter at www.AuthorDiannaLove.com - I only send them about once a quarter and I NEVER give away emails, because that annoys me, too. ☺

Thanks so much!!

Dianna

AUTHOR'S BIO

New York Times bestseller Dianna Love once dangled over a hundred feet in the air to create unusual marketing projects for Fortune 500 companies. She now writes high-octane romantic thrillers, young adult and urban fantasy. Fans of the bestselling Belador urban fantasy series will have two new books soon - Witchlock and Rogue Belador (April 2016). Dianna's Slye Temp romantic thriller series launched to rave reviews and more are coming soon. Look for her books in print, e-book and audio. On the rare occasions Dianna is out of her writing cave, she tours the country on her BMW motorcycle searching for new story locations. Dianna lives in the Atlanta, GA area with her husband who is a motorcycle instructor and with a tank full of unruly saltwater critters.

AuthorDiannaLove.com or Join her Dianna Love Street Team on Facebook and get in on the fun!

A WORD FROM DIANNA...

Thank you for reading Witchlock! Rogue Belador will be available in April 2016.

No book is possible without the support and love of my amazing husband, Karl.

Writing a book is a solitary job, but handing readers the best version of that book depends upon my terrific team. Cassondra M reads the first draft, the middle clean up and makes a last pass through, catching large and small issues, plus she constantly checks lots of continuity details on the series, which is a tremendous help in providing a smooth read. With my focus on the big picture of this story, plus what will happen in the next one and the next one, it's easy to miss something significant.

A huge thanks to my long time brainstorming partner and good friend, *USA Today* bestseller Mary Buckham (MaryBuckham.com), who writes the bestselling Invisible Recruit urban fantasy series. Eagle-eye reader Joyce Ann McLaughlin jumps in on the second round of reads before the copy editing has happened and always sends me a list of typos and details that make it a smoother read, too. Judy Carney is an enthusiastic and skilled reader who is one of the last two people to review the story line-by-line to catch those pesky typos and other grammar issues.

Some of my other readers who are always ready to put fresh eyes on the stories are Steve Doyle, Sharon Livingston Griffiths and Kimber Mirabella – huge thanks to all of you.

A special thanks to the wonderful staff at Stone Mountain who answered questions as I walked the mountain for the opening scene and to the staff at *Metro Diner Cafe* – both places should be on your must-visit list if you live here or when you travel to the Atlanta, GA area.

I want to give a special shout out to my Street Team: I spend a lot of hours alone writing and it's such a pleasure to jump out during the week and visit with all of you. You're a tremendous support for my books and me, but more than that – you are my reading family who mean so much to me. You give me joy all year long by sharing your time as well as your love of books. Thank you from the bottom of my heart. ☺

"*Time Trap* is amazingly original and unexpected... I loved every second of reading it!"
  ~~ **Alexandra Fedor, 15,** who has read The Book Thief, The Hunger Games, andAnna Karenina.

Please enjoy an excerpt from
TIME TRAP
Book 1 of Red Moon Trilogy

By *USA Today* Bestseller Micah Caida

(Free for limited time as ebook)

CHAPTER 1

Painful starbursts exploded behind my eyes.

I clawed awake, tumbling forward, bouncing against a rough surface. Heat scorched my arms and legs. I tucked my head and shoulders. Sharp stones gouged my back and sand coated my sweaty body.

Slammed to a stop, I was flat on my face. Ears ringing. My next breath wheezed out, mouth dry as the hot dust singeing my body.

What was happening?

No answer. Brain scrambled.

"Get up, girl, *if* you value your life," someone demanded in a deep male voice that sounded old.

Don't push me right now if you value yours. I opened my gritty eyes to blinding light and a cockeyed view of an endless desert. Not a person in sight.

"Get. Up."

If he yelled one more time, he wouldn't be happy when I did make it to my feet. I bit back the snarl curling to my lips. Who was he anyway? My head still spun and my stomach wasn't much happier. Gravel bit the palms of my hands as I pushed up on shaky knees.

Every muscle screamed misery, my body battered as a kickball. I twisted around one way then the other, searching in a full circle. Still no one. Now I was dizzy.

Had I imagined that voice?

Where am I?

Blinking against the harsh sun, I struggled to my feet, weaving where I stood. Confused thoughts banged my aching skull. I rubbed my eyes, then focused and looked down at myself. Feet tucked inside short boots made of tanned skins. Familiar, but not. Buckskin material covered me from shoulders to skinned knees and I had a leather thong tied around my waist.

I swallowed, waiting for some memory to rise up from the empty gap in my mind and offer help. The longer I waited, the more nauseous I got.

Nerves had me brushing hair off my face and breathing fast, then I paused, clutching a handful of hair. I pulled the strands into view. Black. Long, thick and black.

Why didn't I know that? My heart thumped hard and picked up speed. I took a quick glance at the barren landscape.

Was this home?

I didn't know. *Why can't I remember?*

Trembling started in my knees and traveled up through my chest. I forced a deep breath through my lungs, anything to stop the rising panic. *Panic kills.*

Someone had told me that once. Who?

Still no answers. Squinting, I looked for something familiar.

Mountains. Red mountains. Wait. I *knew* those. *Think.* I begged my mind to give me something. To remember.

Nothing. Closing my eyes, I tried harder.

Bright colors flashed behind my eyes and a sharp ache stabbed my skull. Grabbing my head did little to ease the throbbing, but the pain did clear some of my brain fog.

Sandia.

The name of those mountains. Sandia. Relief flooded through me so quickly my skin tingled. *I'm just disoriented.*

"You waste time, Rayen."

I froze as I opened my eyes. *I better see him when I turn around this time.* And who was Rayen? I made a quarter turn to find the owner of that gravelly voice.

An old man. No, the shimmering *image* of an old man, an elder. This whole thing just shot up a level on the weird scale. With white stringy hair, light gray eyes and gnarled limbs, he flickered before me, the red and tan cliff rocks visible through his translucent body. Beyond that, an unbroken sky stretched overhead, wide and empty and *so* intensely blue it hurt my eyes.

The ghost man *floated* above the desert floor, legs crossed.

I was feeling a whole lot better until I saw that. "Who

are–"

The ground beneath me vibrated and shifted, cutting off my words. I stumbled sideways.

"Listen," he ordered, his voice tense and urgent. "Three things you *must* know." The ghost spoke louder with each word, competing with a heavy, shuddering sound not that far away.

I chugged in a deep breath, as if that would keep my rising fear at bay, and smelled a rotted stench. Cloying decay and smoke. A warning smell I couldn't place, but something I sensed deep in my bones. Danger. I moved my head to look around, but the old man shouted, "You listening?"

Like I have a choice?

The spooky elder was determined to get his message said.

Nodding at him, I swallowed, not a spit of saliva in my mouth. The pounding of the ground seemed to come from a distance, reverberating through me. Adrenaline stirred my blood, urging me to be ready. But for what?

"First thing," he enunciated as if I was slow. "You die if you eat peanuts and you are seventeen."

Peanuts? Who cares about nuts, and isn't that technically two things? I sniffed at the air. The burning stink thickened. I reached for a knife that wasn't at my hip, but something told me it should be.

"Second. Your name Rayen."

Rayen? I'm Rayen?

If I could believe a crazy hallucination. Fear snaked through me with icy fingers, paralyzing me. *I don't know my name...or what I'm doing here...or where here is, other than recognizing those mountains.*

The ground shook harder, dust and pebbles scattering everywhere. I widened my stance to keep my balance.

That's when I caught the distinct sound of hooves pounding.

Hard. Behind me...and gaining speed.

I looked over my shoulder. A beast. My muscles clenched at the sheer size of the thing. A hairy, rhino-hide gray creature blotting out the desert landscape behind it. Barreling forward, rocking back and forth on three legs, wide head low to the ground. Scary fast, churning geysers of sand and dirt, eating up distance quicker than anything its size should.

Air backed up in my lungs. "What the – "

"Third thing, Rayen," the elder shouted, his voice nearly drowned by the rumble. "*Run!*"

CHAPTER 2

Ghost Man vanished as I took off running.

Something clicked in my head, some instinct. I ran, arms pumping, and rocketed away from the beast. A quick leap over thorny bushes. My heels slammed hard rock, feet racing as if hell itself chased me.

Quick check over my shoulder.

The beast was gaining, yellow eyes burning for blood.

What *was* that thing? Shouldn't I know?

Didn't matter. Right now I had no place to hide and no idea how to escape. No trees large enough to dash behind. Nothing.

Except the mountains. They were my safe haven. I knew that, somehow. *But how do I know?* Was there a place to hide in those rocks up ahead? Maybe that beast couldn't follow me up a sharp incline.

Keep moving.

Ragged breaths chugged past my dry lips. Hot air scorched my chest. I gagged on the creature's nauseating smell. I could hear it gaining on me. Shaking the earth beneath my panicked feet.

I'm running too hard. Won't last at this pace. My lungs were going to burst. *Have to find cover.*

Where?

Stinging sweat poured into my eyes when I lifted my gaze, searching boulders that had tumbled into a monolithic pile along the nearest ridge, as if stacked by a giant's hand.

Tell me that beast can't climb.

If I could just get far enough ahead. Reach the peak on the other side of those boulders.

I veered slightly left, pistoning my arms and breathing as hard as a small prey run to ground.

Fifty feet. *Run faster.*

Thirty feet. *Not going to make it.*

Ten feet. *Come on.* Almost there. Almost.

A roar screamed through the air.

I leaped from ground to rock. Slammed a knee. Slapped raw palms against jagged surfaces baked by the sun. Heat seared my skin. *Ignore the pain.*

Climb, climb, climb!

Scrambling like a lizard, I reached for crevices, grinding my knees and thighs.

Another scream, higher pitched this time but farther away. The thing pawed the ground. Dust erupted, choking the air.

I stretched for the next handhold and risked a quick glance back. What *did* that thing want?

At the base of the rocks, it started morphing from a huge, low-to-the-ground Rhino beast to a tall, thin whippet shape with a short, sleek coat of sand-colored hair.

And talons.

No way. No way in blue blazes. *I'm so dead.*

I bit my lip, tasting blood. *Can't quit now.* I sucked in a blast of baked air and clawed my way up the next rock. Sunlight poked through crevices. Maybe on the other side there'd be someplace to hide. Or people.

Like me? Where were my people? Friends? Family?

Did I have any?

Worry later. Right now, I'd take help from anyone I could find.

The sun roasted my exposed skin and beat down on my back. Muscles burned the harder I climbed. Blood pounded in my ears. I jammed the toes of my boots into whatever crack I could find and shoved my body higher, faster. My fingers clutched sandstone and slipped. I dug in deeper and scrambled hand-over-hand.

Hot breath licked the air around my legs.

The beast was almost on me.

A space between rocks gaped to my left. Crunching my shoulders as thin as possible, I plunged into the narrow V opening, raking my back raw.

A shaft of blue sky yawned on the other side.

Deadly panting echoed right behind me. Closing in.

Fighting panic, I scrambled forward and lunged for the far side...and too late saw nothing below.

Just air.

My feet flipped over my head. I tumbled. An ocean of sky and rusty-brown rocks blurred through my vision.

I hit hard, face planted on dirt.

Knocked the breath out of me. My head spun and every bone reverberated. I took a wheezing gasp that hurt.

"Son of a bitch!" a strange young male voice called. "Hey, dude, we got a skydiver."

Did I know the name Dude?

I opened my mouth and groaned. The only sound I could make.

"Hey, babe, where's your chute?" the same voice asked, closer.

Babe?

"Idiot, she fell from the rocks." Another voice that sounded just as young and male joined the first. "She's a mess. Leave her."

"No way she fell. From those rocks?" First male's voice. He whistled low. "Should be dead." Then he whispered, "Hey. Maybe she is. We better go."

We'll all be dead if that beast follows me. I twisted my head just enough to look up at the cliff face I'd just dove from.

There. In the crevice of dusty-red boulders loomed a shadow. Long and thin. Waiting.

Even from this distance, I felt the danger. Predator eyeing prey. But what kept it from attacking? The other people? The distance? Could that thing not shift from land animal to a winged creature and swoop down?

Beware the beast whispered through my mind.

As if I hadn't figured that out. That voice stirred a memory, almost. A female voice filled with worry. *Who is she? Why can't I remember?*

The flicker of knowing slid away faster than dust through my fingers.

Fear coiled in my chest. *I'm so confused.* The blank spots in my mind threatened me on a gut-deep level, far more than the beast did.

But I'd gotten my wish. I'd found people.

I rolled onto my back, sucking air at the pain that movement caused. My entire body complained. Body slammed twice and feeling as if I'd been squeezed from the inside out.

The second voice called from a little further away. "Come on, Taylor, move it. We gotta get out of here before—"

A high-pitched screeching noise blasted over the top of the stranger's words, followed by the echo of an older male voice. Not the ghost's voice, a different one. His words boomed through a mechanical amplifier, shouting, *"Stay where you are. Hands in the air. Stop!"*

But instead of stopping, bodies swung into action. I angled my head to figure out who was doing what. I'd thought there were only one or two people nearby, but a dozen plus young ones erupted around me. Running in all directions. Dust devils with legs.

The booming voice barked more commands. *"Stop where you are. Down on the ground. This is the APD."*

I had no problem complying. Flat on my back, I stared up at an empty, vast sky. Breathing was about all I could do.

Wonder what an APD is?

As if in answer, gravel crunched under approaching steps. A weathered face with skin as dark as mine hovered into view, indigo blue pants with a knife-sharp crease and dust-covered boots. One boot kicked my hip.

I gritted my teeth to hold back a groan of pain. *A warrior never lets a threat see you flinch.*

Had that been a random thought? Or did I know this as a truth?

"Stay right where you are, kid. No funny stuff and you won't get hurt."

Too late. Everything ached right down to the roots of my hair. And why had he called me kid? Was that anything like a dude? I dug around in my mind and came up with kid as a baby goat. Maybe I'm not the only one with scrambled brains.

The boot nudged me again. "Get up. Slow and easy."

I eyed that boot, considering what would happen if I spun his foot to face the wrong way. But he had a black metal object on his hip that could be a weapon, and I still didn't know where I was or what was going on.

Breaking his ankle didn't seem too smart.

Rolling to my side, I shuddered to my knees. That settled it. I was in no shape to fight anyone right now. I'd made the right decision not to antagonize this person. Bracing myself, I lurched up to stand and anchored my feet shoulder width apart. Wiping at my arms was a mistake. Sand and grit clung to my skin so all I did was grind it into the raw places.

The man I faced stood barely taller than me. An elder I estimated to be three times my age if that old ghost had been right about me being seventeen. Age seamed this man's face and voice. Eyes like coarse stone. "What kind of damn outfit you wearing, girl?"

He said *girl* as if I reminded him of a maggot. As for my clothes, what about *his*?

Couldn't place what he wore, but I sensed the meaning behind his words and attitude—authority.

All the elders milling around wore the same covering—blue pants, light blue shirts, everything regulated and unyielding except for the sweat stains at their armpits and lower backs.

I cast another glance at myself. No one was dressed like me. Not even the others my age. They wore a different type of uniform—unusual words and designs across their chest coverings-PMS, Mad Cow Disease, Rangers. Loose pants that sagged at their hips, colorful footwear too short to be boots. The more I looked, the less I understood. I searched my memory for what was normal or how I'd ended up here.

And found only a cold emptiness filled with dark shadows.

Nothing. How could that be?

Fear turned into a rabid animal in my chest, fighting to get out.

With no idea who I was or where I belonged, what would these people...

"You going native?" the man asked me, guffawing. He shouted over his shoulder, "Hey Burt, we got one thinks she's Pocahontas. Looks Navajo, like that other kid you got cuffed."

Pocahontas? Could that be my name, too? Judging by the way he'd treated me so far he didn't know me and didn't care. The crazy old ghost had shown more concern.

The other elder this guy called Burt had clasped metal rings on the wrists of a scrawny boy younger than me–a kid?–who looked more malnourished than dangerous. What had he meant by saying we looked Navajo? What was a Navajo? I fingered my hair again. Straight and black like the skinny kid. Was my face as sharp as his? Were my eyes brown, too?

Nausea boiled up my throat.

I didn't even know what I looked like.

Panic darted across the other young faces, but not like mine. They didn't appear confused over who they were or why they were being captured.

And no one here recognized me.

Blue lights flashed on top of a dirty white box with wheels. Was that how the elders had arrived? That form of travel seemed wrong, but I couldn't pinpoint why.

Who were these people? What did they want?

I scanned the cliff face again. The beast appeared gone. Or merged so deep into the shadow of the rocks as to be invisible. Unless?

Turning around, I eyed the male and female elders rounding up the struggling captives. Could the beast thing morph into a human? And if so, what were my chances of escaping?

"You got a name?" the man at my side barked.

I whispered through cracked, dry lips. "Rayen."

"That a first name or a last?"

I shook my head. Big mistake. Pain shot through my battered skull. The elder waited for me to answer, but the ghost hadn't given me more. "Don't know."

"Can't hear you."

"I *don't* know." Talk about the scary truth. An icy ball of terror jackknifed around inside me, but I kept my face passive, trying to figure out what to tell him. My eyes watered, but I blinked against tears. I was not one who cried. Strange, but I *knew* this.

Never expose a vulnerability rolled through my thoughts.

I might not know who I was, but some deep-seated instinct told me to trust myself to know how to survive.

"Where you from, kid?"

Just keep asking me questions I can't answer, chewing up my insides. I shook my head.

"Don't have a last name? Don't have a home? Wrong

answers, kid." The elder reached for something in his belt. "Turn around. Hands behind your back."

What choice did I have? There were too many of the blue uniforms with the black metal devices on their hips. I knew something discharged from a unit shaped like that. And even if I did try to run, that beast was out there, somewhere. I could feel its presence bone deep.

So I turned, willing to wait for my chance to escape. A narrow strip of rigid material looped against my bruised wrists. Tightened with a sharp tug.

"That'll keep you." The man sounded pleased. "Where's transport, Davis?" he shouted to someone.

"On the way," came a female answer.

"Captain's going to be glad to know we got this gang corralled before they disappeared into the Sandias," the man next to me bragged. "You were right about these kids holing up this side of the Del Agua Trail."

Del Agua. I knew the name of that trail.

Another positive sign, right?

"Folks out at Piedra Lisa Park will be happier," another laughed.

Piedra Lisa Park? I didn't know that name or what they were talking about.

A sudden jerk on my arm sent me stumbling. I couldn't swallow the groan that slid out this time.

"Keep up, kid. No lagging. We got room for one more in this van." The man spoke out of the side of his mouth as he half dragged, half-shoved me toward one of the dusty boxes with wheels and iron mesh windows. This one already jammed full of snarling, angry prisoners. All who looked my age or younger.

Wary glares taut with anger and fear sized me up, judging me.

I stiffened at the thought of being caged and helpless. And no telling when that beast would attack again. Could it get inside these boxes? My instincts warned me this wasn't a good idea, but those same instincts didn't offer help on how to get out of this situation.

Stalling, I asked, "Where're we going?"

"Why we're taking you to the Hilton Albuquerque." The man snickered.

A Hilton Albuquerque? Could the beast get to me there? I shoved a quick look up and over my shoulder again, searching. A shadow moved down the rocks, closer. "Where?"

"Don't be a fool, girl." The man thrust a meaty hand on the top of my head and shoved me inside toward the only remaining single seat. The taint of fear and sweat filled my nose. Heads hung down, shoulders hunched. I had the sense that the others knew where we were going and that knowledge had them trembling.

I tried once more. "Where *are* you taking me?"

"Where do ya think we take juvenile delinquents who steal twelve-thousand dollars worth of valuables and destroy a business just for fun?"

Stealing? Destruction? I wrenched at the tight bond around my wrists.

I wasn't a criminal.

Was I?

MORE BOOKS FROM DIANNA LOVE

Rogue Belador
Book 7 – April 2016

Tzader Burke uncovers a secret within the Medb coven that threatens to trigger an apocalyptic war plus cost him the only woman he loves – Brina Treoir, the Belador warrior queen. Unfortunately, his only battle plan means going into the heart of his enemy's stronghold—*TÅµr Medb*. As leader of all North American Belador warriors, he's willing to die to protect those he loves, but his close friend Evalle Kincaid, her mate Storm and a tight circle of friends will not stand by and allow him to face that battle alone. With their lives also on the line and a tenuous peace at stake, Tzader has never had more at risk with so little chance to survive.

Belador urban fantasy series
Blood Trinity
Alterant
The Curse
Rise Of The Gryphon
Demon Storm
Witchlock
Rogue Belador (April 2016)

Slye Temp romantic thriller series
Last Chance To Run
Nowhere Safe
Honeymoon To Die For
Kiss The Enemy
Deceptive Treasures

Stolen Vengeance
Fatal Promise (2016)

Micah Caida young adult Trilogy
Time Trap
Time Return
Time Lock
To read excerpts, go to http://www.MicahCaida.com

Printed in Australia
AUOC02n0719291215
272698AU00015B/59/P

9 781940 651705